ROCK

NOLA REBELS MC

NEW ORLEANS
BOOK 6

MACKENZY FOX

Copyright © 2024 Mackenzy Fox

All rights reserved. No part of this publication may be reproduced, distributed, or transmitted in any form or by any means, including photocopying, recording, or other electronic or mechanical methods, without the prior written permission of the publisher.

Please purchase only authorized electronic editions and do not participate in, or encourage, the electronic piracy of copyrighted materials. Your support of the author's rights is appreciated.

This book is a work of fiction. Names, characters, places, brands, and incidents are the products of the author's imagination or used fictitiously. Any resemblance to actual events, locales, or persons, living or dead, is entirely coincidental.

Cover by: mosadesigns.com.au
Exclusive cover: Eric Battershell Photography
Model: Josh Lamech
Formatting by: thenovelassistant.com
Editing by: Mackenzie: nicegirlnaughtyedits.com
Proofreading by: Kiki Edits
Alpha reader: Michelle (The Outgoing Bookworm)
Beta Readers: Dakotah F, Angelica H, Kylie T, Anshul S

*Please note. This book is written by me (Mackenzy Fox) I do not use AI to write my books or in any book content, nor do I use AI for book covers. Any book you pick up that is copyrighted by me - is written by me - and always will be 😊

For all you readers (yes, you know who you are!) Who begged me for Rock's book so he skipped ahead of the other biker boys… this is for you!

AUTHOR'S NOTE

CONTENT WARNING: Rock is a steamy romance for readers 18+. It contains mature themes that may make some readers uncomfortable.

It includes: violence, trauma, mentions of child abuse (not detailed) foul language, torture, stalking, gun violence and the male MMC suffer anxiety as well as possessiveness. If you don't like your bikers possessive, I'd step away now. It also has very graphic, steamy sex scenes that are smoking hot.

Rock was such a joy to write, he's everything a biker boy should be and more. Yes, he is a little over the top with how much he watches over Aspyn (he takes his job very seriously LOL) but he's also a tattooed cuddler and makes up for his shortfalls in other ways. Aspyn has an acid tongue and is quick with the quips, I really hope you enjoy the banter with these two. I had a big grin on my face through most of writing this book.

If you loved my best-selling Bracken Ridge Rebels MC series, you're sure to love this new spin-off too.

You also don't have to have read Bracken Ridge to enjoy this new series as it is written to be read stand-alone.

BLURB

Rock

I kept everything locked away
The parts of me that weren't broken, they were under lock and key
Forever
Or so I thought
When I'm sent to protect a mysterious woman
Everything I thought I knew changes
Everything I felt before her is a lie
It's not just the fact she's beautiful
She embodies all the things that I'm not
And now it's my job to keep her safe
I didn't know that she'd be the one to break me
To bring me to my knees
To see myself like I never have before
And when evil comes to threaten her
I know there is nothing I won't do to keep her safe

Aspyn

The man I'm not supposed have feelings for
The man whose protection borders on unhinged
He's the one I never knew was missing from my life
When I'm sent to the NOLA Rebels MC
I never imagined that I'd be babysat by a biker
But that's exactly what happens
Nothing could've prepared me
The second I lay eyes on him, the feeling burns deep within
I try to fight it, but in the end I give in
I let myself be caught up in all things Rock
Even if there is a deadly game of cat and mouse
One that may cost me my life
I know he'll never let anything happen to me
I'm under his skin
I'm in his blood
I'm etched into his soul
And that's exactly where I want to be
Forever

SYNOPSIS

NOLA Rebels MC - (New Orleans Series Book 6)
Rock is a possessive MMC, forced proximity, heroine in hiding, unhinged hero, biker MC romance with all the feels. The men of the NOLA Rebels MC will do anything for their club. They're a brotherhood, a club who stands mighty, and above all else, they take care of business, New Orleans style. The bikers may rule this city, but the women of the club have their hearts, and the men will do anything to protect what's theirs.
It is part of a series but can be read stand-alone with a HEA. This book is recommended for mature readers 18+

NOLA MC COMMITTEE MEMBERS

Cash – Founder & President
Ryder – Vice President
Harlem – Enforcer
Tag – Sergeant at Arms
Jett – Treasurer
Hawk – Road Captain
Riot – Secretary
Nevada – Tail Gunner
Bronco – Tail Gunner
Priest – Club Chaplain

Other regular club members:
J.J.
Bullet
Chains
Haze
Brew
Bandit

Current prospects:
Pipes
Giggs
Rodeo

PROLOGUE

Rock
The Past
17 years old

I stare at my twin brother Jett.

We've always been close, even when we share a difference of opinions. But people say my brother is sweeter than me, that I'm the harder nut to crack.

"What you think?" I give him a chin lift as I hold the punk up against the wall. "We leave him breathin', or we fuck him up?"

Jett gives me a look. He's always been the calmer between the two of us. If I had completed high school and had a picture in the yearbook, it'd say something like: Most likely to fuck up.

Jett, on the other hand, he'd be most likely to be able to talk himself out of any situation. Calmly.

I scoff at the idea. Talking is overrated. I hit first, talk after.

"Fucked him up enough," Jett replies, rolling his eyes.

"You think?"

"Since he's barely conscious, I'd say yeah."

I check his pockets and relieve him of all the cash in his wallet, plus a nice-looking pocket knife.

"Had it comin'," I mutter.

"Who is he, anyway?"

"Punk owed me money."

"You dealin' again?"

I ignore him. Sometimes my brother's 'holier than thou' attitude drives me crazy.

"Rock?" he presses.

Since when did he become a saint?

Our eyes meet. "Dealin' ain't takin', brother. Don't tell me you don't know the difference."

"Don't want you endin' up like Lazy Pete."

I snort. "Lazy Pete did needles. I don't do that shit." I shudder at the thought.

"You know what I mean. In the end, he crossed everyone in this city until there was nobody left. Now he's six feet under."

I frown. "Who am I crossin'?"

My brother has always had this moral dilemma. Even when he knows justice has to be served for those who cross us. It's the only way they'll learn.

"Just sayin'."

I grip the back of his neck and press my forehead to his. "Thought we were in this together?"

"We are."

"Doesn't sound like it. You goin' soft on me?"

He doesn't answer.

"What is it?" I prompt, pulling back. He's been acting off for weeks.

"Cash."

I try not to roll my eyes. "What about him?"

Cash is the MC President for the NOLA Rebels MC, and I know that he wants Jett and me to join.

Rock

"He wants us to prospect for the MC." He says it like I don't already know.

I try to suppress a groan. I know Cash seems like a decent enough man, but I don't trust him. I don't trust anyone.

"So what?"

"So, we won't have to live like this anymore."

I frown. "Live like what? I thought we were makin' our own rules?"

Jett shakes his head. "Aren't you sick of runnin'?"

I stare at him.

Why does this already feel like a loss... Like I'm losing my brother for good?

Jealousy courses through me.

Jett and I have had plenty to argue about over the years, but we're street smart. We know these dirty holes better than anyone, and I don't like the idea that Jett would need anyone else but me. We've always been there for each other.

I don't like this one bit. It makes me anxious.

"You know what my answer is," I say. "That hasn't changed."

"Why are you bein' so stubborn about this? It's a chance for us to get back on our feet. To get off the streets, start a new life."

I step back like he's slapped me.

He knows how I feel about men in positions of power. We don't mix.

Not after our childhood...

It's the same way I feel about the man who molested us as children, which is why I don't trust anyone, especially men within an MC. They don't have anyone's best interests at heart except their own.

Everyone is a goddamn liar until proven otherwise but, unfortunately, my little brother has a penance over his head and tends to believe outside influences. I'm not interested in that, and I'm not interested in Cash Hudson or his club.

"What's wrong with how we live?" I question, knowing that how we live is no picnic.

"Rock, come on. This is no way to get ahead; we're always hungry. We steal to get by. We have no real home. This is a chance for the both of us… Cash can help us."

"I don't need anybody's help, brother. I told you that a long time ago."

He runs a hand through his hair. "I'm tired of runnin'."

"Tired of me?"

"Didn't say that."

"You think Cash and a bunch of bikers are gonna take your side when shit hits the fan? As a prospect you're nothin', Jett. Lower than dog shit. You're more than that to me."

"I'm lower than dog shit now, though. The difference is we could be part of somethin', a true brotherhood."

I almost snarl at him. What the fuck has gotten into his head?

"A *true* brotherhood?" My anger flairs.

"That isn't what I meant."

"I'm not a good enough brother for you? You need more?"

Nobody can hurt me. Nobody. Except my twin brother. He holds all the power to destroy me because he's the only thing I care about in this godforsaken world.

And I thought I was the same to him.

We needed each other once. When both of us had nobody else, we had each other. That's all that mattered. My, how the mighty have fallen.

Hearing about the NOLA Rebels MC over and over is driving me insane.

I don't want to hear about anything that is going to take my place and leave me out in the cold. I won't conform for him or for anybody.

"I don't need more, but Cash is a good man. He'll look after us, make sure we never have to return to the streets." He kicks the guy who we've both left slumped on the pavement. "Shit like this gets old, Rock. You know it as well as I do."

I shake my head. "Look after us? We're grown now, Jett. You're talkin' like we're kids again."

He stares at me for a moment, trying to gauge if I'm being serious.

Oh, but I am.

Deadly.

Then he says, "Maybe we need to grow up."

I have plans for my life and those plans don't include being stuck in a one-horse town, being an asswipe for the NOLA Rebels. Not happening.

My brother trusts the wrong people, always has.

"You walk away now, we're through."

"Can't keep doin' this. Gonna end up in a concrete box with no windows, or a goddamn early grave."

Betrayal runs through me.

He's choosing Cash Hudson over his own flesh and blood.

"I thought our pact meant somethin'?"

"It does. You're bein' dramatic, brother. We can do this together…"

"*Dramatic*? You wanna join an MC, even though you know that'll mean we'll be split up? And they'll treat you like shit. You won't be doin' anythin' you're not doin' now and yet you'll have to give all the money you make to them. And don't pretend you don't care about me."

"I'm doin' it because I *do* care about you! I won't live like this…" He points in my face, and I push him back. "I can't, Rock."

"I'll fuck you up. I swear to fuckin' God!"

He stands his ground, knowing my temper well. "I'd like to see you try."

I pull my fist back, ready to punch him in the face, but then I stop. I'm being childish.

A part of me has always been the protector out of the two

of us, I don't know why. Maybe it's the fact I'm slightly bigger than my brother, or that I just have a goddamn death wish. I was always the one to take the brunt of the beatings, not because Jett was any less of a target, but because I didn't want him hurt too. He was smaller, so I acted as if I were the big brother, when really there's half an hour between us in age.

Who fuckin' knows, but the jealousy coursing through me is gonna make me do somethin' I might regret.

"Don't do this," he says, determination in his eyes.

I don't like that, either.

"You're just dyin' to be rid of me, so may as well not delay the inevitable," I snarl back at him. "Since your own flesh and blood isn't good enough anymore."

"I never said that. Stop bein' a dick."

I back off, not willing to hit my brother, but I also don't want to be around him anymore. I know he'll pick the MC over me. It's been coming for a while.

The life I promised the two of us when we ran away from foster care never happened.

Life on the streets is as hard as it sounds.

"Give me a call when Cash chews you up and spits you out," I say, walking backward.

"Where are you goin'?" He frowns. "We can talk about this."

Except we can't. I don't want to join the MC and Jett does. I don't like authority, and I won't be shit kicking as a prospect. If my brother wishes to go down that path, then I can't stop him. But I'll be damned if I'm gonna sit here and take it.

"Sayonara."

I turn and walk away, leaving him and the unconscious asshole on the sidewalk.

"Rock?" he calls after me.

I give him a two-finger salute.

Fuck him.

Rock

Fuck everyone.

I can go wherever I want. Do what I want. I'm never gonna have anyone telling me what to do. Ever.

"Rock!"

Pain hits my chest when I walk away. I've never done life without my brother, but I know that I have to sever the cord at some point. He's better than this. Better than me. Maybe I knew that all along and that's why I kept pushing him away.

Jett is destined for better things. He doesn't harbor the past like I do.

He doesn't hate like I do.

He's the good twin. And though I wouldn't consider myself the evil twin, I'm no Boy Scout.

I ignore the ache inside me that he is no longer by my side, and when I get far away enough, I turn to look back and he's gone.

Empty space.

He left me for dust.

I guess that's what happens when time charms the fuck out of you and you think you have nine lives. But in the end, there's nothing left inside you except an empty shell.

1
ROCK

Six years later
Aged 23

I bounce the ball against the wall, just like they do in the movies.

Waiting to get out of jail isn't fun, especially when you're not sure if anyone's coming to bail you out.

Of course, I wasted the only phone call on my brother, namely because his is the only phone number I know.

To say things have been strained between us these last six years is an understatement. We've seen each other, but things have never been the same after he joined the MC.

I walked away without a second glance and Jett accepted his fate.

My brother has thrived, something I'm pleased about, because despite what he thinks, I still want what's best for him. My jealousy stems from him not needing me and instead turning to the MC like they're his family.

Childish? Maybe.

Do I hold grudges? Freakin' A.

At least I'm consistent. I don't play games. I have no agenda.

What you see is what you get, and because I came from nothing, I have nothing to lose. Except Jett.

He harbors resentment toward me for walking away all those years ago. I didn't hide my anger, and he didn't change his mind, so I figure we're even.

Now I'm waiting in the hope that he'll remember his blood and not leave me here to rot.

I've been in the joint plenty of times for petty theft and dumb shit, but if they knew half the stuff I've done, they'd lock me up for good and throw away the key.

I don't know how long I bounce that damn ball for, but when I hear the warden come to the front of the cell and call my name, I feel relieved that I don't have to spend another night in this hell hole. It's dirty and smells like piss.

He unlocks the door and rolls it back as I step out.

Though I didn't touch anything in here, I want to go bathe in disinfectant.

I follow him down the hall, ignoring remarks from the other lowlifes in custody, and before I know it, I'm collecting my contraband and making my way past reception.

My brother stands on the other side of the door looking very unhappy.

I grin.

He looks about the same. I haven't seen him for years but nothing much changes with the two of us. I'm a little more unkempt than him, but that's because I don't have pussy at the ready like he does; sweet butts cleaning his room and cooking his meals for him.

Maybe I'm a dumbass for not following him into the Rebels all those years ago.

He rolls his eyes as the door is unlocked and we're face to face.

I try not to balk at the fact he's wearing a cut that reads: Jett, Treasurer - NOLA Rebels MC. So he's had a promotion?

Rock

His hair is long, like mine, but I wear mine up most of the time.

The chicks dig it, along with the multitude of tattoos I have all over my body. The things I've had to do in order to afford ink…

I've always had a big build as well as being tall, and since we're identical, Jett's the same. If we want to split hairs, I'd say I'm a little more defined, but he'd argue the point.

"Brother," I say, giving him a rueful smile. "It's been a while."

"Yeah, it has."

"Told you I'd write."

He shakes his head. "Not funny."

"Well, if you know I'm callin', it means I'm not dead."

He ignores me. "What did you do this time?"

"What does it matter? I'm out now." I hold out my arms. "No brotherly hug?"

He glances around and I laugh even more.

"Still ashamed of me?"

He nudges me hard in the ribs with his elbow, the closest I'll get to a hug, not that I deserve it.

"Shut the fuck up," he says.

"Gladly. Need a beer."

"It's ten o'clock in the mornin'," he says. "Don't tell me we need to add Alcoholics Anonymous to your ever growin' list of day trips aside from jail."

"Ain't no cure for what I got," I tell him. "Anyways, they kicked me out. Apparently, you're not supposed to fuck in the bathrooms."

He looks at me sideways. "You're full of shit."

"I swear to God it happened."

I mask a lot by joking. It keeps me safe from harm, even if that harm is usually self-inflicted.

We both know that we don't need to go there.

Being abused as children never leaves you. Somehow

you learn to cope with it and tuck it away somewhere. Usually, my beast unleashes when I'm in a fight. My opponent has no fuckin' clue what they're in for until I'm in full anger mode.

Most of the time, I'm pretty placid. I don't go looking for trouble.

When crime isn't permeating my everyday waking life, I tend to chill out the only way I know how. Drinking, smoking, and pussy. In that order.

I guess those things come freely to Jett now that he's patched in and doing well for himself. Not that either of us have to work hard to land chicks. We never have.

That's what happens when you have a pretty face and long hair. Keeping my body lean and trim doesn't hurt, either.

"You gonna drop me home?" I give him a chin lift when we head out toward the parking lot, pulling out the cigarette from behind my ear.

"Where do you call home now?"

"Got a place above a pizza joint. Cheap rent. Shit neighborhood but better than a park bench."

"Sounds classy."

"Probably better than that piece of shit room at church."

"Plenty to keep me there."

I grin. "You gettin' easy pussy. That's the only reason you fuckin' joined the Rebels." Of course, I know that's not true. I just like to rile him.

"That so?"

I shrug. "Probably a good move."

He gives me a chin lift. "How've you been?"

"About the same."

"You need money?"

"Why, you got some?"

"Not for drugs. Not today, not any day." He gives me a warning look.

For some reason, Jett just never fell into that trap. I wish I could say the same.

I give him a look, the self-righteous son of a bitch. "Don't do drugs."

"Nah, you just sell 'em."

"Hey, I'm just the middle guy takin' all the risk."

"For fuck's sake, don't try to smuggle it anywhere. Can't bail you out of the state pen or fuckin' Columbia."

"You think I'm stupid?"

"I got the brains, let's just say that."

I snort. "You sayin' I'm prettier? Louder for those in the back."

"You know why you get into so much trouble?"

I roll my eyes behind his back. "I'm sure you're gonna enlighten me."

"It's because of that smart mouth."

I rub my chin. "Really? I thought it was because of my devastating good looks or my huge cock."

"Please never reproduce."

"We're twins, Jett. What you say about me, you only say about yourself."

I won't tell my brother, but I got caught with some dope on me. Not enough to be charged, but enough to have a night in the slammer.

Not that I give a fuck, but he'll only give me that look he always does, like he's some goddamn saint and I'm some major fuckup.

"Maybe I should've taken up with the MC, then I'd have pussy on a platter just like you."

"Bummer you chose the hard road, but it's never too late." He's always pulling this card. Like the MC is the best thing in the universe.

I'm too stubborn to skulk backward with my tail between my legs. Not gonna happen. I'd rather eat shards of glass. If I don't have my pride, what else do I have?

We head toward his truck, and I whistle low between my teeth. "Nice ride."

"Thanks."

"You pullin' tricks?"

"Nope."

"Fuck," I laugh. "Earnin' an honest wage kinda suits you."

"Glad you think so. Put that cigarette out before you climb in."

I roll my eyes, but do as he says, muttering, "Pussy," under my breath.

Once I hop in the passenger side, he guns the engine to life.

"Surprised you came." I smirk.

"Thought twice about it."

He reverses and I keep my eyes ahead. "No, you didn't. We're blood, Jett. No matter what, you'll always come for me."

"Now's probably a good time to discuss your emergency contact," he mutters.

"Twice in six years ain't that bad. Anyway, who else am I gonna put down as a contact? You're the only one who pretends to tolerate me."

"Got that right." He glances at me. "You look like you need a shower."

"Glad we've got that cleared up. That also explains why the guys in the cell didn't want a piece of me."

He shakes his head. "Not funny."

"Got a knife in my shoe. Cops are dumb as fuck." Anyone touches me, they're gonna bleed. I glance back at him. "You cleaned up alright."

"We just gonna pull each other's dicks the whole ride?"

I grin. "Never could accept a compliment."

"You need money?" he asks again.

"I like how you assume I don't have any."

"You didn't make bail, remember?"

"Doesn't mean I don't have money. Just means I have a brother who thinks I don't."

"Smartass."

I go to light up another smoke.

"Hey, no smokin' in here, remember?"

I roll my eyes. "For fuckin' real?"

"Don't want my cage smellin' like shit."

"Jesus, someone has your pussy whipped. Is it Cash or some chick?"

"Nobody. Just don't want my truck smellin' like you."

"Ouch, that hurts."

We turn out into the mid-morning traffic.

"You gonna invite me to one of your parties one day?"

"You gonna stop gettin' into trouble?"

I smirk. "I didn't know you cared so much."

"How many times have you been to jail, brother? I've lost count."

"A few. But are you really initiated unless you've been in the slammer at least six times?"

He runs a hand through his hair. "I worry about you."

I frown. This isn't like Jett. "You sure you haven't been drinkin'?"

He sighs. "Don't ever wanna get that call, Rock. You never text me. I never know where you are."

"You made shit clear in the past. This is how you wanted it."

"Fuck you. I should stop and make you get out and walk."

Fuck no. My place is miles from here and I've no money for a cab.

Keeping my mouth shut, I look out the window.

Me and my brother have always had this love-hate relationship, and I'm the first one to admit that I hold a lot of resentment. I don't just let things slide like he does. I'm proud to say I'm not the better brother.

"We ever gonna get past this?" Jett goes on after a long moment of silence.

"Get past what?"

"Don't pretend like you're not pissed at me still."

"Well, who else would I talk to if you bailed on me for good?" I am still bitter. Blood is thicker than water.

"You called me because you know I'm the only one who gives a shit."

"Touche."

I've learned to bury how I really feel, now it just comes naturally.

Jett is the only person I truly care about, even if years pass and we don't talk. Aside from him, there's only our grandmother, not that we got to see her growing up because she was on the other side of the country. She's senile now and wouldn't even know who we are.

I often wonder what would have happened to us if we'd had a loving home with parents who cared about us.

Would we still be the men we are now?

Would we have had a fighting chance at being better people?

I snort and Jett looks at me.

"Somethin' funny?"

I shake my head. "Just thinkin'."

"About?"

"When we were kids, and we first discovered drinkin'."

He takes a moment, then laughs too. "Fuck, we were little shits."

"Not exactly our fault. Just thinking about our foster homes still sends chills through me."

We don't talk about that. It's not like we wanna sit around feeling sorry for ourselves because we had a mom who couldn't care less about us and every adult after her was worse than the last.

That made me dislike women for a long time. I was angry.

I've never hit a woman, nor would I ever, but I can't say I've been that nice to them either.

We bang, hard, and then she leaves. That's all I have the capabilities for, and it works for me. The chicks I hang out with are into it.

I feel him looking at me in my periphery. "Let's not go there."

"Just meant the shit we got up to. We should've come with warning signs."

He shakes his head. "Pretty sure it was a given."

"Do you forgive her?" I don't know why I blurt that out. Maybe my overnight stint in jail has made me soft in the head.

"Who?"

I roll my eyes. "Our mother."

He grips the steering wheel hard. "Do you?"

I don't even hesitate. "No."

Another long silence.

"I think she was too stoned to do her job as a parent," he says eventually. "That's what I tell myself, anyway. If she would've been sober, she would never have let..." He trails off, and I continue to stare out of the window.

Jett told me he had therapy one time, but me? I just hit it out in the ring and hope for the best.

I have anger issues, but at least I can admit to it.

"I think there's a special place in hell for people like her." We never mention *him*.

I thought about looking for him on more than one occasion, but we had nothing to go on. We were fuckin' children. We didn't know then that our mother got paid to be a whore. That even men in designer suits would visit and then leave. Sometimes she was beaten, other times just used. We were too young to know what was going on.

The one thing I've never understood is how someone can sell their body for money. I'd like to say I don't judge, and each to their own and all of that shit, but I'd be lying my ass off if I truly believed it. As low as I've ever been in my life, my dignity is not for sale. I've also never paid a whore.

Pity my mom was for sale and she preferred dick so she could keep sticking needles in her arm instead of feeding her children.

Rummaging in a dumpster isn't just one of the memories I've tried hard to break, it's the tip of the iceberg.

"I think that's one thing we can agree on," Jett says, his voice low.

I give him a chin lift, wanting to change the conversation. "So, have you been promoted yet?"

He rubs a hand over his chin, his lips curling up slightly. "I'm Treasurer now."

"What does that mean?"

"I look after the books. Now the club has acquired more businesses, it won't be long before they need a good accountant."

"You goin' back to school?" I scoff.

He shakes his head. "Nah. Don't have the patience for it, but I am lookin' into security cameras and surveillance as a sideline. We were both always good with tech shit."

I laugh. "You mean hackin'."

He glances at me. "You still do that?"

I shrug. "Pays the bills."

I had a friend from the wrong side of the tracks who taught me everything he knew about hacking. And then I got good at it. Really good.

It's no surprise to hear about my brother's plans. If I had the dough, I'd be doing that too. Unfortunately, the jobs I do don't amount to much, but that's largely because I'm pretty new to it. Long as I don't get caught, life may start to look up a little in the not too distant future. If I can get outta dodge and find a better place to live.

He opens his mouth, then closes it again. I'm sure he was

about to lecture me on coming to work with him, as that's his usual repertoire after grilling me, but maybe today he thought better of it.

"You seein' anyone?"

I grunt a laugh. "Lots of someones."

He shakes his head. "Right."

I glance at him. "I got the looks. I don't chase pussy, pussy chases me."

"*You* got the looks? We look the same, asshat."

"Fuck that shit. You wearin' your hair weird like that doesn't do you any favors, by the way."

"Weird?"

I tug on the back of his man bun. Seriously, he's embarrassing. "What is this shit? You too good to be wearin' a ponytail now?"

"Shut the fuck up."

"Mean it. Don't wanna be seen dead with you sportin' a man bun."

"Since you got the looks, that doesn't matter, right?"

I narrow my eyes on him. "How'd you know where I live?" I ask when we pull off on the right exit to my neighborhood.

"You think I came here unprepared?"

"I'd be sorely disappointed if you did."

"Not the greatest of neighborhoods. Don't go out after dark."

"Thanks, *mom*. Didn't think I'd get your stamp of approval."

"You know, in all the years we've been apart. I've never heard you whine like a little bitch more than you are right now."

I grin. "I guess old habits die hard."

We pull up not long after and he idles at the curb in front of the shop.

"I'd invite you up..." I start, waving my hand in front of the pizzeria. "But you might get your shoes dirty."

"You're an ass."

I give him a salute as I step out of the car. "Thanks for the ride."

"Don't get locked up again."

I wink. "Why? You'll still come get me."

"Don't count on it."

I shut the door and flip the bird as he pulls out onto the street and eventually disappears from view.

One thing we both know is he'll always be there. We're magnets, drawn together whether we like it or not.

He may act like I'm nothing to him, but if that were the case, he would've let me rot in jail.

When I can no longer see his car, I move toward the side entrance that leads up to the apartment.

It's a shithole, but at least if anyone breaks in, they have to get past hundreds of pizza boxes before they get to my apartment. Not that there's anything in there to steal.

I have fuck all. It's easier that way. When it comes time to leave in a hurry, I need to be light on my feet.

Just as I'm turning the key in the lock, one of the kids from the neighborhood shouts my name. I turn and give him a chin lift.

"Jimmy Deal told me to tell you there's a fight tonight, good money in it."

Instantly, my interest piques. "Who's fightin'?"

"Rick "Turbo" Mullins."

I snort. He's the best fighter this side of the Mississippi, but then again, he hasn't met me yet. "That's all they got?"

The kid shrugs. "Undefeated in his last ten fights."

"That so?"

He nods, then, "Should I tell Jimmy you're in?"

It takes me all of two seconds to decide.

What's life without a few jabs to the head? Besides, after

that conversation with my darling brother, I think I need it. It may knock some sense into me.

"Tell him I'm in."

He grins and starts to take off, but then turns back around at the last second. "Rock?"

I'm halfway in the door when I stop. "What?"

"You don't even know what they're paying!"

I lean back and give him a sly grin. "Some things in life are worth more than money, kid, just you remember that."

I take off inside to shower and get ready to get my head pounded in.

It's the only thing I can do to tame the beast inside me that simmers like a lion ready to pounce on the deer. I feel it in the pit of my stomach. One day, he'll emerge. And won't the shit hit the fan when that happens…

2

ASPYN

Present day

I throw the remote control across the room.

How long do I have to be kept cooped up in this house?

And why am I even listening to these people? The police, that is.

Granted, my father is one of the men I love and respect, and I usually do what he says, but it's been three days of staring at the wall. I'm done.

I've watched enough YouTube videos to last me a lifetime. Netflix sucks, and don't even get me started on Facebook. My publicist told me to stay off social media, at least until the scandal dies down.

I sigh, not caring about what the hell the media says about me.

I was in a reality show called Tail Spin, where a bunch of girls, who don't know one another and come from privileged backgrounds, all live together and try their hands at activities they've never done before. Like operating a washing machine.

It's the modern-day answer to the Simple Life, and even lamer. Bad trash for those who care about heiresses and how dumb they can act. Not that I acted dumb, but some of the girls were complete airheads. And didn't the viewers lap it up? You bet they did.

As much as I tell myself I did the show for charity, the reality was, I wanted this.

An escape. Something to sink my teeth into and get away from these four walls. To get my dad's attention, too? Maybe. He never notices anything.

Yet, all I did was escape one prison cell for another.

I was pretty popular on the show, even though everyone thinks I'm something I'm not. The entire show is scripted and cheesy, but it paid off. Or it did until I got booted off because of a brawl.

My now ex was caught up in a cheating scandal with one of the dumb girls, Lisa, on the show, and I lost my mind on camera. I'm proud to say I stuck up for myself and ultimately that led to a cat fight. Of course, it helped with the ratings but not so much my persona of shaking off the 'bad girl' image.

I ripped out one of her extensions and made her bleed. She's probably going to sue me for all I'm worth because my dad's rich. Apparently, one way to never have to work again in your life, not that she needs the money.

I claimed self-defense, that she was provoking me, and after the producers decided to drop the bombshell, I lost my shit.

It's been a slow progression of the last twenty-three years, and unfortunately this chick copped the brunt.

It also doesn't help that I've been in the public eye since I was small.

My dad is very well known in LA Tommy Huntley. He's a financier and a realtor, owning one of the first successful real estate businesses in Beverly Hills and turning it into an empire.

Huntley Realtor Group.

My dad has connections, including the motorcycle club,

where I'm being shipped off to until this scandal dies down. As if that wasn't enough, my stalker is back.

I had a mild scare a while ago when some random number sent me scary text messages and told me I was going to die. The cops couldn't find anything because whoever this person is, was using a burner phone. I had to change my number countless times and it only further fueled my dad's paranoia about keeping me safe.

He has this fear of me being abducted and used against him.

To make matters even worse, my cheating ex, Dylan, can't seem to stay out of the headlines. You'd think he'd know when to quit, but it seems he couldn't keep his dick in his pants when we were together.

That's what you get when you hook up with a pretty boy actor who spends more time getting ready to go out than you do. He wasn't interested in anything except getting wasted and going to parties. The sex wasn't just vanilla, it was the sugar-free version. I snort a laugh and my cat, Pirate, looks up at me.

He's my pride and joy. The only thing in the world I love, aside from my best friend Tara. I'm not even allowed to tell her where I'm going, supposedly for my own protection. The cops are downstairs now, talking with my dad about the emails that were sent telling me I'd be abducted if I appeared on television again.

My dad is beside himself.

Even though I'm twenty-three years old — a child in everyone's eyes — nobody treats me like a woman who can make my own decisions, and since my life has been mapped out for me, I won't have a choice in this, either. I'll go along with it so I don't upset dad.

He only wants what's best for me. He still hasn't forgiven me for not telling him I was going on a reality TV show.

My only claim to fame is making some rich girl bleed

while my cheating ex tells everyone that I was the kind of chick that made him "want to quit life."

That's Dylan for you, anything to take the heat off himself.

My parents divorced when I was small and my mom distanced herself. Maybe her lack of interest in my upbringing made me super jealous of other kids who had both parents, or maybe it just made me resent the fact she never even tried.

She had issues, mentally, and when she went away for treatment, she never came back. She's never tried contacting me over the years, and I don't think my dad ever got over her. He can be a handful, but he's not a bad man. He loves me.

He'd do anything to protect me, which is why I'm being sent away until the cops and my father's PI can get to the bottom of who is threatening to kill me.

Oh, there's never a dull moment in the Huntley household.

There's a knock at the door. I sit up expectantly, hoping they let Tara in. She's the only one who knows the real me and the only one I can talk to about any of this.

When I see it's my dad, I roll my eyes.

I'm mad at him, and though he's trying to make my exile sound like a trip to Disneyland, what the actual fuck am I going to do in a motorcycle clubhouse?

I wonder if he's lost his damn mind.

"Honey?" he says, his voice low as he enters the darkened room. "It's me."

Who else would it be?

"I'm tired," I lie.

He sits on the side of my bed. "The police are gone."

"Good. Can I leave my room now?"

He looks at me gravely. "Aspyn, you know the rules. You had it your way and look what happened. The one time I trusted you and you lied to me. Not only are you facing criminal charges, which I'm trying to have dropped, but now somebody wants to hurt you because of all of this."

I didn't tell him about Tail Spin because he never would have approved.

I wasn't trying to bring disgrace on him, or myself, but I've never seen life outside of this protective bubble.

Poor little rich girl.

"This is just how it is when you star on a reality show," I tell him.

He sighs. "Aside from it being ridiculous, you're a national disgrace."

I snort. "Most of the people on social media agree with me, Dad. I took back the power."

"By breaking a girl's nose?"

"Her nose was ugly. They saw what happened, they applauded me.

He gives me a look.

"I can probably get the charges dropped with a little smooth talking or a settlement. But you start acting out again…" He shakes his head. "What can I do to make this better?"

"I'm acting out because I'm a prisoner," I say, not that he hasn't heard it before.

"You have your charity work."

"Dad! That's barely twice a year, plus fashion week, and that trip to Paris where I had bodyguards following me around everywhere. It's like being babysat with a bunch of Rottweilers."

Rottweilers that are all fired up because nobody can do their jobs.

This whack job stalker got into my dressing room…and I don't know what they did. Nobody will tell me.

"I have threats on your life. Do you not understand how serious this is?"

I stare at him.

My dad is my hero. He always will be, but he's wrong on this front.

People will always extort wealthy people for money no matter who they are. Unfortunately, I happen to be his daughter. It has nothing to do with the show.

"I do," I say, lowering my voice. "But this isn't the first time, and it won't be the last. Some nutjob is pissed because they don't like me and I'm your daughter. What happened in the show came after. It has nothing to do with that. If anything, people love that I stuck up to Lisa and smashed that fucking slut's nose in."

He still can't get his head around the fact that the one time I defied him, led to all of this.

It's a bad look for Huntley Realtor Group.

"Language, Aspyn."

My dad has always worried about me, but now he's really going overboard.

"Is this about getting my attention?" he goes on as my eyes widen.

"Is *what* about getting your attention?"

"Telling me one thing and doing another. The minute I let you have an inch, you take a mile."

"Dad, it's like living in a prison cell. I'm an adult now. I don't have to do what you say."

"Don't be so dramatic. Do you know how many girls would kill for this lavish life you lead?"

"The same can be said for a poor girl who has freedom, Dad." I know it's not the same thing, but he doesn't get it.

He stares at me. Of course, he comes from a line of well-to-do successful businessmen who were all born with silver spoons in their mouths. I'm not saying I dislike privilege, but how can I compare when this is all I know?

"You can have freedom, when this is over."

"I've heard that before."

He sighs. "This is for your own good."

"Do you really believe those threats?"

"Yes, and so do the police. They're taking it very seriously. This all came full circle after the show aired your brawl. Until the police can interview everyone on set, you'll be in hiding. I'm not backing down on this."

"Why a fricking motorcycle club?"

"Because I trust nobody."

"Except Cash Hudson?"

"He owes me, and yes, I trust him. Otherwise, I wouldn't be sending you there."

I snort.

He frowns at me. "What's so funny?"

"You trust a bunch of bikers over industry professionals."

"It's either that or the mafia."

My eyes go wide.

"I'm kidding," he says, and I don't want to ask.

My father is involved with other rich, successful people, but I've never questioned his moral high ground because he's my dad. He's known as a bulldog in the industry, but to me, he's just my overprotective father.

"Do you ever wonder if maybe this is about *you*, and not *me*?" I say, the words flying out before I can stop them.

"Of course I've thought about that, but going on that show didn't help."

I cringe at his face of disappointment. My father's a handsome man. Some would say a silver fox who any red-blooded female would love to lock down, but that just makes me want to gag thinking of him like that. Even though he's never settled down with anyone since my mom.

He sighs. "The police will look into everything, so will my guys. For now, this is what's going to happen, Aspyn. Don't fight me on this. This wild streak of yours going on a reality show and airing your dirty laundry on television isn't from my side."

I stare at him blankly. He means *her*.

If only he knew. My bark is worse than my bite. I've had to put on this front my entire life. Rich girls aren't allowed to have any issues. Life is perfect when you have the best schools to go to. The best clothes to wear and your father drops you off at school in his Bentley.

"Why bring her up?" I mutter, shifting uncomfortably.

He shrugs. "Because it's the truth."

I pull my knees up and hug myself. "Are you sure the wild streak doesn't really come from *your* side? I've read the tabloids, Dad, you're a lady killer. A real catch. You bed a lot of women." My cheeks flush at my words, but he needs to know I read the papers too.

The frown deepens but nothing derails my father. He's a man who can hold his own in a room full of rich businessmen in suits. But even I know I'm the apple of his eye.

"Don't talk like that."

I roll my lips. "Silver fox?" I make a gagging sound.

He relents and chuckles. Dad's better when he's being playful, which isn't often.

"I don't even want to know what that means. Stop changing the subject."

"I should be the one screening all these women you date, Dad. That way, your heart won't ever be broken again."

He looks at me with all sincerity and says, "You can't break something that's unfixable, Aspyn. My heart isn't up for the taking."

My lips part and the words get lost as I watch my dad's sad face. He loved my mom.

When she left, she never reached out to either of us, as far as I know. She was just gone. I never really knew why.

Maybe she felt like a bird in a cage, too. In some ways, I know exactly how she feels.

I wonder about her, and over the years I'd invent ways in my mind of her trying to contact me. I asked my father on many occasions where she was, but he shut down the conversation and said he didn't know, only that he'd heard she'd moved to Italy.

Fucking Italy.

"As long as you're being…you know…careful," I say, not relishing the idea of having a sibling at twenty-three.

His eyes go slightly wide. "Thanks for the tip, but I'm good."

"There are plenty of gold diggers out there," I go on, waving my hands in the air. "Just saying. Some women will do anything to pin a rich man down."

He pinches the bridge of his nose and shakes his head. "What the hell am I gonna do with you?"

I smile. "Hide me, for my own protection?"

His eyes meet mine once more. "I'm sorry I have to do this. If there was any other way…"

I nod, knowing that there's a lot he's not telling me.

A death threat is one thing, but this is something else. I've never seen my father so rattled.

"Why so far away? New Orleans?" It's a far cry from LA.

"I'll be purchasing an apartment downtown so you'll be safe."

That's a relief. For a second there I thought I'd be staying at the biker clubhouse. Something that makes my nose wrinkle at the very idea.

Of course, my father doesn't believe in renting.

"If I didn't love you so much, I'd think you'd lost your marbles," I say.

"Coming from my wayward daughter, I'll take that as a compliment."

"Can we Skype?"

"Of course. But you'll need to change your cell."

"Why? Nobody has texted me on this number."

"Just a precaution. It can still be traced."

"Can I call Tara?"

He goes to rise, then he stops as he sits back down and

holds my chin with one firm hand. "You can call her and text, but Aspyn, this is really important. I know she's your best friend, but you can't tell her where you're going. Nobody can know, do you understand?"

I swallow hard. I don't keep secrets from her. I never have. She knows everything about me.

The good. The bad. The ugly.

"But Tara…"

"No buts. If anyone knows, then this whole move will be for nothing. We have to flush out the perpetrator and bring them to justice," he says. "I will not have my daughter in the firing line. Until this mess is dealt with, you're to stay put and do as I say. Then when this is over, we'll talk."

"What if I don't like the NOLA Rebels?"

"You won't be around them long enough to care. My team is closing in. The minute this maniac is locked up, you can come home."

I don't know why every time I say NOLA Rebels, my heart skips a beat. Then I want to laugh at myself. This isn't Sons of Anarchy. And I seriously doubt there are any cute guys. They're probably all pot-bellied, beer drinking slobs. I try not to screw my nose up.

"Dad, that could be ages."

He lets go of me. "So be it."

I look down at my hands. "Should I be worried?"

He leans up and kisses me on the forehead. "No. You're in the safest of hands. And if that asshole Dylan messages you, I want to know about it."

Just hearing his name makes me angry.

He tried his hardest to get out of what he did, spinning some tale about being so drunk he didn't remember what happened. That didn't excuse all the other girls who came out of the woodwork. Damn asshole.

Deep down, I should've known that he couldn't be

trusted. His wandering eyes are legendary. I guess I believed the lie that he really was a good guy.

Good guys don't treat you like this.

"You hear me?" Dad prompts when I don't reply.

I nod. "Yes."

"Which won't be possible anyway because you'll have a new number."

Clearly, Dad is a little slow when it comes to social media messaging channels, but I don't say anything.

Tara will not be happy that I'm being exiled and she won't be able to see me. We've been like two peas in a pod since we were little kids. I trust her implicitly.

What would be cool is if Tara could've come with me. That would have made this trip all that much better.

I nod. "I never want to speak to him again." Which isn't a lie. He's a deadbeat and he's getting a lot of shit for what he did to me with Lisa.

I've watched the re-run of me belting Lisa, and it never gets old.

Her shocked face when I yanked out a handful of her hair and punched her in the nose, will go down as one of the things that made me happiest in life.

I hate liars. And I hate cheats.

"Good. Glad to hear it. When this is over, we can discuss boundaries," Dad says. "I never want you to feel as though you can't live your life. I just don't want you to ever be hurt because of who we are."

I know he has my best interests at heart. I don't want to seem ungrateful, but he is holding me hostage, after all. I have a right to be mad about that.

Still. If it keeps my dad from blowing a gasket, then it's the least I can do since my debacle.

"I know, Dad. I didn't know that it was going to go down like this. But if you agree to give me some more freedom when this blows over, then maybe I wouldn't have to sneak around behind your back."

We're so much alike. That's what scares the crap out of him, I realize.

"Let's just get through these next few weeks, Princess."

He also does that a lot too… Sweeps things under the rug to be sorted out later.

Something that never seems to happen.

I'm not a porcelain doll. I can't be kept in a locked cabinet, on a shelf to be stared at and admired for the rest of my life. He's always been overly protective, but things have stepped up since the stalking incident.

Then again, going to New Orleans could be the break I need. Even if I'm not exactly frothing at the mouth at the prospect of being there with a bunch of bikers.

I should ask him who will be watching me while I'm there.

How long will I be gone for? When will I see him next? But none of those words spill out of my mouth.

My dad will have it all planned out. Just like the rest of my life.

At least this time I'm happy I'm leaving.

I don't want any more reminders of this town. I need an escape.

And New Orleans might just be the place to do it.

3

ROCK

PRESENT DAY

Pain hits me between the eyes.

I shouldn't have drank so much. You'd think after all these years I would've learned by now, but some habits die hard.

I'm also still sporting a shiner from a fight I got into last weekend. While I don't get paid anymore to brawl, sometimes trouble just finds me.

Luckily, it was at my club brothers' Brew's and Haze's family bar, so no harm, no foul. Not that their older brother Hustle was impressed.

Dammit.

My head hurts even more when I sit up and throw the comforter off.

I sleep naked. Spreading my legs, I tug on my dick a couple of times, annoyed that I didn't indulge last night. It's been a little while, and not because I can't get pussy easily, but because I've been so goddamn busy.

Ever since the NOLA Rebels bought into my business; Rocks Truck N' Haulage, shit's only gotten busier. Now that I'm not there as much to oversee, things are getting messed up.

Cash has found better use of my time by getting into security and surveillance with my brother.

You could say we made up after my last stint in prison. The one that landed me six months in the clink with murderers and pedophiles; men I have a personal vendetta against.

What they don't tell you in the real world is that sickos are well protected by isolation in the joint, so getting to them is never easy.

As traumatic as that time was, when I got out, I learned our grandmother had passed away and left her estate to us. Me and Jett got a pretty hefty payout, and I was able to start my business. .

It's taken a little time, but me and Cash are good now. Back when I was in my twenties, I couldn't see the forest for the trees. I was too lost in my own anger and fear to let anyone near me. I can't say that has changed dramatically, but I've learned to let the wall down for certain people... Remembering the time I got shot defending Jett recently, I know it changed things between all of us...

"You've always been like sons to me," Cash said. "Both of you."

I've hidden my feelings for so long, afraid of letting anyone in, in case they got too close.

"I never wanted to join this club," I admit. "Though now I'm thinkin' you need me more than ever."

Cash snorts. "Is that so?"

I've been thinking of getting investors into my business to try to expand. I never even dreamed the Rebels would be interested. I don't have the extra cash to buy more trucks. That shit costs money. And the club has never done wrong by either of us.

"Hackin' is what I'm good at, let's face it."

"You sure you won't miss drivin' trucks?" Jett scoffs.

I give him an eye roll. "Like a hole in the head."

We've been on better terms lately, but after I took a bullet for him, things changed with my brother. We've made changes and now we're close again. I've always wanted what's best for him, believing he was better without me, but he's made it clear that I'm a part of his life, no matter what. Now he has his ol' lady, Summer, who I adore. I'd say my little brother has it made...and for the first time in a long time, I'm happy...

I take a piss and run the shower for a minute before stepping in.

I don't live at the clubhouse, instead I've opted to live in the apartment above the truck shop. It's not ideal, but it's a waste of money getting a place when I spend half my time at the clubhouse anyway. Plus, I don't have an ol' lady and don't plan to rectify that anytime soon.

Pussy isn't hard to get, especially at the clubhouse.

The Rebels MC has an array of women who come and go from the club. Most of them are just there for the bikers, but some like the added perks that come with the job. Free grub. Booze. And dick. Pretty much in that order.

I said I'd never join the MC, but that was before my life turned upside down and went from bad to worse. The only thing that mattered was making good with Jett again after our grandmother died. We came full circle and I'm glad. I was also glad when he finally had the guts to take Summer as his. He crushed on her for years when she lived in Arizona, but was too chickenshit to do anything about it.

I chuckle when I think about the time I sat at the bar and Summer didn't know we were twins, namely because he never told her, and she wrapped her arms around me one day and kissed me. Of course, I didn't know who she was then, but she sure as fuck didn't fit the title of a sweet butt.

To say Jett wasn't too happy about it was an understatement. Summer's embarrassment over her error, however, was priceless and something we still laugh about. Not that Jett joins in on the funny side of it.

We get along well, and I like her for my brother. She's calm and patient and doesn't cause any drama. When my time comes to find my ol' lady, I've often wondered what will come my way. I'll know when I find her, that's what they say, anyway.

I glance at my phone and see several texts from Cash.

Great.

That's all I fuckin' need on a Monday morning.

I've been sharing an office with Jett while we've been installing surveillance cameras around all the club's businesses, as well as doing my own detective work when the club needs it. I shouldn't be so good at it, hence the reason I haven't been at my own shop for a while.

I soap up my body and ignore my morning wood that won't quit. I don't have time for that, but since I haven't been getting any snatch lately, my balls are telling me I'm gonna have to do something about it soon.

I shower quickly, dry myself and get dressed, tying my hair back into a short ponytail.

By the time I head out, it's almost eight.

My new receptionist is being trained by my old receptionist Luna, the club's Sergeant at Arms' ol' lady. Tag is one mean motherfucker, but his ol' lady gives him a run for his money. It won't be long until she's running things with Jas, the club's accountant, whose office is next to mine and Jett's. She keeps everything under control, as well as the Road Captain, Hawk, her old man.

I smile to myself as I think about all the brothers tied down to one pussy. Not saying that one woman ain't good, but I'm just getting started in the club. There ain't no way I'm settling down with one woman when there's scantily clad women throwing themselves at me whenever there's a party or a get-together.

I jump on my sled, something I treated myself to after I got my half of the inheritance. Even before I joined the MC, I've always shared Jett's love of Harleys. I never dreamed I'd have one of my own.

I take the short trip across town and park my Harley in front of the clubhouse.

Cash is in the meeting room we call church; it's where all important decisions are made.

I'm not one of the committee members, so I don't get to sit in on any of the meetings, but Jett pretty much fills me in on everything anyway.

I stick my head in the door and Cash looks up.

"Rock," he says, giving me a chin lift.

His VP, Ryder, is sitting to his left.

I give him a chin lift and say, "Everythin' good?"

I mean, it wasn't good until six months ago. It was far from good. But now I'm thirty years old, I've realized it's time to grow a set. I know the Rebels aren't the devil. For one they're not a one percent club so they don't do illegal shit.

The only thing shady is the hacking and surveillance, which me and my brother take care of. Other than that, the club is clean.

"Remember how we discussed you not havin' to prospect all those months?" he says as he notions for me to sit at the table.

Uh oh. I already don't like where this is going.

"Distinctly," I reply, taking the chair to his right.

"And that we may need a favor?" Ryder puts in helpfully.

I try hard not to roll my eyes, a boyish habit I've never been able to break.

Cash Hudson demands respect, and as an MC Prez, he gets it. Even from me.

I can see how far my brother has come in the thirteen years he's been with the club, and Cash has been like a father to him. The father we should've had.

I missed out on so much and that was to my own detriment.

"Glad I'm sittin' down," I mutter.

Cash slides a file over to me. "Aspyn Ashley," he says.

I frown. "What's one of those?"

Ryder snickers as I open the file and say, "Oh, need me to fuck a nice piece of ass. Don't have to ask me twice, Prez."

He doesn't laugh. "Very funny. This is one piece of ass you'll keep your hands off," he warns. "Her father is Tommy Huntley, one of the biggest realtors and financiers in LA This is his kid."

"I'm sensing the point bein' made sometime soon," I mutter.

"He always like this?" Cash asks Ryder.

"In my defense," I start. "It's early, Prez. Had no pussy for a few weeks and I'm all outta coffee this mornin'. Got a new chick startin' at the office this week and Luna is already stretched between the two places, cussin' at me as if I'm the one who's makin' her leave…"

"You done?" Cash shakes his head.

"Sound like a little bitch," Ryder agrees, smiling across the table at me. "I think this is the perfect job for him."

Cash snickers too. Clearly, the two of them are in on this horrible task.

I ignore them, grinding my teeth and looking down at the file.

The picture, a mugshot, no less, shows the prettiest girl with pale skin, a small smattering of freckles across her cheeks and long, ice-blonde hair hanging over to one side. But it isn't even that which captures me, it's the eyes. They're so blue that I'm sure they can't be real. She looks like trouble with a capital T.

She has a stubborn look on her face, which I guess is a given when you're posing for a mugshot. Her eyeliner is smudged, giving her that 'I don't give a fuck how I look because I know I look hot anyway' attitude. She permeates the kind of rage that I used to see in myself, and I wonder immediately what happened to her.

"She's a reality TV star… Or was," Cash explains. "Ever heard of Tail Spin?"

I look up at them. "Nope."

"It's a reality show," Ryder clarifies, barely containing his laughter. "Rich chicks from all walks of life livin' in a house together, tryin' to operate fancy appliances and failin' badly."

"Do I look like the kind of asshole who watches reality TV?"

"You do kinda look like a Real Housewives kinda brother," Cash observes as I throw him a glare.

"Are we gonna get to the point?" I so need a fuckin' coffee.

"She got kicked off the show for brawlin' with some other chick who hooked up with her boyfriend," Ryder goes on. "Then she was stalked and started gettin' death threats. Apparently, it's not the first time."

"I'm a good friend of her father," Cash explains. "We go way back. I said she could come down here until all this shit gets sorted. I need you to watch her."

I frown. "You want me to babysit this chick?"

"Yeah."

"With all due respect, Prez, can't Harlem or Tag do that?" Harlem is the club's Enforcer. Surely, if anyone was going to be someone's personal fuckin' bodyguard, it should be one of those guys.

"They're out lookin' for Forger," Cash reminds me. "Goin' down this weekend, but the aftermath is gonna require cleaning up. She'll be here Sunday."

The beef we have with our rival club, the Devils Ink, has recently resurfaced. We dealt with them a while back, but then some of the club members survived the fallout and went underground.

I know why Cash wants to keep me away from all of that and it's because I got shot recently and almost died. Not only that, it was his fuckin' step-brother who shot me, the former

Prez for the Devils. Now Forger has taken over, back from the dead. He's also Indigo's ex, she's Harlem's ol' lady.

Trouble is, he's been flying under the radar for a little too long. Once he's found, he's a dead man. He even kidnapped his own daughter, Indigo's kid Cami, and she almost burned to death in a crypt. The club was in lockdown for a few weeks, but now that we have a location to where we think the members are meeting secretly, we have half a chance at fuckin' them up for good.

"Shit," I mutter.

"You know Harlem and Tag both have vendettas against Forger," Ryder says. "Only fair they get first dibs at him."

That is understandable.

Turns out, Luna's ex-boyfriend was funding the Devils Ink with stolen money from her father's firm. That's how they were able to re-establish so fast. That guy's been taken care of now. Feeding those alligators has become a little pastime for all of us of late.

There's definitely some well-fed reptiles in the swamp down in the bayou.

"They get any leads on the stalker?" I ask, turning the conversation back to where it needs to go.

"The ex-boyfriend is the main suspect, Dylan Maloney, though it doesn't look like he could fight his way out of a paper bag," Cash mutters.

"And her father doesn't have security on her?"

Cash shakes his head. "They're useless. Trust me, this is a last resort. She's had death threats and had a stalker. The stalker left a bunch of photos of Aspyn all over her dressing room with the eyes cut out of all the pictures. There was also a note saying they'd be seeing her soon. Aspyn was never aware of it since it all got cleaned up before she came back." He pauses. "She'll be safe with us, and she has no ties to New Orleans. Nobody will be lookin' for her here."

"What kind of chick is she like?" There isn't much to go on

in the file. Just basic information, and that photograph that I swear to God will haunt me for the rest of time.

Mystery girl.

That's what she is. And trouble.

Though, from the sounds of it so far, she's only defended herself and smacked a girl in the face for cheating with her boyfriend. She sounds like my kinda chick.

"If you're askin' for an open pass to nail her, that's a no," Cash states firmly. "I told her pops we'd hide her. The press is all over it and she needs to lay low. She has no ties to the MC and frankly nobody would come lookin' here for her. If they did, we would have the manpower to protect her."

"Takin' it her pops is rich if he's some big mogul in LA?"

Cash nods. "She's his little princess."

I groan. "Awesome, you've stuck me with a brat."

"Owed him a favor," Cash goes on. "One that makes us even. When we were younger, we got into trouble a lot. This one time, I was cornered in a dark alley with three guys tryin' to beat me with a baseball bat. It was a case of mistaken identity, but they didn't care about that. Let's just say he saved my life that night."

"Am I gonna be able to do my other work?"

"Not at the shop, but if she wants to try her hand at drivin' trucks, why not?" Ryder pipes up.

Even though I've only just laid eyes on this chick, I know for a fact she's never done a day's work in her life. She has that look. I know her type and she's gonna be a handful.

Still, how hard could it be? I mean, if I get to sit around babysitting and working from a laptop, why not?

Cash gives me a chin lift. "Can still work security while you watch her. Do what you need to do. You won't get any trouble out of her."

I snort, looking up at him from the file. "You really think that's true?"

"She's scared," Cash says. "As much as she tells her father

she isn't, he knows her better than anyone and she'll do what he says. They have a strained relationship and she never told him about the show. He had to see it on national TV."

"So she's a daddy's girl?"

"Could say that. He spoiled her, so expect a little backlash. She's used to gettin' her own way. But her bark's worse than her bite, or so I've been told." He scratches his chin, not looking one bit sorry for me.

"There really is nobody else?" I wince. I mean, she's hot, but it's not like I'm gonna fuck her. She's too young, for one. Her profile says she's twenty-three.

Even if the idea that she's completely off limits makes my dick stir.

Those pretty eyes...

Cash shakes his head. "Don't trust that Nevada or Riot will stay out of her pants and that would be an issue."

She couldn't be a virgin, for Christ's sake. Hell, she might even enjoy it.

"You sayin' you trust me to stay out of her pants?" I smirk.

Cash stares me down. "If you know what's good for you, and just so we're clear; fuckin' her is off the table. I don't need her whinin' to daddy that you've gone and fucked with her and broke her heart. For fuck's sake, don't need any more drama."

Well damn. There goes the fun police. "You've said it three times, boss. I got it."

"Good."

"Not my type anyway," I mutter.

I smell Manny's BLT before he even appears and my stomach growls.

The man can cook, that's for sure. He works here full-time and loves to experiment with recipes and we're the lucky recipients.

"Knock, knock," he sing-songs.

This man is the only person I know who's so cheery first thing in the morning.

"Oof," he says, when he places the plate in front of Cash, but his eyes are on me. "Have a bad night, *handsome?*"

He's also bi and doesn't have any bones about letting everyone know, not that you'd have to guess with the getup he's wearing to cook in; patent leather pants, a canary yellow shirt, and smudged eyeliner under his eyes that make him look like a pretty punk rocker. Everyone in the club loves him and the chicks adore him like lovesick little puppies. He's a good guy, but I shit stir him a lot, and he gives it right back.

"Actually, no," I lie. "Couple chicks kept me up all night, that could be why."

Of course, within an MC you have to keep up appearances, even if nobody has seen you with a chick, or in this case two chicks, in weeks.

"Uh huh." Manny gives me a chin lift. "Need to work on a little more shut-eye. Don't want people saying your brother is better looking."

Ryder hoots with laughter, and Cash runs a hand over his face as he chuckles. I think his new baby Caprice has been keeping him and Deanna up. Fatherhood suits him; he has always been a protective motherfucker.

"You done?" I shake my head.

"I'll whip you up a protein shake," he says with a smile. "I'll even add some collagen, it'll help with the hangover."

I did have a few beers last night, but I wasn't totally shit faced.

I frown. "I'm not hungover, and how about some of what Cash is havin'?"

"I'd love to, but that was the last of the bacon." He shrugs, though I'm sure it's bullshit. Fuck knows what I did to piss him off.

Manny always has the fridge well stocked, just in case he

plans on a Gumbo cook off, which he's been known to do randomly, not that any of us mind.

His cooking is amazing, which is why he gets away with half of what he says and does. Nobody is ever gonna fire him.

"Right." This place just sucks the pickle. "A round of grilled cheese will be fine."

He clicks his fingers. "What's the magic word now?"

I roll my eyes. "Is he always like this?" I ask the brothers opposite me.

"Pretty much," Ryder laughs.

Cash tucks into his BLT that looks like it just jumped off the page of a food magazine photoshoot.

"I can still hear you, you know," Manny says.

I glare at him, my stomach practically growling. "Pretty please with a cherry on top."

Manny claps his hands as he laughs. "See now that wasn't very hard, was it?"

He doesn't wait for an answer, disappearing out the door before I get a chance to put my coffee order in, not that he'd make me coffee, but I just like stirring the pot.

I turn back to Cash and Ryder. "So, Sunday?"

Cash nods. "She'll need pickin' up from the airport. Jas may come with you. It may be a little overwhelmin' for her if you and the prospects show up with her name card."

I pull on my cut lapels. "Why, what's wrong with us?"

He snorts. "Do I even need to answer that? Now get the fuck out of here. Jas or Luna will email you the flight details."

"Okay." I go to stand.

"Oh, Rock?" Cash says, just as I turn to leave.

"Yeah?"

"I meant what I said, and this is no joke. She's twenty-three. It's your job to keep men away from her. She'll be a novelty if she comes to the club. Anythin' happens to her, I'll hold you personally responsible."

I try not to roll my lips with amusement. "Got it."

I grab the folder and take off. The smell of grilled cheese hits my nostrils as I wander into the kitchen.

So my mystery girl is daddy's little princess.

Great.

Just what I don't fuckin' need.

4

ASPYN

THE PLANE HAS BARELY HIT THE TARMAC AND I CAN FEEL THE heat and the smell of the humid, swampy air, but maybe that's just my mind playing tricks on me.

Needless to say, Tara isn't happy not knowing where I'm going. I feel weird lying to my best friend, but to be honest, I'm not minding this whole idea of being incognito. It's kind of exciting, now that I have my head wrapped around it.

Remembering the shitstorm a few weeks ago with the show, and everyone wanting me to do interviews to find out what really went on, has me feeling nauseous all over again.

I don't want to rehash it. And I definitely don't want to think about it, let alone talk about it on national television.

Lisa is a goddamn piece of shit and Dylan is a liar who I'm glad to see the back end of. I always fall for the bad boys. I don't know what the fuck it is about my nature that makes me think I can fix people. I see a man in a suit with a pair of pretty eyes and I'm ga-ga. No matter his background or financial status, or even his last name. I'm a sucker for a pretty face, what can I say?

Maybe being around bikers will be a good thing. They're

all old guys who are probably slobs who won't give two shits about me being there. Hopefully, that'll mean I get to do what I want. My dad is a little over the top with his rules.

That's just the way it is, but he also has to understand that I'm a grown woman and I'm capable of making my own decisions. He just doesn't realize that. I'm sure he still sees me as a twelve-year old with pigtails.

We pile off the plane and I head toward the baggage claim.

It's gonna be nice and awkward, but I have to put those thoughts aside. I'm only here for a few weeks, I hope, and in that short time it won't be long enough to form any kind of relationship with anyone. Not that I'd want to, but surely there are women in the motorcycle club?

I get visions of biker clad broads with garish makeup and wild hair and I giggle to myself. I mean, I'm not a snob, I'll pretty much talk to anyone. I don't judge, but the idea of me fitting into the NOLA Rebels MC is kinda laughable.

Still, I'm up for anything that gets me out of the house.

Maybe my dad will have bigger ideas and send me back on the first flight out tomorrow. Still. He trusts Cash Hudson and that says a lot. I've never met the man, but I know they go way back, and for dad to put my life in another person's hands is telling.

My dad is many things, even been called a tyrant by some, but I know he loves me. His way of showing me is wrapping me in cotton wool and sending me off to New Orleans to hide.

I have to admit, none of this sits well with me. I've had that awful feeling in the pit of my stomach for weeks, and I'm still coming to terms with what Dylan did. I'm sure my dad's keeping things from me about the stalker.

That's what you get for opening your heart. What a goddamn joke.

Rock

Now I'm the poor little rich girl who got cheated on. I haven't even gone online to see what people are saying but Tara has told me it's a mixed bag of emotions ranging from:

She's a sad little rich girl, probably making it up for publicity.

He's too hot for her anyway. I heard she sucks in bed.

Then... **I feel sorry for her. She has no real friends. How could he do this to her? What a douchebag.**

She did the right thing. That bitch had it coming.

I swear to God, that reality show is the fucking bane of my existence.

Trust me to go and do something completely extreme. just to prove a point, and have it all backfire in my face. My dad thinks I'm a complete idiot. Not only that, but I went against his wishes and a part of me knows he doesn't trust me.

You're a grown woman, I remind myself.

I know, I know. I just have to keep reminding my brain of that every time I torture myself. Which is often.

Of course, nothing went right on this flight. Not only did I get stuck next to a Chatty Kathy in first class, but the air vent wasn't working properly, making me a sweaty mess by the time we landed. I don't know how people in coach do it, cramped together like that with no room to move. At least Pirate behaved in his pet carrier by my feet.

I grumble when I remember my dad giving me a send-off. He promptly told me I was basically cut off from spending until he could trust me again. I like how he waited until the day I was leaving to drop that bombshell.

I'm not a diva. Not by any means, but that's a little harsh, even for him.

I'm also an only child so I've never known what it's like to have a sibling, whereas Tara comes from a big family and they're not all that well off. Her father had to work two jobs so she could go to the best schools, and sometimes I ask myself if she truly appreciates it. Tara has always been down to earth, and she's been very grounding for me.

She has a nice family but acts like they're the worst people in the world. At least she gets to see her parents often and have dinner with them every night. I'm lucky if I see my father twice a week. He's a busy man.

Resting my cat carrier on the trolley, I stroke Pirate through the cage as he purrs against my hand. He's a good traveler, thank God. There was no way on earth I was going anywhere without him.

When my luggage finally finds its way onto the conveyor belt, I screw my nose up as I see one battered end of my Gucci suitcase. *Fuckfaces.*

I should've just brought my cheap luggage, knowing that airlines are notorious for wrecking people's shit. I lug the case onto the trolley I just paid five dollars for and wait for the rest. I didn't exactly pack light and now I'm wincing at the fact that most of my luggage probably looks demented and unrepairable.

My father does have his own plane, but it's currently in transit, something he was annoyed about. I assured him I'd be fine flying commercial. Nobody knows I'm going and my driver took several wrong turns to ensure nobody was following us. Maybe my dad needs to keep him on board.

I pull my phone out while I wait for the carousel to chug along.

Tara

> How are you? I miss you already x

I smile, replying quickly.
Me

> Just landed. Tired. Hungry. My luggage looks like it went three rounds with Mike Tyson, but other than that I'm good. Miss u too x

Rock

The gray bubble appears as I glance up at the conveyor belt. It's beeping loudly, indicating something's gone wrong… That's all I damn well need. More delays.
Tara

> Why can't you tell me where you are? It's not fair. I'm not going to tell anyone

I've thought about this a lot, and I know I will cave eventually because I can't hide things from my best friend. But I worry that someone will use her as a target, and the less she knows the better.
Me

> I know, but dad is really worried. He doesn't want to implicate anyone close to me for their safety, babe. We talked about this

The bubble appears again, and I start to get a pain throbbing in my temples. She's overprotective, a lot like dad, and isn't afraid to tell me.
Tara

> What if something happens and I can't be there?

I smile to myself. Sometimes I feel like my best friend is really the only friend I have in the world and certainly the only one that understands me. She means well.
Me

> Stop worrying. I'm fine

My dad knows some pretty shady people. He still hasn't given me all the details and I'm not as dumb as he thinks I am. I know that he isn't telling me everything, like what was in the dressing room and how someone got in there. I know that this time the threats were real.

Real enough to send me to some stinking, low-down, motorcycle club where they probably have stripper poles and the men drink shots off women's asses.

I cringe at the idea.

Thank God my dad got this apartment. At least I won't have to live in and amongst that kind of caper in the clubhouse, not that I would have agreed to it.

Sharing my space with dirty bikers is where I draw the line. I hope at least one of them is cute…

One of my suitcases sails past, and I lunge after it, missing it. I stumble and almost trip over the damn trolley.

Two strong hands grab me by the shoulders, preventing my fall, and as I turn to thank whoever it was, he's already yanking my suitcase off the carousel.

My eyes go wide when I see his back. A black, leather motorcycle jacket with NOLA REBELS MC and a huge emblem of a skull and crossbones greets me.

I swallow hard.

He has long, dark hair and it's tied back in a messy ponytail. My eyes glance down at his ass; damn he looks good in those ripped jeans. *Ding-dong*.

If only his face is just as nice as the rest of him… suddenly his dark, ochre eyes meet mine as my eyes go wide and my lips part. *Holy fucking shit.*

This guy is gorgeous, like really fucking hot.

He has a sizable beard, long at the front and short at the sides. A perfectly straight nose. Dark eyebrows that frame his beautiful face. Not only that, but he towers over me. He has the perfect body size and shape and it's clear by the look of his broad chest and shoulders that he works out. I immediately feel the heat rising up my neck to my cheeks. One annoying thing about me when I get flustered is I turn red.

Rock

This can't be happening… Have I hit the jackpot?

I glance down at the emblem on his breast pocket, which spells his name. At the same time as I read it, he says, "Hey, I'm Rock." His voice is deep and low.

Jesus, he has perfect lips too. I suddenly wonder what that beard would feel like between my… *No!*

My lips part, my throat drying up like the freaking Sahara desert as I squeak, "Hi, uh thanks… for the suitcase-near-miss fiasco."

He frowns.

I'm such a loser.

"It's no problem. So, you must be Aspyn."

Way to go, idiot. Don't even tell him your name.

Of course he knows who I am. My dad probably sent him my mugshot. I'm quite proud of it, actually. The photo went viral, and I was called "the hottest mugshot since Paris Hilton." I'll take that as a compliment.

But, I am a well-bred girl from a wealthy neighborhood and I can't even remember basic manners.

I nod like a damn idiot. "Yep." That's it. That's all I can come up with.

He gives me a chin lift. "This it?"

"Uh." I clear my throat. "Not exactly. I have another five cases to come."

His surprise shows as one eyebrow arches up, and I bite down on my lip.

He is smoking fucking hot. There is no denying it. My heart races at how he towers over me.

Is he the guy who's going to be following me around everywhere? Or is he just here to escort me to the apartment and then I'll meet my new bodyguards? So many questions and my dad didn't tell me shit.

I hope it's him.

I could spend my days just checking him out, or making

out… That could be fun. It's been a while and I've not been with anyone since Dylan.

Maybe I'll pretend I work out at the gym so he gets to show off those muscles…

He's staring at me, and I realize he's still talking.

"Sorry?" I mutter, embarrassed that I'm acting this way.

"I said, I'm glad I ditched the prospects so we have room in my truck. They're gonna tail us."

I frown. "What's a prospect?"

He loads my case onto the trolley. "Someone who doesn't need to be here."

I sigh. "So there's…just, *you*?"

He looks up at me. "Don't worry. I'm packin'."

My eyes go wide. "Really?"

He snorts. "You're safe with me."

So, does that mean…he's my new bodyguard. And he does or doesn't carry a gun?

Could the gods be so kind?

I give him a look. "That's what my last two bodyguards said, and now they're working security at a mall in Spokane."

His lips twitch. "Obviously, they didn't know what they were doin'."

"Clearly." I flick my hair over my shoulder. I've always been nice to my dad's staff.

I don't treat them like they need to wait on me hand and foot or anything, but do I have to be nice to *these* guys?

I mean…I can't see this Rock guy cooking my meals and washing my clothes. Suddenly, everything is becoming more and more apparent.

If my dad really wanted me to have a good time on this trip, he would've sent staff with me. Then again, maybe the penthouse comes with staff? That would make more sense. I mean, I'm all for getting my hands dirty, but I've never really had to use the kitchen before. I try not to ponder on that horrible thought of trying to cook food.

He glances at my cat cage. "Who's in there?" He peers around the cage as Pirate blinks at him. He can be a sassy cat if he doesn't like you. And if he doesn't like you, you know pretty quickly.

"Pirate," I say proudly. "You're not allergic, are you?"

He shakes his head. "Animals love me."

I roll my lips. I'm sure they do.

I'd love to see him stick his hand in the cage, just to see what Pirate does, but he thinks better of it.

"Gonna need another trolley," he mutters. When I fish out my credit card, our eyes meet again. "You don't pack light."

I steel my back. "I'm from the city." Like that explains everything.

"The City of Angels, clearly."

What in the fuck is that supposed to mean?

I tuck a lock of hair behind my ear and then I see another suitcase bobbing by on the belt. "My case!" I yelp, but he's quicker than me.

He reaches it in two long strides and yanks the thing off swiftly like it weighs nothing.

His lips twitch when he says, "What you got in here, a dead body?"

"Just the essentials," I tell him. "I really don't know how long I'm going to be here for, after all."

He gives me a chin lift. "Give me the card. I'll get another trolley."

He's not asking, it's a demand. And it's so fucking hot.

Stop it.

Now is not the time to be crushing on this dude who not only looks like he just stepped off some magazine cover for Bad Boys Ink, but who also might just be the reason I want to draw this trip out for as long as possible.

Wait until I tell Tara. She'll never believe it. Not that she'll approve, as she hated Dylan and every other guy I've ever been with. Nobody is good enough for me in her eyes.

I hand it over, and as I do, our fingers touch and I feel a jolt. I steel my jaw and press my thighs together at the same time. *Jesus.* As he turns, I get a whiff of his cologne and my ovaries just about explode. It's musky, almost peppery, with a hint of woods.

It's very him.

Mr. Dark and Dangerous.

He might have a pretty face, but the vibe I get coming off him is all wrong. Not wrong in a bad way, like I feel uncomfortable with him, but in another way. Like he's lived a hard life. Like he's seen it all.

I check out his ass as he walks toward the trolleys and avert my gaze when he returns back.

Even the way he walks commands attention. And people are looking.

They're probably wondering what I'm doing with this guy. If it weren't me, I'd be thinking the exact same thing.

It takes another fifteen minutes of standing in awkward silence until all my luggage is finally loaded. Thank God nothing looks as damaged as the first suitcase.

We push the trolleys out together through the exit, and I follow him to his truck.

It's as expected, a large four-wheel drive, black with tinted windows.

It looks like something a biker would drive, when they're not on a motorcycle.

I stand by as he loads all the cases into the trunk, and then lays my hand luggage on the back seat.

"Hop in," he says, nodding to the passenger side.

I do as he says, taking Pirate's cage and placing him on the floor, then I pull myself into the cab as I glance around. It's neat and smells like him.

Holy fuck.

I clear my throat for what feels like the millionth time as

he swings his way into his seat, the car rocks with his weight and he starts the engine.

"Nice ride," I say, staring ahead.

I feel his eyes on me. "Thanks."

"Do you ride a Harley normally?"

"Sure do." Then I turn as he leans his arm over the back of my chair to reverse.

Holy mother of God. This man shouldn't be legal.

It's a simple enough move, guys do it all the time. But with him, it's so fucking sexy.

I press my legs together again. It's been a while. Sue me. And being locked in his cab with that woodsy smell permeating my nostrils might just tip me over the edge.

I'm sure as fuck feeling things in my nether-region and this Rock guy could be just the one to relieve the tension…

"So, have you ever been in this neck of the woods?" he asks.

He's hot, smells amazing, has pretty eyes and he's chatty? Surely, he must have some flaws…

"Uh, no. I can't say I have. The brochure says you have a lot of mosquitos and alligators."

His lips turn up into a devastating smile. I realize that Rock smiling could actually be my undoing, which is ridiculous, I just met this man… *Breathe, fruitcake, just breathe.*

"Don't worry, the alligators are well fed." He gives me a wink, and I quickly look away.

"Hopefully not from the tourists?"

"Nah. Just bad people."

What the fuck is that supposed to mean?

I wrinkle my nose. "What's that bad smell in the air?"

"We've had marsh fires burning for a few weeks. The wind has shifted to the northeast so it's not as bad." He puts the car into drive and we take off.

"Is that normal?"

He shrugs. "It happens from time to time. Wait until you

get to Bourbon Street, then you'll really wonder if they're keepin' corpses under the cities buildin's. Storm traps filled with grease stink up the place like death. Council said they'd fixed it, but I doubt they'll ever get rid of it."

I have heard that the smell from the city can be bad.

"Sounds like fun."

"It's different."

"How's the nightlife around here?"

I feel him glance at me again before he says, "It's not for pretty girls, if that's what you're askin'."

My eyes meet his. *He thinks I'm pretty?*

Okay... *Keep breathing.*

"So that means it's dangerous?"

"It's like anywhere. There are dangerous places and not so dangerous places. Lead with common sense; it's never let me down before."

So we have a wise-guy. Do I not look smart enough to know that?

A few moments pass by when I ask. "So how long have you been part of the NOLA Rebels?"

He changes lanes and I try not to notice his heavily tattooed hands and the adornment of rings on all his fingers. He also has a thick chain around his neck that's tucked into his black t-shirt. If my dad could see me now, he'd have a freaking heart attack and that makes me smile just a little bit.

He clears his throat and shifts in his seat. "Not long. My brother has been with them for thirteen years."

"Why did you wait so long?"

"I was in jail."

My eyes go wide for the hundredth time as my mouth hangs open. "You were in *jail?*" I repeat.

Maybe my dad should have done reference checks before sending me here. I grasp my seatbelt, like that will protect me.

"Yep, not for the whole time. Longest stint was six months."

Rock

"You've been in jail more than once?"

I let the words hang there, afraid to hear what comes next out of his mouth.

He turns to me again, one corner of his mouth turning up, and I wait in anticipation for his words of wisdom...

5

ROCK

Her pretty eyes flash as I shock her once more.

Taunting Little-Miss-Goodie-Two-Shoes might just be my new favorite game.

She flushes the most delightful shade of pink. For some reason, I didn't expect her to be as innocent as she's acting, or maybe that's all it is…an act?

She's twenty-three, and from what I've read, she's lived a very sheltered life. The typical little rich kid who's never had to lift a finger or do anything.

I'm sure someone like me has her second guessing what the fuck she's doing here, and we're not even on the freeway yet.

"Does that surprise you?"

I like how her eyes blink at me as if she has no idea what to think. I like her innocence. It's a turn on.

Her photo and mugshot do her absolutely no justice. She's hot.

Her hair is the same blonde as the photos but it's more unruly. She has a small amount of makeup on, but not a lot. Her eyes, though…bright blue with flecks of green. She is stunning, even if she is a good foot shorter than me and could do with putting on a pound or two.

"I, uh...it's not really any of my business."

"I'm a truth teller," I say. "Don't like bullshit, and if you ask me a question, you'll get an honest answer. Usually, it's straight between the eyes, but on the flip side, you always know where you stand."

She nods like she's still comprehending my words, then says, "So...you and me..." She flicks her pointer finger between the two of us. "We're...uh, *you're* my new bodyguard?"

I snort a laugh. "I wouldn't go that far, but I *am* the guy who's been assigned to your security for the duration of the trip. So...sorry, *Trouble,* you're stuck with me."

Her lips part as her eyes dart to my mouth, and I divert my gaze back to the road.

Those pretty lips, and even prettier eyes, don't do anything to dull down my erection.

And she smells like buttery popcorn. For fuck's sake. I have no idea how I'm not gonna put my fuckin' hands on her while we're holed up together in this swanky new apartment building that I've been assigned to. This won't be a hardship at all.

"*Trouble?*" She practically pouts when she says it.

I rub my chin. "You look like trouble."

She snorts. "I thought the same thing about you."

I glance at her again and I laugh, too. I can't say I've had this kind of easy banter with a woman before in my life. I mean, chicks and I aren't friends.

We're there for one reason and one reason only.

Aspyn, however, she's a different kettle of fish. I didn't choose to be here, yet I'm glad I am. For now, anyway. She's too good to be true.

"*Me?*" I thumb my chest like I'm the Archangel Gabriel. "Do I look like I'd cause anybody any grief?"

She bites down on her bottom lip, then says, "Only wayward alligators, maybe?"

I snort.

She's funny too. Sassy. Hot as fuck. The whole damn package. No wonder Cash was so adamant. Now I get it.

My wood isn't gonna go down for days.

I don't see how staying away is gonna help me. I'm fuckin' assigned to her day and night.

She's just landed in my lap like some wayward little deer who needs steering back to the herd…not left out in the open for guys like me.

The big bad wolf.

I grin at the idea, knowing I'm not gonna touch her. She'd freak out anyway. She's not ready for a man like me.

Chicks like her only fuck country club types; the ones who already have a fortune before they're even old enough to spend it. They wear their cashmere sweaters wrapped around their necks and drive fancy sports cars that they don't know how to handle.

But if she's uncomfortable in my presence, she sure as heck hides it well.

She seems perfectly at ease.

And she better be, as we're about to get up close and personal in a different way.

I got the logistics report from her father this morning.

I have to sleep at the apartment building, which I guess is a given, but you'd think a prospect on the door would be enough to ensure her safety while I sleep in my own bed, in my own place. It's like Fort fuckin' Knox in that complex. Nobody can get to her floor without the damn code and a pass.

I crack my neck.

It's gonna be okay.

She's off limits. She's off limits. She's off limits.

"Don't worry, where we're goin', we don't have any alligators, wayward ones or otherwise."

"Good to hear. So, I guess a trip out to the bayou is off the cards then?" She quirks an eyebrow as she looks over at me.

"Better believe it."

As she sighs, the sound makes me turn my head. "You good?" I prompt.

She fiddles with her fingers in her lap; the first sign I've seen that she's a little hesitant, aside from the lip biting which is turning me the fuck on.

"I'm fine."

It's none of my business, and I don't know why I care, but I find myself asking, "Why the sigh?"

I can't be sure, but I think she just eye rolled me. "Because it's always the same, no matter where I go or what I'm doing."

Uh, oh. Cash warned me she was a brat. Five minutes in the car and she's already whining.

"What is?"

She crosses her arms over her chest and it's the first time I really notice her tits.

They're not huge, but also not small. Just the right size if we're comparing apples to oranges. I imagine sliding my hand up her torso and under her shirt to feel how hard her nipples are...

"My father's rules."

Here we go... "Sounds like you don't like that."

"You guessed right."

"So why follow them?" I say.

I feel her gaze on me. "What do you mean?"

I shrug. "You're old enough to make your own decisions, Aspyn."

It's the first time I use her name, and I don't know if it's just me, but I'm sure I heard a little intake of breath when I said it.

"That just goes to show you how different we really are because, in my world, if you don't do as your parents say, you'll be outcasted and labeled a black sheep."

"So? All you'd have to do is sell one of your fancy cars and you'd be able to start out someplace new. I'm guessin' you drive a luxury car and have lots of pretty things to sell if you did get cut off."

Probably not the right thing to say, but I've never minced words.

She all but gapes at me. "It's not that simple, *Rock.*"

The way she says my name isn't kind or gentle, but a little on the firm side, and my dick practically aches at the idea that she's already mad at me.

Why am I such an asshole?

I shouldn't be messing with her...but she's just too cute.

"Yes, it is. You poor little rich kids are all the same. But really, you gotta ask yourself this; is he really gonna cut you off? And if so, wouldn't he have done that already?"

"For your information, he *has* cut me off," she all but snarls at me. "For the entire stay. It's like he wants to punish me all over again."

Oh, *mystery girl* has a temper. I like that, too.

"For doin' that show?"

She swallows hard. "You know about that?"

I give her a sideways look. "I know a lot about you, *Trouble.* More than I probably should."

Her lips part again, and I force myself to look away.

Fuck.

This is not going as planned.

She reaffirms her arms over her chest as I concentrate on the road.

"Exactly what else do you know about me?"

"Nothin' much, just what your dad told us." Also, not true. I broke into her college records doing some research of my own to see if there was a conflict with anyone.

Rock

It seems Little Miss Perfect was an honorable student. She graduated with a degree in English, of all things, and as far as I can see, she has never held a job but has been involved in a lot of charity work. So I guess that's something.

I have no idea what kind of job you're supposed to get, majoring in English, but I assume it's more of a socialization and networking thing for rich kids. Something brats who study nothing at Harvard or Yale do. In this case, the latter for Aspyn Ashley Huntley.

I know she's scrutinizing me to see if I'm telling the truth, and the fact that I'm not doesn't worry me one bit. If I want to find out every damn thing about her, I'd probably just have to stalk her Facebook profile. Something I've only glanced at briefly. This girl Tara that she's always photographed with needs to be looked at a little more closely, as does the ex-boyfriend, Dylan Maloney. He looks like a jerk.

Her dad says they're not threats, but everyone is guilty until proven innocent in my book.

She turns to face me and says, "Spill."

I frown. "Huh?"

"Spill what you know since you seem to think you're an expert."

I can't help but smirk.

Temper, temper.

"The basics. What I need to know to protect you, Aspyn *Ashley* Huntley."

I can feel her fury and I revel in it. I'm a son of a bitch, what can I say?

"Surely, you couldn't be as bad as the last two guys I had watching me."

"Like I said, you don't have to worry about that."

She laughs without humor. "I had a whole team. Here… there's just you. I'm sure you'll figure it out."

Her tone mocks me, but I don't care. Anything to keep her

talking, which is weird for me. Usually, I don't like chicks who talk a lot.

"That's where you're wrong. We have a big club. Everyone is there to help if they're needed. You see that truck behind us?"

She frowns, swiveling in her seat to look behind her. "Uh, yeah?"

"Didn't even notice them, did you?"

She turns her gaze back to mine. "Should I? Who are they?"

"My guys. The prospects."

"Oh. You said you ditched them."

"Yeah, from my truck. Then I said they're gonna be tailin' us."

"So...how many of them are back there?"

"Two."

"Do they have guns, too?"

I snort. So she takes everything literally. Of course she does. "I'm not really packin'... Not on my body anyway."

"You have a gun in the *truck*?"

"You ask a lot of questions."

"Can you blame me?" she balks. "I have no idea what the hell is going on here. Just what little information my dad told me. And to be honest, I'm getting pretty sick of being kept out in the cold."

There's that temper again. She flares so quickly.

"What do you need to know?"

"Where we're going for a start."

I frown. Her dad never told her?

"The Platinum Apartments. It's a new complex downtown in an elite neighborhood. Practically need a passport to get in the buildin'."

This seems to settle her.

So her security is an issue. I wondered if she thought this

was all a joke, but it's clear that she's worried, even if she tries her best to hide it.

"Okay, and then what?"

I blink. "What do you mean? That's where you'll be staying, and when you need to go out, I'll be there to escort you."

"All day?"

"Yes."

"And night?"

Now it's my turn to swallow hard. "Yes."

"So you'll be staying there, too?"

"For the most part."

I don't register the look on her face. Is she pleased, or horrified? I can't tell.

She takes a moment's pause before asking, "So, I can go out?"

I part my lips. "Within reason…for essentials."

She sighs again. "Uh huh."

"Uh huh, what?" I'm not understanding.

"I'm under lock and key here, too."

I frown. "It's like that at home?"

"Why don't you tell me?" she snaps. "You seem to know all about me."

Okay, so this is an issue and I'm learning that she gets pissed off easily.

Being under her dad's control is triggering for her.

I'm gonna take a wild stab at the fact she's daddy's little girl, like Cash said — and as if her resume isn't enough to prove otherwise — she's never been let far enough out of his sight to do anything for herself. Except maybe for college, and even then Cash told me she had security.

Her going on that show was acting out. She was trying to get his attention, and probably that of her boyfriend too.

I can see that the brat aspect of Aspyn's personality takes a little time to surface, but that's probably because she's putting walls up as we speak.

Of course, I'm not gonna go into what I know about her. I don't want her to think I'm some kind of weirdo. I'm only researching so I know how to protect her.

This is my job now. I can't fail Cash.

This is important to him, so it's important to me.

"Like I said, your father briefed us on the basics," I go on. "And that nobody knows where you are, including your best friend."

"What's her name?" she challenges.

I let out a slow breath. "Tara."

She shakes her head.

"So?" I prompt. "Does she know you're here?"

Again, she shakes her head.

"But she has your new number, right?"

She doesn't even have to speak to answer that. As if she's going to stay away from her best friend since kindergarten.

Little does she know I can tap into her phone if and when I need to.

The fact her father went to these lengths after the emails I've seen are understandable. One described exactly what he'd do to her if she ever saw Dylan again. Why that mattered I don't know, but this person is definitely obsessed to the point of paranoia.

There are also photos of Aspyn, sent via email, from her stalker.

Photos of her everywhere, unbeknown to her.

Shopping.

At restaurants.

Embracing her friend.

Coffee with other friends.

Getting in and out of her father's limo.

They got too close. Too fuckin' close.

She's smaller in person than she looks on camera. Tiny. Her small frame is no match for any would-be attacker.

Oh, don't get me wrong. Aspyn's a smart girl, but it's worrying that she's not more aware of her surroundings. I know cameras have lenses, but still. This person has been following her for a while now. Tommy is lucky nothing happened before now, though he said the threats have been on and off for years.

"Say it, *Aspyn*. Does she have your new number?"

"She's my best friend," she says haughtily. "She can have my new number if she wants. I'm a grown woman. I don't need my father's permission, or yours, or anyone else's, for that matter. In fact, I'm starting to think that this was a very big mistake."

"You're mad because I asked you if your best friend has your number?"

"No. I'm mad because I don't even know what I'm doing here or why I listened to him."

She has no idea the gravity of how bad things are, yet she still went along with it.

She's got no life experience, which is why she does everything her daddy says, then questions it later.

"He's only tryin' to keep you safe."

"So he keeps saying," she mutters.

I know I should leave it, but I can't seem to stop my gums flapping. "So, you disagree? Then why come?"

"I disagree with most of what my father says, not that it matters to him."

"I think you do matter to him," I say. "Otherwise, he wouldn't have gone to these lengths to protect you from harm."

She snorts. "Yeah, shows how much you know."

So, I've established all is not well at home, no matter how pretty the picture Tommy painted of their relationship.

"I know a lot about bein' someone who people don't worry about," I say.

The second the words leave my mouth, I regret them. *Why*

are you saying these things? She doesn't need to know your life story.

I feel her eyes on me once more. "Are you close to your parents?" she asks.

I almost balk at the idea. "My mom was a crack whore who overdosed when me and my brother were little, just after we got taken into care. My dad was a sperm donor. Don't even know who he is."

Her mouth falls open as I grip the steering wheel hard. I don't need to divulge my secrets to this woman I don't even know.

The notion is ridiculous.

"I'm sorry," she whispers.

The last thing I want is her pity, for fuck's sake. I don't want anyone's pity.

"Don't be. I turned out alright, considering."

"That's debatable."

I shoot her a look, and she smiles softly. She's kidding.

It melts at the ice I've built around my heart just a little.

"Wiseass."

She settles back into her seat, and the notion that she's comfortable with me settles my temper. Little does she know, I do have one. Not that I'd ever aim it at her, but my job now is to protect her. And I take my job seriously.

Whatever Cash wants of me, I'll do. Whatever her father wants of me, I'll do that, too.

Aspyn is stuck somewhere between a baby bird who doesn't know how to fly and a sultry vixen who has the power to render any man to his knees.

That combination is hard to find.

She saw me raw for a moment and instead of staying mad, she tried to cheer me up.

Not that I have any cure for what I have.

No, I don't.

And I also don't need Aspyn thinking I'm some kind of nice guy.

I'm nothing of the sort.

Maybe I know right from wrong, but I'm not very good at staying on the right side of the law.

I'll toe the line. I'll do as I'm told. But I'm rotten inside. I have darkness inside me that is untamed and unpredictable.

One day, the beast may be let out.

When I care about someone, there is nothing I won't do to protect them, but I'm doing this for Cash. Not her.

I just hope she doesn't piss me off too much, or get too close.

It's in her best interests if she just goes about her daily business and we converse only when necessary. This banter has been way too familiar. I need to control myself better.

As I glance at her once more, she's chewing on her nails. A bad habit that shows every bit of nervousness that's going on inside.

There are many layers to my mystery girl, and I have no intention of getting between those layers.

I'm best off on the outskirts looking in. That's what I do best. When I'm just there to be seen and not heard.

That's where I belong. And that's where I'm going to stay.

6

ASPYN

I cannot sleep with my security. I cannot sleep with my security.

For heaven's sake, is my father completely stupid?

He's not old. He also doesn't have the beer belly like I first imagined. And he's damn easy on the eyes.

Why would he pair me with this gorgeous man? Maybe he didn't know, which I find hard to believe. Then again, if he'd known that my new bodyguard has been in and out of jail, I can guarantee he wouldn't be placed in my care. Again, he trusts Cash.

Or maybe my father thinks I'll behave like the good little girl he raised.

What he doesn't know is that I'm getting more and more tired of his strict rules.

I only let him boss me around because I felt sorry for him, and he's told me on more than one occasion how lonely he gets. He has a bevy of women, don't get me wrong, but even I know that must get old after a while.

All those gold-digging women smiling at him, and acting as if they're important when, really, all they want is his money…and sex. I cringe at the thought. I'm not an idiot.

Rock

I know that my dad is an attractive man, and women of all ages flock to him. But when you're that rich and that well known, how do you ever find a woman who you can be yourself with? The answer is you can't. Hence why my dad has been a single bachelor for as long as I can remember.

The building to Platinum Apartments is as impressive as it sounds. And I get the entire penthouse. I guess that is the safest option, even though I've no idea what I'll do with all that space.

Rock pulls all of my suitcases out onto the sidewalk, and the doorman helps with my luggage. I carry Pirate as he purrs. I already let him out for a pee on the grass outside, holding his lead so he didn't get scared with the traffic. He's fully toilet trained, but I know he'll take some adjusting to get used to the new place.

This building has facilities that are top notch.

A full gym.

Two pools.

A sauna and spa.

A tennis court.

Private parking.

It even has a cafe on the street level that opens out onto a magnificent terrace.

Once we're in the elevator and heading toward the top floor, Rock says, "Cash will be comin' over in a few to introduce himself."

I frown. "I won't be going to the clubhouse?"

Rock looks at me strangely. "You want to?"

I shrug. "Sounds like a walk on the wild side. Why not?"

"Excuse me for sayin', but you don't exactly strike me as the wild type."

I glare at him. "Why not? You've known me all of five minutes and you think you know me?"

He smirks. I try not to notice how his whole face lights up when he smiles, and this isn't even a full smile.

My heart beats rapidly, and I know it's stupid.

"No, but I know your type."

I snort. "I doubt it."

"What's that supposed to mean? You think the only chicks I know are ones who hang around the clubhouse?"

I turn to him. "Aren't they?"

He shakes his head slowly. "Somethin' about me seems to appeal to the good girls."

My mouth goes dry at his words...*good girls.* Is that what he thinks I am? *A good girl?*

"You think I'm a good girl?"

"Bad girls don't go to Yale, sweetheart."

I exhale slowly, trying not to let my temper surge. "Yes, they do."

He shakes his head. "Don't think so."

I fold my arms over my chest defensively. "Have you ever been to Yale?"

He smirks. "You know the answer to that."

He has no idea how badly I want to be a bad girl. There is no good girl in me whatsoever.

"Why do you think good girls are attracted to you?" *So he thinks I am, too?*

He shrugs. "Could be the ink."

I glance down at his body, not that I can see much of his ink with all those clothes on.

"How many do you have?" *Why the fuck am I asking that?*

"A lot."

"You don't keep count?"

"At least twenty..."

"Oh."

"What about you?" His eyes dip to me as I stare straight ahead, trying to not picture him with just his tattoos and nothing else...

"I only have one."

"You do not."

"Do too."

"Where?"

I swallow hard. "Somewhere you'll never see."

He snorts. "That sounds more like a challenge."

I can't help feel that the air in here is feeling pretty thick. I mean, is Rock as attracted to me as I am to him? If so, then why does he keep teasing me?

"So when you said good girls are attracted to you, you meant me?"

"Trust me. There is nothing attractive about me if you really knew me."

My heart races about what a bad boy he must be in his real life.

Yet, he has kinda been sweet to me this whole time.

I can't help but wonder what kind of lover he'd make.

Would he be hard as a rock, just like his name. Taking me hard and fast. Or a slow, attentive lover who pleases me any which way he chooses? I press my legs together and hope he doesn't notice. I'm going to have to do something about letting off some steam tonight when I'm alone.

"I'm sure you have some redeeming qualities."

He laughs. "Redeeming? They teach you that at Yale?"

"Yes, they did, actually."

"Let me ask you somethin'?" He doesn't even wait for me to agree. "What kind of job does one expect to get with a degree in English?"

I open my mouth, then close it again. "I... My father wanted me to work for him in the family business," I say, though that still hasn't eventuated.

"So you work for him?" I love how he asks when he already knows the answer.

"No."

"Then what do you do all day?"

I take a slow breath. Why does it sound like an accusation?

"I spend time on my charity work, mainly," I say. "It's something I'm passionate about."

The elevator finally dings, and I'm relieved when Rock holds the doors open while he allows me to step out first into a massive foyer.

This place is so new I can smell the fresh paint.

He rolls the suitcases out one by one, and I look around, impressed.

Rock whistles low between his teeth. "This place is nice."

I turn to him. "You've never been in here before?"

He shakes his head. "First time. They have state-of-the-art security. Nobody can get up here without ID, not even the prospects. Only myself, Cash, and the club's Enforcer and Sergeant at Arms. They're trustworthy."

"Are you completely sure they *all* are?" I give him a cheeky smile and his eyes dip to my throat for half a second.

I see a storm in his eyes…like he's holding back. Could it be that I'm making Rock nervous? I almost laugh at the notion. As if a man like him would be intimidated by little old me. He probably thinks I'm a good girl freak who has a crush on him.

And while he may have that crush part right, he has no idea I feel like a ticking time bomb that hasn't gone off yet. I feel it in the pit of my stomach. All the rage. All the pain. All the hurt. It's all mounting.

Maybe it's a good thing I am here. I can fall apart without the media circling, and in a few weeks, it'll all have died down. Everyone will have forgotten all about it and hopefully this stalker business will be a thing of the past. Some crazed fan who moved onto greener pastures.

"You flirtin' with me, *Trouble?*"

I shake my head. "Wouldn't dream of it."

He spreads his hand out in front of him. "Ladies first."

I smile, pushing the foyer doors open to a beautiful expansive living room, the kitchen and dining combined, and it all overlooks the city.

Giant floor to ceiling windows, and sliding doors that lead out onto a huge patio. The view is impressive.

I walk toward the large bunch of yellow roses in a vase on the dining table. There's a card. It reads: **I hope you enjoy your new apartment, princess. It won't be long until you're back home. I promise. Dad x**

At least he left a note. I lean forward and take in the glorious scent.

Yellow roses are my favorite and it was a nice touch. I will, however, have to go shopping for some candles and other decor items because, while it's nice here, it's very beige and boring. The only color are the cushions on the couch, a deep blue and white stripe that match the rug.

Everything is opulent, including the large chandelier dangling over the kitchen table.

It can seat twelve people. I shake my head.

I put Pirate's carrier down, unlatching the door, and he sprints out, darting across the living room and down the hall.

"I need to get his litter box organized," I say.

"You have that in your luggage?"

I turn to him. "Of course. Well, just the crystals. My dad had the box delivered ahead of time. What kind of cat mama would I be?"

"There's also a rooftop lap pool," Rock tells me. "Or so I'm told, and a sun deck."

"You read the brochure?" I quip, running my hand over the plush couch.

It's so clean and immaculate that I already feel right at home.

I'm impressed but not at all surprised. My father does nothing by halves.

"Not just a pretty face, sweetheart."

I walk toward the kitchen and wave my hand around. "There's a lot going on there."

He leans his hands on the kitchen island and looks around. "What? It's just a kitchen."

I turn to him. "Don't laugh."

He puts a hand over his heart. "I would never."

I roll my eyes. "I don't cook."

He stares at me blankly, "That's gonna be an issue."

I frown. "No, it won't. The staff…"

His face turns from amusement to confusion. "*Staff?*"

"Yes. At home, we have a chef, a maid, a butler…" I trail off, swallowing hard. "There are no staff here, right?"

He shakes his head slowly. "No, sweetheart. Just me. And I don't cook. I don't clean either. Unfortunately, I didn't take after my twin brother."

I frown. "Twins?" *Oh, God. There's two of them?*

"Calm down, he's taken." He smirks as I shake my head.

I can see that Rock isn't gonna be hard work, and I should be thankful that at least we're getting along. Even if he is getting under my skin just a little bit.

"Ha-ha." I swallow hard then ask. "What about you? Are *you* taken?"

He stares at me, his eyebrow lifting slightly. "Why? Interested?"

I shake my head. "No. I'm just wondering what you're going to tell him or her about why you're out every single night, at another woman's apartment."

"*Her*," he states. "I'm into chicks."

"Never can tell these days," I say. "Didn't want to offend."

"None taken. And if Cash says you do somethin', then you do it. No questions asked."

"Sounds severe."

"That's the life of a biker. Cash is a good man," he tells me, looking suddenly serious.

Rock

I run a hand over the cool marble and then wander onwards, toward where the bedrooms must be.

"What do you do, Rock?" I ask. "As your day job?"

I feel his proximity so close behind me and now that I'm locked inside this huge apartment with him, it's kind of exciting. More exciting than it probably is, but being out of my dad's house with absolutely nobody else here, *except us*, sends exhilaration through me. It's like being free.

"I own a truckin' company."

"Oh?" I say, surprised. "And you're not needed there?"

"No, I've got it covered. I also do more security for the club than I ever have, so I'm needed there more at the moment."

"Bodyguard stuff?"

"Surveillance. This is a one off."

I like the idea that he hasn't done this before. That he hasn't been trapped in some apartment with some other girl who finds him attractive. Which just goes to show you how naive I really am. As if this man can't get any woman he wants or would be interested in someone like me.

I may have money, but I don't buy into the Hollywood fishbowl. My boobs are my own and I'm proud to say I don't have silicone shoved into my lips, or Botox, for that matter. Which is sacrilege amongst my other friends in LA who swear by it. Here it feels like I can let myself completely go and not care who notices.

What a thrilling thought.

And having Rock here with me, even if my slight crush on him is completely one-sided, doesn't worry me.

I've made this a fleeting fantasy, instead of the reality it is. Two people being forced together into a situation neither of them can get out of.

Well, I can pass the time however I damn well want.

The one thing my father doesn't own is my mind. And it's gonna stay that way.

He may have my free will, and make all my decisions for me, but he can't have this.

My thoughts are my own.

"Oh." *Why do I keep saying that?* I do like the idea that this is a once off.

It also means Cash trusts him implicitly.

Pirate skits past me and I try to catch him, but he jumps up on the couch instead.

"He's a little wayward at times," I explain, glad that he hasn't hissed at Rock or tried to bite him. "Especially new places."

Rock snorts. "He'll get used to it."

I push open the first door I come to. It's a nice spacious room and has a queen bed and a bathroom attached with a large walk-in closet. Again, there are views of the city from the window. The decor is neutral with a plush, fluffy throw and lots of pillows.

I can see that my father had a decorator in because these are all my colors.

There are also more yellow roses in a vase on the side table. I smile to myself.

Though, if Rock is staying here, I doubt he's going to appreciate it.

The next room is the same carbon copy of the first room, decorated the same. Opposite that is an office set up with a computer sitting on an expensive looking mahogany desk and bookshelves galore. There's also a small laundry room. I wince at the fancy washer and dryer and Rock notices.

"Don't tell me…"

"Shut up."

"Do you know how to work one of these things?"

I roll my eyes. "Of course I do."

"Show me then."

Before I can think, I punch him on the arm and he laughs, pretending to be hurt. "Ouch."

"That didn't hurt."

"You're right, it didn't, which has me thinkin'... I should show you some self-defense. You ever done anythin' like that?"

I turn to look at him. "No," I lie. "Do I need to know that? Isn't that what I have you for?" A new plan starts to brew in my head.

He gives me a disapproving look. "Every woman needs to know self-defense. Do you at least own pepper spray?"

I shake my head. That part is true.

He does not look impressed. Not one bit.

"*Aspyn*," he says, and the way he says my name...it shouldn't feel like a caress. It shouldn't feel like anything. I just met this man. "Not even in a place like LA?"

"I've always had..."

"Protection," he finishes. It's not a question. "Still. You should know the basics. Trust me, it's not that hard. Even someone of your slight stature..."

I give him a double blink. "My what?"

His lips twitch. "Okay, I was bein' polite. You're short, but that doesn't mean you aren't capable of defending yourself."

"Thanks for the reminder."

"Just bein' honest."

"You know they say sweet things come in smaller packages, haven't you heard?"

"Yeah, like poison?"

"Ha-ha. Like diamonds. And chocolate covered candy. And..." I wave a hand. "Other shit."

"Uh huh."

"You're a smartass."

"I've been called worse."

I avoid any more talk about the washer and dryer I don't know how to use and glance up the hallway toward the final room. The main suite.

I walk toward it, and when I push the double doors open, I gasp in surprise.

The bed is huge. A super king with a plush pink and white Versace bedspread and lots of cushions and pillows. I make a note to send my father's assistant, Alana, a thank you gift.

She clearly did all of the organizing in this place. I can't give my well-meaning, but hopeless dad, all the glory. He just picked the penthouse. Alana does all the hard work.

"Wow," Rock mutters.

The carpet is plush and new. It also has views of the city from the wrap-around windows that expand the entire way around the bedroom, stopping at the open-plan bathroom.

I see it has a massive jet tub, a large two-person shower with all the gadgets under the sun, and a separate toilet. It's all white with silver penny round tiling on the floor and subway tiles on the wall. The gold taps and matching hardware make the space look elegant and expensive. It screams class.

"I may never leave," I mutter.

Rock moves over to the sliding doors and opens one side. "Another patio," he says. "Nice place to have a mornin' coffee."

"You gonna make it?" I tease.

He turns to look at me and grins. "I think we're both gonna have to order in, *a lot*."

I turn to look at him. "So, you're really staying here? You weren't kidding?"

"Unless Cash changes his mind."

"But it seems pretty secure to me."

"Still. I have my orders."

Is that the only reason he's staying? Duh, of course it is.

A deep, dark notion surges through me at us being here alone together.

This man is the epitome of sex on a stick.

Rock

He's so fucking hot...and I'm here all alone with him in this big swanky apartment with a private pool and a sun deck? What in the world do I have to complain about? It's more like a self-imposed holiday, rather than a prison camp. Maybe I should send my dad a quiche and a bottle of wine.

I hug myself. Maybe this won't be so bad after all.

I join Rock out on the patio, looking down at the city traffic. We're so high up it makes me dizzy.

"You don't like heights?" he asks, nodding toward me.

I shake my head. "Never have."

"Yet you're in a penthouse."

"Safest place in the building."

His lips twitch again. "Guess that's true."

I stand in the doorway and avoid looking over the edge. It makes my legs feel weak. "So, what's for dinner?"

He cocks his head. "Shit on a stick?"

"That doesn't sound appealing. I'm sure we could hire a chef to make meals."

He shakes his head. "Nobody else is allowed in the apartment," he tells me, tone firm. I look at him in surprise. He's not kidding.

"Not even DoorDash?"

"Nope. You want take-out? I've gotta go get it."

"Like my little errand boy?"

He steps toward me, and I don't move back. He's so close to me that I forget how to breathe.

"Do I look like the type of man who's a little errand boy, *Trouble?*"

My heart rate accelerates. "Maybe."

He doesn't move and we're toe to toe. "No maybes about it. I don't run around for anyone, got me? I'm not here to be your maid."

I try not to smile, but I can't help it.

"You think that's funny?" He quirks an eyebrow.

I shake my head but fail at smiling. "Sorry. I'm not laughing. It's just…the image of you in a maid's outfit…a frilly little apron on…" *Holy fuck… What the fuck is wrong with me? And I haven't even been drinking…*

His eyes dip to my lips and my breathing hitches in my chest. *Oh, fuck…* His eyes look heated and his breathing is rapidly increasing…a lot like mine.

Is he… Is he attracted to me, too?

"If I were your maid, *Aspyn,* I wouldn't be botherin' with clothes, sweetheart. Just so you know."

My eyes go wide as he smirks, stepping around me as I realize I'm pressed right against the glass of the window behind me.

That bastard.

He knows what he's doing.

He knows he has me all in knots, and I'm a rookie at this flirting with a biker shit.

Still, that doesn't stop me.

What he doesn't know is that my panties are soaked. That for the first time in a long time, I'm actually looking forward to having a break from my 'real' life. And I get to spend it here, with him… Mr. Dark and Dangerous.

Maybe my luck is changing after all. Maybe all of the bad stuff in my head is just that.

It feels better already.

Even if I warn myself that this isn't some fairytale with a happy ending.

But I push the warning signs aside.

This is my fantasy, after all, and I can do with it whatever I please.

7

ROCK

"I'm sure you'll be happy here for the time bein'," Cash says, glancing around the room after his meet and greet with Aspyn.

"I'm sure I will be," Aspyn says. I frown at her tone. Cash doesn't get sassy Aspyn. All of a sudden, she's sugar with a cherry on top with Cash. "And I have my new security to make sure that nothing happens to me." She smiles sweetly.

What in the actual fuck?

She sounds like Mary, Mary quite fuckin' Contrary, or however that dumb as fuck nursery rhyme goes.

I want to facepalm myself.

His eyes meet mine and I give him a chin lift. "Everythin's in place," I tell him, trying to keep my voice even. "Apartment security are also on alert, and Mr. Huntley has assured me to call him, should anything change."

Cash nods. "The prospects?"

"One is outside at all times; Rodeo or Bandit tonight, and Pipes will take the inside shift."

Rodeo has just joined the club, and Bandit is Indigo's younger brother, Jonah.

Cash frowns. "Inside the apartment?"

"Only if I'm not here."

"But you will be here. At all times."

I glance at Aspyn, who looks as sweet as pie as she smiles at Cash once more.

She acts like an innocent angel, but I know her type. It's always the quiet, seemingly harmless chicks who surprise you. And the ones you have to worry about.

"Of course. I just meant in case somethin' else comes up…." I'm referring to Forger and the Devil's Ink mess. Something else we really don't need right now, but that's out of our hands.

Harlem and Tag did some networking on Saturday night, and we're closing in on the nomads that continue to haunt us. The quicker this is dealt with, the better. Though, I am kinda pissed that I have to miss out on the action. Saturday night turned out to be a bust because all I did was sit in a car with J.J listening to him whine about how much pussy he was missing out on being stuck in a car with me.

Cash frowns at me even more. Turning to Aspyn, he says, "Nice to meet you, Aspyn. You have my number. If you have any concerns, please give me a call."

"Okay, thank you, Cash. I'll do that," she says, stroking Pirate as she moves toward the kitchen. We ordered take-out after all, since neither of us can cook.

She seems to be on cloud nine after arriving, something I didn't expect. It has thrown me off a little. *Why would anyone be excited about this?* She's basically being kept prisoner for her own good and isn't allowed to do anything without her father's say so.

Only the few people from the clubhouse know she's here, and have overheard that she's a lot to handle. She definitely lives up to her reputation of being a pistol as well as difficult.

I make a mental note to stream some episodes of Tail Spin to see exactly what everyone is talking about, along with the infamous episode of Aspyn punching the chick who slept with her boyfriend. Now that I've met her, I can certainly see how it happened with that fiery temper. Sweet but spicy. I make a conscious effort not to chuckle.

"Rock?" Cash says, continuing what he was going to say. "A word."

I give him a chin lift and follow him out to the foyer.

"Sup?" I say. He has that look in his eyes, and I have no clue what I did wrong this time. I always seem to put my foot in it somehow.

He turns to face me. "When I say nobody is to come into this apartment but you, I mean it. The only thing I'll allow is a change of shift. You're expected to be here, and if you need to check on the shop, then she goes too." His tone is firm, reiterating the fact that this is important to him. "Since I'm puttin' you in charge, you can work the shifts out with Tag and the prospects. I need a copy of the schedule to send to Tommy. Better yet, email it to Jas and she can forward it on after briefin' me."

"Got it."

"Oh, and one other thing." He points in my face. "Stay away from her."

I frown. "Little bit hard, boss, considerin' you don't want me to leave." We've had this discussion already.

"Don't be a wiseass, you know what I mean."

I palm the back of my head. "She's not my type."

"She's pussy. She's your type. I'm not kiddin' around. I told her father she was safe here."

"And I told you she *is* safe. I'm handlin' it. Not short of hearin', Cash. I think I know when I can get my dick wet and when I can't."

He stares at me for a moment, and I don't look away. "Good. Tommy and I go way back. Last thing I need is her goin' back cryin' to daddy because some punk broke her heart."

"Not gonna happen."

He thumbs behind him. "She shouldn't give you too much drama."

I snort. "You buy that little act she's got goin' on?"

He chuckles. "Not really. Which is why we're not takin' any chances. Not with Forger still on the loose."

"This shit has to end soon."

"When he's bein' protected by the underworld crime syndicates, things take longer than usual."

"The Irish mafia gonna get involved?"

The club has called on them before when shit went down with Cash's brother. Now I proudly wear the scars to fuckin' prove it.

"Not unless it's completely necessary, though the Devils aren't formin' any alliances with them anytime soon."

"Swear to God, Forger is a fuckin' phantom."

"Tell me about it." Cash looks stressed every time this subject comes up.

The fact this asshole keeps going underground and nobody can find his, or the club's, permanent location is driving us up the wall. No matter how much surveillance I hack into around the city where I know he's been seen, he always seems to fly under the radar. Something isn't right, I can feel it in my bones.

"I'll text you with any important updates. In the meantime, I'm gonna look into her background, check out her ex and her friends, see if I can come up with anythin' that may have been missed."

I know the cops already ruled Lisa out because the threats began before Dylan started the affair.

He gives me a chin lift. "Anythin' changes from Tommy's end, you'll be the first to know."

He leaves, hitting the elevator button, and I head back inside.

I see the tail end of Aspyn disappearing around the door... *Was she eavesdropping?*

Rock

I secure the latch on the foyer door and put the alarm on.

When I say this place is like Fort Knox, I'm not even kidding.

I saunter toward the bags of food on the counter. I try not to eat a lot of junk food, preferring to pick food up from the Whiskey Bar and Grill, the restaurant the club owns on Bourbon Street. They make good food and it's reasonably priced for that neck of the woods.

I open the bags.

Aspyn wanted dumplings and noodles, so I opted for the meat version and extra fried rice. Not all of us are like Manny or Harlem who both cook well. Word got out after he dated Indigo that Harlem's a whizz in the kitchen. I guess having to bring up two kids on your own meant that he had no choice.

Cooking just isn't one of the things I take an interest in. And neither does Aspyn, so that's going to be interesting.

"Hungry?" I call out.

A few moments later, she appears. The cat nowhere in sight.

I tried making friends, but he ran away to hide under the bed. I feel sorry for animals that move to a new space. It must be weird for them to get used to.

As she plonks at the other side of the island bench, I glance up.

Is she expecting me to serve her? I almost laugh at the idea, but I guess handing her a take-out box isn't completely beyond me.

"Chopsticks?" I say, holding a pair out to her, which she takes.

"Smells good."

I slide her two boxes across to her and admit that it does smell amazing, but maybe that's just because I'm hungry.

"Gotta ask," I say, undoing the lid to my rice. "Were you listenin' to my conversation with Cash?"

She frowns, her eyes purposely avoiding me. *So she was.*

The little minx.

"No," she lies. "I was trying to stop Pirate from escaping." *And inadvertently listened in at the door.*

"Huh." I tuck into my food with a plastic spoon. There is cutlery in the drawer, but I'm not one for washing dishes, either.

"So... Cash seems cool," she says.

I watch her eating daintily. She doesn't dig into her food like a maniac, like most people do. She takes her time, probably chewing twenty-six times or whatever that stupid rule is for good digestion. Again, I remind myself how very different our upbringings were.

"Yes, he is."

"And you all have businesses, right?"

"Yep."

She pats the stool next to her. "You can sit down, you know. I don't bite."

I stare at her for a fraction too long, my eyes dipping to her lips. She's gonna be the death of me.

"I'm good."

Her bottom lip almost juts out at my rebuttal. The words from Cash ringing in my ears. I may have lied about her not being my type, but I still need to wipe this fog from my brain where she's concerned.

Get your head in the game.

"So... what *is* your type, exactly?" she blurts out of nowhere.

I almost splutter my rice everywhere but manage to choke it down my throat.

"So, you were listenin'?" I say, shaking my head as I reach for a glass from the cabinet and run myself a glass of water from the tap.

"I didn't mean to... I really was trying to stop Pirate from running out there."

Rock

I cough, banging my fist against my chest. "I'm not sure that's somethin' I should be discussin'."

"Why not?"

I shrug. "It seems inappropriate."

She frowns. "You're the one who told me you'd been to jail. You also don't seem to follow rules, so I figured it was okay."

"You thought wrong."

She rolls her lips. "By the way, you order a mean take-out, so you're not totally useless." *Trying to butter me up?*

I place a hand over my heart. "Thank God you said somethin', now I can sleep tonight."

She narrows her eyes. "Don't avoid the question."

I sigh. "I don't have a type."

"That's not what you told Cash."

"You should mind your own business."

"Come on, don't be boring," she whines. "We should get to know one another, since we're kinda stuck together. Here. I'll go first. I'll tell you my type."

"And I care, because?"

"We have to get along these next few weeks. It'll be better if we know things about each other. Then I won't do anything to piss you off."

I snort. "You have a staff of eleven back home. I'm sure you're not too fazed about pissin' anyone off."

Her mouth parts as she stares at me. "You did do your homework." It's not a question.

I give her a devilish grin. "Oh, *Trouble,* I always do my homework."

She clears her throat. "So, I'll tell you something about me, and then you do the same, okay?"

I give her a withering look.

She doesn't wait for my reply. "I cheated on a math test in the sixth grade, and then got presented with an award for doing so great. Then I had to stand up in front of the whole class and accept it, knowing what I'd done."

I burst out laughing. "It feels like you've waited this long to get that off your chest. Well done." I give her a clap.

She rolls her eyes. "That was a pretty big confession."

I lean on the counter as I rub my chin, trying not to lose it. "Is that the worst thing you've ever done?" Fuck me.

She thinks about it. "Aside from smashing one of my dad's cars into the garage door when I pressed the accelerator instead of the break…pretty much."

I know she doesn't have a criminal record. She's clean as a whistle.

"Ouch."

"Yeah, he wasn't happy."

I give her a chin lift. "What's your type?"

She gives me a sarcastic smile. "So, you're allowed to ask, but I'm not?"

"I am kinda in charge here."

She sputters a laugh. "Oh my god. You actually looked serious when you said that."

I can't say I have too many chicks laughing at me like that. Most are just trying to get my pants off in the first five minutes of me meeting them. Not that I mind that so much.

"I don't see anyone else around here securin' the premises."

"He'd have to be Spider-Man to get up here," she throws back, and I admit, she has a point.

"Don't change the subject." I throw her words back at her. "Your ex looks like a regular do-gooder type. Does he go to church?"

He looks like a little bitch. Another typical little rich kid who can't fight his way out of a paper bag, much less find somethin' like her clit. I'll bet he's the type to completely miss it, and in the end, she just ends up pleasing herself.

I don't like him, and not just because he's been inside my mystery girl.

"He pretends to be. Not now, though. His reputation is shot."

"So, you didn't know he was a player before you went into the house?"

She shrugs. "Maybe I didn't want to believe it."

"He's too squeaky."

She rolls her lips. "Squeaky?"

"Yeah. Too fuckin' perfect. Those are the ones you gotta watch out for."

"So, you're an expert on relationships now?"

"Nope, but I know an asshole when I see one."

"Then you'll know how embarrassing all of this is for me, not that I want a pity party or anything."

"He hurt you. It's okay to be mad about it."

She sighs. "The thing is, as mad as I am, I'm glad that I didn't find out before I wasted too much time on him, ya know?"

I watch her carefully. She's opening herself up to me, and I understand now that she trusts far too easily. She doesn't know me, and she has no reason to trust me or tell me anything, but yet here she is, sharing intimate details with a man she just met.

"So, what did you tell him? When you confronted him?"

She smiles wickedly. "I threw a vase at his head. It was the closest thing I had within my grasp."

"I hope it made contact."

"Sadly, he ducked and it smashed against the wall. He tried to make out he was sorry. Stress and all of that. Basically, I wasn't giving him enough attention. So it was my fault."

I laugh. Some of these kids have no fuckin' clue what being stressed even is.

Try hunting through a dumpster in order to feed yourself.

"Sounds like a typical gaslighter. How long did you date him?"

She shrugs. "A year."

I wonder how deep her feelings run for this asshole. She doesn't seem that cut up about it.

"Did he stay in touch?"

She nods.

"And he doesn't have your new number, right?"

She shakes her head.

"I don't want you messagin' him," I say out of nowhere. "We can't risk him findin' out where you are. If he's still hung up on you, and it sounds like he is, he may very well have had somethin' to do with those threats."

She looks at me sharply. "He wouldn't do that."

I stare at her. "Everyone's a suspect, *Trouble*. I've seen things that would make your head spin, in and out of prison."

"He's too much of a pretty boy to have any brains about stalking me," she says around a mouthful of food. "I'm not at all worried that it's him."

Once again, I remind myself she doesn't know the brunt of the threats.

When I saw how detailed and descriptive those messages were, that's when I knew this asshole meant business. They were specific, down to cutting her up into little pieces.

I point my fork at her. "First thing tomorrow, we start self-defense." That has her frowning.

"Why?"

"Because you need to know the basics." I hold a hand up to stop her butting in with the same spiel she gave me earlier. "And it'll keep your mind sharp. Nothing makes an easier target than lettin' your guard down."

"Nobody knows I'm here, except my dad and you guys." She sighs. "But I suppose I could do with a few lessons." Something flashes in her eyes and I can't work out what it is.

"Good."

"Can we do something after that? Like check out the apartment block."

"What for? You're not gonna be socializin'."

She looks at me sternly. "I still have to live my life, Rock. I can't just trade one prison for another."

My eyes go slightly wide. "Prison?"

"I meant...*home*."

"No, you didn't." I stare at her for a long moment while she digs around in her take-out box.

"Let's just drop it, okay?"

"Fine by me."

I don't need to know what the fuck is going on in her head anyway. It's doubtful even she knows.

A few moments go by. "So?"

I glance up at her.

Her pretty clear blue eyes stare back at me. I never usually notice women's eyes.

I always notice tits, ass and curves. But I couldn't tell you any chick's eye color from the club. But Aspyn...she's not like other women.

"So?"

"What's your type?"

I shake my head. "You're like a dog with a bone, has anyone ever told you that?"

She smiles triumphantly. "Actually, yes, they have."

I sigh. "I already told you..."

"But you told Cash I wasn't your type, so that indicates that you *do*, in fact, have one." She won't let it go.

"Nope. Just said that so he'd get off my back."

"I'm not completely repulsive to you then?"

My lips part. "Why would you say somethin' like that?"

She shrugs. "No reason. I just honestly wondered if a guy like you only went for racy women."

"Racy is overrated."

She looks down at her food. "Yeah, I guess it is."

"Aspyn?" She glances up at me. "There is nothin' wrong with how you look. You're hot. But this..." I flick my finger between us. "*This* can't happen."

Her cheeks flush. "I didn't... That's not what I meant!"

I run a hand through my hair.

Why do women always have to get angry and inevitably shout at me? I'm just trying to do the right thing.

I can't tell her that she is *exactly* my type, even with the platinum hair that washes her out and takes away from her pretty eyes. I can't tell her that her body is smoking hot and I've wondered for the last few hours how a guy like fuckface Dylan should be the one to enjoy it.

I can't tell her that she isn't just pretty, she's absolutely stunning. There is nothing she has to change for that asswipe, or anyone else, for that matter.

But I keep my mouth shut.

"Okay, we're good then."

She stares at me with humiliation on her face. "You're just like the rest of them."

I open my mouth, realizing I've embarrassed her, and that wasn't my intention.

I just don't want her crushing on me, making things all the more awkward.

I also question my own hypocritical thoughts because I haven't been able to keep a straight thought in my head since I caught her suitcase off the baggage claim.

She slides out from the breakfast bar.

"Aspyn..." I start. "I didn't mean it like that..."

She stomps away, cussing at me as I let out a deep sigh.

I can never be myself. I always have to think about people's fuckin' feelings. And I wasn't even intending to be an asshole.

Maybe I should take a page out of Tag's book and be stone faced to everyone and grunt one-word replies.

Rock

My eyes dip to her ass in her sweatpants as she retreats and my dick hardens. Not that the damn thing can stay down around her, and that is a problem.

I don't go running after her as she's probably used to that.

I'm not some damn errand boy. And I'm not someone who gives a shit.

She's a job.

Nothing more.

I did the right thing by telling her no.

She can't keep flirting with me.

Stay away from her. I snort at Cash's warning, even though I knew exactly what he meant. He smelled trouble too.

At this point, I could be in for the longest fuckin' few weeks of my entire life.

8

ASPYN

I CRY LIKE A BABY IN THE SHOWER.

I don't know what's gotten into me lately, but I blame the stress of moving as the main culprit.

So now Rock thinks I'm crushing on him? He has some damn nerve.

Even if I was, I wouldn't waste my time on him now.

I noticed his demeanor changed the minute he came back in from speaking to Cash.

I'm not stupid, I know they had words, and it was about me.

She's pussy. She's your type. I'm not kiddin' around. I told her father she was safe here.

I cringe at the word "pussy." God, is that how all men speak behind a woman's back?

What gets me the most is Rock's reply and his irritated tone.

And I told you she is safe. I'm handlin' it. Not short of hearin', Cash. I think I know when I can get my dick wet and when I can't.

Before that, we'd been getting along, and if my mind serves me correctly, we were flirting a little.

It felt good, because for a second there, I thought he actually liked me.

Now I realize that wasn't the case. He probably felt sorry for me, especially after all the stuff he's likely read about me online. All in the name of research.

I feel more pathetic now than I ever have.

And simply because I trusted a pretty face.

Everyone warned me about Dylan, but I shook it off, thinking that I knew better. Thinking that I was *the one*. God, I must've looked so pathetic.

It just goes to show that I really don't know anything about men whatsoever.

I run the bath with the Chanel bubble bath that's sitting on the shelf.

Alana really went all out.

As I'm waiting for the bath, I tap into my phone and add a gift reminder in my calendar. She likes candles and chocolate. Just because I am in exile, doesn't mean that I'm totally cut off from the world.

Rock's words suddenly flash through my head. *This…this can't happen.*

Urgh. Kill me now.

I don't think I've ever been more embarrassed in my entire life, aside from, you know, my ex cheating on me on national television. That's kind of hard to live down.

I need to keep myself busy while I'm here, I realize. And stay out of trouble.

I can't be moping around thinking about Dylan. He's not worth it.

That's just being a victim. All of this media and speculation has made me realize that I was never really in love with him. I liked him, but it wasn't love.

Or maybe that's just something that exists in the movies or in romance books. It's not like Dylan was rushing in on a white horse or asking me to marry him. We didn't even live together. I almost snort at the idea. As if that could ever happen. He's way too focused on his own appearance to share a bathroom with me.

All of these things I already knew, but I decided to look past it. Ignoring the red flags, because that is what most guys in LA are like. When a man takes longer than you to get ready, that says a lot.

And now Rock thinks I'm a total loser. Not that I give a shit what he thinks.

I text Tara.

Me

> This blows

I wait for a couple of minutes and then I see the gray bubble appear.

Tara

> oh, no, what happened?

Me

> My new security guy is a douchebag – and he's a biker

Tara

> A biker?

Me

> It's a long story

Tara

Rock

> I thought you said he was cute... What happened?

I texted Tara earlier, letting her know how hot Rock was, and how this wasn't going to be a hardship at all. It looks like I jumped the gun on that one.

Even though she's my best friend, I still feel weird about telling her the whole story. It's lame.

Me

> Nothing I'm just bored

Tara

> Spill

Me

> I think he thinks that I have a crush on him, and he kind of told me that it wasn't gonna happen...

So much for not telling her the whole story.

Tara

> Well if he's a biker, babe, it's probably for the best

Me

> Yeah. He probably has women throwing themselves at him with their fake tits. You should see this guy, T. But that's no excuse to make me feel dumb

Of course, in Rock's eyes, he probably thinks I'm just

being a spoiled brat. Because girls like me, they couldn't possibly have feelings, right?

Even if I am acting a little childish, his comment came out of the blue. And I don't like to be caught off guard. The trouble with me is I never learn. I give out way too much information, and then it gets used against me.

No wonder so many people have hurt me in the past. Is that my fault for being so naive? I know the answer to that.

Tara always tells me it's because I'm too trusting. That not everybody is a good person, which I get. I'm not a total dummy. But I'm also not the kind of person who walks around on eggshells, saying one thing, and doing another. It's so pointless.

Tara

> Pretty boys are the worst. Forget him. You'll be home soon

Me

> ugh, you've no idea

Tara

> I wish I was there

Me

> I wish you were here too. It would be so much more bearable. Maybe I'll work on my dad, and convince him to let you come down here

Tara

Rock

> That would be amazing, babe. Think of all the fun we could have.

I always have a good time with Tara. Even if she is a little bossy at times and doesn't like me doing certain things. I know it's only to protect me. She's quiet and reserved, but we somehow get along just fine. She also hated Dylan with a passion. In fact, I'd go as far to say that she despised him. When we broke up, she was the first one to tell me "I told you so." It wasn't like she was meaning to be cruel, it was more like, why didn't you listen to me?

Thanks to Dylan, I'll certainly be a lot more vigilant in the future.

I turn the taps off once the water is high, inhaling the mesmerizing scent from the bubbles.

Once I strip off my clothes, I test the water with my foot. Leaning over to the taps, I add a little more cold water before sinking in.

It's been a long day. I set the jets on low and slide down deep into the water. This is what I've been looking forward to all day.

The jets soothe my aching muscles, and it's one of the few ways that I like to relax.

I don't drink very much. Which I'm glad about. Ever since my dad told me that my mom had alcohol problems, I never wanted to upset him by having alcohol in the house. I know my mom battled with mental health, and I have some serious abandonment issues with that. Maybe that's why my dad overcompensates?

All of these feelings and emotions rush to the forefront of my mind whenever I'm upset or angry. It's like I just need to punish myself even more, so I can truly feel.

Maybe Rock's rejection hit a nerve deep inside me. This really has nothing to do with him. I don't even know the guy.

But just the idea that someone like him would think I was attractive made me feel good for half a second.

Now I'm just mad. I don't need his approval. I don't need anybody's.

I grab my Kindle and get lost in the book I'm reading until the water starts to get cold. Sighing, I step out of the bath and wrap myself in one of the new fluffy towels. I don't go back out into the living area, in case he's out there.

After I'm dried with my pajamas on, I head over to the door and listen out.

I don't hear any movement out there. Maybe Rock went to bed.

This is really ridiculous. Can I not even walk through my own apartment without fear of running into him? Maybe I acted impulsively. I never should have spied on him.

I mean, this is *my* home. Not his. He should be the one to leave.

And I need a glass of water, and I'm not going to deny myself my basic human rights.

I tiptoe down the hall. All the lights are off, but I can still see because of the huge windows and the reflection of the city below.

Rock must have gone to bed. I make it to the kitchen, and I see that the take-out containers have been put away. I'm annoyed I didn't even get to finish my noodles. *Asshole.*

The next time I decide to stomp off in a huff, I'll remember to take my food with me.

I go to the fridge and take out a bottle of cold water.

Rock drank from the tap earlier, but I don't know what the water is like around here. I wouldn't want to risk it.

I walk over to the large, sliding doors to get some air.

Unlocking the latch, I pull the door aside and step out. The cool night air hits me, and I welcome the breeze on my clammy skin. I only take one step out, as that's all I need.

My bath made me feel about ten times better. It's like all

the weight of the world on my shoulders has subsided just a little.

I don't head any closer toward the railing, but I look out across the city. All the traffic and sirens below in the distance seem like white noise compared to LA. The lights are not as blinding, either.

I don't know how long I stand there for, but when a ripple of cold makes its way up my arms, I shiver and turn back, yelping as I run smack into Rock's body in the doorway.

"Holy fuck," I say with a gasp. "Jesus! You scared me!"

"I thought you didn't like heights?" he says simply, my heart racing ten to the dozen.

"I don't. But I needed some fresh air, if that's okay with you?"

As I step inside he reaches behind me, sliding the door closed and latching the lock back into place.

I take those few moments to flick my eyes down toward his bare chest.

Holy fuck.

He's standing there in his black boxer briefs with nothing else on. Zip. Zero.

His chest is large and muscular, and completely covered in tattoos. His beautiful bronzed skin makes me want to reach out and touch him. To feel his muscles and how smooth his skin is. To trace my fingers over his tattoos as I snake my hand south of the border. I know it's dark, but even I can see he has a serious bulge going on.

My mouth is dry instantly. I clutch the water bottle in my hand, trying not to squeeze the contents. It's either that or squeeze my legs together, and it feels like I've been doing that a lot today.

Rock is gorgeous.

Not only that, but he has his hair out. It's just above the shoulders, hanging in long, dark waves.

He ignores me. "Is everythin' okay?"

"Why would you care?" I blurt out, still annoyed.

"Aspyn," he starts, his voice a mixture of irritation and controlled calmness. It's like he can't work out which way to be with me. "You don't have to get all haughty on me just because I said somethin'."

Haughty?

Oh my god, this man has the nerve!

"Haughty?" I repeat.

"Yep. It's a word."

"For your information, haughtiness is the least of the problems that you should be worried about with me."

"Is that right?"

"Yes. I'm not as dumb as I look, which may come as a shock to you, since you're probably used to women who have silicone instead of a brain."

"Never said you were dumb. And I'm not that much of a fan of silicone."

"Really? How surprising."

"I think you'd be surprised by a lot of things if you knew me."

"How cryptic."

"Not really. Just sayin' it like it is."

I snort. I should move, but he makes no attempt to back off, so neither do I.

"What's so funny?" he prompts.

"You certainly have no problems telling it like it is."

"I find it's the only way to be. Saves fuckin' around."

"I guess it does. If you're you."

"Meanin'?"

"Oh, nothing."

I go to skip past him, but he moves the same way. "Elaborate."

Holy fuck. His voice is so deep...husky...

I hate the way my body reacts to him when all I want to do is run away.

Rock

"No."

He grins. "Why? Scared?"

I steel my back. "Nope."

"Your body betrays you, doesn't it, *Trouble?*"

The way he says that. I wish it was a lie...

I fold my arms over my breasts as his gaze lands there. It's no secret my nipples are pebbled, but he needs to keep his eyes at eye level, not on my chest.

"Have a good look?" I counter.

His lips twitch as he folds his arms over his chest, mimicking me. "Not nearly enough."

I shake my head. "Why play games?"

Now it's his turn to frown. "I didn't think I was."

"Then let me by."

"You're free to go."

I go to move the other way, and so does he.

"Rock!"

"Listen. I didn't mean to upset you before. That's all I wanted to say."

"You know what?" I snap, pointing a finger in his face. "You think you're in charge of me because my dad said so, but you're not. Nobody is."

"Is that right?"

"Yes!" I jab my finger into his chest, and he slowly looks down at it. "I bet you enjoy flirting with girls and then shooting them down, don't you, Rock? Coming out here with nothing on." I wave my hand at him.

"Is that what this is about?"

I'm acting childish, that's what he's saying. "And for the record, as if I'd ever let anything happen with us. Ugh."

When his eyes meet mine again, they're heated. Really fucking heated.

"Uh huh?"

"Yes."

He smirks. "You can't even say it. Can you?"

"Yes, I can."

"So do it."

I open my mouth.

"You ever seen a man this naked, precious?"

My mouth is so fucking dry... "Of course I have."

"Really? Then why do your eyes keep flickin' down to my dick."

Instinctively, my eyes dip down there.

When I'm met with his expression, I roll my eyes. "Is that the reason you came out here? To flaunt your hot body at me? *Puh-lease...*"

He smirks again. "Actually, I was just comin' out to rescue your cat."

I frown. "My cat?"

He points behind me, and I shriek. "Shit, he's outside."

I locked Pirate outside!?

Rock moves fast, sliding the door back as Pirate hops up onto one of the chairs, dangerously close to the banister... My heart does a little flip as he likes to climb.

I cuss as I watch Rock pick him up and pass him to me. My hands trembling all the while.

Tears spring to my eyes and escape down my face.

Rock stands and stares at me as I wipe my tears away.

"Pirate," I say, rubbing my face in his fur. "I'm so sorry. Mommy's really sorry. I wasn't thinking..."

"He must've followed you out without you knowin'," Rock says, his tone gentler.

He pulls the door closed again and runs a hand through Pirate's fur. To my amazement, Pirate lets him.

"He's cold," I say, shaking myself with what I just did.

"Don't get so upset, he's fine."

"He can jump up on the railing, Rock," I cry. "He's been on our roof many times. He could've plummeted to his death."

He gives me a sad look, knowing it's true. "I'll fix it."

"How?"

"Don't worry about it. Just keep him inside until tomorrow. I'll build something."

Build something?

"He isn't used to high rises."

"I'll make a cat enclosure," he says. "So he can come out here and so you don't have to have a heart attack every time he wants to play."

"But how?"

He smiles. I like his smile. "I've got skills."

I nod gratefully. "Thank you."

Something about my tears has Rock staring at me with a new look in his eyes. I don't need or want his sympathy, nor do I care what he thinks about me crying in front of him. I love Pirate. He's my only friend right now, and I locked him outside on the top floor of a tall ass fucking building.

I try not to lose it.

"Come here." He pulls me into his chest, and I'm engulfed by him. *All of him.*

He smells like soap and that same musky scent as I smelled earlier in the car.

His body is warm, his hair damp as it touches my skin, indicating a recent shower.

My heartbeat accelerates, leaping and bounding all over the place at his close proximity. Even Pirate stays completely still as I try to gather myself.

"I'm sorry," I mutter. "I'm not usually this...emotional."

"I get it. He's important to you."

"I'm so stupid."

He pulls back, his hands settling on my shoulders as my breath hitches. "No, you're not stupid. It was an innocent mistake that anyone could make. Pirate is fine, and tomorrow I said I'll fix it so you don't have to worry, okay?"

I nod, feeling about as small as a person can get. I almost killed my fur baby.

Maybe he would have survived the night waiting to be let in, but I know how curious he is. The thought makes me woozy. This is exactly why I hate heights.

"Okay."

"Go back to bed."

I realize my hands are skating dangerously low on his hips. I didn't even know I was touching him.

When he glances down, I do too, and my eyes grow wide when I see his erection.

Oh, my...

He clears his throat.

"I should...go back to bed."

He gives me a chin lift, and I swallow hard as his hands leave my skin.

It feels like he's burned my skin where he's touched me. His hands are so firm, and commanding.

I wonder how firm he'd be somewhere else.

His cock... Jesus. That thing can't be real. I know it's dark and all, but there was no mistaking he was hard. I felt it when he hugged me. His body was so warm.

Was he hard just because of me? Or is he just one of those sexual guys who has it up all the time? I've only been with two guys. I'm not as experienced as I like to make out. In fact, people think I've slept with a lot of men because I guess that's what most young people do. I've just always been in a relationship. I've never had a one-night stand or anything close. I imagine lying down on my plush bed with Rock on top of me and I squirm.

"Aspyn?" he calls as I turn, halfway toward my room.

I don't answer, I just stare at him as I hold on to my cat for dear life.

"And I didn't answer your question earlier because I lied to Cash."

He lied? What does he mean?

"Don't believe anythin' that comes out of my mouth when

I'm outside these walls. My job here is to protect you, but I'm also a man. I can't be tellin' Cash what I really think…"

I'm his type.

Is that what he's saying?

I nod, racking my brain for something to say to that.

"Thank you," I say, gesturing to Pirate. "For rescuing my cat. I… He's really grateful. He let you touch him. That's a good sign he likes you." It's lame, but it's all I have.

"No problem."

I scurry away to the safety of my room and lock the door before I can get myself into any more trouble tonight.

Sinking back against the door, I sigh.

Trouble.

At least he got the nickname right.

I may never leave this room ever again.

9

ROCK

"The gym?" I stare at her.

"Yep."

I narrow my eyes. I don't know what game Aspyn is playing at, but I sincerely doubt her narrow little butt has seen the inside of a gym.

"I guess…"

"Then you can teach me some self-defense."

I don't know why I fuckin' suggested that, because now I'm looking for excuses to get out of it. Especially now that I'm faced with Aspyn in her sports bra and tight yoga pants.

Should that kind of attire be legal?

I don't know how I'm gonna get through a gym session with her in that outfit, but I keep my eyes from dropping to her tits.

Fuckin' perfect.

And after last night's display in her itsy-bitsy nightgown that clung to her body, I'm gonna be going to hell for what I did to myself when I got back to my room.

I couldn't sleep, so naturally, I did the only thing that I do when that kind of insomnia happens.

When I sprayed cum all over my stomach, I pictured

Aspyn's mouth taking my cock as I rammed it down her throat. She swallowed me down, too. Just like the bad little girl she is.

She stares at me now as I try to keep myself composed.

"What do you usually do at the gym?"

She shrugs.

I sigh. "Have you ever stepped foot in a gymnasium before?"

"Yes!" she says, that haughty tone back again.

Huh. "When?"

"Not so long ago. I take step class, for your information, and I use the treadmill."

"Step class," I snort. "Sounds riveting."

"It's cardio," she explains. "Not that I'd expect you to understand that. What do you lift, anyway?"

"A lot."

"Scared of a little competition?" she taunts.

I snort, then I can't help the laugh that leaves my chest. "Does this mean we're friends again?"

"Only if you order us breakfast, I'm starving."

"Workout first," I say. "And we can grab something from the cafe downstairs."

"I need to go food shopping. I have no snacks."

Food shopping. We sound like an old married couple.

I clear my throat. "Cash wanted me to drop in at the clubhouse later. I thought you might like to come along, to meet the girls."

Her eyes go wide. "For real?"

I nod. "Yeah. Jas wants to meet you, and Luna, and Cash's wife, Deanna. They're cool chicks, I'm sure you'll get along."

"Wait." She stops, then cringes. "Are they gonna ask me about the show?"

I shrug. I don't tell her I watched her for hours last night and my slowly growing obsession with her may be amping up.

I saw the fight with Lisa. In fact, I rewound it so many times I lost count.

I try not to let the amusement show on my face. She's got some spirit, I'll give her that.

"I have no idea. I don't know if the girls even watch the show," I say honestly. It's probably something I should've asked Cash about.

I can tell the idea of going to the clubhouse excites her.

What I don't like is seeing her cry. Tears of sorrow does something to me. She loves that damn cat, and I have a plan to make an enclosure so that Pirate can be safe, and we won't have any splattered cats on the sidewalk below.

Even though I don't know her, I'll do anything to not see the tears well in her eyes like they did last night.

Frankly, I was concerned when I saw her walking out onto the balcony, knowing that she hates heights. Not that I thought she was gonna do anything stupid, but under my watch, I don't like the idea that she's out there, all alone. Even if we are on the top floor. And when she just stood there, staring out at the city, she looked so lost.

I realize that I have been judging her. Labeling her as a spoiled, poor little rich girl. What if she's so much more than that? What if I've got it all wrong? More to the point, why do I care?

So far, I know that she has a sense of humor. A feisty side. And she's emotional. None of those things I am easily equipped to deal with.

I question again why the hell Cash put me on this job.

But now I'm invested.

I have to see this through.

I've never quit anything I've ever done, and I'm not about to let this woman get under my skin to the point that I can't do my job.

If she wants me to take her to the gym, I'll take her to the goddamn gym. She won't last five minutes anyway.

"Lead the way." I fling my arm out toward the door and her eyebrows raise in surprise.

I was going to go for a run, but she doesn't need to know that.

She walks in front of me as I try to keep my eyes on her shoulders, instead of her ass. But that's a trying task.

Everything about Aspyn draws my eyes to her curves. I swear this woman would look good in a paper bag.

I run a hand through my hair. I tied it back this morning to keep my unruly strays out of the way.

When we're in the elevator together, heading down, I keep my eyes laser focused ahead.

"Sleep well?" she asks.

"Like sleepin' on a cloud," I tell her honestly. When I did finally get to sleep, it was probably the comfiest bed I've ever been in.

Better than that piece of shit mattress I have at home.

She makes a noise in the back of her throat that goes straight to my dick.

"Tell me about it," she purrs.

Is she purposely doing this?

Is she purposely trying to talk to me? What for?

As if this isn't hard enough.

Jesus Christ. I need to get laid. But not with Aspyn.

As the elevator descends and we get closer to our destination, I'm starting to believe that this was a really bad idea.

The gym, as expected, is empty, and I'm intrigued to see what equipment Aspyn decides to try first.

Step class? Is that some kind of joke?

To my surprise, she walks over to the stationary bike, adjusts the seat, and hops on.

All the equipment in here is brand-new. And for a small gym, it's pretty impressive.

I may as well do some lifting, if I'm gonna be stuck here,

waiting for her to finish. So I won't hold my breath. She'll probably last ten minutes, if we're lucky.

I head over to the free weights and start a set of bicep curls.

Focusing on the mirrors in front of me, I avoid looking at Aspyn, whom I can see in the mirror behind me.

I distract myself by thinking about what I've got going on this afternoon, but my mind quickly wanders to our visit to the clubhouse. Maybe it would've been easier to keep her away from the MC. Then again, if the club is called in to protect her further, it's best if she shows her face at least once. Not that I like the idea.

The less people who know about her, the better. And it's gonna make my job one hell of a lot easier if people think she's just a blow-in.

Once I complete four sets, I glance at the clock on the wall. It's been about ten minutes, and sure enough, Aspyn moves off the bike and starts up on the treadmill.

I remember what it was like in my early twenties. Never having to work out, and barely watching what I had to eat. Those were good times, but those days are long gone.

I'm not one to ogle women in the gym. Not that her cute little outfit isn't a distraction, my dick certainly thinks so, and I'm pretty sure she got the idea last night.

Note to self: pull jeans on when investigating noises around the apartment.

After about another five minutes, my eyes divert over to her. She moves off the treadmill and goes over to the side table to grab a hand towel and pats her pretty little forehead with it. I chuckle to myself.

She wanders over to the lat pull-down, and I wince when I see her reaching for the bar. The person who had it last kept it on a high weight. She'll never be able to lift that, and she'll hurt herself trying. I drop my hand weights and turn just as her hands grip the handles.

"Wait!" I say, moving to her quickly. She stops, turning to frown at me. "Have you ever used that?"

She shrugs. "Can't be that hard."

I roll my eyes and move toward the pin. Pulling it out, I move it up to the lightest weight. "Doubt you can lift ninety pounds. That's more than you weigh."

"I weigh more than that. It's not my fault the Incredible Hulk was on here before me."

I snort. "So what you want to do is pull it down all the way behind your head as far as you can, slowly."

"Got it."

She reaches up again and grabs hold of the handles and plants her ass down on the seat, bringing the bar with her. I hover behind, but don't touch her. The last thing I want is for her to hurt herself, but I also don't want to be right up in her business.

"That's it," I say as she completes one. Then another. After the third, she sighs.

"This is hard."

"Uh huh. Not meant to be easy."

Four.

Five.

"Okay, I'm done." She lets the bar go too fast and it clunks loudly as the weight drops and the bar spins around above her head.

I shake my head. "Maybe we need to look into step classes?"

She turns and smiles. "What about self-defense?"

I pull out the pepper spray from my pocket. "Got you this."

She frowns. "You already left this morning?"

"I get up early for work."

"Huh."

My eyebrow quirks. "Does it surprise you I'm an early riser?"

She shrugs. "A little. So is this lesson one?"

"It's lesson two."

"Oh, what's lesson one?"

"Think smart. It's sad to say that puttin' yourself in a position where you're alone at night, for example, isn't a good idea. Especially not for a woman."

"I won't be doing that."

"Not while you're here, but you won't have security on you forever."

She stands. "So? How would I get away from an attacker?"

"Best thing to do? Make noise." She stares at me as I elaborate. "Would-be attackers don't like the idea of anyone seein' them or bein' heard, and whatever you do, don't ever drop to the ground if they get you in a hold."

"That sounds scary."

I give her a chin lift. "I teach this stuff."

She frowns. "For real?"

"Yes."

"Where?"

"At the community center."

"Since when?"

I let out a deep sigh. "Since a friend of mine was raped when I was eighteen. She didn't get away."

Her throat bobs as her eyes go wide. "Oh my god. That's horrible."

"Yes, it is. Ever since that day, even when I was goin' through shit of my own and in a bad place, I tried to help where I could. I've always done martial arts or fightin' of some sort, but most people, especially women, aren't fighters."

"Scary world," she mutters.

"Right again." I point to the pepper spray. "Carry this everywhere. I don't wanna scare you, but let's face it, this will work until you can get away."

Rock

"Rock?"

I look down as her gaze meets mine. "Did your friend… recover?"

I shrug. "Eventually. But she'll always have that memory, you know? She'll never really be healed, not when she was violated like that."

I don't elaborate further on why I'm so passionate about that, and it isn't just because of my friend.

When Cash set up BADVA, Bikers Against Domestic Violence Association, helping victims of abuse, including children during court sessions, I knew I wanted to be involved. My commitment to this is solid. I've been there. As a defenseless, helpless child with nobody coming to help.

I shake it off.

Aspyn stares at me, her eyes watching my face. "What is it?"

I shake my head. "Nothin'."

"So what would I do?" she goes on. "If you came up behind me."

"Well, the thing you have to remember is, it isn't always about size. You can still get away if you hit correctly." I point to my eye socket. My throat and nose. My under arm. My foot. And finally, my crotch. "If you can gauge an eye socket, stamp a foot, or better still, a swift kick or knee to the balls, it'll drop a man every time."

"I get to kick you in the balls?" Her lips turn up into a smirk.

"In theory." I point to the mat.

She walks over and stands there, hands on her hips. "So, let's do it."

"You wanna use the underside of your palm," I tell her. "Not a fist. Your knee or foot are also a good option."

She braces and I shake my head. "You need to walk, like you would normally."

"And you'll come up behind me?"

"Well, as a potential attacker, you don't know which angle you'll be attacked from."

She nods. "Right."

I stop. "Do not spray me with pepper spray," I reiterate.

She rolls her eyes. "It's in my pocket."

She starts to walk, and I come up behind her and grab her with my arms wrapped around her chest, like in a bear hug. "Now you wanna stamp my foot," I say as she squirms in my arms. "Save your energy."

She tries and I wince when she makes contact, breaking my hold just a little. She's a determined little thing as she swings her foot back and I just cup my balls in time to feel her heel brush past me.

"Good," I say. "But I think you were really gonna kick my balls there for a second." I let go of her. "Wanna try it again?"

"Sure."

I come up behind her again, and she turns before I reach her, using her foot behind my knee to trip me as I fall to the mat, bringing her with me as I grab her hips. I hit the mat and she's sprawled on top of me. I groan.

"I took martial arts as a kid," she says.

"Glad to see some of it paid off. Thanks for tellin' me," I mutter.

She smiles down at me triumphantly. "Can't give away all of my secrets now, can I?"

My dick is hard in my pants, and I hope she doesn't notice.

She sits across my lap, and I admire her face for a brief second. It makes me feel a lot better that she knows how to get out of a hold. For a small little thing, she's actually got a pretty good throw. It got me flat on my back.

"Admit it," she gloats. "You're impressed."

I don't hesitate to gather what's left of my manhood as I roll her off and pin her down. "What did I say about not gettin' down on the ground?"

Rock

Her chest beats rapidly as I stare down at her.

Playing with fire, asshat.

"I could still kick you in the nuts," she tells me with a sweet smile.

I let go of her wrists. "Don't even think about it." I push off her and go to stand. Once I adjust my dick as discreetly as I can, I reach down to help her up.

"So gentlemanly of you."

I snort. "That's the first time I've ever been called that."

She takes my hand, and I yank her up as she rights herself. "Well, that was fun."

"I think we've had enough trainin' for today."

"I read the lap pool is heated," she says, like it's Christmas morning.

I do not want to think about mystery girl in a bathing suit. Nope. I've enough of a raging hard-on going on in my sweats right now without adding to it.

"So you're goin' swimmin'?"

She shrugs. "I swim a lot at home. That's my usual modus operandi for working out."

Fuck no. I can't… Swallowing hard, I pretend that doesn't affect me. "Figures."

"Hey. I did okay, didn't I?"

"Twenty minutes without breakin' a sweat isn't exactly a workout."

"Says you." She shrugs.

"I think I need to go order breakfast," I mutter.

"Great. Bring it to the pool."

I glare at her. "I'm not your fuckin' errand boy."

"Fine. I'll go down and get it myself."

I run a hand through my hair. Of course, I can't let her do that.

"Remind me we need to stop at the grocery store. Can't be orderin' in every second of the day."

"Why not? I'm paying."

"It's not convenient."

I do not look at her ass in those tight yoga pants as she walks in front of me. Her ass is so damn fine…

"For you, no, it probably isn't. But it is for me."

"That's because you're used to having servants wait on you hand and foot."

She turns and gives me an eye roll. "They're not servants. They're staff, and I don't treat them badly."

I have a vision of her screwing her nose up at dinner time and demanding another meal instead. Is she really that much of a brat? Or is she just a rich kid with a heart of gold?

I haven't quite figured that out yet, but from what I've seen over the years with spoiled kids who used to buy from me, most of them are all the same.

"What do you want for breakfast?" I never thought those words would come out of my mouth.

"Eggs Benedict, organic, of course, with fresh smoked salmon and hollandaise sauce is what I usually have." She presses the elevator button impatiently.

"You're shittin' me?"

She rolls her lips, and I shove her in the shoulder lightly. "Oh my god, your face," she laughs.

I run a hand through my hair. "It's the only face I have."

The elevator doors open, and a tenant hesitates before stepping out. He's a fresh-faced looking dude with pale skin and a skinny frame. We move aside and I follow him with my eyes as he makes his way into the gym.

He swipes himself in with the keycard as we step inside. Aspyn presses the Penthouse button and scans her card at the same time.

I don't like that she could be down here alone and some guy could come wandering in. It makes me realize even more that I have to be more vigilant than I've planned for. Sure, nobody knows her here, but at the end of the day, we don't know if she's been followed.

She eyes him as the doors close. "I didn't think anyone else lived in this building," she laughs.

"Yeah, it is pretty quiet. Especially where we are."

The elevator whirs its way efficiently back to the top of the building. "So, breakfast?"

I shake my head. "You like surprises?"

"Not usually, but I'll make an exception."

I can't believe I'm doing this, but she seems to be in a happy mood. And a happy Aspyn is better than a sad or angry Aspyn.

Plus, she's gonna need to keep her strength up if she's meeting the girls today.

That took all of one day before Deanna probably told Cash to invite her over. It's inevitable that the nosy women of the club will want to get to know her, even if it is only for a few weeks.

Her prisoner comment still rattles around in my brain.

She deserves to see things other than these four walls.

And that's what I'm here for, if she behaves herself.

10

ROCK

I let myself in, holding two bags of the best bagels in town.

Luckily, we're in the type of neighborhood that is famous for ridiculously priced food that I'd never usually order. Since I've got a credit card without a limit and Tommy Huntley is paying, I go all out. I'm also carrying a tray with two coffees.

She never specified what she likes, so I just went with a cafe latte. I think that's what chicks drink.

I make a mental note to stop by the hardware store, too. When I pass by Pirate, I give him a scratch on the head and he purrs. After last night, I don't think he sees me as a threat anymore.

The thing with cats is letting them come to you. I've been around enough stray animals over the years to know how it works. And animals generally like me.

I make my way up the stairs toward the deck, unsure if I'm ready to see Aspyn in a bikini, and it turns out I'm right.

She's doing laps. The lap pool isn't huge but big enough for a penthouse.

I watch her glide through the water effortlessly. She

doesn't have a swimmer's body, so I don't know how often she truly swims, but her form is pretty good.

After a few minutes, she slows her pace and swims to the edge.

She rips her swimming goggles off and wipes her face, looking up at me.

I dangle the bag as her eyes go wide. "You weren't gone long."

"That's because I know people in low places," I tell her.

She rolls her eyes and I avert my gaze from her breasts. I mean, could she find a bikini any smaller?

When she hauls herself up, my eyes drift to her ass. *Holy fuck.*

I know she's teasing me. Flaunting herself at me, just like she did in the gym.

But I'm not gonna fall for it. I can't... However, my feet have a different idea.

I should move away, in fact, I should get as far away from this siren as possible, but I don't move.

"Could you hand me that towel, Rock?" she asks pleasantly.

I arch an eyebrow. "You think I'm your personal chef and bellhop now?" I shake my head. "I don't think so, princess."

"I think I liked *Trouble* better."

I can't have her thinking she's leading me around by my dick, even though I'd gladly let her. Hell, at this point, I'd break every single rule of Cash's just to suckle on those titties, which is why I divert my gaze, acting as if she has no effect on me.

It's probably the hardest thing I've ever done. My dick is so hard that I know I'm gonna have to deal with that again in the shower. It seems like it's becoming a regular occurrence around her, and it hasn't even been twenty-four hours yet.

She leans across me toward the end of the sun bed, her tits

dangerously close to my body as she swipes the towel. Her eyes stay on me the whole time. "You're no fun."

"I know what you're doin'."

I'm rewarded with a small smile. "Oh really, what am I doing?"

My eyes flick to her breasts and that does nothing for my swollen dick.

She dabs her face with the towel, still not covering herself.

"Flauntin' your body in front of my face." I stare at her, unyielding. "Trust me, you don't want anythin' to do with me."

I'm delighted when she glances at me in surprise. "I'm not flaunting myself," she says, instantly annoyed. "I'm swimming…" I wait for it, because I know she can't help herself. "But while we're on the subject, why don't I want anything to do with you?"

Keep your eyes on hers…

"You're in my care, for one."

"So what? Hypothetically, people can still fuck, Rock."

My lips part.

She. Did. Not. Just. Say. That.

For once, I'm completely lost for words.

"Cat got your tongue?" She smiles, pleased with herself.

I recover quickly, stepping into her space. Her breath hitches in her chest as she steps back, but there's nowhere to go except back in the pool.

"Is that what you want, *Trouble?* For me to fuck you?"

She gives me that tight little smirk again. "No. I just meant hypothetically. I didn't mean *us.*" She says *us* like she's flicking something bad off the bottom of her shoe.

She's such a goddamn liar.

"You're so full of shit," I say, watching her face as she tries to stand her ground.

It's so fuckin' hot how she thinks she holds all the power, when really, she's at my mercy. She just hasn't figured that out yet and I'm too much of a "gentleman" to take what I really want. I snort at the idea. "You can't keep your fuckin' eyes off me."

"Listen to you." She laughs like I'm hilarious. "You sound like you need to take a chill pill."

I roll my eyes. "*Chill pill*? Really? Isn't that like nineteen ninety-five all over again?"

"I don't know," she scoffs. "I wasn't born back then."

I shake my head. Beads of water run down her face as I struggle to keep my eyes on hers.

She's beautiful. There is no denying it. But she's here to tempt me, and now that things are on the up and up with Cash and we're getting along, I don't want to fuck things up. The other part of my brain tells me that I'm a grown man and I can do what I want and fuck the rules. It's not like I've ever listened to them anyway.

But she also just insinuated we fuck.

"*Back then*," I chuckle. "You make it sound like it was fifty years ago."

She stands there and dries herself off right in front of me. Her towel moves over her breasts and down her torso as my eyes trail her movements.

Walk the fuck away.

"I'd rather hear about how I *should* stay away from you. That sounded more fun."

"There ain't nothin' *fun* about me, let's get that straight right now."

She glances down my body very obviously, her gaze landing on my crotch. "I bet that thing's fun."

She's baiting me. That's what she's doing.

I smirk, keeping calm, even though my palms are itching to touch her. To pull her bikini strings aside and devour those tits until she begs me to fuck her.

"You won't be findin' out."

She rolls her eyes. "Too good for it?"

"Nope. But once we fuck, you'll be ruined for any other man."

Her eyes flick up to mine as her lips part, and she starts to laugh. "Do you practice that line in the mirror?"

I smirk. "Do I look like the kind of guy who needs to practice anything in the mirror?"

She shrugs. "Maybe you do."

"No, but the last chick I made come watched me fuck her in the reflection of a ceiling mirror. I guess you could say that was *fun*. I fuck hard, princess." Okay, that was a year ago, but she doesn't need to know that.

Her lips part, eyes sparkling. "You're a bad boy, Rock," she whispers, clearly turned on by my words.

I snort. "Don't romanticize it. I'm not good, Aspyn. Know that. Hear it. You don't want this." I don't mean to make it sound so harsh, but there is truth to it.

She's serious for a second. "I... I don't believe you're bad. It's not possible."

"You've known me for seventeen hours. You can't possibly know that."

"Yes, I can," she argues. "I get vibes."

I chuckle. God, she's cute. "Vibes?"

"Yes."

I can't resist asking. "What vibes do you get about me then? Little Miss Mouthy."

"You have a lot of nicknames for me."

"Don't change the subject."

She finally wraps the towel around herself, thank God. Keeping my eyes off her feels like a crime in itself.

"You're a tough guy, from the wrong side of the tracks, but you have a good heart." When I scoff again and give her a look, she ignores me and continues. "You care more than you let on, maybe not about me, but definitely about Cash and your club, which means that you're loyal. Your downfall is your mouth. I bet it's gotten you into more trouble than any given lifetime, but you get away with it because of your pretty eyes and your hot body…"

My throat is dry. "Pretty eyes?" I try to laugh it off. "All the better to see you with?"

"You're not the Big Bad Wolf, Rock. But I do believe that you fuck hard, and if you want, we could be good together. Let off some steam while I'm here…"

Holy fuck.

Did she just???

Abort mission.

Move your fuckin' feet, asshole.

But I don't run away from women. Even if this little pistol is on fire at the moment.

She really has no clue what I'm capable of. I'm not a good guy, despite what she thinks. She's living in cuckoo land if she thinks anything about me is redeemable. There ain't no absolution for me.

I lean in closer. "Get your clothes on, *Trouble*. Gotta eat and then head to the clubhouse. Don't wanna keep Prez waitin'."

It takes all of my strength to turn on my heel, tossing her bag on the sun lounger as I saunter back to the stairs.

"So that's it?" she hollers.

"Clothes!" I yell back.

She's not gonna fluster me or make me do something I'm gonna regret. Don't get me wrong, fuckin' her wouldn't be a chore, but the aftermath? I don't know if it would be worth it. She's high maintenance.

She doesn't know what she wants, and she thinks she can just play me and I'll roll over like her little bitch and drool.

When I said I fuck hard, I wasn't playing. She doesn't want any part of this because she may think she wants a wild night with a biker, but she has no clue what that entails.

I don't know if I could be gentle with her, and I guarantee she's never been fucked like I could fuck her. That's just the truth.

I can't go running to Cash to be removed from the job, I have to suck it up.

I mount the stairs and don't look back.

Her taunts mean nothing to me. At least, that's what I tell myself.

It's a little hostile when we ride to the clubhouse. Cash said to come during the day so nobody will be there aside from him, Ryder, Jas, and Luna. That way, things can stay relatively incognito where Aspyn is concerned.

She's wearing white jeans and a midriff sweater that shows off her lean stomach and a little too much skin, if you ask me.

Sweeping her hair up into a bun, she keeps her face completely bare of makeup.

Huh.

I thought all high maintenance chicks took hours to get ready to go out. Not that Aspyn needs makeup. She's naturally beautiful, and I think makeup would only hinder her.

But what the fuck would I know?

"The bagels were nice," she says, five minutes after leaving.

I grunt.

"Are we not friends now?"

"We were never friends."

I see her pout in my periphery. Maybe she's just trying to be nice to save face, because I had to set her straight, again. Not that Cash would know. It would've been so easy to slide those bikini bottoms aside and…

"I was kidding," she says, looking out the window. I don't know where this sudden confidence came from, but it's a stark contrast to the quiet woman I drove yesterday and ran into last night when I saved her cat. "Breaking the ice. The truth is, I've never had a one-night stand in my life."

I glance at her. Her words pique my interest. "Seriously?"

She sighs. "Pathetic, right?"

"Who am I to judge?"

She hugs her knees to her chest. "You've no idea the assumptions people make about you when you're the daughter of the most successful businessman in LA. It kinda sucks sometimes."

"Is that why you went on a reality TV show?" It comes out sounding a little harsher than I mean it to.

"No. I did it to prove a point, and I know to you I'm just some spoiled little rich girl who goes running to her daddy every time things don't go her way, but life isn't as uncomplicated as you might think it is, just because I have money."

Here she is again, opening up to me. Does this girl really have nobody else to confide in? I know she has this friend Tara, but her tone is sad, like she's trying to get her head around the concept. I can't exactly tell her to shut up.

I'm intrigued.

"It isn't?"

She shrugs. "Sure, for most people, money fixes a lot. But your problems aren't non-existent just because of your financial status. It doesn't make them go away."

"Huh." I've never really looked at it like that. I always thought the more money you have, the more problems you can solve.

She turns to me. "You don't believe me?"

"Never really thought about it, to be honest."

Our eyes meet, and she says, "Did you watch the show?"

I clear my throat and don't answer.

"You did, didn't you?"

I roll my eyes. "Only because the girls were goin' on about it via a group text last night. It was annoying."

Her eyes go wide. "The girls?"

"Luna and Jas. They're big fans, apparently." It's the first I've heard of it.

She puts her face in her hands. "Oh, no. Is it too late to turn around?"

"Relax," I say. "They're cool. Between the two of 'em, as well as Cash's ol' lady, you'll fit right in."

"What are they like?"

"You'll see soon enough, but probably nothin' like you imagine."

Just like that, all sexual tension has evaporated. I don't know which way is up with this girl.

She looks out the window again and says nothing more, even though I know she's burning with questions.

You're not the Big Bad Wolf, Rock. But I do believe that you fuck hard, and if you want, we could be good together. Let off some steam while I'm here...

I keep thinking about her words and trying to push them out of my memory for good.

Jesus Christ.

She shouldn't talk to me like that, which is why it's not a good idea that Cash put me in charge of her. I'm attracted to that smart mouth.

I could shut her up, teach her things... I could also do the letting off steam thing in a heartbeat, but I get the feeling Aspyn isn't as brave as she appears. But she sure does like pushing my buttons.

When we pull up into the lot out front, Aspyn stares at the building with some kind of awe on her face.

"You good?"

She snaps out of it, unbuckling her seat belt as she grabs her purse and slides out of the truck.

"It looks more like one of those saloons in an old Western movie," she says, a little smile on her lips. She's not wrong, even if the inside has been completely gutted and renovated, courtesy of Deanna.

"Wait till we get inside. They removed the stripper poles in honor of your visit."

She shoots me a look, and I can't help but laugh.

As it's mid-morning, not much happens around here this early.

Cash makes sure the staff clean up regularly and keep the place looking tidy.

We jump out and Aspyn looks around as we mount the steps and I push the double doors open. Waiting, I let her go ahead of me. There's nobody inside at the bar and it smells freshly cleaned.

"Wow," she says. "It's actually pretty nice in here."

"Cash's ol' lady renovated and decorated the place last year. Was a bit of a shithole back then."

"Hmm, I can imagine."

She eyes everything like she's never seen a bar before. I get we're inside a clubhouse, but it's not really that different from a bar with extra seating and lounges. There're also pool tables, dart boards, and a large flat-screen TV for when the boys wanna watch the game.

"Follow me," I say as we head toward the meeting room doors.

We barely get a couple of feet when I hear, "Well, lookie who we have here... Little Miss *Laguna Beach*." Manny, of course.

I roll my eyes. I forgot to warn her about Manny.

She turns around, looking at him curiously.

"You must be Aspyn," he says, walking toward us, a big grin on his face.

He hasn't toned down his attire today.

His hair is messily disheveled, a cross earring dangles from one ear, and he has more bracelets and rings than I've ever seen on anyone, females included. His AC/DC t-shirt and designer ripped jeans are more casual than his usual patent leather.

And he gives her a shit-eating grin.

I groan internally.

I don't need Manny crushing on my mystery girl. He can go fuck right off.

"And you are?" Aspyn raises a brow.

"Manny." He pats his chest. Giving me a quick glare over her shoulder, he says, "I take it Rock didn't give you the courtesy of explaining who all the important people are?"

"I guess not." She shrugs.

He holds his arms out toward her, and I groan internally.

"I'm a hugger," he says. "Could we just…" He invades her space, and I feel a low rumble in my chest.

Manny eyes me as they embrace, giving me a smirk. *Asshole.*

My jealous streak raises its ugly head.

"Uh, nice to meet you," Aspyn says, politely.

Again, I'm dumbfounded by her.

She's spicy. She's shy. She's nervous. She's verbose. She's flirty. I can't seem to get a handle on her. Yet, she opened up to me pretty quickly. Offering herself like a lamb to the slaughter before we'd even had breakfast.

I feel a tightness in my chest, wondering if she'll be offering herself to anyone else so easily. Manny, included. He may swing both ways, but Aspyn is an attractive girl from out of town. 'Fresh meat' for want of a better description. And if he doesn't get his hands off her in the next five seconds, I might rip his arms out of his sockets.

I don't think she's easy. In fact, I'm fairly certain she's not. She did say she'd never had a one night stand.

But she's young, and she's just gotten out of a relationship where the dude cheated. That can't be good for your self-esteem. Though I don't know her, the idea that she would jump into another man's bed, other than mine, makes me want to commit blue murder.

After one squeeze too long, Manny untangles himself.

Rock

A soft flush of color pops on Aspyn's cheeks and I stare at her. Is she embarrassed? Or turned on? I don't like the fact that Manny put that color there.

I glare at him.

"I'm the cook," Manny sing-songs, ignoring me. "I specialize in NOLA cuisine local to the area. Rock will tell you I make the best Gumbo this side of the Mississippi."

"I've never had Gumbo before. What is it?" Aspyn says as Manny gasps.

He holds a hand to his chest. "Never had Gumbo? Oh. My. God. That's sacrilege. I have to educate you." As he shifts his eyes to mine again, I know what he's doing.

Why he thinks I'd give a fuck, I don't know. But then again, one look at Aspyn and it's enough to drive any red-blooded man wild. I need to get this over with so I can get her out of here before any of the boys arrive.

Oh, they'd have a field day with her.

"While we'd love to be *educated...*" I drawl the last word with heavy sarcasm. "We're here to see Cash."

Manny snorts. "*You* can see Cash. I think Aspyn needs to try my Gumbo."

I open my mouth to protest, and Aspyn says, "See ya," then flounces off toward Manny, who's heading to the kitchen.

She just ditched me the second she could. Nice.

I watch on after them, annoyance riding a wave through my body that feels nuclear.

I'm not a jealous man when it comes to chicks. Heck, I've shared women before, plenty of times. But not Aspyn.

And it's not gonna be with pretty boy Manny. Over my dead body.

She might act like she wants a walk on the wild side, but I don't really think she understands what that entails.

If she did, she'd be back on that plane to LA as fast as her legs could carry her.

11

ASPYN

I don't miss the pissed off look Rock gives Manny as I follow him into the kitchen.

I half expect him to come bursting in here after me, and I'm a little disappointed when he doesn't.

I'm wet. I have been since he made that comment about him fucking hard.

Once we fuck, you'll be ruined for any other man.

I have never in my life been spoken to in that way. And I don't know what's making me so brave now. Maybe the fact that I'm so comfortable around him could be part of the reason. Or maybe it's just because he's a full-blown hottie. I mean, I'm not that experienced, but I wouldn't say no to a roll in the hay with Rock.

The idea thrills me.

And I have absolutely no doubt that he meant every word he said. Aside from the fact that he's not a good man. That part, I don't believe.

Everything I said to him, I meant. I may be blonde, but I'm not a total dummy. My father trusts Cash and this club, and that means something. My father would never put me in

Rock

harm's way. In fact, he's the one who's protecting me from everything, except myself.

Maybe he should be more worried about that. I'm sure he never expected my security to be someone who looked and talked like Rock. I can't help but smile.

My father is keeping me in the dark about a lot of things. He hasn't even let my publicist, Beth, have my new number.

"So. Have you fallen for Rock's charms yet?" Manny sing-songs as I follow him into the kitchen.

I balk. "Uh, no." I don't know why I sound so fricking guilty.

He turns around, leveling me with his gaze. "*Ooh.* Is something going on there?"

My eyes are wide. *Is this guy some sort of psychic?*

"Nope. I've only been in New Orleans for less than twenty-four hours. I'm still finding my bearings."

He zeros in on my face, and I realize that this man is a force to be reckoned with. And there's probably no point in lying to him. Not that I need to wear my heart on my sleeve with every single person I meet. I've already said enough to Rock to get me in a whole world of trouble. There's that word again. *Trouble.*

"Well, don't give your cookies up too soon. Gotta make him work for it. Not that Rock screws around the club that much. In fact, he's one of the better ones."

My eyes go round. "I have no intention of making him work for anything," I say, narrowing my eyes. Maybe it was a bad idea that I followed him in here.

He seems to have intuition that is scarily accurate. "Let's cut to the chase," I go on. "I'm here because I'm being stalked. You've probably heard. Rock told me there were a few fans of the show in the clubhouse who think I'm here because of the fight I had on national television with the whore who slept with Dylan, my ex."

Manny stares at me, agog, then he claps his hands

together and purses his lips. "I'm sorry if I'm being so intrusive," he says. "I've never really met a reality star before. Nothing very exciting happens around here, so excuse the giddiness. I promise we're not a bunch of weirdos who gossip. Well, except for maybe Nevada and Riot."

"Who are they?"

He waves a hand. "Nobody to be concerned about."

I think he's just nervous, which is kinda sweet. But who am I in the grand scheme of things? A girl who went on TV to try to get a life because she doesn't have one at home. Pretty pathetic, really.

"So, how long have you been working for the club?"

"A coupla years. I got the job through the club's Enforcer, Harlem. His daughter, actually. I'm good friends with Stella. You'll love her. If you're here long enough, you might get to meet her, as well as some of the other girls who are big fans of the show."

My face must pale because he looks at me and his grin slowly fades. "Are you okay?"

I take a long, deep breath, sighing noisily. "I guess I brought it upon myself going on that stupid show. I just never expected things to pan out the way they did. Now I'm up on assault charges, that my father is desperately trying to get me out of. Add to that my ex-boyfriend cheated with that skank, Lisa, who now has to have a new nose job, so that's all the media seem to want to talk about. Not if my broken heart is doing okay."

"I love how you smacked her. She deserved it. How much of that stuff is preplanned?"

It's not. That's why the ratings went crazy after the scandal. "That part definitely wasn't, I can guarantee it. It's clear that the producers wanted to push the ratings. I'm not normally a violent person, but after the last twenty-three years of being under my father's lock and key, that was the final blow. I snapped. Everyone has a breaking point and that was mine."

"I hope your dad can get you out of the charges. That bitch had it coming. In fact, do you ever think she might've done it just to cause some controversy in the house? Some chicks will do anything to get famous, even make themselves look bad on TV."

I sigh once more. "I don't know. I keep going over in my mind, and the more I think about it, the more I realize that she knew exactly what she was doing. And my idiot ex-boyfriend was dumb enough to fall for it."

"He's such a dick for throwing you away." He sounds genuinely upset for me.

"Thanks for saying that."

"And don't worry, I'm not makin' a pass at you. I like guys and girls, for the record, but I get that you've come here to regroup and probably find yourself."

He turns away and starts to pull things out of a large refrigerator as I stand there watching him.

Suddenly, I feel like I've known this guy for a lifetime. He's easy to talk to, but I don't want to be naive, as Tara always tells me I am.

"I got my heart broken too once. I was really into this dude, in fact, I think I was in love with him, and he threw me away like I didn't matter. Like all the things he told me were just a complete lie to get what he wanted. It didn't help that I come from a small town where being bi or gay isn't accepted. God, even wearing leather pants and smudged eyeliner gets you half a dozen Hail Marys. I always imagined LA would be kind of open minded."

"You've never been there?"

He shakes his head. "I've never really been anywhere. Someday, though. I don't travel well."

I smile softly. "LA is not all it's cracked up to be. Yes, it's open minded, to a degree. But when you're in the public eye, it also comes with scrutiny that just isn't normal. If I knew then what I know now, I never would have gone on Tail Spin. It was the worst decision of my life."

"Then why did you? If you don't mind me asking."

Yes, part of it was to annoy my father and try to branch out and do something different. But now it just seems like I was attention seeking. Maybe I was in a way, but I didn't know I was doing it, so does that really count?

"To piss off my father, mainly. He means well, but he's overbearing. I've never been able to do anything on my own, ever. I wanted to do something reckless. But it all backfired on me in the end."

"I wouldn't say that. You're here now. There's nothing wrong in taking a break from your real life and trying something different."

"I'm not exactly facing the music."

"So you will, when things die down. Your safety is first, *Laguna Beach*. That's my new nickname for you."

I smile. I know he's trying to make me feel better and it's working.

He's right. I know that I have to get back at some point and make a statement. My publicist was going on about it for ages. And we released a watery, very heavily lawyer-induced response to the charges. I still don't know if I'm going to get out of it, but at least they let me leave the state temporarily, based on the grounds of the threats.

I'm not hiding out from the police.

"Yeah, well, the stalking isn't something that I predicted," I admit.

"I'm sorry about that. How awful for you."

I watch as he starts to ladle something into a bowl. It smells pretty good. I know I just ate breakfast, but I have a high metabolism and I eat all day long.

"That's pretty much the reason I'm here. Because my security was useless and my father trusts Cash. They're investigating and that also means interrogating my friends. Another reason to leave LA. Maybe I am burying my head in the sand to avoid the confrontation, but I can't deal with all of this." I wave my hand around. "Maybe someday I will go back to my real life. Even if I don't really know what that is right now."

He looks up at me with sympathy, and I can't meet his gaze. I don't want anyone feeling sorry for me. That's not what I meant. I just wanted someone to know the truth.

He pops the bowl in the microwave and turns back to me. "I'm sorry that things are so shitty at the moment. But if you want to hang out with me and the girls, I promise we won't pry too much. Might take your mind off things."

God, I've been here for five minutes, and he already knows my life story.

Am I just this sad little girl who has nobody to talk to? Other people have it so much worse than I do. I've nothing to complain about.

I'm also not completely alone. I have Tara.

Even if I have had visions of myself being an old cat lady who never leaves her house. "That sounds kind of fun. I'd like that."

"Take a seat, the Gumbo won't be too long. Usually, I heat it up on the stove, but by the look on Rock's face, he wants to get you out of here quickly."

I frown, lowering myself onto one of the stools on the other side of the bench. "Why do you say that?"

He smirks. "Have you seen yourself lately?"

I look down at myself. "What's wrong with me?"

He laughs. "There's nothing wrong with you! I meant, you're gorgeous, Aspyn. So I'm not so sure that Cash made the right move with Rock."

"I'm sure that's not true."

"Don't get me wrong, he's a great guy. But he's a *guy*. And you're exactly the type he goes for…"

"That's funny, he told me I wasn't." I omit the part where

he told me he lied. I want to hear more information on what Manny knows about Rock.

Manny's eyebrows perk up. "Ah, you've had the conversation already, then?"

I hold my head in my hands. "I shouldn't even be telling you this."

He snorts. "You'll find I'm kind of the Agony Aunt around here. A role I've taken on quite proudly. Apparently, there's just something about my face that makes people want to confess all their sins." He laughs at the idea, then adds, "Though it could be worse; Priest is the one you really want to avoid."

"There's a biker called Priest?"

He snorts. "Yep. And before you ask, no, he's not really a priest, but he is the spiritual advisor for the club, a chaplain, amongst other things. And he has this way of getting information out of you easily. Makes me wonder if he wasn't with the FBI or the secret service in another life."

I blink a couple of times. "This club is nuts."

He laughs. "A little." Then he gives me a chin lift. "So, what shouldn't you be telling me?"

I shake my head. "Just me and my big mouth."

The microwave pings and he retrieves the contents. It smells amazing.

I love how he's feeding me even though I didn't tell him I was hungry or agree to eat his Gumbo. I think Manny likes to take care of people. He has a sweet nature and a nice aura about him.

"Well, I'll say this, don't be worried about Rock. Despite the hair and the tats and the impressive beard, he's a pussycat once you get to know him."

"Apparently, he fucks hard."

Manny almost drops the bowl as he cusses and dumps it on the bench, some of it swilling over the side. "Holy fuck, woman!" he chastises. "A little warning before you shock me with your potty mouth."

I snort. "It's not *my* potty mouth you have to worry about, though I did kinda proposition him, as a joke, and he said no." I tell myself it was a joke, to save face, but I can't deny how my body reacts to him.

Manny's eyes go wide as he wipes the side of the bowl with a cloth and slides it over to me. "He said no? That can't be right. What the hell is wrong with him?"

I probably shouldn't have said anything, but my self-esteem is a little shot after Dylan and Lisa's little stunt. "God, this smells delicious."

He smirks. "Wait until you taste it. You might be propositioning me." He gives me a wink when my eyes meet his, and I laugh.

"I'm not one to brag, but it's won prizes," he goes on.

I dip the spoon into the stew-like dish served over white rice and take a mouthful. When I groan loudly, Manny's grin widens. The flavors... Wow, it's amazing.

"Oh my god."

"I take it, you approve?"

"Oh yes. It's delicious." I nod, taking another mouthful. "What's in this anyway?"

"Lots of stuff. Meat. Chicken. Sausage. Vegetables and shrimp, mainly. It's my grandma's recipe."

"She's an amazing cook."

"She was."

I look up. "I'm sorry."

He shrugs. "It's alright. She lives on in my kitchen. I'm just glad you got to experience the best before you try it elsewhere."

"I'm sure it won't compare."

"The boys like it plenty."

I make more appreciative noises as Manny watches me eat. "So, Rock?" I press.

"Right," he laughs. "I'm intrigued to hear the rest of this story."

"I'm an idiot, that's all I can say. I was trying to goad him, then shoot him down. I don't know why, but it backfired."

"You're not an idiot. And it's not possible he'd really mean no. Unless Rock's taking what Cash said seriously."

My eyes go wide. "What did Cash say?" Although, I kinda already heard it when I was spying.

He gives me a pointed look. "That you're off the table. His good friend's daughter. Told him to keep his hands off, that kinda thing," he says, waving a hand around. "And Rock only just joined the club not long ago, so he's still trying to prove his worth to the boss. Trust me, he wants to."

I shake my head. "I shouldn't have said anything like that to him. The truth is, I don't sleep around. Now he thinks I'm just as big a Jezebel as Lisa."

Manny snorts. "He doesn't think that. He's a biker. Trust me, he'll be stewing over it. Rock's a deep thinker, like his brother."

"I heard he has a twin?"

"He's a little more chill than Rock. Though Jett has the nickname 'the Beast' when he gets going, usually he's placid. Takes a bit to provoke."

I laugh. "So I have the evil twin?"

He smirks. "You could say that. But getting back to Lisa... God, I'm so happy to hear that you rearranged her nose. Is it true you broke it?"

I nod sagely. Not my finest hour. "I wish I could say I feel sorry, but I really don't. Apparently, she was having an affair with a married man before this."

"Ew."

"I know. What is wrong with people who cheat? Do they think they're never going to get caught? I don't get it."

"Ugh, neither do I. There is no room for lies in any relationship, even a short-lived one. I can't stand it. Just be who you are. If the person doesn't like you for you, then walk away. Find someone else. Be honest, but don't cheat."

I can tell right away this is a sore subject for him, just as it is for me.

"I hear you, trust me. I have trust issues myself now."

"I mean, your ex is cute and all, but what an asshole. I guess he showed his true colors."

"You've no idea, and get this, he even wanted to get back with me!"

Manny's face is shocked as he leans on the bench with his elbows. "Get out?"

I shake my head. "I'm not kidding. He was all like, *we can work it out. Give me another chance. I can't lose you. Bla bla bla.* He didn't give two shits about losing me when he had his dick buried inside Lisa's Jezebel hole."

Manny rolls his lips to save from laughing.

I glance at him. "You can laugh if you want to, I am pretty funny."

He does and I grin too.

"*Lisa's Jezebel hole,* oh, I'm saving that for poker night."

"You have a poker night?"

"Me and the girls do. If you haven't figured it out yet, I hang out with them more than the guys. The men in this club can be a little overbearing and, truth be told, boring as bat shit. But the chicks in the club are cool and they don't make demands about what they want to eat."

"The guys make demands?"

"Oh, you have no idea. I once went on strike, but it lasted all of an hour. Cash made them apologize, and from then on, we've been cool. I'm not here to be anyone's slave. Start as you mean to go on, that's what my grandma taught me. She's the only one in my family I had anything to do with after I left."

"I'm sorry. Your family must be a bunch of idiots if they don't want you in their life," I say.

He grins, and before I can say anything more, the door bursts open and three girls come running in.

They stand there like schoolgirls as I take them in.

Must be Jas, Luna, and Deanna.

"Ladies," Manny says, a little smirk in his tone. "Nice of you to finally join us."

"Aspyn?" the fuller-figured one says. She's pretty with shoulder-length chestnut hair and big eyes. "Oh my god, Hi! I'm Luna. This is Jas, and that's Deanna."

Jas is tiny with thick-rimmed glasses and a skirt suit. She looks like a lawyer. Deanna has ripped jeans on and a tank, her long, dark hair flowing down her back.

None of these chicks look like Gemma Teller, nor do they fit the idea I had in my head.

"Pleased to meet you," I say, greeting the other girls.

"So, how does it feel to be out of the house?" Deanna asks. She's the braver one, I note, moving to come stand next to me.

"My house, or *that* house?"

"*That* house." She smiles.

I shrug. "It's good. I was just telling Manny I have a lot of regrets."

"Let's just leave the pecking for another time," Manny chastises. "The woman is trying to eat."

It's okay, I mouth.

Jas sizes me up. "I thought you'd be taller," she says. "You're such a slight little thing." She can't talk, I'm taller than she is.

"I get that a lot," I admit.

"Don't worry," Luna goes on, rushing at me. "All your secrets are safe with us. Nothing you say leaves this room... but we may have to tell Summer. She's trustworthy."

"Who's Summer?"

"Jett's ol' lady," Jas clarifies. "She's a big fan, too."

I gulp. I had no idea they'd even know who I was.

I roll my lips. "Okay, thanks for..."

"But there is a party on Friday night," Jas pipes up. "For Crystal's birthday. That's Ryder, the VP's, ol' lady. We're having a few drinks to celebrate, you should come."

"That's nice of you. I'll think about it."

"She's meant to be incognito." Manny rolls his eyes. "I'm not sure how that's gonna go down."

I'm touched that a man I just met is concerned about my welfare. They really do seem close-knit around here and I like that. It feels like a family.

"Actually," I say. "I have been thinking about a change lately." I flick a lock of my hair up in the air. "I'm getting tired of the bleach and my roots are starting to grow out. The blonde is easily recognizable."

Manny's eyes go wide. "For the love of God, I'm so glad you said it." He puts a hand over his chest. "I mean, you're gorgeous, don't get me wrong. But I know people. You'd look amazing with darker hair and a little sun...a couple of inches off the ends would work wonders."

"I have been cooped up lately," I admit. "I kind of hid just after...*the incident.*"

"How are you feeling?" Luna asks, looking sympathetic. "I'm so sorry that happened to you."

The girls nod in agreement.

I shrug. "I had no idea he'd go and do that, *obviously.*"

Again, I don't want anyone to feel sorry for me. That isn't my intention. But I'm also not a troublemaker. Lisa showed absolutely no remorse and was so smug about it. Like she couldn't wait to get it off her chest for the cameras.

"You're way prettier than her," Deanna tells me. "Like a million percent."

I smile. "Thanks."

"We should all go shopping," Luna says, excitedly.

Manny frowns again. I smile at the fact he's worried about me going out and he's taking it seriously. It seems I don't just have Rock and Cash in my corner.

"We'd have to run it by Cash," Jas says.

"That won't be a problem." Deanna smirks. "When works for you, hon?"

Girl time is what I need, though Manny tagging along won't be a hardship. I can already tell he's working out what hair color might suit me, and I'm glad to have a change. This might be fun after all.

"I've got all the time in the world," I say, tucking back into my meal. "Lead the way to transformation heaven."

12
ROCK

Jett

> How's it hanging?

Me

> Fine, thx

Jett

> How's the blonde?

Me

> She's cute, if that's what you're askin'

I sigh. Of course my brother wants all the details, just like everyone else. Right now, there isn't much to tell. And what I do know, I'm confused by.

Jett

> Saw that when Summer showed me her picture

Me

> She's better in real life

Jett

> You tappin' it yet?

Me

> Nope

Jett

> You wanna tap it?

Me

> Fuck off. Do you want something?

Jett

> No. just checkin' in

Me

> She's been taken hostage by Manny and the girls. God knows what they're doin' to her out there

Jett

> Least she's in safe hands. If you can keep them to yourself.

Me

> There is no point you texting if it's only to bug me when I'm busy

Jett

> Since when are you ever busy?

Me

> Just shows what you know

Cash was no help whatsoever. Not that I went into the meeting room and whined to him that I can't control one little twenty-three-year-old brat.

I changed my mind the minute I saw he had bigger fish to fry with Forger...

"Gonna need your help on the weekend, probably during Crystal's party. It'll keep the girls distracted and all at the club."

"So, I'll bring Aspyn here?"

"Yes. Then when we finally bring this motherfucker down, life can go back to normal."

I rub my chin.

Now is not the time to complain about needing to be away from Aspyn.

Cash will have my balls for being such a pussy.

Fuck doing the right thing, anyway. Since when have I cared about that?

If Aspyn propositions me again, I'll show her exactly how I roll; bent over the nearest flat surface. That might shut her smart little bratty mouth up a little.

"That's all?"

He gives me a chin lift. "You look…stressed."

I shake my head. "I'm good."

"You sure?"

"Yep."

"What did she do?"

Got my dick hard by wrestling me to the ground, then swam around the pool in a G-string and itty-bitty bikini top that covered nothing. And I can't handle it.

"Nothin'. You said to bring her here to meet the girls, and Manny."

Cash rolls his eyes. "Never hear the end of it if I didn't."

Like clockwork, Deanna appears in the doorway.

"Hey, Rock."

I turn. "Hey, D."

"Baby?" she says, walking over to Cash.

He gives her a look as if to say, 'What is this gonna cost me?'

"I'm baby now? This mornin' I was 'it's too early for this, we'll wake the baby.'" *He laughs.*

A little too much information…

She slaps him on the arm as she sits in his lap. "Aspyn would like to change her hair."

Cash looks at her, confusion in his eyes. "Good for her."

She plants a quick kiss on his lips. "So we need to go to a salon to do that."

He frowns. "I don't know…"

"We'll all be there, Rock too." *She flings her arm out to me but keeps her gaze locked on Cash's.* "And we'll promise to be good little girls."

I roll my lips.

"You think you can use that sexy voice and push those tits in my face to get your own way?"

She shrugs. "Worked in the past, didn't it?"

He chuckles. "She's not a prisoner, babe. But I'm glad you thought to ask. We need to keep in mind she's in a dangerous situation. This isn't fun time for the MC. We're the ones responsible for her, plus all the shit goin' on with Forger and the Devils."

"It's a salon," Deanna goes on, her tone a little firmer. "Nothing bad is gonna happen. It's hair color, for heaven's sake."

He stares at his wife, and I almost feel like I should make myself scarce. Then he says, "Fine. But you know what you owe me later."

"Kick Rock out and I'll give it to you now," she croons.

I stand, my palms up in the air. "And just like that, I'm outta here."

So I kept my pussy-boy thoughts to myself about complaining about Aspyn. Cash has enough headaches going on, and if it means I get to kick some ass on Friday, then it'll be worth it. Aspyn will be safe at the party, and I'll collect her later.

We left shortly after. I had a cat enclosure to make, though I didn't finish until the next day. Aspyn spends the day talking to Manny on the phone, making a Pinterest board for her new hair makeover. I seriously question Manny's loyalty to this club sometimes.

Working on the enclosure is easy. I bought some clear Perspex and glued it to the existing railing, so we can still see out, but the cat can't escape. The pet shop had some elaborate cat runs, but since Pirate is old, I didn't think he'd be into that. It looks pretty good, and it'll mean he's safe and Aspyn will be happy.

I glance at my phone and see my brother is texting me again. I sigh.

Jett

> Heard the new girl has your balls in a sling.
> Way to go

Me

> You again?

I roll my eyes.

I'm waiting for Aspyn to hurry up and get out of the damn shower so we can go eat. I said I'd take her out since we've had take-out the last three nights. It isn't a goddamn date, but she disappeared over an hour ago.

Jett

> Just makin' sure you saw the footage on TV

Me

> Do you ever let up?

The gray bubble appears as I wait for his reply.

Jett

> Better watch out, she packs a mean swing. Though, your nose is already a little crooked from being broken so many times

Ha fuckin' ha.

Me

> Fuck off

I sling my phone on the couch just as Aspyn appears in the kitchen.

My eyes almost bug out of my head when I see she's wearing a skintight pair of jeans and a top that barely covers her tits. I'm not one to judge, but I feel like wrapping a cardigan around her shoulders so other guys don't look at her. Just as I'm doing.

"All dressed up and nowhere to go?" I tease.

She turns to look at me. She's kept her makeup simple but has done something to her eyes so they look bluer than ever. I think it's the eyeliner. She also has red lipstick on that instantly makes me think about her pretty mouth wrapped around my cock.

Looking over my shoulder, she says, "Pirate!" She dashes for the door, almost tripping over herself.

"Relax," I say, shaking my head. "He's safe."

She swings the door open and then stops. "Oh."

"See. He can sit out here and not go splat."

She picks up her beloved cat and kisses him on the head. "I hope you said thank you to Rock?" She turns to look at me.

I shrug. "He rubbed up against me, I think that means it's okay."

Her face is genuine when she says, "Thank you, Rock. I really appreciate it."

"That's alright."

"I like how you kept the view for us."

Us. Should that sound so fuckin' hot?

"Well, chicken wire looks tacky." *Who even am I right now?*

"Now you're speaking my language." She gives me the brightest smile as she squeezes my arm, taking Pirate inside.

I swallow hard. Her hot little hand touching me isn't what I need.

I close and lock the door behind us.

"You ready?"

"I just have to pick some shoes."

I sigh. "This isn't a date, *Trouble.* We're pickin' up dinner, remember?"

She frowns. "So we can't eat there? I'm getting so bored of take-out. I need a home-cooked meal."

I can't exactly deny her that, even if she is used to having a personal chef. And if we go to the Grill, we'll be under the club's protection. I don't think Cash can shoot me for that.

"Fine. The Grill and only for an hour. It's my ass on the line here."

She smiles, happy that she got her own way.

I've been doing a lot of research about her over the last few days. I'm starting to wonder if she actually is some kind of saint.

She was a straight-A student. And president of her sorority in college. Excels in all her charity work, which I have to admit was pretty impressive. Aside from that and a few fashion week photos, she isn't out a lot. And doesn't have a criminal record.

Her only crime is dating the wrong kind of men who are completely unworthy of her. She seems to be good at it. I've seen a string of men she's rumored to have been romantically involved with. There are multiple pictures of her on the arm of some pretty boy type. Each one just like the next. Yet, I'll bet my last dollar that she's never been fucked like she truly deserves.

My dick stirs at the thought.

At least she's in a good mood about the cat enclosure.

She coos and talks to Pirate like he's a little kid, kissing him on the head while she places him in another one of his fluffy cat beds. He seems to have a lot of those.

I glance down at the shoes she just retrieved from her room.

They're sky-high red stilettos, the same color as her lipstick, and I withhold a groan as I imagine her wearing those shoes and nothing else.

Oh, I've pictured Aspyn in a range of positions over these last few days. Manny and the girls seemed to do the trick as she hasn't come onto me again, and she hasn't pouted once.

She even burned me some toast this morning—accidentally, of course. So we've both agreed we need to just stay out of the kitchen.

"Ready?" I prompt, glancing again at my watch.

"Are you in a hurry?" She slides her heels on.

"Nope."

"Got another date to get to?"

"What do you mean *another*? This isn't a date."

She puts a hand over her mouth. "Oops. Okay, Rock. We can sit down and have a meal and chat without calling it a date."

"I don't chat."

It's true. These last twenty-four hours I've been holed up in the office, researching. When I had to leave earlier, she stayed put with Pipes outside.

I'm amazed that she hasn't tried to leave the building. Ever since she told me she lived in a prison at home, I figured I'd have trouble with her. But she's compliant.

She does as her daddy says.

"Okay." She doesn't let my gruffness deter her, it seems.

My eyes are glued to her ass as she sashays toward the front door and we finally leave.

I jab the button half a dozen times.

"You seem agitated," she notes as the elevator doors swing open. I let her climb in first.

"Nope. Just tired."

"I know a good remedy for how to bring sleep on, if you're having difficulties."

I do too, and it involves squeezing my dick until I'm spraying cum all over myself thinking about her in the next room.

I side-eye her. "You do?"

"A relaxing bath with lavender Epsom salts is really soothing." *So is my cock driving into your tight little pussy or that perky ass.* "Or magnesium. Have you had your magnesium levels checked?" *Or putting her over my knee and spanking that ass for suggesting stupid shit.* "I've also tried smoking weed, but it didn't agree with me." *Or I could just shove my cock down her throat to stop her from talking...*

I snort. "You smoked weed?"

She looks at me with narrowed eyes as we begin to descend. "Why is that so funny?"

I shrug. "You seem so...*vanilla*."

She frowns. "I am not!"

"Remember, I have access to your records. There's not a lot I don't know about you, Aspyn. Then again, I could just go to Facebook and find everything out. I bet you're one of those types who posts about having a bad day so people will ask what's wrong." I'm grumpy because I'm depriving myself. It isn't all her fault.

"See that's where *you're* wrong," she sing-songs, undeterred. "I deleted my social media right after the incident."

I glance at her. "I'm a hacker," I remind her. "I can get into anythin'."

Her eyes go wide. "Anything?"

I nod. "Yup." Now I've got her thinking.

"So you could, like...hack into a bank or a government agency?"

"That's classified." I hold in my laugh, but she doesn't.

"You could tell me, but then you'd have to kill me?"

"Somethin' like that."

"Oh my god, Rock." She holds a hand on my bicep to save from falling over in those ridiculous heels. "You can be funny when you try."

"I'm glad I keep you amused." *Stop touching me. I'm fuckin' hard enough as it is.*

"That reminds me, Manny said I have an appointment tomorrow at the salon."

I already heard. Does she think I don't have ears?

The girls, and Manny, want to take her out and do some shopping after too.

Not for the first time I wonder what the fuck I'm doing here and why I don't just tell Cash to go shove it.

I take a deep breath. *Don't let her get under your skin.*

"Rivetin'. Could do with a wash and blow dry."

To my surprise, she reaches up to my hair and pulls on a

strand. "Could probably do with a treatment. The ends feel a little dry."

She's fuckin' touching my hair now?

I suppress a groan. I love it when chicks touch my hair. I dig it when I'm ramming into them or eating them out and they tug.

"Thanks for the advice, but I'm good."

She keeps assessing me. "Do you use beard oil?"

I turn and stare down at her. "What the fuck is beard oil?"

"That's a no then. I'll get you some. I've heard that it works wonders."

I keep staring at her as she looks straight toward the doors. "Works wonders for what, exactly?"

"Softness."

I scoff. "Softness? Not sure if you're aware, but bikers don't really give a shit about beards bein' soft."

"Well, chicks might not like it."

"Never had any complaints."

"*Yet.*"

My eyes almost bug out of their sockets. "You really are somethin'," I mutter.

She maintains her composure. "I just meant…like…it can get scratchy."

I laugh. "Like you'd know. You've never dated a man with a beard."

She turns to look at me. "Been checking up on me?"

I hold her gaze. "That's my job. You seem to have a type, if we're 'chattin'.'"

"What is that supposed to mean?"

I shrug, looking to the front. "Pretty boys."

She snorts. "That's completely ridiculous."

"Okay."

She jabs a finger at me. "I was just trying to be helpful because I can't imagine that any woman wants to feel a rough beard on their skin. Sorry for trying to help."

"I don't need any help, and my beard is just fine, thank you."

"Let me feel."

I balk. "You're shittin' me?"

She turns to face me. "What's wrong? Scared I'll get too attached?" The sarcasm rolls right off her with ease.

"No. I just don't like people touchin' me."

"Even me?"

I swallow hard. I can't bring my lips to form the words.

She smiles. "Are you hard right now, Rock?"

My lips part. How much more can a man take?

I turn to face her. "I bet I'm not as hard as you are wet."

Her lips part this time as her eyes flick to my mouth.

I reach over and press the stop button. The elevator comes to a halt.

"What are you doing?"

"Let's see," I suggest.

Her eyes go wide. "What?"

"You wanna see how hard I am? Fine. Go for it, babe. But in return, I wanna feel how wet I make you."

"You don't make me wet." I don't know if her voice is meant to sound hoarse, but I smile in response. She's affected.

"Really? I bet you fifty bucks you're drippin' thinkin' about me goin' down on you with my *rough beard*."

A little gasp leaves her mouth as my hands ball into fists by my side. I want to touch her. I fuckin' need to touch her.

"Oh." She dips her eyes to my crotch and then back to my face. "I can see you're hard."

"Feel it."

"Rock."

"Feel. It."

"You're being very demanding."

"You wanna know. Go right ahead."

I don't expect her to do it, for fuck's sake. I'm just trying to embarrass her so she'll shut up talking about sex. But then I see the determination in her eyes and her tongue peeks out to catch between her teeth as her eyes flick south again.

Does she want to touch it?

Before I can turn away, she reaches between my legs and cups my dick.

A groan leaves my chest as she smiles in triumph.

"Wow."

My heart rate goes up about a thousand notches as she massages my cock through my jeans. *Holy fuck.*

"You're big," she whispers. "I knew you would be."

I swallow hard. "You done?"

There's that little smirk again. "I bet you'd like me to drop to my knees right now, wouldn't you? Is that what your little minions do at the clubhouse for you?"

"Minions?" With her hand on me like this, I'm so close to losing it, it's embarrassing.

"Those club sluts the girls talk about."

"Hey, they have feelin's too, you know."

She bites down on her lip again, and I reach out and tug it free. "Don't do that," I warn.

As she looks up at me, her chest heaves. "Why not?"

"Because it makes me wanna pull your jeans down and fuck you up against the wall of this elevator every time you do it."

Her breath hitches again. It seems I shock her easily.

I grab her wrist and pull it away. Anymore and I will do exactly that.

"Your turn." I smile.

Before I can do anything, she leans past me and taps the stop button again, the elevator swings back into motion, and in two seconds flat, the doors are opening on ground level.

She grins at me. "Better luck next time, Rock."

When she sashays out of the elevator, I adjust my cock, just as two old people waiting to get in witness the display.

Great. Now I'm a fuckin' pervert.

I should haul her ass back upstairs and finish what we started. My dick is so painfully hard, there is no way I'm gonna get through this dinner.

My eyes are on her ass all the way to the parking lot. But I have a surprise for her.

One that might even give her what she needs because I've been told that the rumble of my bike's engine can cause a woman to climax. I like the idea of Aspyn coming on the back of my sled.

She stops, eyeing the bike parked next to my truck. One of the prospects dropped it off earlier today.

She turns. "Are we going on your motorcycle?"

My dark eyes find hers, and she backs up a step.

I can't fuck her here, but she's not gonna get away with what she just did to me, whether I wanted it or not.

Now I have to walk around with a giant wood in my jeans for the rest of the night and there ain't nothing I can do about it.

"Yep."

I reach for the saddle bag and pull out her helmet.

"Is it safe?"

"Only if you ride with me."

Her cheeks are flushed, and it'd be so easy to sit her on my bike and finger the fuck out of her pussy right now. I bet she's wet as fuck. But I'm not gonna give her the relief she so desperately wants. Not till she's begging for it.

If she wants to play stupid little games with me, then game on. I'll play.

She just may not like it when she realizes that she's not the one in charge.

I am.

I fix her helmet, trying my best not to touch her.

Her eyes are shining brightly with excitement. She's

forgotten all about getting my dick hard just five seconds ago. I'm gonna let it slide for now.

"You like teasin', don't you, *Trouble?*" I whisper close to her ear.

She shudders ever so slightly. "Only when it's you because you're so highly strung."

I balk. "You won't be sayin' that when we get to the Grill. In fact, I think you'll be pleasantly satisfied. Hop on."

I sling my leg over and fix my helmet and goggles. Patting the seat behind me, she climbs on board.

Feeling her hands slide around my waist without having to tell her makes my cock even harder than it was when she was touching me. *Fuck's sake.*

Now I've got to ride all the way to the Grill with her tits pressing into me and her warm body heat teasing me and testing me for all I'm worth. Sassy doesn't even cut it with her.

She doesn't get time to talk as I roar the engine to life and rev it unnecessarily.

My baby is a beast and I'm proud of it. This motorcycle represents how fuckin' hard I've worked and how far I've come in the last couple of years. A present to myself for keeping on the straight and narrow, so to speak.

I wish I could say the same about wanting to put my hands all over this little vixen who's wrapping herself around me as tight as she'll fit.

If the almighty sent her down as a test, then I know this is one task I'm sure to fail.

13

ASPYN

Tara

> You barely know him

Me

> Yes, I'm aware of that. But if you could see him… and the ride on his motorcycle…

I think I know what Rock was talking about, as the rumble of the engine had me on the edge. The throb between my thighs is even more needy than it was before.

Tara

> Send a photo

I snort. Rock went to say hello to the kitchen staff so I take the opportunity to message Tara back. She was pissed I haven't been checking in. Accusing me of having too much of a good time, which, to be honest, I can't really deny.

Rock has his back to me, but I see him checking on me in

his periphery. I'm always in his line of sight, which sends a little tingle up my spine.

Me

> I can't just snap a pic of him!?

Tara

> Clearly, you're not trying hard enough. Does he have FB? Then we could stalk him a little

Me

> I don't even know his last name, and he doesn't seem like the social media type. He's not on his phone much.

Tara

> And you're thinking about sleeping with him???

I told her what happened in the elevator.

I don't know why she's on such a high horse. I know this is hard for her. We've had an on-off friendship for years. Off when she became too overbearing and fiercely protective, something I've since grown to love and understand that's just how she is. She's never steered me wrong before, and she hated all my other exes who all turned out to be douchebags. Maybe if I beg Dad, she can fly on down here and we can have a girls' weekend.

Meanwhile, I'm not going to tell her about going out with Manny and the girls tomorrow. She'll get jealous and then I'll have to answer more questions. It's best to just keep those things to myself. Tara can be insecure at times, and while I understand she has abandonment issues with dickhead

boyfriends, there's nothing I can do about my current situation until this blows over.
Me

> I never said that. But what would be so bad with that anyway? It wasn't even a full hand job...

Most friends would be encouraging and asking how big his dick was and what he said or did while I was massaging him through his jeans. But Tara is old fashioned.
Tara

> But that's what he's going to expect, babe. Sex. I'm just looking out for you. He's a biker. Aren't those guys like outlaws or something?

My dad gave me the big spiel on how the NOLA Rebels are different than outlaw clubs because everything they do is above the line of the law. They all have legit businesses and don't sell or deal drugs or guns and all the bad stuff that's always in the news.
Me

> No. they're just a club that likes to ride motorcycles. They have legit jobs. Rock has a business

I can just imagine Tara snorting and telling me not to be so naive. Maybe she's right. Maybe I shouldn't be so stupid to believe anything that comes out of Rock's mouth.

Nothing more was said about what we did in the elevator, yet I can't stop thinking about it.

How hard his dick was.

That look of lust in his eyes.

How his lips parted as I fondled him.

He's a big boy and he was right; I was dripping wet for him. It wouldn't have been a hardship spreading my legs for him and getting off... My God. The idea of somebody like Rock inside me and what he could do to me makes my core ache.

The pulsing between my legs won't go away. I need friction.

Still. Typing to Tara is distracting me.

Tara

> Sounds fishy to me. I just don't want you to be another notch on this guy's belt, that's all

She's sweet for caring about me, but I'm the one who's been pursuing him. Not the other way around. I'm the one who's been provoking him to get a response and hoping that he'll take me up on my proposition, even if a tiny part of me is terrified of being in bed with him.

A guy like Rock knows a lot.

I haven't had a whole lot of experience, but sex is pretty basic. Surely, I could keep up?

Me

> It's nice of you to care... and it's big btw

Tara

> 👀

Me

> No, more like 🥒🥒🥒

Tara

> I have no words for you

I don't know why she's so weird about sex. As best friends, we're supposed to be able to be open about these things, but I do like teasing her.

Rock comes back to the table, and I put my phone down. I don't want to be my usual self and have my nose stuck in my phone all night. I'd rather look at him…

He hands me a drinks menu. "Did you choose your food yet?"

I tap my chin. "I was thinking about the shredded chicken tacos."

"Good choice."

He's been a little distant ever since we got off the bike. I wish I knew what he was thinking and if what I just did was crossing the line, though I'm sure most red-blooded males wouldn't be so quick to say no.

That heat in his eyes… I've never seen anything so damn sexy.

He's probably right. Handling him in bed would be like nothing else. I'm sure he bangs super damn hard, and after the dud of a boyfriend I've had recently, I think a good hard rollicking is in order.

I snort at the idea.

He glances up at me.

Oops.

"You good?"

I nod. "Sorry. My mind was elsewhere."

I look back at the menu, though I feel him still staring at me.

"What are you going to have?" I ask, ignoring the heat rising to my cheeks.

He takes a few moments to answer, but I keep my gaze on the menu that I'm not even reading.

"The Grill burger with the works."

I smile. Of course he's a meat eater.

Finally, I give in and look up.

"Can I eat some of your fries?"

There is no amusement in his face. "No. Get your own."

I pout. "Meany."

"What do you want to drink?"

"A vodka martini, please."

He frowns.

I roll my eyes. "Would you like to check my ID?"

"Maybe I should?"

I lift my purse off the chair and pull my wallet out. "I'll show you, just so you know you're not going to get in trouble supplying a minor with alcohol."

My license photo is cute, so I don't mind showing it off. "See."

I fling the wallet at him, and as I do, a couple of receipts, a coffee card, and a condom packet fly out of the compartment. I keep forgetting to buy a new damn wallet.

I slap a hand over my mouth and say, "Shit." When I scurry my hands forward to retrieve the offending item, he beats me to it. Rolling the damn thing around his knuckles as I die of embarrassment.

"I swear to God that was an accident," I mutter between gritted teeth. "Give it back!"

"You think you'll be needin' this while you're here?"

My cheeks flush. "I... I didn't even realize that was even in there."

His eyes darken as he continues to taunt me with it. "Sure, you didn't."

I roll my eyes. "I'm not sure it'd fit you, though," I go on, trying to save face. I'm rewarded by a quirk of his eyebrow in that sexy way of his. "It's not XXL."

His lips twitch. "You caught that, huh?"

I lean forward. "I can't say I've ever felt a dick that big before."

He swallows hard. I love feeling like I make him squirm,

even though he's the one making *me* squirm. "You go around feelin' a lot of dicks, do you?"

I shrug like it's nothing. "I told you. I'm a good girl, Rock. I've only been with a couple of guys. I probably don't know… the *things* you know."

His jaw steels. He doesn't like me mentioning anything about other guys, and I didn't miss the glares he gave Manny when we embraced. I get the feeling that my personal bodyguard is a little possessive.

The idea that he's jealous and wants me for himself is a fantasy I may have created in my head, but I have to keep myself entertained somehow.

"I don't believe that for a second," he mutters, shoving the condom in his top pocket.

"Hey, that's mine! I want it back."

"It's mine now."

I smirk. "Afraid I'll use it?"

He leans closer to me. "Nope. You're all talk, *Trouble.* Like I said, I know how girls like you work."

I don't back away. "You just have me all figured out, don't you, Rock?"

"Pretty much."

"Well, you should be so lucky."

He takes a long breath. "There's more than one way to shut that smart mouth up."

Snatching my menu out of my hand, he leaves the table to go and order.

I turn and watch him leave, my eyes glued to his ass.

Jesus. If I get through this meal, it'll be a damn miracle.

Rock is quiet during dinner, though I do a lot of the talking.

I tell him about my boring life in LA and he listens. He's

good at listening and never once tells me to stop talking, even if he may be thinking it.

"Luna is always lookin' for people to help at the shelter," he says, when I tell him how boring it is in the apartment. There's only so much YouTube and Housewives of Beverly Hills you can watch.

"She is?"

He smirks. "Don't look so horrified. Though, it is manual labor. Cleanin' cages. Bathing the dogs. Takin' 'em for a walk. Buyin' food and shit."

My heart rate kicks up a notch. "Really? I mean, I could do that. I've never been to a shelter before, but I know I could do it."

He looks like he doesn't believe me, and now I'm even more determined to show him that I'm not just some spoiled princess. Not that I care what he thinks.

"It's dirty work," he says.

"I'm not afraid of that."

"Some of the animals that come in aren't always in the best condition."

My eyes go wide. "As in, mistreated?"

He nods. "Pretty fuckin' sad, if you ask me. People are assholes. We took a leaf out of our brothers' book in Arizona and shut down several puppy mills. Luna's very vocal about it. If you wanna help, talk to her about it tomorrow."

I nod. "I will." My heart aches for those poor babies. Why would anyone mistreat an animal? What is wrong with people?

I guess not everyone has the kind of life Pirate has. He's such a delight that I can't imagine life without him.

"You done?" He gives me a chin lift.

"Yes. Thanks, Rock." Our eyes meet. "For letting me sit down and eat at a table, around other people."

He clears his throat. "It's nothin'. But we better get back."

I smile. "Is it past your curfew?"

His lips twitch. "No, but I'll bet it's past yours."

I only had one martini because I'm not a heavy drinker. Rock drank water the entire time. When I asked him why he wasn't drinking, he said his grandma was killed in a car accident by a drunk driver. He never drinks and drives.

I didn't know what to say after that.

I can tell that his grandma had a big impact on his life, and though he hasn't said anything about his family life, I can sense there's sadness there. A dark cloud hangs over him, and I can't figure out what it is.

We ride home in silence, and I revel in how being on the back of his bike makes me feel. I press my body into his and wrap my arms tighter around him.

He smells so good. The way he handles the bike. His big, strong arms gripping the handlebars while we race through the city.

It's like nothing can touch us.

I remember his muscular body the night he rescued Pirate and how ripped he was. I imagine him coming over the top of me, caging his arms over my head as he pounds into me, making me moan.

Shifting on the bike, the humming between my legs only gets more powerful. I squeeze my knees against his outer thighs, so much so, he turns his head slightly and rests a hand on my outer thigh. I think he's asking me if I'm okay... I can't answer... I'm in the throes of... *Oh, God.* I see stars as I climax. My arms tighten against his belly as I moan softly, his name falling from my lips as his grip on my knee tightens.

I press my head against his back, hiding my face as my climax goes on and on.

Holy fucking crap.

He just made me come and he didn't even touch me?

When it's over, I'm panting wildly, my face still burning as the pressure of his hand on my knee keeps up. I want him. I need to have him. I need to have him tonight.

Still, he keeps driving until I feel the bike slow. When I open my eyes, he's pulling into the parking lot and then we come to a stop.

I'm shaking with the force of what just happened, though I've no idea if he knows.

He kills the engine. Shakily, I climb off and begin to unfasten my helmet. He swings his leg over and does the same, then he leads me abruptly to the elevator by my elbow as I look up at him. His face masks what he feels. Surely, he's affected by what just happened, right?

I hold in my smile as he presses the elevator button rapidly. There's movement behind us, and I feel Rock's arm touch the small of my back as he turns to see who it is. It's just a middle-aged couple back from a night out.

He ushers me inside and keeps his hand on my back as the couple enter. Hitting the PH button, he swipes his card. The couple swipe their card and hit their floor.

We take off in silence, and when I take a peek at Rock, he's staring down at me. Fury in his eyes.

Uh oh, what did I do wrong now?

I look away quickly, my cheeks flushing with embarrassment that he could be ticked off that his bike just made me come. It's not like I can help it, that's one big ass powerful machine. Mixed with the sexual tension and how he looks and smells, can one blame me?

When the elevator stops and the old couple get out, the doors close again, and Rock's grip moves to my hip as he pulls me closer to him. "Did you come?"

The elevator takes off, and I stand there in silence.

"Aspyn?" he prompts. "Answer me."

"Yes," I whisper. "The movement. The sensations. The tension…" I look up at him. "It felt so good, Rock." He grinds his teeth, and it prompts me to ask, "Are you angry with me?"

His face softens slightly. He shakes his head. "No. I'm

just…" I wait as he runs a hand through his hair. "I wanted to be the one to give you your first orgasm, not my sled."

My lips part. He's jealous over his fucking motorcycle? This man.

"Now. Now. A little healthy competition is a good thing, right?" I tease.

His intense glare tells me this isn't the time to be making jokes.

When the elevator stops at the apartment, the doors open, and we both stand there and stare at each other. You could cut the sexual tension with a knife.

Neither of us moves.

The doors close again.

Rock hits the open button and the doors fly open. "Out," he orders.

I do as he asks, unsure what has prompted this mood.

He's dark. The energy rolling off him feels different, and I can't work out if it's good or bad.

I can't help it when I ask, "Rock, what's wrong?"

He ushers me inside, and then locks the door that leads out into the expansive foyer.

When he turns around, he stalks toward me.

I take a step back. "Are you mad that I got off?"

He shakes his head subtly. "No. I'm mad at myself that I can't control this thing between us."

I swallow hard. "It's alright, Rock. We can…like I said… uh, *fuck*… Friends with benefits?" It sounds lame, and I bite down on my lip.

He reaches out, swiping his thumb over my lip as he tugs it free. I squeeze my thighs together as he parts my lip. As he slides his thumb into my mouth, I start to suck it.

Oh, God.

"Stop sayin' that."

He pulls his thumb out to caress my lips, his eyes watching me intently.

"Why? We're grown adults. We can have sex if we want to." Then I remember his words. "Do you think you're too big for me, Rock? That I can't take you?" There's mocking in my tone, and I'm a bitch for hoping that antagonizes him.

His lips part as I bite down on the pad of his thumb. "Fuck," he mutters.

"Anyway," I whisper. "If you're so worried about your precious Prez, we can do other stuff...without...actually fucking."

I can't stop using the F-word. It's so erotic when I use it around him. I can feel how wet I am from my orgasm and from my dirty words and the way he's looking at me.

"Jesus. Fuck, Aspyn. You're makin' this so fuckin' difficult for me to be good."

I lick the pad of his thumb. "Nobody has to know. It could be our little secret."

His eyes heat as he says, "Get on the couch. Lie down. Spread your legs."

Holy shit.

My lips part as he cups one side of my face. "You really wanna fuckin' push my buttons, don't you, *Trouble?*"

I shake my head. "I'm not..."

"*Yes.* You are. And now you've got this to deal with." He cups himself, and my eyes flick down to the huge bulge in his jeans. Uh oh.

I guess I did ask for it.

Am I really about to have sex with him?

Heat flares in my body at getting my wish. Along with a little bit of fear because he's so much bigger than me and he's not like any other guy I've been with.

"What are you going to do to me?" I manage, my voice cracking on the last word.

He smirks, pushing me back against the cushions. "Whatever the fuck I want."

14

ROCK

She lies back against the cushions, and I stare down at her in awe. Her cheeks are flushed. Her breathing ragged. Her eyes watch me with lust and mixed with a little caution. And she'd be right. I'm not a man to be trusted, not that I'd ever hurt her.

But I do want her.

I want to fuckin' possess her. Own her. Make her mine.

In the back of my mind, I know I promised Cash that I wouldn't touch her. But for fuckin' real, she's been egging me on this entire time. Feeling my dick in the elevator. Flaunting her hot little body around the apartment any chance she gets. Coming on my sled. She knows exactly what she's doing.

And she keeps saying "fuck" every five minutes. Even when I know that she's less experienced than she makes out, it's still cute.

"I did try to warn you," I say, bending to my knees. "Didn't I, Aspyn?"

She nods.

"What did I tell you?"

She swallows hard. "That you fuck hard and that I couldn't handle you."

I smile. "Good girl." I move my hands up her thighs as I undo the top button of her jeans, my heart racing.

I need to see her tits, but I also wanna see her pussy too.

My bike made her fuckin' come, and I should burn the damn thing to hell for taking away what's mine, but at the same point, she was that pent up that I had an idea it might happen.

"Pull your top off."

Her lips part as she hesitates, then she does as I say, pulling her top up over her head and tossing it aside. My eyes dip to her tits. They're barely contained in the tiny bra she has on.

I don't suppress my groan this time. "Do you know how fuckin' perfect you look?"

She shakes her head.

I unzip her jeans as she watches me like a poor little lamb. Oh, I'll be her Big Bad Wolf and I meant what I said about ruining her for all men. I want her to say it too.

I want her to scream my name.

Grabbing the sides of her jeans, I yank them. She lifts her hips to accommodate me, and I'm greeted with a pair of black lace panties that are mesh and high cut, leaving nothing to the imagination. I can see her pussy and I can also see the darker patch of heat where she came.

"Bet you're so damn wet, aren't you, *Trouble?*"

She bites her lips, nodding, as she grips the cushions on either side of her.

I look up at her, knowing she needs to come, but I'm gonna draw this out for her. Make her realize that she can't go around teasing a man like me.

It has consequences.

"Did you touch yourself thinkin' about me?"

She nods again.

I grunt. "All I can think about is you," I admit. "Fuckin' day and night."

Her breath hitches, and I pull her by the hips to the edge of the couch. I bury my face between her legs, inhaling as she groans, my nose running through the seam of her panties. I smooth my hands up her outer thighs and up her torso to her tits.

As I hold them in my palms, she spreads her legs wider, sticking her chest out.

I cup and squeeze them, enjoying how they fill my hands. I love natural tits. Especially ones as perfect as hers.

Yanking one cup down, I move my mouth to her nipple, and she makes the most delicious sound as I take it into my mouth. I toy with the hard pebble as I grip the other one and tug gently. Her hands reach into my hair as I begin to suckle.

I love tits. I love pussy too, but fuck me… I run my chin over her nipple as she moans, my whiskers skating across her skin. Remembering what she said about beard oil makes me chuckle. I palm her other nipple, playing with it as she gasps and whimpers.

She has no clue how much I love foreplay. I could do this for hours.

I'm gonna make her so fuckin' wet that she's gonna be begging me for my dick.

I yank the other cup down and take that nipple into my mouth, too, laving it with my tongue as she squirms against me. I know she must need relief right now, but I'm not touching her pussy on purpose.

"Rock," she cries out.

I grin. "You could come just like this, couldn't you, babe?"

"Yes!"

I keep at it. Tugging. Nipping. Suckling. Her grip on my head only increases, and when I move a hand south and slip it into her panties, when I feel how wet she is, I groan.

"Babe, you made a mess."

"I need your mouth," she whispers.

I look up as our eyes meet. "Tell me, *Trouble*. Tell me what it is you want me to do to you."

Her eyes widen.

Little Miss I've Never Had Anyone Give Me Choices.

Oh, she's got more than one choice right now, and I'm intrigued to hear what she wants.

"It's okay," I reassure her. "You can tell me."

She pants, her eyes full of lust when she whispers. "Your mouth on me."

I cup her pussy. "Here?"

She nods.

I grin, sliding a finger through her slit as she cries out. Her clit is swollen, and I'm dying to get my lips wrapped around it so I can send her to heaven and back.

"Do you… Are you sure you want to…"

I glance up at her.

"Why wouldn't I?"

She frowns slightly. "Most guys…they just want a blow job, but don't want to reciprocate."

"Oh, don't worry, babe. You can reciprocate all you want. But right now, this is about you and you bein' in charge for once. And for the record, I love eatin' pussy."

Her lips part. I love how she does that.

I rip her panties down her legs to sit with her jeans around her ankles. Then I get annoyed and pull her shoes off. I rid her of her jeans and her panties, then I carefully put her shoes back on.

"You… You like those?"

"Oh, yeah."

She stares at me as I push her legs farther apart, and I groan at the sight of her bare pussy. Of course she's well groomed. Would I really expect anything less?

I waste no time settling back between her legs as I continue to grope her breasts with one hand, and I part her lips with the other. When I lick through her folds, she practically levitates off the couch.

I blow on her sensitive flesh as she whimpers, one hand reaching into my hair.

My dick is so hard that I reach down and undo my belt, the top button and finally the zipper.

I start to eat her out as she tries to close her legs, but I push them back open, my eyes meeting hers. "Watch me," I mutter against her flesh. "Watch me eat this sweet pussy, *Trouble.*"

I lick through her again, my eyes on hers as she watches me, her eyes heated.

Swirling my tongue over her clit, she cries out. I flatten it against her sensitive flesh, inserting one finger inside her.

"*Rock,*" she groans.

I start to finger fuck her slowly, lapping at her clit, enjoying how she tightens her hold in my hair. She's so wet for me, and I fuckin' love it.

"Come, Aspyn, come on my tongue."

She squeezes her eyes shut and starts to move her hips.

She's so beautiful. Her breasts perfectly perky. I want to come all over them, marking her as mine, because that's what she is.

I don't give a fuck that it's only been five days.

That's how long it's taken for her to get right under my skin. Now there is no way out.

I'm having her.

Her face flushes pink as she comes, gripping my head so she's grinding against my face. I insert another finger as she cries out, calling my name over and over.

My dick is so hard that I need relief soon, but I'm having such a good time, my own release can wait.

When she comes down from her high, I pull back and watch my fingers disappear inside of her. I pump her a little harder as she groans. She's so slick, she's leaking everywhere, and I can't wait to feel how tight she is when I slide my dick inside. All of my and Cash's rules have gone out the window.

"Such a pretty pussy," I mutter against her flesh. "My baby's so wet for me."

"God, Rock."

"Put your heels on the couch. Open up wider."

She does as I ask, completely bare to me as she rests back on her hands. I scoot her even closer toward me, right where I want her.

Reaching down, I suck on one pussy lip, then the other. Jesus, I need my dick in her and fast.

I move my hand under her legs to cup her ass. "Anyone ever fucked you here?"

She shakes her head.

I smile. Good. At least I can be first at that, at least.

I taunt her puckered hole with my finger, spreading her cum around to help.

"Relax," I tell her. "It'll feel weird at first, but really good."

"Are you going to put your dick inside my ass?" she whispers.

I glance up, cupping her face. She looks worried.

As I press my forehead against hers, I realize I haven't even kissed her lips yet. I don't kiss a lot. It's too intimate, but with Aspyn, I seem to be breaking all my rules.

"Not tonight."

My lips brush against hers as I taunt her asshole with my fingers and rub her clit with my thumb.

"But soon?"

I grin. "You really are trouble, aren't you?"

She pants as I press my finger to her hole and insert the tip. "*Rock...*"

"Relax. Do you want me to fuck your ass with my finger, babe?"

I lick her bottom lip, and she groans. "Yes," she whispers.

Good. I want that too.

"What else do you want me to do to you?"

"Fuck me really hard."

I laugh, then without warning, I capture her lips with mine and shove my tongue into her mouth. At the same time, I slide my finger in her ass even more, enjoying how tight she is. Knowing nobody else has ever been here.

Our tongues wrestle as I move my other hand to her entrance, and I insert two fingers into her pussy. Fingering both her holes as I tongue fuck her.

"*Rock!*"

"Come for me," I groan, my dick straining to get out of my pants. I can feel precum leaking from my tip, and I know I'm not gonna last a few more minutes of this.

She does as I say, and as she lets go, I slide my finger into her ass even farther until it's in all the way. She wraps her arms around my neck and buries her head into my shoulder when it all gets too much.

I revel in her moans, in how her body responds to me and how slippery she is as my finger slides in and out of her ass easily, my other hand still working her pussy as she comes over and over again until she's spent.

"Good?" I whisper, my nose brushing hers as she nods.

When our eyes meet, she surprises me by saying. "I want to suck you off, Rock."

I groan, reluctantly pulling my fingers out of her as I bring the two fingers that were in her pussy up to my mouth. I suck on them, and she stares at me, shocked.

"Want to taste?"

She shakes her head.

I laugh. She pushes me back so I slide onto my ass. Quickly removing my shoes, I sit on the floor with my back against the couch as she crawls into my lap.

I shove my jeans and boxers down my thighs as she stares down into my lap, my dick pointing at her.

"Crap," she breathes.

I grab her hand, needing her to touch me again. "He won't bite."

Placing her palm on my cock, I reach up and shrug my t-shirt over my head.

"You have such a good body," she tells me, gripping my dick harder as she settles on her knees.

Reaching back, I grab a cushion and hand it to her. "For your knees."

She gives me a look as she places it on the floor and kneels on it. "And you told me there was no good inside you."

I laugh. "Shut up and get my dick in your mouth."

She looks down at my cock with heat in her eyes as I spread my legs. As she bends over into my lap, I move her hair to the other side so I can see what she's doing.

Taking the tip to her mouth, she licks the end softly.

A groan escapes me as she swipes the precum off the end and then sucks.

Holy fuck.

Her hot little mouth is even better than I expected. Her lips stretched over my length is a sight to be seen.

She keeps my dick in place as she starts to bob her head, and I watch her with hooded eyes.

Her body is so hot. Her tits swing as she takes me...all of me, and I'm impressed when I hit the back of her throat. But she doesn't let up. *Shit, yeah.*

I rub my hand over her ass cheek. Then I give it a little slap as she mewls.

Moving my hand between her legs, I feel all the way from her ass to her pussy, enjoying that she's dripping wet. Knowing that I got her in this state and I plan on doing so much more.

"So big," she groans when she pulls out, her tongue lapping at my slit as I curse a string of profanities just watching her. That little tongue of hers flutters away as my balls begin to draw tight. *Not yet.*

I can't come yet, though I wonder if Aspyn is the type of girl to swallow. I smile to myself. I guess we'll find out.

"That's it, babe, take my dick. I'm so hard for you. Look what you've done to me."

She grins around my girth, and I can't help it, I yank her off for a second to capture her mouth, my tongue sliding inside. She mewls as our tongues wrestle.

I keep fingering her from behind, working two fingers inside her pussy as I spread my legs wider.

"Love making you lose control," she whispers.

I move my hand to the back of her head and grip hard. "And I love makin' you come. In fact, it could be my new favorite pastime."

She smiles as I let go and shove her back to my lap. She grips my dick again greedily, running her tongue up the underside as I groan, knowing that I can't last much longer.

My first time with her ain't gonna be shooting my load into her pussy. Nope. It's gonna be shooting down her throat while she chokes on it.

I slap her ass again, and she cries out, her hand grabbing my balls as I grunt.

Oh, fuck yeah.

This chick knows how to drive me completely wild.

And I'm wild for her.

I need her so fuckin' bad.

She caresses my sac, fingering my balls lightly as my heart hammers in my chest.

"My bad little bitch," I growl. "Where'd you learn to suck dick like that?"

She shrugs, her eyes meeting mine. I pull out and hold her chin.

"This mouth is mine," I tell her.

"Yes," she whispers.

I continue to plunge my fingers in and out of her pussy. "This is also mine."

"Oh, *Rock*."

"Is my baby gonna come again?"

"Please," she whines. "Please let me come, Rock."

I smile as her hot little hand still grips my dick and she pants as I continue to fuck her with my fingers.

"This pussy was made for me. I wanna hear you come while you suck my cock," I say, steeling my jaw.

She nods, eager to please me.

When she takes me back in her mouth, bobbing her head, I groan. I finger her harder, watching her tits bounce as I reach my hand under her body and play with her tit. As I tug on her nipple, she yelps.

My girl is so fuckin' responsive. It turns me the fuck on.

I can barely take it when she cups my balls and squeezes. I'm so fuckin' close.

Watching her mouth take me, her ass in the air while I plunge my fingers inside her, is too much. Every single cell in my body is wired. I know I'm gonna shoot streams of cum in that pretty little mouth of hers.

She starts to groan, and I know she's close.

But I have some new instructions for her when she comes this time, and I can't wait to see if she complies.

15

ASPYN

Oh my god. This man. *This man...*

His hard, thick cock is so freaking big. My entire mouth is swollen as I take him in, his length hitting the back of my throat as his fingers punish me from behind.

I've no idea what's happening, but I've never come that hard in my life. No guy has ever gone down on me like that. He's so good with his mouth and his fingers that I have no doubt his promise of ruining me for all other men is true.

He already has.

I'm so wet for him it's embarrassing, but he seems to love it.

I'm moaning his name like a whore, but every time our eyes meet, I see how much he wants me in their reflection.

"So beautiful," he coaxes, holding my chin as I bob my head up and down. Swirling my tongue over his tip. God, I love this so much.

His taste is salty but intoxicating.

And his fingers…plunging in and out of me as my tits bounce all over the place. I've never been so turned on in my life.

"Gonna come in your mouth," he tells me. Oh, Rock doesn't ask. He tells.

He may have asked me what I wanted, and I unashamedly told him, but I know he wants to come in my mouth. And I want that too.

I nod, blinking back tears as he starts to thrust his hips. "You're gonna come too, and after you've swallowed my cum, I'm gonna paint your tits with the rest."

Oh, holy Jesus.

I whimper as his words make my pussy throb.

I'm so slick, so wet, that his hand slaps against me loudly, and I start to move my hips in turn. I need him inside me. I need to ride that fat cock and be as close to him as I can get.

He tilts my chin. "Eyes on me. Don't look away."

I grip him at the base harder, eager to please as he rams in and out of my mouth. I see stars as I gag, but I hold on. His hand works furiously behind me, and I've no idea how he's coordinating this, but now isn't the time to ask dumb questions. I just roll with it.

"*Fuck,*" he mutters. "Fuck, babe..." I love it when he calls me babe, and baby, and Trouble and anything else he wants to call me.

I'm so close. He moves his hand, and his thumb grazes my clit, and I go off like a rocket ship. He follows suit as I feel streams of cum hit the back of my throat. He keeps pumping me, stilling as he empties himself, then he pulls out, and just like he promised, he continues to stroke himself over my hand as the rest of his cum sprays on my tits. I lean back so my hair doesn't get coated and, finally, he stills.

"Jesus," he pants.

I glance down at my chest, and I've never seen anything so hot. What Rock does next shocks me to my very core.

He starts to rub his cum into my tits, spreading it around so it coats my nipples.

I watch in fascination as he leans down and sucks on my nipple. Gasping, I watch him taste himself as he moves over to the other one.

Could this man get any hotter?

He glances up, a smirk on his lips. "Shocked?"

I shake my head. "Turned on."

He grins, swiping his tongue between my breastbone, licking all the way to my chin as he presses his cum-soaked lips to my mouth and I lick it off him.

I feel myself ready for more, and I feel like we've already done a lot.

"You suck cock a little too good," he tells me.

"Thanks."

He pulls me into his lap and holds me there. "Your body's so hot. I'm in so much fuckin' trouble."

I laugh. "Touché."

Just then, his phone rings, and he glances at it and groans. "Sorry, gotta answer. It's Cash."

I sit in his lap as he punches the answer button on his phone with one finger.

"Boss?"

I listen as he talks to Cash, the man who said that I'm off limits…yet here we are, both naked after pleasing each other.

Then I hear, "Now?"

Uh oh. Our night of debauchery may have come to an abrupt end. Not that I'm not sated enough, but his dick… I still haven't had him inside me yet.

He palms the back of his neck as I run my hands down his chest. His eyes meet mine, and I revel in how he's looking at me. Like a hungry wolf.

He wants to fuck just as much as I do. And I want to make it even harder to resist.

"Alright… No, it's fine. Just…hangin' out, gettin' some work done…"

I think Cash just asked him what he was doing. And he lied...

I stifle a laugh. He reaches to me and puts a hand over my mouth, his lips turning up into a smile.

Oh, I like that.

"No problem. Okay. Well, Stella and Manny can? Don't wanna freak her out..." What are they saying? "Yeah, I will. I'll wait until they get here. The prospect stays outside."

Cash says something else, then he's pulling the phone away from his ear.

"Everything okay?" My hand slides down to cup his dick, already at half-mast again. He groans.

"Gotta cut it short, babe," he grumbles.

I frown. "Why?"

He runs another hand through his hair. "Gotta go to work."

I pick up his phone. "But it's late."

"Yeah, that don't mean shit."

Disappointment floods me. "But..."

He smiles, bringing me closer as he presses his lips to mine. "Like how your red lipstick is now all over my dick."

I glance down and then laugh. He's so right.

"I could clean that off for you."

He grins. God. He's so gorgeous when he lets that mask slide just a little.

"So eager for more of my dick?"

I nod, unashamed. "Can you blame me? That thing is a monster."

He grips my ass. "Trust me. I'd love to continue, but Stella and Manny are comin' over to watch you while I'm gone. One of the prospects will stay outside."

"So, Stella is Manny's friend?"

"Yeah. You'll like her."

I frown. "Why do they need to come over?"

"A precaution. They won't annoy you."

"Why do you have to go?" I tiptoe my fingers up his chest.

"'Cause when my boss calls, I have to do it."

"I'll be fine here by myself."

He shakes his head. "No."

I frown. "Did Cash offer Stella and Manny so the prospect won't come in here?"

One look at Rock's furious face tells me all I need to know. "He said they wanted to come over."

I stare at him. "What if the prospect was..."

"He's not comin' in here."

I cup his face. "I'm not gonna do anything with anyone else, Rock."

He stares at me. "We're not a thing."

"No. But we're a thing while I'm here. Deal?"

He nods, his hand cupping my pussy. "This is mine. Nobody gets to fuck this except me. If I find out that you let another guy..."

"Manny?" I laugh. "Not my type." I should slap him one for suggesting that I'm so easy, but somehow, I think it's coming from a place of possession, rather than implying I'm a slut. I know I'm not. It's just I've never wanted anyone as badly as I want him.

"I don't know, he can be pretty persuasive."

I shake my head. "I don't sleep around, Rock."

He stares at me. "You're pretty."

I smile. "So are you."

He shakes his head. "Keep that pussy on ice for me."

I roll my lips. "Seriously?"

He rubs his nose with mine. "We better get dressed. They'll be here soon, and they have no manners."

I reluctantly move off his lap with a sigh.

He lets go of my hips, and the minute we're not connected, it feels cold without him.

Rock

God. *What am I even saying?*

Tara's right. I am just another notch on Rock's belt. I know that, but I just don't seem to care.

The way he caressed me softly. The way he painted my breasts and then sucked his cum off me... What in the fuck? I'm still slick just thinking about that.

He tosses me my t-shirt and I thumb behind me. "I should take a shower."

He watches me as I lean down to collect my jeans. "Wish I could join you."

I smile regretfully as he shucks into his jeans and pulls them and his boxers up, tucking his dick back inside as I mourn the loss of him.

"Let me ask you somethin'," he says, as I pick up my panties and bra.

He moves toward me, cupping one side of my face as I still stand there naked in front of him.

"You haven't once argued about not bein' able to go out, why is that?"

I stare at him, surprised by the question. "Uh, because I'm not allow–" I stop.

He comes closer. "Aspyn, you're a grown woman. You *can* go out. I know your father wants you safe, but I'm certain we've never been followed, nor does your stalker know where you are."

"But... I don't wanna piss off my dad even further."

"You've got me. I'll protect you."

I stare at him. "You'd dive in front of a stray bullet?"

He nods. "Though that's extreme and highly unlikely, that's my job. That's why I'm here." Then, I watch as he points to his chest. "Took a bullet right here one time."

I gape at the red scar on his skin, surrounded by tattoos, and look back up at him. "You really got shot?"

"Yep."

"How?"

"My brother... Someone was tryin' to kill him."

"So you...you took a bullet for him?"

He shrugs. "Of course I did. He's my brother. He'd do the same for me if it were reversed."

I look back down at the jagged scar and shake my head. "I thought this club was supposed to be safe," I mutter.

He leans forward and kisses me on the head. "It *is* safe. Now go and shower. When you come out, I'll be gone, but I'll be back as soon as I can."

I don't want to look or sound like a baby, but I also can't help but feel pouty.

"Fine. But you owe me."

He smirks, pressing his lips against mine. "I owe you?"

"Yes."

"I think I just gave you enough to dream about."

I feel so warm and safe having him here. I can pretend for a while that my father didn't send me here in exile. That Rock cares about me and what I think. That he thinks I deserve to be let out for once. I'm not just some pet that can be kept locked up in a tower for the rest of my life because he worries about me.

I've only been gone five days and I feel like it's been a lifetime.

I nod. "You have."

He presses one small kiss to my lips, and I suppress a groan.

Now isn't the time to be needy.

I give him a dirty look before I spin around and walk across the room toward the hallway leading to my bedroom. Completely naked. My clothes in my hands, Pirate hops off his perch and runs behind me to catch up.

I know Rock's eyes are all over my ass, and I can't be sure, but I think I hear him groan.

Rock

Rock never comes home.

Not that this is *home*.

It's a designer penthouse that I'm calling home. I've never had to clean before, so that's going to be interesting.

I do have fun with Stella and Manny, though. We watch movies and Manny makes popcorn, which he somehow manages to get absolutely everywhere. Stella is fun to be around, she seems like a cool chick.

Luckily, Stella is too interested in talking about everything to do with New Orleans for them to bother with asking me too many pesky questions. I'm too heavily involved trying to get the vision of Rock spurting all over my breasts out of my mind.

That had to be the hottest thing I've ever seen. His face distorted in pleasure as he tasted himself off my skin.

I've never, ever had an experience like that before. Especially when he fingered my rear end. It felt different to how I imagined it would, and not at all as painful as I thought it might be… I enjoyed myself. Oh, boy did I.

So when I took myself off to bed and had one of the best nights of sleep I've ever had, I wasn't surprised. I'm thrilled when I wake feeling refreshed. It makes a change from the usual tossing and turning. I lean over and grab my phone and immediately see several messages from Tara that I didn't reply to last night.

Tara

> Babe? How'd you go, did anything else happen?

Tara

> I've got all night…

Tara

> Seriously... you can't keep me waiting!? Did you guys fuck?

I snort at her question. It seems Tara's had a change of heart.

Tara

> Going to bed now, message me when you get this x

I sigh, tossing the phone onto the bedspread. I groan into my pillow, wishing I was waking up in Rock's arms, which is completely stupid because he probably isn't one to usually sleep over. In fact, I sincerely doubt it.

Tara's warning keeps popping up in the back of my head as I swat it away.

You're just another notch on his belt.

My phone beeps again and I don't check it. A few moments later, another message.

I turn my phone over and my heart accelerates when I see a message from Rock.

When did I put his number into my phone? I think for a second. Nope. I come up blank... I never put his number into my cell.

My cheeks burn when I think he may have taken my phone and... Oh my god, did he do this? What if he read my messages? I mean, he's a hacker, I'm sure he knows how to get into people's private business, including their phones and computers.

I swallow hard. I've had my cell on me the entire time... It's practically an extra body part.

Rock

> Good mornin', how'd you sleep?

Rock

This badass biker, who said he has no redeeming qualities, is asking how I slept?

I stifle a laugh. He's so full of shit.
Me

> Like a baby

I'm excited when I see he's typing back.
Rock

> I'll be back this evening

I pout. *That long?* That's like a whole day.
Me

> K

Rock

> Miss me bad, huh?

I roll my eyes.
Me

> Nope. Barely remember your name

I grin to myself, thinking I'm cute.
Then I gasp when his messages bounce back fast.
Rock

> You seemed to remember it when I fucked you with my mouth last night, Trouble.

I slap a hand over my mouth.
Me

> I'd had a martini, sue me

Rock

> How do you explain what you did in the elevator then?

Me

> I blame you. No man should look as good as you do

I'm only telling the truth, after all.
Rock

> I'm still pissed my sled got you off before I did

I grin, warmth spreading through me. Is he really jealous over his motorcycle?
Me

> Don't worry. You can make up for it tonight

My heart flutters at what we might get up to in this big-ass apartment when we're all alone again. I've never craved anything more.
Rock

> I plan to

Holy shit. I hug myself as I try not to let the shit-eating grin spread across my face. But it's a little hard not to.

And today I get to have my hair done. I'm ready for a change.

Rock

After being booted from the show, I lost my mojo. I didn't leave the house for weeks, so there was no point in trying to look good for anyone.

That was my excuse, anyway. Now I look at my dark roots and groan. It's time.

After I pull my robe on and use the bathroom, I wander out and smell the most delicious scent of something cooking.

Of course Manny has taken it upon himself to cook up a storm in my kitchen. Though Lord knows how he's rustled together the ingredients to make pancakes.

"That smells amazing," I say, stifling a yawn.

"Well, good mornin', *Laguna Beach*."

I smile at his words. It seems the men of this club love giving me cute nicknames, even though the way Rock says *Trouble* sets my insides on fire.

"Morning." I smile back.

"Sleep well?" He gives me a devilish grin, and my heart skips a beat thinking he knows something's up. But how could he? There was no evidence left behind, and I didn't tell him and Stella about me and Rock.

I walk to the coffee percolator and pour myself a cup.

Stella is outside on the patio, talking on her phone.

"I did."

"Well, today is makeover day. The only poo-poo is that Priest is coming over."

My eyes go wide.

Manny laughs. "Don't look so worried. Rock's needed at the club, and Priest was available. They're taking this security thing to new heights, honey. Just go with it."

"Noted," I say, dumping sugar in my coffee and adding creamer.

It feels weird without Rock in the apartment. Even though that's silly, as it hasn't even been a week.

But we've gotten into this little coffee and breakfast ordering ritual.

"So, are you excited about your new hair?"

I nod, sitting down at the island. "I honestly can't wait. It's long overdue."

"What color are you thinking you'll go with?"

I shrug. "My natural hair color is dark mahogany."

"I think you'd look so pretty with darker hair, but you do you, boo."

I roll my lips and idly wonder what Rock would think.

Does he like my hair as is?

Will he still like me if I dye it and cut some length off?

I chew on my thumbnail as Manny's eyes meet mine.

"You okay, sugar?"

I nod. "Fine."

"My friend does spray tanning too. It's where I get mine done."

I smile at his honesty. "You put a lot of effort into your appearance," I tell him. "I like it."

He flips the pancakes and then turns back to me. "Nice of you to notice."

He runs a hand through his messily styled locks. He looks like he just stepped off a magazine cover.

"Thanks," I say. "I mean, for arranging this for me. I will pay."

He grins. "It's my pleasure. I told the boss he can't keep you cooped up in here all day, it's not healthy."

In my texts, I wanted to ask Rock what he was doing all night. Jealousy hits me when I think that he could have been back at the clubhouse, with another woman. I mean, he did come, but still, we didn't actually do it. Maybe he needed more. He was ready to go again when he tucked himself back into his jeans...

"Where did Rock go?" I ask innocently.

He pulls out some plates as I fiddle with my mug. "Cash needed him for a job. It happens from time to time. He wasn't happy about it." I look up and meet his taunting eyes. "Seems like you may have made an impression on him in all of five days."

I roll my lips. Do I deny it? Is there any point?

"I mean, he's hot," I whisper. "But that's it."

"Uh huh."

"We didn't fuck," I clarify, which is true.

"Woah, honey, it's not even eight a.m. and it's dinner and a show. For the record, you don't have to explain to me, but I don't think I've ever seen Rock whistling while he works."

My eyes go wide. "I'm sure he's just…"

He winks at me. "Your secret's safe with me. Don't worry."

He looks over as Stella opens the door from outside and gives me a smile.

"Hi, *Laguna Beach.*"

I groan. "Not you too."

She laughs, then thumbs behind her toward the man-made cat enclosure. "Uh, did Rock make that?"

I swallow hard as my eyes meet Manny's. "Yeah. Just so my cat doesn't go flying off the roof. Pirate got out on the first day, and I was worried he'd jump up and fall."

Manny's lips twitch as I give him *shut the hell up* eyes.

"Sweet," she says.

It was sweet.

Just like everything about Rock.

He can deny it all he wants, but there isn't a mean bone in his body.

I know it. Not only that, but I feel it.

I can't wait to see him tonight. The fact he texted me…that has to be good.

I refuse to believe that I'm just another notch on his belt. I don't care what Tara says, or how naive I'm being. She has it wrong.

Rock isn't like that.

Even though a deep, dark part of me really doesn't care if he is.

16

ROCK

I punch him again in the ribs, hearing the crack as Jett winces next to me.

It's just like old times.

"Think he's had enough?" Jett gives me a chin lift.

"Nope. He spoiled my fun with a beautiful woman. So I think he can go a little longer."

We're at the shipping yard, which is where we go to conduct business that we don't want anybody else seeing. Such as torturing potential suspects over information they may have on Forger and the Devils Ink MC.

I revel in this. In the pain. In making them suffer. It's not like they're good people.

Fuck that. They're not.

I've always thought something fishy was going on from the start with the Devils Ink.

Okay, so they had a financial backer who wasn't as smart as he thought he was. Luna's ex had a price to pay, and he paid it. He was also getting a cut of whatever Forger made on drugs and guns, but it still didn't explain how Forger went from shit to Shinola so quickly. I guess scum helps scum and loyalty means nothing anymore. Not in the underworld crime syndicate.

I don't get to do this as much as I'd like, mainly because that's Tag and Harlem's job, but since they're not here and me and Jett are, now seems like as good a time as any to get under the fucker's skin.

All these assholes are scumbags. If they weren't, they wouldn't be involved with the likes of Forger. A man who left his own child in a crypt for her to burn to death.

Sick son of a bitch. We've all been instructed that if we capture Forger, he's to be left for Harlem. And I almost pity the idiot because he won't walk out of here alive.

"Don't know…" the man sputters as I pull his head back by his hair.

"You don't know? How about I cut your nuts off and see how long it takes for you to bleed out? Would that spark your memory?" I snarl angrily in his face.

"We don't get details, locations. We don't…"

I punch him again.

We have a fuckin' location. We're goin' tomorrow night, undercover. What I need to know is who is really behind this. I don't believe for a second that this is cut and dry. Forger ain't the sharpest tool in the shed.

Something stinks, and until we get to the bottom of it, we all have to do what we gotta do.

"Gettin' tired of hearin' excuses," I mutter. "I sharpened my blade this mornin', chump. And it would slice through your skin like butter."

"Do it. I'm dead anyway," he spits.

"Who is Forger workin' for?" I repeat.

Jett looks at me dubiously. He thinks this is all useless, but I could always smell a rat better than he could. I can thank prison for that one.

I cut his cheek with my blade, and he cries out like a pussy. I can't kill him. Harlem and Tag would kick my ass.

But since they're not here, and we're on a timeframe with this thing, I don't think they'll mind too much what I do.

"Fuck, man! I don't know shit. I'm one of the runners, that's it."

I frown. "What's a runner?"

He pants, hands tied behind his back, sitting on a wooden chair.

Frankly, I'm running out of patience.

I'm pissed I got dragged away from Aspyn last night babysitting this asshole because Tag and Harlem were out of town chasing down a lead.

Jett kicks his chair. "Answer him!"

"I run the drugs," he says. "I get it ready for the deal and distribute accordingly."

"So he's the one who cuts the drugs with cheap shit and passes it off as pure," Jett scoffs.

I shake my head. "Did you ever see that other scumbag that we caught a couple of weeks ago?" I ask, as he looks from Jett to me. He wouldn't have, the assholes at the bottom of the swamp.

"No, I don't know who you mean…" he stammers.

"He was yours. *Was* being the operative word. He was also a runner. Do you remember, brother, what we did to him?"

Jett smirks. "Right. I almost forgot. The alligators had a feeding frenzy that day. Had a bit of meat on his bones."

The man's eyes go wide, and we both laugh. Works like a charm every time.

I doubt these idiots know anything. They're bottom-dwellers in the grand scheme of things.

Forger is being protected, not just by the underworld criminals, but it's something so much more… I've even thought about the Irish… Would the mafia really betray Cash? I doubt it since their leader, Ronan, almost got shot the same night I did. We have an alliance with them and the Mexicans.

As long as they stay out of our territory, we'll look the other way.

And the Irish have at least been helpful. The cartel... maybe not so much, but then again, getting too involved with them could only lead to more trouble. Cash won't deal in anything illegal, especially now that he has Deanna and their daughter, Caprice.

He's not risking shit and hasn't for years. So keeping the cartel and the Irish at arm's length unless we need them is for the best.

"Alligators?"

"The bayou," I sigh. "Take it you're not from around here, bud?"

He shakes his head.

"That may be a good thing," Jett says, side-eying me. "If he doesn't see what's comin'. Snap, snap."

"No! I swear..." Blood drips down his face.

"If I hear you swear one more time..." I warn.

Jett shoves him back. "Any piece of information, no matter how small, can be useful. I'd start thinkin' if I were you, my brother isn't known for his patience."

He shakes his head, and I shake mine at what a pussy he is.

"Should we leave him for Harlem?"

The man's eyes go wide. Clearly, he knows who I'm referring to.

"No!" he begs. "If I tell you somethin' I heard, then you'll let me go? I have a family."

"So did Indigo when Forger kidnapped their daughter and she almost died in an inferno," Jett reminds him. "Think about that before you open your goddamn mouth again."

He writhes around. I wish we didn't have to wait for Harlem and Tag. This is getting tiresome.

"If you start makin' up shit," I warn him. "I'm gonna start

slicing your fingertips off one by one, then I'll move to your toes. Then I'll start on your nuts."

He shakes his head. "*Please…*"

"Out with it, then we'll decide if you live or die, or if we just leave you for Harlem."

He blinks a couple of times, looking like he's going to pass out. "I heard a name. It's probably nothin'. It was only one time."

"Spit it out, fucker!" I yell.

"*Caruso.*"

I blink.

Caruso?

Haven't heard that name in a long time.

It's an old Italian mafia last name. The Carusos were notorious back in the day, I'm talking the 19th century. The name fizzled out years ago with the Irish taking reign over the French Quarter and the Carusos moving on to bigger and better things, like Texas.

I feel Jett's eyes on me. "Is he for real?"

"I think he's lyin'."

"So you know who I'm talking about?" the man frets. "I swear to God, I only overheard it. I don't know shit. Carlo Caruso's name came up a couple of times…"

"He's the head of the Houston crime family," Jett mutters.

"I know," I reply. "Didn't go to school for long, but I know all the mafia outside of New Orleans."

The man smiles, like he's done something good. I don't know what he's got to smile about. His days are numbered.

Trouble is, they'll notice another runner has gone missing. Not that Cash cares about that, but Forger will know we're closing in.

"Good. Now think." I tap his head with my knuckles. "What did they say about Caruso?"

He frowns. "I don't… Okay, I never heard the whole conversation…"

I round the back of him to where his hands are tied. "You're makin' me do this," I warn. "You have pretty fingers, or should I say...*had.*"

I hold one hand and slice the top of his finger off of his pointer and he screams in agony.

"Fuck, that blade's sharper than I thought," I chuckle.

"*Think!*" Jett yells at him. "What can we do with a name? Fuckin' nothin', asshole. We need more."

"There was talk," he pants. He's a slobbering mess. I should just put him out of his misery early, but I don't wanna be on the outs with Harlem. "The Carusos want to move back to the Quarter. The Irish are not real happy about that..."

"I'll bet," I snort.

But this is news.

Jett and I share a glance. This ain't good. We don't wanna be in on the beef of two mafia rivals, but if Forger is involved with the Carusos, then where the fuck does that leave us?

The more I think about it, the more I realize this is news Cash hasn't heard. Nobody has. I run a hand down my face.

"What else, asshole?" Jett kicks his shin. "Hurry the fuck up, you've already taken up too much goddamn time."

Jett hates blood, and this guy's finger and head is dripping continuously.

"The Carusos want in, from what I heard," he stammers. "And I don't know for sure, but they could be backin' Forger. Ever since his contact in the city mysteriously disappeared, so did the funds. But talk goin' around is that the Caruso's plan on claimin' back what was rightfully theirs. What they walked away from years ago."

I pinch the bridge of my nose as Jett's eyes meet mine.

Jesus.

I'll call Cash, I mouth.

Jett nods.

Walking away, I pull out my phone.

I see another text message from my girl, and I smile when I see the subject line.

Trouble

> How did you get your number into my phone?

I wondered when she'd query that.
I quickly tap out a message.
Me

> That's for me to know...

Good, that'll keep her wondering. It's amazing what one can do when the woman of your current obsession is sleeping and you Face ID her so you can punch your number into her contacts without her knowing. Not exactly rocket science, but since she practically has her phone glued to her side, she'll likely think I hacked into it.

I also read all her messages from her best friend. She seems like a pill.

I smile at the texts where Aspyn said I was hot and she propositioned me. She kept talking about it. My dick grew so hard seeing her words, knowing that she finds me attractive and was asking her best friend what to do. I wouldn't take Tara's advice.

She didn't seem keen on the idea about me and her best friend fucking.

I also checked there were no other assholes messaging or emailing her, but it seems Aspyn is actually a good girl and was telling the truth. No ex-boyfriend. No publicist. No other friends. She literally only has her best friend messaging her.

So my girl can agree to rules, it seems. I find that equally arousing as it is disturbing.

She's a grown woman and she's still doing everything

daddy says. That's a habit she's gotta break at some point, when this stalker is found.

I rub my chin and click off to dial Cash.

He answers on the third ring.

"Boss?" I say. "We got somethin'."

"Spit it out."

"Carlo Caruso."

A pause, then, "What about him?"

"Fuckface heard the Carusos want to move back in from Houston, shoot the Irish down, and claim back the French Quarter."

"Are you fuckin' kiddin' me?"

"Unfortunately not."

"Fuck, that's all we need."

Then again, it could be a distraction…

"I doubt this asshole is clever enough to make up somethin' this elaborate," I go on. "Took a little bit to get it out of him, but still, I think he's tellin' the truth."

Cash sighs. "Harlem, Tag, Hawk, Ryder, and Bronco are en route. They'll be there shortly."

"Okay."

"Rock?"

"Yeah?"

"You sound exactly like your brother on the phone."

"Fuck off," I mutter. It's not the first time I've heard that.

He chuckles. "Good work, but keep him alive. H won't be happy if you slice him up too bad."

I smile. "Got it."

I quickly tap out another message to Aspyn.

Me

> So hard for you

I smile. I like teasing her and I think she enjoys it. Strolling back toward my brother, I wonder how much I should actually fuck him up. Should I feel guilty that I enjoy hurting bad people? I mean, I don't go out of my way to do it, but when the opportunity presents itself, I don't hesitate. It isn't as if this guy is a stand-up citizen.

It also helps with my anger problems and the dark part of me I bury that wants to punish anyone who does wrong by people. I can't help it.

It's gonna be a long afternoon, but at least I have my girl to look forward to when I get home.

The adrenaline coursing through my veins at hurting this man, mixed with her sucking me off and me eating her out, makes my dick hard.

I'm having her when I get out of here.

I don't give a fuck about Cash's rules. Her dad's rules. Or even her fuckin' rules.

The minute Aspyn landed in New Orleans, the stars aligned.

She may be my new obsession, but it's not like I won't make it good for her.

If she'd let me, I'd worship the ground she walks on. Being on my knees for her is not a hardship. I'd gladly do it over and over. But if she thinks she can flaunt herself around like she has been and I won't notice, she can think again.

I'll make what I did to this guy look like a jamboree at a Boy Scout outing if any other guy so much as looks her way. Manny, included.

I grind my teeth.

I'm a possessive asshole when it comes to what I want. Not that she's gonna want to hear that after having a stalker who threatened her life. This isn't the same thing.

I'd never hurt her. I can't say I want what's best for her, because I'm not what's best for her in any way, shape, or form. But I'm here. And I will stop at nothing to make sure that she's out of harm's way.

I need to get back to her.

But first…

"Let's see how high he can scream," I say to Jett, waggling my eyebrows.

Jett's hand over his mouth softens the roar as I split him open once more.

It's late when I pull up to the apartment.

I'm tired.

We had to wait for Harlem and the boys to arrive before debriefing them. Then I had to work on some shit for Cash, which I planned on doing back at the apartment, but of course, that didn't happen. While I was out, I also showed my face at the shop. Luna was out for lunch with the new receptionist and all the drivers were out doing deliveries. To say it's a well-oiled machine is an understatement. So at least that's one thing I don't have to worry about.

When I pull up, I see Rodeo loitering near the elevators.

I give him a chin lift. "All good?"

I never replied to my girl's next text, which read:

Trouble

> When will u be back?

My dick hardens when I think about her pining for me. I want her to want me; there is no mistake about that. And keeping her hanging on the line excites me.

I want her needy for me.

"Nothin' goin' on, dude," he says.

"Good." I nod.

"Priest is up there with her."

I hide my annoyance as anger boils my blood.

Fuckin' Priest. He's anything but holy.

He claims he made a vow of celibacy after getting out of the joint, but I see sweet butts all over him all the time. I can't actually say I've seen him take any of them upstairs, or anywhere else secluded, for that matter, but that don't mean shit.

He's not a real priest, more like a chaplain, and usually he's a stand-up guy. Just not when he's hanging around my girl without anyone else around.

I crack my neck side to side, trying not to envision Aspyn doing anything with Priest.

Women like him because he's mysterious. He knows a lot just by looking at you and I don't like that. He's tried to get in my head a few times, but I just tell him to fuck off.

I don't need no goddamn therapist.

I press the elevator button and swipe myself up to the penthouse.

I do not like the idea of Priest being alone with her. The more I think about it, the more my mind gets carried away.

I've never felt this kind of jealousy in...well, ever. I knew Aspyn was different when I first laid eyes on her, but what I didn't know is that, apparently, I am too.

Anxiety sweeps through me as I will the elevator to go faster.

What if I catch them at it?

Would I be able to refrain from choking Priest to death?

Would she honestly do that to me? She seems kinda innocent but also not. She has been a vixen flirting with me shamelessly... feeling me up in public and getting off on my motorcycle. I left her hangin' for my dick last night...

All of these possessive thoughts swirl through my mind, making me feel all the more agitated by every fleeting second that passes.

Is the elevator going slower than normal?

I slam my fist on the side of the wall, annoyed that I got called away.

And my girl has been out today. It annoys me that I wasn't there to protect her.

What if something happened? And I wasn't there...

My heart pounds in my chest.

Breathe.

I feel my head starting to spin.

Sometimes I get anxiety attacks but they're not often, and I haven't had one for a while.

Now...I can't seem to get air into my lungs.

Aspyn...

She's in trouble...

I shake it off. It's Priest... He would never hurt her...

The elevator pings, and I dash out the door into the penthouse a little too fast, but then I stop, my vision blurring as Priest turns from his position at the kitchen table.

They're...*playing battleships?*

Is this some kind of joke?

"Woah," Priest says as I steady myself against the door. "You drunk?"

I shake my head, leaning over as I try to catch my breath.

I see Priest stand and I hear a far-off voice that sounds like Aspyn, "Oh my god. Is he okay?"

I feel hands on me, and I'm being ushered over to the couch.

"... Anxiety or panic attack..." Priest says. "Happens from time to time. Could be the confines of the elevator..."

"Can I do something?"

"Open the sliding door. Let some cool air in, that'll help."

I glare sideways at him. "I'm..."

"You just need to breathe, motherfucker."

I wave a hand. "Yeah...the elevator," I lie. It has nothing to do with confined spaces, but I don't wanna look like a pussy in front of him.

He nods. "Just breathe. Put your head between your legs."

"Fuck off."

"Do it." He yanks the back of my head, forcing it down.

I take deep inhales as I start to feel less lightheaded as the seconds pass.

What a fuckin' pussy.

I should be ashamed of myself.

I want to punch this asshole in the face for taking up my time with Aspyn, and here I am sucking in lungful's of air with my head buried near my crotch.

Do I even deserve to be a biker?

"Rock." Aspyn dives to my feet, concern on her face. "God, is he gonna be okay? He looks pale and all clammy..."

"It's claustrophobia," Priest explains. "He'll be okay in a minute."

I breathe as he tells me to, and then he says, "I'll get him a stiff drink. That'll help with relaxin' him."

I don't tell Priest that alcohol rarely ever works even when it's used as a depressant. It doesn't make things worse for me, luckily, but the short-term relaxant might just help me get my breathing under control.

"Rock," Aspyn whispers.

I stare at her.

Her hair is...*different*.

She looks completely different.

Her hair is chestnut, her skin has a more subtle golden hue.... Those lips, though, they're still the same...

"I need you," I whisper.

Her eyes go wide. "You have me, Rock. I'm here. I'm not going anywhere."

17

ASPYN

I nod as Priest leaves, giving me instructions on what to do if Rock has another episode.

I'm glad he was here. I would've had no idea what to do, which annoys me.

That's another thing about living a sheltered life... I don't know what to do in emergency situations. Like, if someone was actually choking or something, what the hell could I do? Holler and scream for help? Dial 911. Someone could die in my hands, and I'd never be able to forgive myself.

He sits back on the couch, his eyes closed as he starts to get some color back in his cheeks.

This wasn't the reunion that I envisioned. Far from it, but this isn't about me.

My heart races a mile a minute as I wait for him to say something.

He holds the glass in one heavily tattooed hand. It's half full of amber liquid which smells like whiskey.

I was playing a game with Priest because we were bored, and Rock hadn't replied to my text, when he came bursting in the door looking furious.

"Rock?" I whisper. "Is there anything I can get you?"

Finally, he says, "I'm good, *Trouble.*"

I rub his back with the flat of my palm, soothing him as I try to will him back to me.

I've never seen anything like this before. He was so…out of it.

"Are you still dizzy?"

He shakes his head. "Just need another minute."

"Do you really hate confined spaces that much?"

He shrugs.

I frown. I don't know what to do for him, so maybe it's best I leave him be.

"Have you been sleeping okay?"

He frowns.

"I mean, you said it was the elevator, but we've traveled up and down the thing heaps of times…"

"It was you," he blurts out, shocking me.

My eyes go wide as I tuck my hair behind my ears. "Me?" I'm not sure what he means.

He moves his hand to glance sideways at me. "Yes, *you.*"

"Wait, what did I do?" I squeak. "You're the one who didn't reply to my message…"

He clears his throat. "Doesn't matter."

"No," I say sharply, earning me another glare. "Don't do that, Rock. We've been able to be honest with one another. Let's not change that now. Tell me what I did."

He sighs. "You didn't *do* anythin'. It's me."

I frown. Then it clicks. "Were you… Were you worried about me…and *Priest*?"

He takes another long breath. "I let my mind get away from me."

I frown, my voice small when I say, "You really think I'd jump into bed with another guy? After what we did?"

He looks away. "I don't know, I don't know you, Aspyn. The thought angered me."

I know he's being serious when he uses my proper name, and now isn't the time for kidding around.

"Talk to me," I say gently. I'm annoyed he thinks I would do that, but I keep that inside for the moment. I can yell at him when he's better.

"I'm a fuckin' pussy," he says, his voice low. "I usually have this under control."

"What can I do to help?"

"Nothin'."

I take a deep breath, then ask, "Why do you think I'd sleep with anyone else when it's you I want, Rock?"

He shifts his gaze to me again. His lips part but no sound comes out.

"I would *never* do that," I go on. "I know we're not exclusive, even though you told me my pussy was yours." I roll my lips when his lips twitch in turn, fighting a smile. "And I told you I don't sleep around, that was all true. Maybe it doesn't seem like it because I flirted with you like a harlot, but it's only because I wanted you to notice me."

"Oh, I noticed, *Trouble*. C'mere."

He pats his lap, and I gladly crawl onto it.

Staring down at him, he cups my face, one hand running through my newly colored tendrils. "You changed your hair."

"I wasn't sure… I didn't know if you'd like it…"

"I love it," he says. "Better than blonde."

I feel a relief in my chest that I know I shouldn't, but I like pleasing him.

"Really?"

He nods. "Brings out the blue in your eyes more."

I feel his hard cock as I press my body closer, my arms wrapping around his neck.

His lips brush mine, but he doesn't kiss me.

"I missed you," I whisper.

"*Aspyn,*" he mutters against my mouth. His whiskers tickle my lips. "What are you doin' to me?"

"I know you broke into my phone," I say.

"Had to make sure…"

"Did you read the messages from Tara?"

He doesn't hesitate to answer. "Yes. She doesn't like me very much."

I *should* see red… I *should* feel a lot of things, but all I feel right now is this strange sensation coursing through my chest as my breath quickens.

He's a possessive asshole…and I think I like it.

"That's quite stalkery behavior."

"That's not a word."

"I made it a word."

"I'm not stalkin' you. I'm makin' sure the stalker stays away."

"By breakin' into my phone?"

He shakes his head. "No. I went to put my number in…"

"By Face ID'ing me while I slept?"

He bites his bottom lip, and my eyes drift to his mouth. *Holy fuck.*

"Yeah, about that…"

"So you came into my room?"

"No, you fell asleep on the couch that time."

I adjust my words, knowing that I know the truth. "Have you watched me sleep?"

He swallows hard. "Yes."

"And that isn't stalking?"

"Nope. I was makin' sure you were okay and not feelin' scared."

My heart warms as he says the words, even though I should be a little terrified he's been sneaking into my room…

"How many times?"

"Just the once."

I level him with a stare. "Okay, twice. I didn't stay long. The first time your cat was makin' a racket that you seem immune to." Like that's any excuse.

"Rock?" I don't wait for him to answer. "I want to be with you. I want you inside me. Do you understand?" I don't say the word fuck, because that isn't what that is, and he knows it. This is so much more. "I don't want Priest or any other guy. Just you."

"You want my dick?"

I shake my head. "I want you."

"Why?" He looks so lost. "I'm broken, babe. I don't know if I can ever be fixed."

I frown, realizing we've gone from panic attacks to something else.

The darkness, I realize. That cloud that hangs over him.

"Did something bad happen to you?" I let the question linger between us.

He swallows hard.

"Rock?"

He nods.

"Do you want to talk about it?"

He shakes his head.

My poor Rock. *What the fuck happened?*

He looks so fucking lost that it breaks my heart... I don't know what to do for him....

"I want to run you a bath," I say out of nowhere.

He frowns. "What?"

I press my lips against his, forcing a kiss from him as I let go and fall out of his arms.

"When Priest was helping you, I googled it, and it said that a hot bath can be therapeutic for anxiety and help calm your nervous system." I walk backwards as I explain, then I turn and dash down the hallway to my bathroom and start the water running, squeezing my Chanel bubble bath under the flowing stream of water.

I smile at my own idea. I get to bathe Rock and get him naked at the same time.

Win-win.

Rock

When I move back into the lounge, Rock is still in the same place.

He lets his hair down as I move toward him softly. It's like if I make any sudden moves, it might set him off again.

"Don't do that," he says out of nowhere.

I frown. "Do what?"

"Act tentative around me. I'm not gonna break that easily."

I crawl back into his lap, and I relish the feel of his hands around my waist.

"I'm not."

Pressing my lips against his once more, his tongue slides into my mouth as we kiss. I push my tits against his chest as his hands settle on my ass cheeks, effectively holding me against his hard cock.

He squeezes my ass and we kiss for so long, I lose track of time.

I'm wet for him. So ready to have him, but I also want him to relax. He's still so pent up and his grip on my ass is almost painful, not that I let him know that.

"We better not start something before we can finish it," I pant. "If you're a good boy after I bathe you, I might suck your dick."

A slow smile spreads across his face. "I think I like the lead up to that."

I smile too. "You like the idea of me washing you, don't you?"

He squeezes one cheek, and I yelp. "No, but I like the idea that I get to be naked with you."

He stands, taking me with him as I wrap my legs around his waist.

We kiss again. It's so passionate. So raw. Everything about this man makes my senses feel like they're tingling.

When we reach my bathroom, I slide down his body, my hands landing on his belt buckle. I want to undress him.

I undo his belt, his top button and then I unzip him. My knuckles graze his hard cock as he hisses. I shrug his jeans and his boxer briefs down to his thighs and then look up at his smirk.

"Sit, please," I say. "I need to deal with those boots."

Surprisingly, he does as I say and sits on the edge of the tub as I get on my knees and untie his laces.

When I glance up, he's watching me, his eyes dancing with a delicious mix of surprise and lust. I always want him to look at me like this, and while my head is telling me not to get too attached, my heart is telling me to shut the fuck up.

I yank them off, along with his socks, and while I'm down there, I tug his jeans the rest of the way off. He doesn't move to help me with his motorcycle jacket or his t-shirt.

I leave them on as I divert my gaze to his dick that is now bobbing in my face.

I run my hand down his thick length as he hisses, one hand automatically landing on the back of my head. He doesn't move it, or force me anywhere, he just rests it there.

I don't know why I find that soothing, but it calls to me on another level.

It brings something out in me that almost feels feral.

My badass biker.

As I swipe my tongue over his slit, his chest rumbles in approval.

I do it again, murmuring, "Does my baby need some attention?"

I smile to myself as I suck the end of his tip, looking up at him as he watches me with hooded eyes. I flatten my tongue, loving how his eyes darken when I take him farther into my mouth. *Goddamn.*

"Jesus," he mutters. He shrugs off his jacket, and then yanks his t-shirt off, dumping them on the floor.

I let him go with a loud pop. "I can't get you too excited," I say, standing as I lean over to turn the taps off now that the tub is nicely filled. "We just got your breathing under control."

He grabs me by the hips and drags me back to his lap. He's shaking his head, amusement on his face. I'm glad to see him smiling instead of the rage that he showed me earlier. "You're bein' a bad girl, *Trouble*. I should put you over my knee."

He's jealous and possessive. I try to reason with myself that it's because he cares, but is that the reason?

I ignore that thought and brace my hands on his shoulders. He wants to spank me, and to be honest, I'd let him.

He pushes his head between my breasts as I run my hands through his hair.

I revel in the feel of his warm body against mine, even if I am still fully clothed.

"You smell so fuckin' sweet," he says, as I groan when he grabs my ass.

"Not as sweet as you taste," I murmur.

He pulls back and looks up at me. I know he wants me, but I want to look after him.

I've always been a nurturing person.

When our housekeeper once brought her sick kid to stay in the pool house while she worked, I watched out for him and we played games and I made sure he got food and plenty of hydration. This is really no different.

Even somebody as tough as Rock needs some TLC.

"But…I promised to get you in a calm place."

"I am calm," he says, and I see the lust in his eyes. "I need your pussy, *Trouble*."

I squeeze my legs together. It'd be so easy to let him lead me over to the bed and fuck exactly like I know he wants to. But drawing it out also turns me on just as much.

I wag a finger in his face. "I'm in charge now."

A shit-eating grin spreads across his face. Once again, I'm

reminded just how pretty he is when he smiles like that. The whole world lights up.

"Is that right?"

I nod, moving my fingers to my blouse as I start to unbutton it.

"Why don't you hop in?"

His lips press together as he watches me undress. "How about I stay right here?"

I shake my head. "You need to relax."

"Smells like a perfumery in here."

I laugh. "Chanel will do that to you."

The tub is like a jet spa. There is plenty of room, which is gonna be good because I think Rock has plans for us...

"Do you want the jets on?" I prompt.

He shakes his head.

I watch as he stands, tugs his dick a couple of times as he turns and steps into the tub, settling back against the far side facing me. "Keep goin'," he tells me, nodding to my chest.

I bite down on my lip as I undo my blouse, keeping it loose as I reach down to pull my socks off and then my jeans and panties. I had a fresh Brazilian while I was at the salon today, along with my new tan and hair.

Rock notices, his hand disappearing under the suds, and I know he's touching himself.

"Turn around," he drawls.

I shuck my blouse off my shoulders and let it drop to the floor. Turning, I shake my ass at him as I bend over, pretending to pick something up.

I know he can see all of me like this, and I'm not afraid to show him. In fact, I want him to see.

I'm still a little raw from the wax, but the warm water will help. If I ever make it that far...

Turning, I see Rock's hand moving up and down his cock as he stares at me.

"So fuckin' beautiful," he tells me.

Rock

I unclip my bra and fling it with confidence across the bathroom floor. My tits spring free as his eyes move to them, devouring me with his gaze.

Moving toward the tub's edge, I grab a sponge and the shower gel and climb in.

"C'mere, *Trouble*."

I shake my head. "I have to get clean first. Then I'll do you."

He smirks. "Oh, you'll be doin' me, babe, don't worry about that."

I bite down on my lip and squirt shower gel on my sponge and start to move it across my breasts. My nipples are pebbled and hard as his eyes watch my movements, his hand still working his cock as I tease him.

"So wet for you, Rock," I whisper, his eyes flicking to mine momentarily as I pinch one nipple.

"*Aspyn*," he growls. "Get. Over. Here. Now."

I smile. "My baby's very bossy."

"Need you to comfort me." Oh God. His damn words. My ovaries practically explode.

I grin. "Why didn't you just say so?"

I scoot toward him as he catches me, his mouth on mine instantly.

He spreads his legs and I move between them. His hard dick bobs between us in the water. I know he wants me to touch it, but I want to tease him a little longer.

"Do you like how I touch myself, Rock?" I mutter against his lips.

"You drive me fuckin' crazy," he groans when I lick his lips.

His hands find my ass, and he presses his dick against my stomach.

Still holding the sponge and the shower gel, I squirt out some more and I start to work the sponge over his chest. He makes a noise that sounds feral.

I place the shower gel on the side and make a big show of soaping him up. The sponge moves in one hand, and the other slides down his rock-hard abs as I brush his cock.

He groans, grabbing my hand as he places it on his dick.

I tsk. "That's very naughty when I'm tryin' to lower your blood pressure."

He grips me by the back of the neck and pulls me toward him as our lips touch. "Set my blood pressure off bendin' over like that, babe."

I smile. "I wanted to show you my fresh Brazilian. I'm taking it that you approve?" I tug on his dick harder as I hear that rumble in his chest again.

That damn sound does it for me.

"*Fuck*," he mutters.

"Problem?" I can't help but feel smug. I've got him in this state of arousal and it's so fucking hot.

I slide my palm down his length as I tease him, working the sponge over his nipple.

He slides the hand on my ass up the side of my body to cup one breast. Dipping his eyes, he rolls my nipple as I gasp.

"Sit in my lap," he demands.

I comply, moving so I'm straddled over him now.

I move the sponge under the water to gently massage his balls and he loses it.

"Fuck, Aspyn." He pulls me to him, and when his mouth meets mine again, his kiss is lustful and hungry.

I drop the sponge and wrap my arms around him. His cock rubs against my pussy as I moan quietly.

When he moves his mouth to my neck, I'm dying for him to play with my breasts.

And he wastes no time in doing that.

Both hands cup me as he moves his mouth to one nipple, his eyes watching me as I groan in pleasure. My hands reach into his hair as I pull.

He works my nipple, sucking and nipping as I buck

against him, rubbing my pussy over his hard dick. I could come just like this. Now who's teasing who?

He does it so damn well.

"*Fuck*," he mutters again.

I move back a little to reach between us, feeling his cock as he watches. Then I dip my hand to cup his sac. "This feels really full, Rock," I whisper.

He growls, moving his lips to the other nipple as I cry out when he bites me gently.

God, his beard feels so damn good against my sensitive skin.

When I squeeze his balls, he hisses. This time, he stops what he's doing, grabs my hips, holds his dick, and before I know it, he's pushing into me as I slide down.

Oh, my.

He's so big.

It happens so fast. One minute, I'm rubbing against him, and the next, he's seated all the way inside me as I gasp from the intrusion.

A noise leaves my throat that I know I've never made before. He brings the wild animal out in me.

His eyes meet mine. "Now," he breathes as I stare at him in shock. "Let's talk about what I'm gonna do to you shall we, *Trouble?*"

18

ROCK

She's so damn tight.

I'm all the way in as I still, her breath catching in her chest when I gaze up at her.

She's the most beautiful woman I've ever seen.

I wouldn't care what color her hair is, to be honest. None of that matters.

All that matters is that look in her eye and that she wants me. Maybe I'm a fool and it is just my body and my cock she wants, but I can delude myself into thinking that she digs the connection we have just as much as I do. That I mean something even though I know that's impossible.

I never wanted to give a sob story when I told her I'm broken. I am in many ways. In ways that may never be healed. I like hurting bad people, and if she ever found out, what would she think of that? She'd probably run a mile.

I swallow hard.

"Yes, let's discuss that," she breathes.

I don't move, just stay seated deep inside her. Her pussy clamps around my dick like a vise. I can't get enough of this. I never will.

I press my forehead to hers. "You're a bad girl, Aspyn."

She shakes her head. "No."

"Did you enjoy bein' with Priest?"

She shakes her head.

"Most women like him."

"Not me. He seems nice, but I don't like him in that way."

My jealous streak isn't well known because not many of the guys ever see me with a woman. I keep a lot of what I do away from the clubhouse. Sharing pussy isn't exactly my thing. And with Aspyn? I'd kill someone who dares look her way.

I wanted to throttle Priest for even being in the same room as her.

Playing Battleships?

For fuck's sake.

"You sure?"

She nods, wiggling in my lap. I hold her still.

"I'm a possessive asshole, *Trouble.*" My eyes travel down her body to her breasts.

"All of this is mine while we're doin' this, got me? This body. This pussy. These tits. This ass. Your eyes only see me." I know how I sound, and I don't give a flying fuck.

"Oh."

My throat feels dry as I take in her shocked face. I don't know if it's a good or bad thing.

"That's so possessive, and so...*hot,*" she breathes, her eyes pleading with me to move.

Okay. So it's a good thing.

I lift her hips slowly as she rises until my tip is just inside her entrance. She groans when I slam her back down.

I don't give a fuck about letting her adjust to my size. Her pussy is tight, but she better get used to me pounding her because that's exactly what I'm gonna be doing.

"Hot?" I mutter, pulling out again and slamming back down. "My girl loves to be touched, don't you, babe?"

She nods. "*Oh, Rock.*"

I still her again, moving my mouth to her tits. She whimpers when I suckle, my eyes on hers as she grinds against me. I let her, but only because I'm enjoying her so much.

I don't thrust back, letting her push off me with her hands on my elbows as she starts to ride me. Each time she rises, I suck on her nipple, then let it go as she sinks down.

"This pussy is so tight around me," I grunt. "I need you."

She grinds down again, and I cup her ass. We're not using a condom, but I'm past the point of caring. Maybe I should check if she's on birth control…

As if reading my mind, she says, "I'm on the pill."

"Good," I breathe against her mouth. "Because I wanna spill my cum inside you until you don't even know your own name anymore."

I jerk and thrust as she cries out.

"Are you… Are you clean?" she pants.

"Always use one." *Just not with you because I can't get close enough.*

I want to do her in so many positions, but right now, I need to give her what she wants because, ultimately, I want to please her.

I grab her hips. "Gonna let you come now," I mutter as her lips find mine and our tongues clash. I hold her by the hips and pump her up and down.

"Rock," she cries.

"That's it, baby, scream my name when you come all over my dick. I wanna hear it."

She's close, I can tell by the rise of heat in her cheeks…just like when I went down on her and she came so beautifully.

The water splashes everywhere as she pumps her hips and her tits bounce in my face.

She squeezes her eyes shut as I pound her pussy until she's stuttering her words and crying out. I bite down on my lip as I watch her fall apart, calling my name over and over.

Her eyes open when she's spent, and I hold her still.

"Don't wanna come yet, but you're makin' this so fuckin' hard," I mutter.

"I need you deeper," she groans.

I pull her off my lap. "Bend over the tub," I grunt.

I hold her hand as she steps out, following behind. We don't even bother to wipe the suds off ourselves. She sticks her ass out as she presses her hands against the edge, and I move behind her, grabbing her by the hips as I line up my dick and sink into her.

She groans as I start pumping her hard and fast. My balls hit her pussy as she cries out, the slapping of our skin the only sound aside from her little whimpers.

"I told you what I'd do to you, and how I fuck," I grunt. "Do you believe me now?"

"I'm coming!" she cries, and she lets go so loud that I spank her ass cheek. She's so fuckin' perfect. I can't wait for that, either.

She sticks her ass out, riding out her pleasure as I plunge in and out, not giving her mercy. This entire week she's had my nuts in a sling, and now she's gonna pay for all that teasing. For the time she paraded past me in her bikini, asking me to pass her a towel. For wrestling me to the ground at the gym. For massaging my dick in the elevator, then coming on my sled.

This is her punishment.

"Oh, Rock, *yes*..."

"That's it, babe, feel me. I'm gonna ride this sweet little pussy all night. I ain't done after one time, so don't think that this is one hot, fast fuck and we'll call it a night. That ain't happenin'. I'm gonna eat my cum out of your pussy, and then feed it to you when I'm done. You got me?"

She gasps as I grin, slapping her other ass cheek. I smooth my hand up her soft skin, all the way up her spine until I'm clutching the back of her neck.

All I want in the world is to hear her scream.

"I didn't hear you?" I grunt, needing her to tell me she wants it.

"*Yes,*" she breathes. "Yes, I want that, Rock."

"Good, 'cause you're gonna get it. I'm close, babe. Touch your clit, show me how you do it."

She does as I say, and I move my hand up to her tit and cup it hard. I feel my balls tug, and when she cries, "*Rock!*" I shoot hot spurts of my cum inside her over and over until I still and hold her back to my front, rubbing my nose up her neck.

"You're so fuckin' beautiful," I tell her. "Comin' for me like that. Do you like what I do to you?"

She's panting hard. I continue to fondle her, still seated deep inside as she tries to gather her words. I grin against her neck.

"Yes, Rock. I love it and you're right…"

"About?" I kiss her racing pulse.

"Ruining me for all other men."

That makes my heart happy. A surge of pride fills my chest.

"I'm glad to hear that." I pull out, watching with adoration as my cum drips out of her.

As I run my fingers through her soaked pussy, she groans.

I turn her in my arms. "Look at what I did to you."

She stares at me, her mouth open as I suck on my own fingers, then I swipe her again and hold them to her lips.

She moves her mouth to suck my two fingers, laving her tongue as she swirls. I replace my fingers with my tongue and we're all hands as I reach behind me for a towel. I need these bubbles off her skin so I can fuck her in bed.

"You're so…*dirty,*" she whispers.

I grin.

"You know I'm goin' to corrupt you, don't you, babe?"

"I'd be disappointed if you did anything *but* corrupt me," she breathes.

Rock

I spread her legs and do exactly what I said. I eat her out, smoothing my tongue over her clit as she cries out, mumbling incoherently as I make her come again. I know she's sensitive, but I gave her five generous minutes of me playing with just her tits while she fondled my balls. I didn't intend on making her sore, but I know she's gonna be by the time we're done.

I groan when she erupts as I suck her clit into my mouth, my fingers moving in and out of her as she cries out in raspy, breathless shouts.

I lower my mouth and do as I promised. I lick through her pussy, my cum still running out of her from before, and then I move to her mouth. Her lips part as I spit my cum, mixed with hers, into her mouth, and she swallows.

I groan at the sight, continuing to finger her as she watches me with fascination.

"I want your ass," I tell her.

She nods. "Okay."

I grin. "Just like that?"

"I trust you."

I slide my cock inside her pussy without warning, but it's slow this time.

"Oh, Rock, that's so good."

"Need some of that to coat your other hole," I mutter.

Our lips join again, and I start to move my hips as she lies spread eagled, her hands tugging on my hair in a way I can't get enough of.

I bang her harder, enjoying her tits bouncing on every thrust.

I know I'm hitting her G-spot when I tilt her hips and she screams.

Pumping harder, I grind with a thrust as I move up onto my hands and give it to her.

She scratches her nails down my back, and I hiss. God, I love making her scream.

Pulling out, I lift her up to sit. "On all fours," I say.

She looks worried for a second.

I cup her face. "I will never hurt you, babe. Do you want this?"

She nods. "I want it to feel good."

"It will. I promise it will. I'll make you scream so much harder."

I sit back on my haunches as she moves onto her hands and knees. Spreading her ass cheeks, I bring my mouth to her puckered hole. She gasps as I latch on, using my tongue as I grip her hips and whisper to relax.

She's so wet we don't need any lube. I dip my fingers into her pussy and spread our combined climaxes to her rear end.

"I need it, Rock." I love how impatient she is.

"Love that I'm the first here," I mutter against her flesh. I slide the tip of my finger in slowly and she gasps, gripping me. "Just take it easy, I said I won't hurt you."

She groans when I slide my finger in and out. I need to get her used to the feeling before I go shoving my cock inside.

Wiggling her ass as I play with her, one finger turns to two, then she moves her hips back, wanting more. My dirty, dirty little girl.

"Fuck, if you could see how hot you look from back here," I mutter, working her in and out. "Touch yourself, *Trouble.*"

I watch as she reaches her hand between her legs and fondles herself. I love how responsive she is to me, doing as I say without hesitation.

"Such a good girl."

I shift and grab my cock, rubbing the tip over her back entrance as she gasps.

She's already anticipating what I'm about to do. I'm so turned on, my cock is weeping to be inside her.

Rock

As I prod her ass, she grips the pillows. "Aspyn?" I whisper.

"Yes?"

"You gotta relax, baby. If it hurts, you tell me, but you can't tense up…"

"I'm trying!"

I smile, running a hand up her spine to cup her neck. Bringing her backward for a second, I tilt her head so I can kiss her. My tongue in her mouth. "I will never hurt you. I'll stop if it's too much."

"Hurry, I need you," she groans when I tug on her bottom lip.

I let go of her and rub some more, spreading her wetness all over. I slide my tip in again and she moans. *So damn tight.* When I push a little harder, I'm met with resistance. I'm about to tell her to relax again but I feel her do just that.

"Good girl," I tell her. "My cock is gonna fill you so full, babe. You won't be able to get enough of me this way."

"Oh," she cries when I slide in and out, giving her a little more of my length.

She surprises me by moving her hips back. I groan too as I slide in farther.

"So good," I mutter. As I grip her ass cheeks, she relaxes some more. I pump her for a little bit, enjoying the feel of her but not penetrating farther. The more she relaxes and enjoys it, the better it'll be. "How you feelin'?"

"G-good," she stammers.

I smile. My girl is up for anything, and I dig that. I love how she's so open to trying something new.

I slide in a little more, knowing I'm pushing her limits.

"Takin' me so well, babe," I mutter, rocking my hips back and forth slowly as her hand works busily between her legs.

"Oh, Rock," she cries when I feel her ass clench me. I revel in making her feel good, I realize, and I wasn't kidding when I said it's gonna be my new favorite pastime.

She starts to come, and she goes silent for a few moments, then she explodes as I ride her harder, pushing in farther, in and out, in and out.

Her orgasm goes on and on as I dip my fingers around to her pussy and shove them inside.

"Oh, God!" she screams when I curve my fingers to massage deep inside her, my dick still in her ass as she combusts.

I move my mouth to her ear. "Did my girl just have multiples?"

"Jesus," she whimpers. "Please, don't stop, Rock."

I grin, tilting her mouth as I lick her lips with my tongue.

It's so fuckin' dirty and I can't get enough of it.

"You like me drippin' my cum in your mouth, babe?"

"I love it. I love how you taste."

Hearing that makes my balls wanna explode again. I still deep inside her.

"You like your ass bein' fucked, babe?"

She nods. "It... It feels different to how I thought it would...in a good way."

I know I'm being gentle with her, and I don't wanna be. But I don't wanna make her regret it the first time.

I slide out, then ram in a little harder. She jolts forward with the force, my fingers still buried inside her.

Kissing her shoulder blade, I enjoy the sheen of sweat all over her body. I love making her hot for me.

I pull out and do it again until I'm fully seated and she's gasping.

"Fuck," I mutter. "You've no idea how hot you look right now."

"Rock!" she breathes, her moan drowned out as I pull out.

"Tell me," I demand. "Tell me how good it is."

"So good!"

I pick up my pace, fully fuckin' her ass as I massage her G-spot. She moves, gripping the headboard, lifting slightly as

Rock

I remove my fingers and grab her ass cheeks and ride it home.

"Gonna come," I grunt. I can't hold on, this feels so good. "Finger yourself. Let me feel you, Aspyn."

She moves one hand to her pussy as I ride her ass. "Oh God!"

She throws her head back and screams my name for the entire apartment block to hear, and I love every fuckin' second of it, spurting hot waves of cum in her ass as I pull out and spray her rear end and pussy.

"*Fuck!*" I yell.

She trembles as I still, holding my cock in my hand as I rub my cum and massage her poor little ass gently.

"I... I..." She's lost for words as she pants and collapses onto the bed.

I grin, moving off the bed to grab a towel. We've made quite a mess.

I wipe my dick and then between her ass cheeks, pussy, and thighs. Reveling in the sight of seeing my release all over her.

She's still panting when I return.

I stroke her ass cheek gently as I lie on my side and face her. "You good, babe?"

She shifts her head, looking at me sleepily as she nods. "Oh. So. Good."

I smile, leaning down to kiss her softly. "You took my cock so well."

"I love it," she says, yawning as her eyes close.

My baby needs her rest.

I pull the comforter over her, and she groans in appreciation. I don't want to go back to my room so I slide in behind her, pressing my body against her side as I listen to the sound of her soft breathing. She's already asleep.

I kiss her shoulder, pushing the hair back off her face as I study it.

She couldn't be more perfect.

This woman is mine.

I don't give a fuck about goddamn rules. She's mine.

Mine to protect.

Mine to hold.

Mine to fuck.

Mine to love.

I snort. *Love?* What in the ever-living fuck is going on?

My brother warned me. I'd know when I'd found 'the one' because it'd feel different.

My heartbeat would change. My thoughts would cloud me. My mind would play tricks on me. And he's right, on all accounts. I can't think straight when she's around, and I sure as fuck can't think straight when she's not around. I'm like a rollercoaster, out of control.

I run a hand down her body and cup her ass.

Mine.

I'm gonna get to the bottom of all of this, I swear to myself. *Nobody is gonna come near her.*

Not now. Not ever.

Or I'll fuckin' kill them.

19

ASPYN

THE MINUTE I WAKE, I KNOW HE'S GONE.

I look to the left of me and see the rumpled pillow. When I run my hand under the sheet, his side of the bed is cold.

He spooned me last night.

We cuddled.

I woke up a couple of times in the night, and he was by my side, his arms around me protectively. It spoke to me in so many ways and made me feel more protected…and fuck…more *loved* than I ever have before. Not that I think he loves me, that would be stupid. I know this is just sex…really great sex…that it doesn't equate to love, but Rock has been so sweet and nurturing.

All that crock of horse shit he told me about not being a good guy and how bad he was…it's all lies. I know his heart. I've seen how caring he is.

Oh, my. I wince. I am a little sore, but nothing crazy. When I get up and pee, I can't help but feel a little smug that he did what he did and it felt good. I mean, I've always kinda looked at anal sex as something uncomfortable and just…eww…but when I came, it's never been like that. Rock is a master at sex.

He knows so much more than I do and I'm here for it. I want every damn inch of him all over again.

I go in search of my robe and my poor cat who I neglected last night.

I can smell coffee brewing, and I smile to myself.

When I round the corner, I stop and slap a hand over my mouth.

Dad?

Oh. My. God.

Clearly not who I was expecting.

"Dad?" I say, echoing my thoughts. "What are you doing here?"

He turns, smiling as he takes me in. "Princess?" he says, genuinely happy to see me.

We haven't texted much or talked at all, but that's normal for us. He only checks in every now and again. "What did you do to your hair?"

Oh, fuck. I can only imagine how I look right now.

"Uh, I colored it."

He pulls me into a hug. "It looks great, so much better than blonde."

"Thanks, Dad."

He keeps his arm around me and says, "Coffee?"

"Yes, please."

"You never said anything…" I start.

He leaves my side for a moment to make my coffee. Something of a rarity as I've never seen my father do any such thing. Ever.

"I texted last night," he says with a shrug, "to say I was flying in early. You were sound asleep this morning, so I didn't want to wake you."

I was too busy fucking, Daddy Dearest.

Where the fuck is Rock?

I frown. Something must be wrong. "Is everything okay?"

He hands me my coffee. "Everything's fine. But I have some things to ask you."

I've no idea if his sudden switch to serious mode is because he knows something about me and Rock, or if it's to do with me leaving.

My gut tightens.

I don't want to leave.

Not yet.

Not while me and Rock are just getting acquainted...

"That sounds kinda ominous," I say, sitting at the island as Pirate, the traitor, rubs himself back and forth on my dad's legs.

"You need to talk to me about Beth."

I frown. "Beth?"

"Yes. Your publicist," he reminds me.

"I know who she is," I say. "Why did you fly all this way to talk about her?"

"I didn't. I flew all this way to check on my daughter and the apartment and to make sure that you're happy and safe."

Still, he could've called to ask me that. Something about my dad's surprise visit smells fishy.

"I am," I say. "Rock is doing a very good job." I don't know how I manage to keep a straight face.

In fact, Daddy. He fucked me hard last night, in the ass while I screamed his name for everyone to hear...and he spat cum in my mouth...

He eyes me. "You seem...*different.*"

Uh, oh. Dad is really fucking good at smelling a rat. He didn't get this far in life from being a pushover. And his nose is always on the ground. Hiding this from him isn't something that I thought I had to do thousands of miles away.

"It's the hair, and I got a tan."

He smiles.

Phew. Dad wouldn't be smiling if I'd done something wrong, would he?

I wait for whatever he's flown here to say. "Honey, I'm making sure Beth hasn't tried to contact you."

I frown. "No. I mean, she hasn't got my new number, and I don't have email access. You took it away, remember?"

He frowns. Oh. This is bad.

"Dad?" I prompt. "What's going on with Beth?"

He looks back up at me. "Rock found something."

Rock?

What in the actual fuck? Has Rock been in contact with my dad this entire time?

My heart skips a beat. "What did he find?"

"He traced one of the emails back to a server shared in Burbank, near where Beth's office is."

Rock hasn't mentioned this. He hasn't said a goddamn word about it.

"And you think Beth has something to do with the threats?"

"We don't know exactly, but it seems like it could be someone in her office."

"It isn't her," I tell him pointedly. "Beth wouldn't want to hurt me."

He gives me a look that tells me that I'm naive. It's a look that I've grown accustomed to over the years. "People do very strange things for money, Aspyn. Just remember that. Unfortunately, no matter how much you pay people, greed can often get in the way."

I shake my head. Beth is the sweetest, she would never… and what would she have to gain from threatening me? It's not adding up.

"Dad, you're scaring me."

"Which is why you're here, angel," he says. "Far away from all of that. I just wanted to make sure that there isn't anything you're not telling me."

It seems I can't get away from the persistent men in my

life. And after I heard Rock whispering to me last night, I can't get the words out of my head.

I will protect you, Trouble. Nobody is ever gonna hurt you...

The man isn't supposed to say those things to me.

He's supposed to be someone to have fun with, nothing serious, not someone who I could easily be falling for. Instead, he's already worked his way into my heart and now he's got my head all messed up.

What he tells me about himself is a stark contrast to the man I'm getting to know.

He lied. He *is* good.

He may be broken in parts, but who isn't? I know he isn't the terrible person he makes himself out to be. Maybe he's done terrible things in the past, and he's been to jail, but none of that matters.

"There isn't anything," I say.

I'm the model child, Daddy. Just like you taught me to be.

I always follow the rules, never deviating.

I remember Rock's words about me being a free woman and not living under my father's spell. It may have hurt at the time, but I realize there's a lot of truth in it.

I have been. For so long.

Daddy cares about me, I understand that. But this isn't living.

It isn't just since this stalking nonsense. I've been living like this for so long now that it's become normal to me. After being in New Orleans for less than a week, I can see just how *not* normal things really are. And it has to stop.

I don't want to anger my father, but I'm a grown woman. I haven't been living my own life since...well, since forever. I've been living in the shadows, taking precautions because my father is an important man in LA and has enemies.

All because he doesn't want anything to happen, or for me to leave, just like my mom. He barely ever talks about her.

The pain has always been too much for him to bear. I think it's safe to say that's why he dotes on me so much.

He nods. "I'm glad the apartment is to your liking, even though I'm not fond of Rock being here with you."

I swallow hard, trying to keep my face neutral. "It's fine, Dad," I say. "He seems like a good guy. Cash has his rules, and I understand they have to be followed. It makes life easier for everyone this way, if I do as he says..." I almost bite on my tongue from the lies that spill out of my mouth.

I want to scream to the world that I want to be free.

"You've changed your tune all of a sudden. You were fighting me tooth and nail to stay in LA five days ago."

"Like you said, change is as good as a holiday."

He scoffs. "Would you feel better if one of the women stayed here with you?"

I shake my head. "It's fine, honestly. Rock is quiet..." *Except when he's fucking me.*

"He keeps to himself, mainly..." *When he hasn't got his hands all over me and in my panties.* "In a way, we're perfectly suited. He goes his way and I go mine." *In and out of each other until we're both panting and I'm screaming his name.*

His lips twitch. "Good. I'm glad he's not making you uncomfortable."

I roll my lips. The only thing uncomfortable is how hard he pounded my asshole last night. "It's fine, Dad. I know once this blows over, things will go back to normal, and I can come home." *Lies!*

Returning to my old life seems so outdated and out of place right now. I have no desire to go back to that big, lonely mansion and live whatever pathetic existence that was. I just need time to gather my strength to tell him that, when I get home, I need to move out and learn how to live by myself. He won't hear of it now, and I don't want to anger him since he's flown all this way, but this madness has to end.

"Also, Tara was cleared."

I stare at him, my cup halfway to my mouth.

"What?"

"Yesterday. The police interviewed her and cleared her of any wrongdoing in this mess."

My eyes go wide. "They interviewed *Tara*? What the hell for?"

His eyes meet mine. "Don't get so upset. Everyone has to be questioned. *Everyone.*

Down to our staff. Don't forget the statistics of this kind of menacing act is usually from someone you know."

That does not fill me with confidence.

"Dad, that's ridiculous." And Tara is gonna be pissed. She'll take it personally. I'd be surprised if she hasn't blown up my phone. I feel guilty that I haven't checked it since Rock got in last night, or this morning. And we usually text each other every night and first thing in the morning. If Tara doesn't hear from me in a few hours, she'll send out a search party, God bless her.

"No, it isn't. We're following procedure and taking all precautions," he says, just as I hear the elevator doors.

Oh, is that Rock? Where the hell is he? Did my father send him away?

A few moments later, I turn as he comes through the door, holding two stuffed bags of what smells like amazing goodness.

"Ah," Dad says. "Rock."

His eyes meet mine, and I look away.

I can't face this man. Not after what we did. Not after... *everything.*

"I'm gonna go wash up for a second," Dad says.

"There's a powder room to the right, down the hallway," I tell him as he nods.

Rock sets the bags down on the counter as my dad walks off in the other direction.

As soon as he's gone, Rock asks, "Didn't check your phone, did you?"

I shake my head.

He surprises me when he leans over and quickly pecks me on the lips.

Holy shit.

His eyes glance down at my robe, heating instantly. When they meet mine again, he rounds the counter and pulls me to him. His tongue in my mouth and his hand reaching under my robe to cup my bare pussy. Nope. I didn't have the chance, or the willpower, to even put underwear on.

"Rock," I hiss, slapping his hand. "Stop it."

He groans softly as he fingers me gently. "Haven't been able to get you off my mind, babe," he mutters. "After your dad leaves, I'm gonna fuck you on this countertop."

My eyes go wide as he releases me with one lasting look, and I gape at him while he shifts back behind the bench top.

Who is this man?

I mean, I'm relieved he isn't ignoring me or chalking our experience up to another notch on his belt and then scramming, but I didn't expect *that*.

He just tongue-kissed me and fingered me with my father in the next room.

He whistles as he pulls the containers out of the paper bags, his eyes meeting mine as he gives me a wink.

"Thanks to you I'm dripping again," I hiss.

He grins. "Fuck. Don't say that, or I'll come back around there and…"

"Honey?" Dad calls. "Don't go eatin' my sausage muffin."

I poke my tongue out at Rock before Dad comes into sight.

"Dad, you shouldn't be eating that," I scold when he appears again. "It's not good for your cholesterol."

Rock moves out of the way and distances himself even farther from me.

Rock

"When I'm out of LA, my trainer doesn't know a thing," he assures me.

I roll my eyes.

I wonder what my dad would say if he really knew. It's probably good that Rock put that enclosure up for Pirate, or dad might be inclined to throw him over the top.

As if reading my mind, Dad says, "Nice of Rock to build that for Pirate. I didn't think of that with such short notice."

I smile, glancing at Rock, who's pulling out the food he got for himself, but then he leans over and hands me a Styrofoam container.

"It was nice of him," I say, as Rock's eyes meet mine.

He looks away as I tip the lid up and see pancakes underneath. My favorite.

"Let's eat at the table, sweetie." I know that invitation doesn't extend to Rock.

He takes his food out onto the patio, closing the door behind him as my traitorous cat follows behind.

"Looks like Pirate has a new friend," Dad remarks.

"It's because he has bacon." I roll my eyes.

Dad moves to the table, and I follow him. He's eager to catch up, though in his eyes, I've been holed up in this room by myself. In reality, I've been all over the city.

I plan on keeping that to myself.

"Are you sure you're okay with him being here?"

I shrug. "Sometimes some of the girls come over, they're really nice." I only say that so he won't worry and Rock gets reassigned.

"I hope it won't be for much longer," Dad goes on. "Then you can come back home."

"Yeah, Dad, about that." I didn't plan on saying anything, but now seems like the perfect time to broach the subject about me breaking away. I'm a grown-ass woman.

He glances up at me as I poke my pancakes with my fork. I don't even bother getting a plate.

"What about it?"

"Dad. I've been living like this for so long now," I start.

His frown deepens.

"It's made me realize that I really don't have a life back home. I didn't even know how to work the washing machine!"

"Honey. We have people for that."

I shake my head. Leaning over, I hold his hand. "You've spoiled me, Dad. And I know I'm your only child and all, but I haven't seen anything of the outside world. I've never done anything for myself."

"That isn't true. You have your charity work…"

"That you organize! I haven't even been out of the country by myself."

"Well, it's a scary world out there. This whole stalking debacle should remind you of that." He's getting annoyed.

"No, Dad. Once this blows over, there won't be any threats. There's no reason for me to be living in solitude."

He laughs without humor. "I'm a rich, powerful man, Aspyn. People want to hurt you to get to me. I can't have that…"

"That's *you*, though. It isn't *me*. I didn't choose this. *You* chose it for me after Mom left. You wrapped me in cotton wool…"

He yanks his hand back. "I've been keeping you safe, Aspyn. That's my job!"

"Yes, until I'm an adult…"

"A father's job never ends. Not even after you're an adult."

I try to rein in my temper. I know he only wants what's best for me, but he has kept me under lock and key for far too long. Thinking I'll do what my mom did and leave him all alone. But that has to stop. He isn't my keeper.

"I know that," I say, gently. "But Dad, you have to understand that I have to make my own way in life. I've never had a real job, not one that you didn't organize for me. I've never gotten my hands dirty or done anything that wasn't orchestrated by your staff. I haven't really lived."

He stares at me. "It's a harsh world out there," he says, his voice gruff. "You don't know how cruel people can be. This latest stunt on that stupid show..."

"Dad, all of that was going on *before* the show. It only amplified when I went on there. I should have told you what I was doing, and for that, I'm sorry. It backfired. Going on there was a mistake, but then again, maybe I wouldn't have realized what an asshole Dylan was either."

"He'll never work in LA ever again," Dad mumbles.

"I appreciate everything you've done for me. I know a lot of kids don't grow up like I have," I say. "I am truly grateful for the blessings you've given me, but a part of me thinks you're afraid to let me go because of Mom."

His lips part, and I expect him to stand and storm out of here. He's not usually the kind of man who talks about his feelings.

"Aspyn," he whispers. He runs a hand through his hair. "I knew this day would come."

"What day?"

"The day you'd want to know what really happened."

My eyes go wide. "I do..." I've tried asking before, but he shut me down so many times that I stopped. "But you said..."

"You weren't ready to hear the truth." He sighs. "I never wanted to hurt you more than you already were when she left."

I wait, unsure if I really want to hear this, but I know I need to.

"Go on," I urge.

"Your mother wasn't well," he says after a beat. "I never kept you from her until she...she threatened to hurt you."

My mouth gapes. "That can't be..."

"As I say, she wasn't well. I knew she wouldn't go through with it, but I couldn't take the chance. There was no way I could risk her being around you. She wrote me a letter... I had my lawyers take care of it, and I made sure she sought treatment."

"Postpartum depression?"

He sighs. "She had problems before that, but maybe that played a part." His eyes are glassy when he turns to face me. "I'd never put you in harm's way. Even with her. She never wanted a relationship. She wanted money, even after she was better..."

I had no idea it was that serious.

"So she took the settlement and never came back?" I stammer.

He shrugs. "I honestly don't know. I promised she could see you once she got better, under supervision, but after she got out of rehab, I never saw her again. Over the years, I've looked into her whereabouts. She moved to England."

My heart falters. "She really did leave us."

He nods. "I don't think she ever had any intention of hurting you, for the record. She just used that to get what she wanted. And it worked. I wanted her gone, at any cost."

"Dad, I'm so sorry." I leap up and fold into his arms, knocking him off guard.

"It's...it's fine, it's dealt with," he mutters, embarrassed.

"All this time, I just thought maybe you actually kept her away, out of spite."

He pulls back to look up at me. "You really think I'd do that?"

I shake my head. "No."

"I admit that I've kept you under lock and key because I was worried. Maybe I've been a foolish old man, but I'd rather be safe than sorry. You're all I have." I see the resolution in his eyes and my anger falters. I can't be mad at him. He was protecting me.

"I love you, Dad," I say, knowing that he'll probably balk.

He surprises me. "All I've ever done is because I love you more than life, Aspyn Ashley Huntley. Even if I have been overprotective."

Just a little, but I don't argue the point.

"Then you'll agree to let me live my life when I come back?" I step back, looking down at him pointedly.

He frowns. "Baby steps."

I sit back in my seat. I've never had a real conversation about this. I can't believe it's taken this long for him to finally open up.

"Thanks, Dad," I say. "For loving me so much."

He smiles, it's small, but it's there. "I'll always love you, Aspyn. No matter what. Everything I've ever done is because there is nobody more important in my life. You're my only child."

I try not to stare at him in shock. He's never been this open with me.

"Thank you for your honesty," I say. "But it's really time you found yourself a woman."

He balks. "Let's not get crazy." He smiles wistfully, then adds, "Maybe I've been waiting for you to tell me that it's time. My baby is ready to fly. As a father, I realize I can't be there every time you fall."

I smile softly. "But you have to let me try to spread my wings."

He nods. "I'll try. But I'm an old dog, just remember that."

We have a lot of work to do, but at least this first hurdle has been overcome. Even talking to him like this is a miracle.

"We can navigate it together," I say, the tightness in my chest subsiding. "I promise, it isn't as scary as it sounds."

He reaches for my hand, bringing it to his lips to kiss my knuckles. "Baby steps, deal?"

I grin. "Deal."

20

ROCK

ASPYN'S FATHER STAYS THE NIGHT, MEANING MY GIRL AND I don't get to do anything bad while he's under the same roof. The following day, I'm summoned to the takedown that's taking place tonight.

I'm pissed I didn't get to spend the night wrapped around Aspyn, but we agreed it was too risky. All we've shared are stolen glances and the one and only kiss I took from her while her father was in the next room.

He's none the wiser, of course, and I'm not sure that he likes me all that much.

He trusts Cash, not me. And I'm surprised he didn't take one look at me and demand someone else watch Aspyn. I know I would if she were my daughter.

If I ever have a daughter one day, I'd be exactly the same. Protect her with my life.

I don't, however, like him keeping me from seeing her. I haven't had my fill of her yet, and maybe I never will.

I'm still working on getting more intel on the satellite where the signal came from when those emails were sent from too close to Beth's office. IP addresses aren't easy to crack, even for someone in cyber security like myself.

It makes me scratch my head, thinking about what I know so far about Beth.

From what Aspyn has told me, she doesn't seem like the kind of woman who would stalk somebody. Not that they ever do. But she's successful already. People in the industry respect her and her enemies are few. Could she really be this obsessed with Aspyn? It's more likely, it's someone from her office, or someone who's been watching closely. I make a note to check out internet cafe's close to the Burbank office.

Still. The police haven't cleared Beth yet, not that they'd know jack shit about surveillance or how to find real information, but she did get brought in for questioning.

I know a lot more about Beth St. Michael and her agency than I did yesterday. I've got a list of all current employees, but will the police go and question any of them? Oh, no. They wait until something worse happens before they intervene. A stalking case like this doesn't rouse their investigative skills or their will to catch a criminal, as they've got better things to be doing. Especially since Tommy fired all of his security team.

"You think Forger's gonna go down tonight?" Priest asks me.

While the spiritual advisor for the club doesn't always come out when we have business to deal with, it's all hands on deck while we storm the underground compound Tag's been watching recently.

"I fuckin' hope so."

I feel his gaze on me. "How is the li'l lady?"

Flicking my eyes to his, I see the smirk on his lips and the look in his eye. "Why don't you ask her yourself?" I'm still pissed, even though technically he did nothing wrong. I'm more mad at myself about having a panic attack.

He gives me a chin lift. "Do you have panic attacks often?"

I shrug. "Not in a while."

He turns back to looking out the windshield of the van we have parked down the street. "She's a handful." His words hang in the air. "Got a lot of obstacles in your way with that one."

I roll my eyes, even though he doesn't see me do it. "Don't know what you're talkin' about, brother."

"Right. That's why her eyes light up every time you walk in a room."

"Happens a lot," I say, feigning indifference. "She's only human."

He snorts. "You tappin' it?"

I take a long breath. Normally, I'm not so coy about my conquests but, frankly, it's none of his business. Plus, he's close to Cash, and though he's a brother and all, he'll be less inclined to keep this to himself.

I turn to him. "Am I in confession?"

He smirks. "Do you wanna be?"

"I'm not sure you have enough holy water to rid me of the things I've done, oh holy father."

He shakes his head. "You know, I've heard that a lot."

"Not surprised."

"Aspyn is a smart girl," he goes on. "Does as she's told. Gotta love me a submissive woman." I know he's stirring the pot, but I still don't like hearing her name come out of his mouth.

I clench my jaw. "I wouldn't know."

"Rock. Give it up. I'm not here to judge, I'm here to help."

I snort. "What do I need help with, exactly?"

"Not fuckin' it up."

"She's been here a week. I think we're good."

He shakes his head. "She's worried, you know, about the stalker."

I frown. She's never told me anything like that. Nothing.

I don't like the idea that she's confided in him and not me, even though Priest has been known to get blood from a stone.

"I'm sure she is, but she's safe here."

"Did she tell you this has happened before?"

I frown. No, she didn't. "Cash mentioned it wasn't the first time…"

"Aspyn has had some kind of threat toward her ever since middle school. We can blame her financier father for that one. She's the ultimate daddy's little girl, make no mistake, but I think there's good in her. She hasn't been corrupted by the world *yet*. She still sees the world and people in it with rose-colored glasses on."

Yeah, but she's been corrupted by me…

"Is there a point to all of this? My ears are bleedin'."

"She doesn't see things right in front of her, the bad anyway. Her friends. Her manager. Even her family. Aspyn sees no bad in anyone."

I listen to his words, realizing they're true.

When I tried to tell her I was bad and no good for her, she didn't believe it. She didn't listen. She pursued me.

"I get that," I say, not wanting to sound too defensive. "But she's a grown woman, she knows right from wrong."

"That may be so, but a woman like Aspyn has never lived. She's never been around an MC, hell, she's never been around *people*. The girl is cryin' out for a big, strong man to take her father's place, to make sure she doesn't fall."

I don't like him summing her up like that.

"Are you worried about my virtue, brother?" I pat him on the shoulder. "It's okay. It was gone a long time ago."

"Nope, and I'm not worried about hers. But once the smoke has cleared, there will be choices."

"Cryptic."

"Rock, I think she's in love with you."

I stare at him, confused. "What the fuck? I've known her for a week."

He shrugs. "Doesn't matter. When you blanked out...she was like a mother hen. The way she touched you." He shakes his head. "She cares for you, and I don't want you to blow it by actin' like a fool or treatin' her like she's just another sweet butt. Then you'll lose her for good."

I point at him. "I would never treat her like that!" I growl. "And like I said, it's been a week. Nothin's..." I give up, turning and looking out the window.

"Have you ever felt this way before?" he asks quietly.

I swallow hard. Several seconds pass by before I answer. "No," I admit. "But it's just lust. That's all it is, because I want her so much. She's fresh meat, right? Isn't that how the story is supposed to go? She doesn't mean anythin'..." The lies feel like poison on my tongue. But I can't divulge to Priest how I feel. Fuck that. The only one who gets my words is Aspyn.

"I think you're full of shit," he says, his voice low and dark. "And that you think you don't deserve it. A lot like your brother felt, before Summer came along."

I snort. "He was in love with a woman for over two years before he did anythin' about it."

"My point exactly."

I scratch my head. Oh. "It's not like that with us. We're just havin' fun. Foolin' around. For fuck's sake, don't tell Cash. I'm not plannin' on hurtin' her. We both know what we're doin' here." *Do we?*

"If that's the case, about you just havin' fun, why did you have a panic attack when you saw me in the apartment and glared at me like I was the devil himself. If looks could kill..." He chuckles.

I turn to him. "You wanna know?" My tone is dark.

He nods. "I wanna know."

I lean closer. "Because she's *mine*."

His lips twitch. "Does *she* know that?"

"I doubt it. She's young. She feels something, I think, but

maybe I just have a big dick and that's all this is." I don't like admitting it, but I have to be level-headed about this.

I don't know if she's *that* into me past getting off. "Maybe when she goes home, I'll never see her again." Pain twists in my gut at the thought.

"You know that for sure?"

I laugh. "She's daddy's little girl, like you said. She doesn't know what she wants, and this is just the kind of thing that would piss him off."

"I don't think her rebellion is based on gettin' her dad's attention when it comes to you."

"You don't?"

He looks wistful. "Just sayin'. Don't let a good thing go because you're too scared to admit your feelin's. Leave the past in the past. I know shit's been hard, but you deserve to be happy, just like any other brother."

It's no secret in the club about me and Jett. What happened to us. But I don't want Aspyn knowing about any of that. She'd look at me differently. Like I'm something she can fix, and I can't be fixed.

"Do you think it's wrong? For someone like me to taint someone like her?" I ask with all sincerity. Like I have the willpower to withstand her advances.

He shakes his head. "You deserve a good woman, Rock. You're a good person. I know you don't think so. When I see you, I often see that dark cloud travelin' right along with you. I've seen many bad men come and go over the years, and you're not one of them. The past doesn't have to rule your life anymore."

"I don't know how." I don't even wanna talk about this, but the man seems to be good at trapping me into admitting things. He's right in the fact that I don't wanna lose Aspyn. "I buried everythin' good in me a long time ago. I don't even remember what it's like to feel happy. Until…"

"Until?"

Fuck.

Until Aspyn.

Now who's the fuckin' goddamn sap?

"Rock?" he prompts.

I run my hand over my face. "I don't know what to tell you. Only, I don't want anyone else to have her, yet I know I'm no good for her. She's so far above me that it makes my head spin. Yeah, when I saw you with her in the apartment, I was jealous. I don't know what the fuck any of it means. I wanted to throw shit like a toddler havin' a tantrum."

"It means you have feelin's and that's alright. A lot of the time, men who have been abused as children have a tendency to seek out women who give them comfort, and not in a sexual way, but in a way that consoles them. It speaks to them on another level."

I frown. *Is that a thing?*

I think about how caring she's been. Bathing me after I had my attack and letting me do what I want to her. Sure, she enjoyed it, but I know I've corrupted her just a little.

I also don't know if I should listen to him, tell him he's full of shit, or punch him in the face.

He's headed for one of them, I just don't know which yet…

"A lot of the time, abused children just wanna forget," I mutter.

"That may be so, but also you can't let it sabotage a chance at bein' happy."

I let his words ring around in my head. I didn't know that's what I was doing.

"You always like this? Gettin' under a brother's skin?"

He chuckles. "I've been known to do that. Comes with experience."

I give him a chin lift. "What about you?" Changing the subject might get me off the hook. "You're a man of God. Rumor has it you're abstainin', accordin' to the sweet butts."

He chuckles again. "Ah, the sweet butts. They certainly like to use their mouths more purposely in this club than in some others."

Yeah, they do talk a lot.

"So is that a yes?"

He gives me a look. "Abstainin', at least for a time, can be good to clear the mind."

I shake my head. "Sounds like a whole lot of dick pullin' to me."

"That's because you're a physical being, I get that. But the mind connection is a powerful thing. Like with Aspyn, she's not just ticklin' your nuts because she's hot or has pretty eyes. You're connectin' with her on another level, which is why you said you've never felt like this before. Sex is sex. Anyone can have it. Anyone can do it, but not everyone can connect on that level that makes you want to climb the highest mountain, or give up other women."

Do I wanna give up other women? I know right away the answer to that is yes.

"I don't deserve her," I mutter. "I know that already."

"That's where you're wrong. Despite your flaws, I see good in you, Rock. This whole club does, or else you wouldn't be here."

I give him a small smile of gratitude. "Thanks for the vote of confidence."

"You're welcome. And give yourself some credit where it's due. You can at least admit that you have feelin's for her, if not to me, to yourself."

"If it's that obvious, Cash is gonna start noticin'."

"I just observe well, and I can only tell you from experience, if you don't stop and smell the roses, you will burn out and then you'll lose everything."

I shift in my seat.

I get the feeling he's not just talking from experience; it's coming from a place of pain. I really haven't spent that much time talking to the man, so I don't know much about his background.

"I'll remember to have my panic attacks in private from now on," I mutter.

"No need." He slaps me on the back. "Can always come to confession on Sundays. I'm helpin' out a friend for a few weeks while he's away."

My eyes go wide. "For real?"

"Don't look so shocked. I'm technically Catholic, but I don't preach the Catholic faith. I'm more on a spiritual path. The club has helped with that, but I also help out the church from time to time. Mainly, when they're in a jam."

"I didn't think you were really a priest."

He smiles. "I'm not. I started to do my training, but then I went to prison. It's a long story, bein' in the wrong place at the wrong time. I've tried to stay out of trouble since then. I have to try to live up to some of the promises I made."

"When were you inside?"

He looks wistful. "A long time ago. Can't say I've been a complete saint. But since comin' to the club, I've changed my ways a lot. I've reconfirmed my vows to God."

"Does that mean no pussy?"

He laughs. "No, not forever. It's not as difficult as you would assume."

"Then why do it?" I can't imagine life without sex.

"Like I said. From time to time, it's healthy, and if it reconnects you, then you'll be a better man for it."

Priest is a man who you'd never think has a care in the world. He's the calmest brother out of everyone. I guess that's his job, but still.

"I guess I'll take your word for it."

He snorts. "I guess you'll have to."

I don't know if I should thank him or get down on my knees and pray, but all of a sudden, goddamn Nevada knocks on the window and scares the living shit out of us.

"Open up," he says as I unlock the doors. He climbs in the back.

"It's goin' down," Nevada says, excitement in his tone. "Harlem confirmed the fight tonight, and it's one that Forger has a big wager on. He's been incognito for weeks, but in order to make the next cocaine drop with the miscreants he's dealin' to, he has to show up. Big Papa is all set."

What Forger doesn't know is we have one of the biggest dealers in the city, a man called John "Big Papa" Hastings. A man who runs every underground fighting and boxing match in this city and turned tricks once he realized what was going on with Forger. The man may be many things, but a traitor isn't one of them. He just doesn't like guys who fuck with the system. The system works, and when things get disrupted, it means he loses money. Forger has been wheedling his way in, and something has to give.

He was never on Cash's payroll as an informer, nor was he ever on the right side of the MC, but the man is loyal to a fault, and he doesn't want Forger taking back the French Quarter. It's bad for business. He's in with the Irish and wants to keep it that way. Once the Irish get wind about Caruso and the Italians, it'll be a war amongst them that none of us want to be in the middle of. If we can pull this off, we may just be able to walk away. What happens after that isn't our business.

It's risky. Tag and Harlem want to be here, but they're well known to Forger and the Devils so they've gotta lay low.

I groan. "Well, he better show up. His men have been doin' all the dirty work for weeks. None of them know shit. Caruso motherfuckers."

"That's gonna be a problem," Priest agrees. "But he can't hide forever."

The last thing we want is trouble with the Italian mafia but, hopefully, it won't come to that. It's everyone's wish we can stay flying under the radar and take down the Devils for good.

It'll put an end to this war between the MCs and confirm that the club can rest easy for the first time in over a year.

"This is so fucked," Nevada agrees. "Should be out shootin' pool and gettin' my dick sucked, but instead I'm sittin' out here in the goddamn cold."

"Hold your horses, it'll be over soon," Priest says.

"How can you be so sure?" I frown. "You got connections?"

He smiles. "I feel it in my bones. Change is comin'. Forger will have to pay for the sins he's committed. In the end, we all have to answer to a higher purpose."

"Sounds fucked," Nevada says, wincing.

I shake my head.

Priest's phone buzzes. He pulls it out and reads the message. "Showtime."

When this is over, I can see my girl.

Maybe there's something in what Priest said, but all I can do is take things one day at a time. I know how I feel, and that I've never felt this way before. But that doesn't mean Aspyn feels the same.

Setting myself up for a fall would be stupid, but who am I to argue with reason?

"Holy fuck," Jett hisses. "That was fuckin' close."

We're watching the fight.

All of us are dressed in normal clothes without cuts.

There's nothing like an MC patch to get you flagged at the door.

And if Forger is here tonight, there ain't no way he's getting away.

Me, Jett, and Priest are the three most incognito as we've

never seen Forger before. The others are hidden around the underground platform. It's an old, abandoned station that the underworld criminals have been using to conduct illegal fights and push drugs relatively unnoticed.

"You know the plan," Priest says to me.

Yes. We do. We just got a briefing from the big guys half an hour ago.

We took care of the motherfuckers who were here to collect tonight, and now we're posing as them. Tonight has taken Tag and Harlem weeks to put together, and if all goes to plan, there shouldn't be anything stopping us from getting closer to our goal of eliminating Forger.

We also have help.

Not just Brew and Haze, along with Bronco, JJ, Riot, Hawk, Nevada and the prospects, Pipes, and Rodeo. Cash and Ryder wait in the wings close by. If the meeting abruptly gets moved— which can happen at any moment if Forger gets antsy—then they'll be waiting. Our Prez isn't scared of a fight, but he's easily recognizable.

There's nothing I love more than the adrenaline that flows through me when we're about to do a bust. Not that it happens very often, but these last few days have been eventful.

When Big Papa gives us a chin lift, we follow him past the fighting and into a back room.

Nobody knows Big Papa met with Forger a few weeks ago, before he found out about what he did to Camille. One thing Big Papa doesn't like is men who mess with kids.

He might be the biggest drug runner in this city, a man we never deal with, but if it means ending Forger's short-lived reign, then he's all in. We promised him he'd get to liaise with the Irish himself, and they'd agree to let him keep his side of the city if he stayed out of the French Quarter.

"Motherfucker doesn't usually meet here," Big Papa says. "But he's runnin' out of places to hide. As far as he knows, everyone thinks he left town. I told him I'd spread the word." He shakes his head. "Also told him the heat was off since you took issue with the Irish and bad blood was brewin'. I only hope he bought it. If not, I'm gonna have to rethink my Christmas card list."

We smirk. Priest in front, with Big Papa leading the way.

Two large men stand by the door. Both look like fighters, and if I didn't wanna slit this guy's throat so badly, I might even be impressed by the security here tonight. He's cautious, but I hope he's cocky enough to think he's in the clear.

I know he needs this pay dirt, which is why he's here.

The guards let us through, and Big Papa spreads his arms wide as he says, "Forger! My man, it's been too long…"

21

ASPYN

A FEW HOURS EARLIER

"Oh my god!" I clasp my hands over my mouth as Tara appears around the door.

She smiles tentatively as I stand there in shock.

"What are you doing here?"

She drops her bag by the door and says, "Your dad said I could come and keep you company. Oh my god, what have you done to your hair?"

My hands quickly fly to my locks, remembering I'm about ten shades darker than when I saw her last. "It's a new look, do you like it?"

She gives me a nod. "It makes your eyes look prettier. I like the tan."

I smile.

My dad left this morning and I've had Manny and Deanna here all morning, making a list for the party tonight. It's fun hanging out with them. They look up from the dining table as I fold into Tara's arms.

"I can't believe you're here!" I declare, giving her another hug. It feels like it's been so long.

"Well, someone had to come and make sure you're really okay," she says, glancing around the apartment. "Nice place."

"Dad." I shrug.

"How have you been?" She looks at me with concern.

I nod. "Good. Never better." She frowns, and that makes me frown too, before quickly adding, "It killed me not being able to tell you where I was."

She's still pissed about that, and rightly so. But at the end of the day, my safety is what matters. She knows that. Even if she was questioned by the police.

"I know," she sniffs. "I was so worried. Thank God your dad called. He said it was safe enough to let me come see you and that you were probably pretty lonely out here with nobody to talk to." She glances over at my friends at the table, a little accusingly. "He said you seemed a little…*different.*"

Oh, did he now?

Dad took my little heart-to-heart as me being *different*. I know it's baby steps with me and him having that heavy talk, but I thought our conversation was a good one.

"No. I'm just adjusting to life in New Orleans," I say honestly. "So much has happened. We've so much to catch up on."

She smiles. "We do and now I can keep a closer eye on you. I know you say you're okay, but I know you, Aspyn."

I nod. "I've had Rock."

Her lips part as she whispers. "*Rock?* Are you serious about him?"

I shrug, giving her a sly grin. "Maybe."

She shakes her head. "I seriously can't let you out of my sight for more than a week. You're already planning the wedding, aren't you?"

I laugh. "Don't be silly."

"I'm glad to see you're in good spirits, that's all that matters." She pats my shoulders like my Dad does.

Sometimes I forget just how different we really are.

"Oh," I say, waving my hand toward the dining table as we get closer. "This is Manny and Deanna."

Tara smiles politely but doesn't move to greet them. She's like this a lot and not overly friendly with people she doesn't know. Some people think it's rude, but she's just shy around strangers and a complete introvert.

Of course, Manny stands to open his arms. "I'm a hugger," he declares.

Tara makes a little surprised noise when Manny squeezes her into a hug. Deanna just waves politely and says hello.

I roll my lips and try not to laugh at Tara's startled expression.

"Don't you just look like heaven that fell out of the sky," Manny comments, standing back to admire her. "I'll have to go to LA someday."

Tara tucks her hair back behind her ears, a faint blush rising on her cheeks. She's not used to public displays of affection, and aside from me, she doesn't have too many other friends. I'm used to her quirky behavior, but some people think she's plain weird.

"It's...uh, really something," she says, lost for words.

"Laguna Beach told us all about you," Manny goes on.

"*Laguna Beach?*" Tara looks at me.

"Don't mind him." I link my arm through hers. "He has nicknames for everyone."

Deanna rolls her eyes. "It's so annoying."

"Be quiet, *Arizona*," he laughs. "I think Tara looks like Heaven Sent to me."

I laugh, nudging Tara. "He's a dork."

Tara smiles and turns to me. "Could I use the bathroom?"

"Of course! Sorry, I'll show you around."

Pirate runs past, not even bothering with Tara. He's fickle like that.

"I'll bring your bags in," Manny declares, strutting over toward the door.

"Thanks, Manny!" I call out as I show her to the powder room.

"Who are those people?" Tara whispers when we're out of earshot.

I smile excitedly. "My new friends."

Her eyes go wide... "The boy...he seems really...I don't know...*out there.*"

"Don't worry, he's awesome. You'll love him."

She looks at me dubiously. "Well, you really don't know them that well, babe. I mean, they are part of the biker club, right?"

I try to contain my excitement. "I've so much to tell you about it all."

I wait for her to use the bathroom, and then drag her to my room so I can tell her without the others hearing. "I slept with Rock!" I whisper.

She slaps a hand over her mouth. "Oh my god."

"I know!"

"How? When?"

"The night before last. He had a panic attack, and I helped him get over it and we ran a bath. One thing led to another, and we did it... Oh God, Tara. He's amazing. He's like no guy I've ever been with before."

She stares at me in utter shock. "Holy shit. You barely know the guy. What if he's a criminal? I mean, you don't know anything about him?"

I managed to snap a shot of him on the couch when he wasn't looking.

She agreed he was hot, so what's the issue now?

Tara is old fashioned and comes from a strict family. Her parents are religious, and they've never really let her live on her own accord, a lot like my father but without the religious aspect. I suppose in that way we're both perfectly suited to be friends.

Except she's very judgy. Not liking any of my boyfriends over the years is just the beginning.

"He's not. He's...wonderful," I gush. "We had such a hot night. It's not just about his body or his dick—which is amazing, by the way—but we seem to have this *thing*. I can't even describe it. A connection? I guess."

She looks like she just tasted something bad as I take in her expression. "I, I just think it's a little too soon. You're confusing lust with love, Aspyn. This is what you do. I'm only pointing it out because I'm your friend, and I don't want you to get hurt again."

My heart plummets. "I... I don't think I do that."

She nods. "You do, and it's not a bad thing, on your part. You're a giving person. You can't be held responsible for people who want to use you for sex. Look at you. You're amazing, who wouldn't want to bed you? But I just don't want you to be used."

I feel her words, but they also sting. She's saying Rock isn't good enough, but she hasn't even met him. She wouldn't know the first thing about him.

"He's...not like that, and I'm not being used. I'm the one who pursued him."

She gives me a look. "You've slept with him how many times? Once?"

I swallow hard. She's right in some ways. I barely know anything about Rock.

I shrug, wringing my hands. "We have a connection." My voice sounds small. I'm holding on to it for dear life. *The connection.*

"Just like you did with Dylan, and the guy before that."

I shake my head. "That's not true. I wasn't in love with them."

She gapes at me as I slide onto the bed, feeling the weight of her judgment. "You're *in love* with him?"

I frown. "No." *Yes.* "That's not what I meant!"

Her face softens. "I just don't want you jumping in with both feet," she says, sitting next to me on the bed. "That last asshole did a real number on you, and you had to pick up all the pieces and mend your broken heart. I don't want that for you again. I just want you to be happy."

"I am happy!" I declare.

She looks even more confused. "Your dad sent you away to a strange town to hide amongst a biker club." She shakes her head at that. "And you're holed up in some expensive apartment and you never go anywhere, how can you be happy?"

I shrug. "Maybe it's because I'm away from what I know. The same four walls. The same thing day in, day out. With nobody but my housekeepers for company."

"But it's the same thing here. The four walls may be slightly different but, essentially, it's the same. You're talking like you plan on staying here?" Her expression turns horrified. "You're best off coming home, where we can be closer and you're around people who care about you."

"My dad wouldn't put me in danger."

"I know that, but one has to wonder if he's lost his mind," she says in a hushed whisper. "Plus, it smells bad in this city."

I snort and think, *wait till you get to Bourbon Street.*

"You get used to it."

"You're not staying here, though, right?" She can't let it go.

I shrug. "I had a big heart-to-heart with my dad about him giving me some more freedom after all this stalker business is dealt with, and I think I got through to him."

"What will you do?"

"I don't know, T. But I can't go back to what I was doing. That's not living. It's like being a bird in a cage that can never fly."

She looks pensive for a moment, but she had to know this was coming.

Rock

I put my hand on hers. "I'll be coming back, silly," I say, hoping she'll smile eventually. "But I want to get to know Rock better. We've barely had time to talk about anything…"

"But you had time to fuck him?" She raises an eyebrow.

I sigh. "T. You'll understand when you meet him. Honestly, he's a good guy." I feel annoyance rising in me. *Why does she have to be so judgmental?* "And anyway, I thought you'd be happy I'd stopped moping around."

"Like I said, I don't want you to get hurt."

"I know what I'm doing."

"Do you? Because it sounds like you practically want to marry this guy."

I snort. "Don't be stupid. I barely know him, but I do like him. I thought you'd be happy for me. He's so sweet, T. He makes me laugh. He's protective and he's so good in bed." I throw that last one in because I'm being spiteful, and I know she won't appreciate it.

"It's not all about sex."

"No. But it's an important part. It's not make or break, but it's a bonus that he knows what he's doing."

She looks dubious. "And you know he's not sleeping with other people?"

Panic hits me.

I've never even thought about that. I mean, I've never even asked him if he's sleeping with other people as well as me. But he did say that thing where I wasn't to sleep with anyone else, and I made him agree, too. Does that mean he isn't sleeping with other people?

Am I an idiot for believing he wouldn't?

And what has he been doing on the nights we haven't been together?

Fear and jealousy rise deep inside me, and Tara sees it immediately.

She sighs. "Honey. I'm not trying to be a Debbie Downer on this. I just think it's naive to expect anything more than a random fuck from this dude. Do you even know his last name?"

I swallow hard. I actually don't know his last name. I know nothing much about him, to be honest.

I shift in my seat. "You don't know the connection we have," I say, my voice low. "I may not know him that well, but I know he cares about me."

"I bet he says all the right things, just like Dylan."

I shake my head. "No. It's different, this feels...*different.*"

I wish she'd just be happy for me. If I wanted to hear judgment and scrutiny, I'd just go and tell everything to my father, or some of the other superficial "friends" I have back home.

Tears start to well in my eyes.

"I'm sorry. I didn't mean to upset you," Tara says, her voice matching mine in octave. "I... I'm just worried about you. You've been through so much. This is from a place of love, not judgment."

I decide to keep my inner monologue to myself. I wipe my eyes and say, "We have a party to go to tonight. If you're up for it?"

She frowns. "Whereabouts?"

I smile. "At the clubhouse."

Her eyes go round. "With the bikers?"

"Don't look so petrified. It's not as bad as it sounds, and the girls are really nice. I don't know who will be there, as it's Crystal's birthday. She's the VP's ol'...uh, his *wife.*" I know biker terms will freak her out even more at this point.

"If it means I get to hang out with you, then of course I'll tag along."

I beam, clapping my hands together. It's so much better when my best friend is on board and not mad at me. "I can't wait for you to meet Rock."

She smiles. Even though it doesn't reach her eyes, I know that she's trying. She's out of her comfort zone, and I have to realize this is hard for her, too. "Me too." Her voice sounds a little flat, but I choose to ignore it.

"Great! Well, I'll show you to your room, and if you want to freshen up, I can help you unpack in a bit."

She nods. "Okay."

I pull her into a hug. "This was the best surprise ever."

She hugs me back. "I'm glad. I was starting to wonder if you needed me anymore." She laughs wistfully, and I shake my head.

"I'll always need you. Don't ever worry about that."

But things have changed. *I've* changed. And I feel as though I may have to have a heart-to-heart with Tara in the not-too-distant future.

Baby steps.

It seems like I'm hearing that word a lot lately.

The party is in full swing, and I'm shocked at how many people are in the back lounge area. A loud jukebox plays, and the lights are dimmed.

There's bar staff and a few bikers are shooting pool in the main area, staying well away from the hooting and hollering going on just across the bar.

I start to feel the adrenaline in my veins. Especially when I remember Rock's text messages from earlier...

Rock

I need you

I couldn't keep the wide-ass grin off my face at seeing that.

He needs me?

Oh, God. I need him so fucking much.

Me

> Where are you?

Rock

I'll be there soon

Me

> I can't wait to see you. Not just your dick, though that's a bonus

Rock

Fuck, baby. You're distractin' me

Me

> I am. So you'll hurry up and get over here. I've got no panties on…

Rock

Holy fuck, Trouble

Me

> Also… you're not sleeping with anyone else, right?

I waited so long for that reply that I got worried.

Rock

Why would you ask that?

Me

> I want to know

Rock

> I thought we weren't exclusive?

A sharp pain stabbed in my chest when I read it over and over again.

Me

> I know, but you said I was yours while I'm here... does that work both ways?

I don't know what I would do if he was sleeping with another girl. We had sex without a damn condom!

Rock

> There's nobody else

Relief flooded through me.

Me

> Tara came to visit. You can meet her when you get here x

And that's the last I heard from him. That was hours ago. He never replied, but I assume he got busy doing whatever secret business the men are up to.

In fact, most of the guys are gone. There's only a handful here, and I start to worry when it gets to ten p.m. and I still haven't heard from him.

In the meantime, we join in. Or rather, *I* join in. Tara goes through the motions of meeting everyone, but she glances around like she may catch a disease if she touches anything.

This bar isn't seedy. It's actually nicer than most bars and clubs I've ever been in.

I don't care. I'm having fun tonight.

Tipping back tequila shots with Luna, Jas and Manny makes me feel like I'm floating on air. Tara has a sip but screws her nose up.

"She's a little uptight," Manny whispers in my ear.

I nod. "She's an introvert who's led a sheltered life."

"Maybe we need to try to get that shot down her throat so she'll loosen up?"

I giggle. "Maybe."

"I get it's not her scene. It was nice of her to come see you," he goes on.

I nod. "It was. She's a good friend."

She's been pretty quiet since I confessed about Rock. My words shocked even me.

I denied that I'm falling in love with Rock, but that was a lie.

Maybe I am.

Maybe I'm also stupid, but when I fall, I'm all in.

Maybe Manny will know what's going on tonight and where Rock and everyone else is, so I ask him.

"Trust me, it's best you don't know," he says, looking more worried than I'd like.

"This party is a good distraction, though. Best not to think about it. They'll be back soon."

My first thought is that they're out at a strip club or a bar... As if sensing my fear, Manny adds, "It's club business, nothing to do with other women."

I let out a sigh of relief. "What bad stuff do these guys do for down time?"

Manny shrugs. "I stay out of it. They have beef with a rival MC and stuff's getting hairy. Hence the reason Cash let the party still happen, as it'll keep the women from worrying. Even though most of the ol' ladies, if you haven't noticed, aren't gettin' trashed. They want to be sober when their men return."

I glance around and see Crystal and Deanna talking amongst themselves, and Luna and Jas are nowhere to be seen.

"Is everything okay? I mean, are they in danger?" I squeak.

Manny just pats my arm. "Everything's gonna be fine."

I honestly don't know if his words make me feel better or ten times worse. I know something big is going on, and Rock didn't tell me. Not that he would when I'm not privy to things like club business. The thought of him getting hurt...I can't deal with that.

I make sure I pay attention to Tara, and she loosens up a little. We even dance to the music on the jukebox.

About an hour later, the clubhouse doors bust open, and the men all come walking in.

The music quickly gets turned down when they come into view, and I'm shocked by what I see. Blood. Some of the men have blood on their shirts and they look like hell.

I stand there in shock as Deanna runs up to Cash and flings into his arms as he catches her. Crystal does the same to Ryder as I shake my head.

Rock? Where is Rock?

"Stay here," I tell Tara. "Stay by Manny. I'll be back."

I don't even know my feet are moving until I'm pushing past people to find him.

The blood pumps in my veins, and I don't know what I'm going to do if something bad has happened. I never even got to tell him that I'm falling in love with him.

And now I may never have the chance.

22

ASPYN

When I see Rock I run toward him and fly into his arms as he catches me.

My body presses into his as I revel in the warmth of his skin, how he cocoons me protectively.

We kiss. My arms around his neck as he holds me by the hips.

When we break free, I glance down. He has blood all over him. It's dried, but I can see it plain as day.

"It's not mine," he tells me quickly. "I'm okay."

"Rock? What happened?"

There's a commotion all around us. People are shouting and Cash is trying to call order to the room.

"Who got hurt? Who's blood is it?"

"We're all okay."

I don't know what's going on… It's scaring me.

I cup his face. "Are you sure you're not hurt?" My eyes well up as he stares at me.

"Come," he demands, taking my hand as we push through the crowd. He makes his way to the back, past the mayhem to where it's quiet.

When he pushes the door open to a room, I realize immediately it's his office. All that's in here is a desk and a big computer setup with surveillance cameras.

Leading me inside, he slams the door shut, pressing me against it as I moan when his lips touch mine.

He pulls back, shoving his cut off, and then he rips his blood-soaked Henley over his head. I gasp when he pushes his hard dick into my stomach.

He's covered in blood and he's hard.

"What happened?" I breathe in between kisses, but Rock already has my dress hitched up to my waist and he's reaching between my legs, proving I really didn't wear underwear tonight.

"Fuck, *Trouble.*"

I gasp as he inserts a finger roughly, and I moan into his mouth.

What the hell is going on?

"Are you okay?" I manage.

"I'm fine."

"But you're soaked in blood." I push against him, wanting answers.

He presses his forehead to mine. "I'll tell you, but I need this first."

"Covered in someone else's blood?"

His eyes are dark when he says, "Are you denyin' me what's mine?" As he inserts another finger, his other hand moves up to cup my breast.

I need him so much. I want his mouth on me.

I reach up to unzip my dress, but realizing it's a two-person job, I turn around, and he roughly unzips it for me. I let the top part fall to my waist where it bunches up with the skirt.

He stares at my breasts and groans when I cup his dick through his jeans.

"You're so hard," I whisper.

"And you're so beautiful, Aspyn," he says. "I need to fuck you hard."

"Oh, God," I groan when he curls his fingers inside me, and I press back against the door.

He finger-fucks me and drops his mouth to my nipple as I move one hand into his hair and the other grabs his ass. As he grinds into me, I cry out.

"Give it to me, *Trouble.* Let me hear you scream." He pounds in and out and moves his mouth to my other aching nipple.

His hand and the blood and our sweat and stolen kisses, it's all so erotic and dirty.

I come fast, calling his name as a satisfied smirk rests on his face when my eyes open.

"Put your hands on the desk and stick your ass out, babe."

I do as I'm told, holding my dress at my waist as he flips the skirt up to cup my ass.

"Oh," I cry when he bites down on my shoulder and fingers me from behind at the same time.

"My baby's so wet for me."

He unbuckles his belt and unzips his jeans, pulling his dick out in his hand.

I groan when I see how big and swollen it is. And it's all for me.

"Rock," I whisper. "Hurry!"

He chuckles, lining up behind me as she shoves his fat cock inside me, and I cry out.

This isn't gentle. Not like he has been before.

This is hot, animalistic, rough sex…and I can't get enough of it.

He smacks my ass cheek as he pounds in and out of me, holding me at the nape of my neck as he shoves me down so I'm on my elbows.

I moan with wild abandon. I don't care who hears me. I don't care as long as I'm with him.

"I love you," I whisper.

He stills.

Shit.

Did I just say that out loud?

"What did you say?" he pants.

"Uh, nothing." *Did I really?*

"You said you loved me."

"No."

"Yes. You did."

I panic. "I'm sorry, Rock. I meant...*this*. I love *this*."

He's seated deep inside me as he pulls me up, his arms wrapped around my waist as his mouth reaches my ear. "Tell me again."

"No, I..."

He slaps my ass, and I cry out. "Do you love me, Aspyn?"

Oh, my. *He likes it? Is this turning him on?*

"I...uh..."

"Spit it out." He doesn't move inside me, and I need him to. "Do you love me, my little ball of *Trouble?*"

Pulling out, he slams back in and stills.

"*Yes!*" I cry. "Rock, I love you..."

Bending me back over, my hands plant on the desk.

He groans, pulling out and then thrusting back in. He makes the most delicious sound when I arch my back, resting down on my elbows, sticking my ass out for him.

"Nobody ever told me that before," he grunts as he starts to speed up. "I like it."

He stretches me as he moves in and out. I love the feel of him, of how dirty this is and how turned on I am that he likes me telling him I love him.

Where did that even come from?

"Do you love this, Rock?" I gasp, pushing the limits. "My body?"

"Yeah," he grunts.

"This pussy?"

He grunts again.

"It's yours, Rock. All of it is yours. My mind, body, and soul. It belongs to you."

"Babe," he groans.

"I love you."

"Trouble."

The pressure starts to build as I feel the heat rising up my neck.

"I love you, Rock. Do you... Do you love me?"

"Fuck."

"Do you love me, Rock?"

"Yeah," he groans. "I'm comin', babe..."

I let go and ride the wave of pleasure as I feel his hot streaks of cum spurt inside me and there is no greater feeling in the world.

We still and he buries his head in my neck. "Fuckin' love that."

We're both panting as I reach around to cup his neck. "Me too."

It's then I see movement at the door. Tara is standing there watching, her face aghast as my eyes go wide.

"Tara?"

She slams the door and Rock turns, pulling out of me as I start to pull my dress back together.

"Shit," I mutter. "I left her out there with Manny." But how long was she standing there watching us?

"She's a big girl. She'll be fine. The door was closed behind us, so she decided to be nosy by openin' it."

Still, I feel...a little weird about it. "Can you zip me up?"

He does as I ask, and I kiss him chastely. "I have to go to her."

Tucking his dick back in, he fastens his jeans, pulling his shirt back on, even though it's covered in blood. His cut is next as I sort myself out, embarrassed that Tara saw what we were doing.

He takes me by the hand. "We'll go together."

I nod as he leads me out of the room.

Everyone is still around, and people are talking loudly as we rush through the crowd to try to find Tara.

She's out near the front, looking around, probably for someone to take her back to the apartment.

"Tara?" I call out.

She spins around, her face annoyed and angry. "You just left me there, with those people!" she spits at me, her eyes flicking over my shoulder toward Rock who's just behind me.

"I'm sorry, I didn't mean to... Manny..."

"You were bent over a desk, being fucked like a whore."

Oh. My. God.

"Tara!"

"Now wait a minute..." Rock starts.

I shake my head. "No, Rock." I go to her. "I'm sorry I left you. I didn't mean to, Rock needed me and..."

"I needed you too. I don't know any of those people, Aspyn. And then I find you being bent over a desk while he pounds the shit out of you covered in blood from God knows where! You people are all crazy!"

"I know, I'm sorry. We got lost in the moment."

I feel Rock's protective hands behind me, holding my hips.

"Not a great way to meet for the first time," Rock admits. "But I closed the door for a reason." His tone isn't pleasant, and I turn to look over my shoulder.

"Uh, Rock, this is Tara... Tara, this is Rock." I don't know why I'm even bothering with introductions. It's obvious who everyone is.

"Is this what you get up to?" she sneers. "Being treated this way? By *him?*"

"What way?" I say, my frustration growing. "I'm sorry I left you for five minutes. I get there was a lot going on when the guys came back, and for that, I'm sorry, but you could've just closed the door again. I mean...I'm a grown woman..."

"You told him you loved him?"

Holy shit.

I frown. "You heard that? How long were you standing there?"

I feel Rock's grip tighten on my hips.

"Long enough."

I shake my head. "Why?"

"Is it true?"

"Answer me first," I demand. "Why didn't you just walk away?"

"I… I was shocked. I'm sorry… I had nowhere to go…"

I take a deep breath. "And yes, it's true. I love him. It's crazy, I know. And he may not feel the same way, but I've spent too long holding my feelings in and keeping everything locked inside. I won't do it anymore."

"I do feel the same," Rock whispers in my ear, loud enough for Tara to hear.

Their gazes meet, and Hell could freeze over. But my heart still warms at hearing his confirmation.

She hugs herself. "I want to go back now."

I nod. "Okay."

There's no point pushing the issue, she needs to cool off.

I turn to Rock. He's staring down at her with a look on his face that I don't like. Like he doesn't like her one little bit.

I need to smooth this over. I can't have my best friend hating him, not after what we just shared.

"I can drive us, I have my truck here," he says.

"Why are all the men covered in blood?" Tara asks. "Are the police coming to arrest us all?"

Rock shakes his head. "It's nothing like that and not as bad as it looks, trust me. The assholes deserved it."

Tara screws her nose up and shakes her head. "Are you coming, Aspyn?"

I turn to look at her. "We're all going."

"I think it's best if I go home in the morning," she says.

Rock

"Just so you know, I don't think your dad is going to be too happy to hear about this. I told him I'd keep an eye on you."

Now my anger really boils that she'd threaten me with that. "That isn't *your* job," I tell her. "That's *Rock's* job. My dad knows about the MC…" I don't mean to be cruel, but she's acting like my mom, not my best friend.

"Yes, but does he know that they're thugs?"

I wince like she just slapped me. "Rock isn't a thug!"

"Like you said, you don't even know his last name…" Her words mock me and make me feel stupid.

I get this is scary and there is no explanation for why Rock has blood on him, but there will be a reason. And for her to walk in and watch us having sex? What the hell is wrong with her?

Rock holds me tighter, his eyes never leaving Tara. "It's time to go," he says, kissing me on the back of my head.

Rock

There's silence as we ride in the car.

I'm pissed, to be honest.

I don't know who this Tara chick thinks she is acting this way. I'm in my own goddamn clubhouse, and she's acting as if I personally did something to her.

She doesn't own Aspyn.

If she didn't like what she saw, she should have closed the door and waited until we finished. She was with Manny, Summer and Crystal. It wasn't like she was just left in a corner to fend for herself.

What went down tonight… *Fuck.*

My hands are shaking.

But that shit can wait.

I don't like the fact that Tara spoke to Aspyn like that. I get she's worried for her friend, but I'd never put her in danger or harm's way. That's why she was at the clubhouse, and I was at the location and things turned south…very fuckin' south.

Aspyn reaches across and puts her hand on mine, resting on my thigh. The act in itself speaks a thousand words, and I wish that Tara would ask to be dropped off at a hotel, because I know I'm not done yet with my girl. Far from it. I haven't been this pent-up in…well, forever.

Before I left the club, I told the girls to wait in the car while I went back in to see my brother and Cash.

Both were in the meeting room, talking while Ryder and Hawk tried to calm everyone down.

"This doesn't go anywhere," Cash says, looking at the two of us. "I did what I had to do for you. But the blame will fall on Forger. If we're lucky, we'll skate under the radar."

"What about Big Papa? He'll talk," Jett says. "He won't have a choice."

Cash shakes his head. "Nobody else was there to witness. He's lucky he survived, because of us. He owes us. Not the other way around. If he squeals, we'll gut him."

"Jett's right, if he snitches…" I run a hand through my hair. "It's the mafioso, Cash. If this gets out…"

"Then we'll deal with it," Cash grunts. "You saw the shootout. There's nothin' and nobody left to talk anyway. They won't pin it on us if we were never there. And we weren't. Got me?"

"It's the mob," I mutter, knowing what we've done. "They have spies everywhere."

Jett looks at me. "He's right. We lay low…"

My hands are still shaking wildly.

The Italians just thought they'd come along for the ride when Forger moved things off-site. They wanted to sample the coke.

Cash passes me his mouthful of scotch. I down it in two gulps. I'm driving the girls home so I can't get trashed. Not like I want to.

Cash looks at both of us. "This never happened."

I nod.

"Go home," he says. "Sleep it off. We'll reconvene in the morning."

"What about the pigs?" Jett asks.

"Our favorite cop Callaghan will no doubt come sniffin' around, but we'll be ready for him if that happens." He nods to me. "You took care of any security footage quickly. That's all we had tyin' us to the meetin' tonight. That and Big Papa. Like I said, he wanted the Italians out, but I guess it just happened sooner than we thought. And now Forger is gone, he'll be takin' over."

I shake my head. "This means war," I mutter. "The mafioso will come callin'."

We all know what's going to happen.

Officer Callaghan has been dying to pin something on the club ever since he stuck his nose in with Indigo and Camille. Not that the cops have done anything to find her captors.

Cash shakes his head. "Big Papa is no fan of the mafioso, and he wants to keep the Irish on his side. If he spills, he knows we'll retaliate. There is no war if everybody is dead. The Italians think Forger did this. They'll go finish the rest of the club off and we can sit back and watch it all unfold."

It seems too easy.

"The mafioso aren't just gonna take this lyin' down," Jett says. "They'll want blood."

Cash shakes his head. "Then they'll put their anger to better use trackin' the devils. Forger got too greedy, and everyone will testify to that. If Big Papa squeals, we have enough ammo against him to bring him and the underworld down."

He's right. At least that makes me feel better.

"Go wash up." His words are final...

My hands still shake as I clutch the wheel. I know Aspyn is looking at me with concern in her eyes, and she should be. Shit went down tonight. Shit I may never be able to explain. How could I? We may have just confessed our love for one another, but was that just in the heat of the moment?

Is Aspyn Ashley Huntley really going to come down here

and be my ol' lady? Or will she leave like everyone else in my life?

When we get back to the apartment, Rodeo and Giggs stay downstairs while we ride up to the top floor in more silence.

Tara keeps quiet, avoiding looking at either of us. Hopefully, she'll be gone in the morning because I don't like her. She looks down her nose at everyone, and I can tell by the look on her face that she knows I'm not good enough. Like I need her approval.

"For what it's worth, the assholes deserved it," I say, looking right at her.

She turns to cast her steely gaze on me. "Did people die?"

I shake my head. Now is the time to lie through my teeth. I'm not telling this chick anything about what happened. It's club business. If she runs to the cops, this could be a problem.

"Of course not, but this club protects its own. And when we go after people, it's because they're doin' harm to others."

I feel Aspyn's fingers link through mine, and she squeezes. The comfort I feel from that small touch makes my heart thump in my chest. She's with me. No matter what.

Maybe we don't know one another that well, but I know how I feel.

And I feel everything for my sweet mystery girl.

She says nothing more, and I'm relieved when the doors finally open and I let the girls step through ahead of me.

Tara officially hates me, and this club, and I've no doubt that she plans on making my life hell if I want to be with Aspyn.

Just as I'm stepping out, my phone rings. It's Cash.

"Glad I caught you," he says. "Just got a call from Tommy."

I glance at Aspyn instinctively as she talks in a low voice to Tara. It sounds like she's trying to smooth things over.

"Is everythin' okay?"

"Beth has been arrested."

"What?" I turn away and head toward the office. I feel Aspyn's eyes on me as I retreat.

"The police think the email was sent from her office. They took her in for questioning, but the evidence they found is pretty damning."

I'm pissed at hearing that. If I hadn't been so busy with what went down tonight, something that will haunt me for the rest of my days, I would've uncovered this earlier.

"Fuck, Cash."

"So, we're sittin' tight to see where it goes."

"Alright." I'm too tired to hear any more. Not that this makes any sense.

"You good?"

"I'll get over it."

"Don't overthink things. It's done."

I run a hand over my face. "Okay."

"He's gone, Rock."

"I know."

"Gotta go." He hangs up.

I don't even get a chance to turn when Aspyn's arms are folding around my middle.

"Is everything okay, Rock?" she whispers.

I turn in her arms. I know I need to go shower and wash this damn blood off myself.

"Beth was arrested," I tell her.

Her eyes go wide. "What?"

"One of the emails that was sent to you came from an IP address in her office, babe. Either she or someone who works there could be behind this." I know I checked their backgrounds, but now isn't the time to worry about that.

Aspyn frowns. "That can't be."

I soothe her back with my palm. "Let's go to bed. I'm beat."

She nods. "I'll say goodnight to Tara. She's pretty shaken up."

I lift her chin to meet my gaze. "I get that it was frightening for her tonight, but that doesn't excuse her rudeness toward you, or watchin' us."

"Yeah." She shifts on her feet. "That was a little weird. I think she just freaked out."

Still. I don't like it.

There's being protective of your friend and then being plain creepy. It may make things strained between Aspyn and me, and I don't want that. But still, she has to learn her place.

I peck her on the lips. "Come join me when you're done."

She sees the promise in my eyes and a small smile plays on her lips.

I need to tell her what happened to me. Only then may the demons be gone inside me forever. If she really does love me, when she hears the horrible truth, maybe she'll walk away. Or maybe she'll stay for good.

23

ROCK

A few hours earlier....

Forger looks different in person than his photograph.

The fact he's even here has me on edge, wondering if this is a trap, but Big Papa prattles on as Forger gives us the once-over.

Aside from me, Jett, and Priest, there are three of Big Papa's men, and we're all packing. You don't bring knives to a gunfight, and the adrenaline races through my body that the man that has caused the club so much trouble is actually here. We have him. Even if he is surrounded by several protectors, plus security on the door.

If any of us are surprised that he's here, we hide it well.

"Didn't expect so many of your well-wishers." Forger nods, eyeing us over.

I'm glad Cash made the decision to send us in now. Forger is none the wiser that we're not just goons hired to protect Big Papa. The one card we hold up our sleeves is Forger is never around, and neither are his men, so he really has no fuckin' clue who anyone is. Except Cash, of course, and Harlem and Tag. They kinda stick out.

"Ah, you know me, I never travel light," Big Papa says, his hearty laugh echoing through the small room.

They shake hands.

I stare at the man who has been the sole focus of all the animosity and disruption these last few months and I want to slit his throat. Just thinking about poor little Cami that day makes my blood boil. She must have been terrified. And this man is her own father!

He's a large, wiry man who hasn't aged well. He looks like he's lived a hard life. I can no more see Indigo with this man than I can flying to the moon, but I guess we all do dumb shit when we're young.

I crack my neck to save from lurching across and choking him, noticing Jett glancing at me in his periphery.

"Thought we'd take the party elsewhere, after the fight," Forger says, and I immediately get my back up. *We're leaving?* "I have some new friends you may like to meet."

Big Papa runs a hand over his jaw. He told us this may be expected, because there are too many eyes and ears around, but it also means he could be luring us anywhere.

Still, we have the manpower, they just can't be seen right now.

"Can I take a wild stab at it?" Big Papa jokes. "Mafioso?"

Forger's eyebrow quirks. "I see good news travels fast."

"I heard they were back in town."

"You heard correctly."

"Pardon my French, but are we sure we want to get involved? The Irish run things in the quarter. If we upset the apple cart, the Irish won't be happy." We all know Big Papa doesn't like change, aside from taking Forger out, but now he's piggie in the middle.

"Who said anythin' about the Quarter?" Forger fires back, his eyes land on me briefly.

He commands power, I'll give him that.

"I just assumed…"

Rock

"What the Italians want to do outside of our deal is up to them," he goes on. "They can fight over turf. Maybe it'll shake things up a little. The Irish have had it good for too long." There's clearly no loyalty anymore.

"Not for me," Big Papa grumbles. I guess he has to make a bit of a show of his displeasure. "I'm the one in the middle here, takin' the brunt of it now the Rebels are on the outs with the Irish. If the Irish are on the outs with me, that's bad for business."

"Forget the Irish," Forger says. "The Italians run things differently. They have a setup in Houston they want to expand. I don't give a fuck about the French Quarter. As far as I'm concerned, that shit's between the Irish and the Rebels."

"Then what do you need me for? If we supply to the Italians, then the Irish will be on the outs with us too. Last thing I need is more of a headache."

He shrugs. "The price we take for bein' low lives, isn't it?"

Big Papa scratches his chin. "You're not concerned that the Irish will turn on you?"

"Not if we blame the Rebels. May as well take the fall for that as well. It'll tidy things up nicely."

Maybe because he can't help himself, or perhaps he's now got a cross to bear, I'm not sure, but he asks, "What about that kid? Heard there was a fire at the crypt."

He looks at Big Papa with no expression. Here I was, thinking he might even feel bad about that, but it seems he is a cold-hearted bastard after all.

He shrugs. "Kid got in the way. Wasn't supposed to go down like that. If you wanna point the finger, point it at the Rebels MC."

"Go figure," Big Papa grumbles. "That asshole Cash has had it coming for a long time."

"Can say that again." He goes to stand. "Caruso insisted on a more secure location."

"Understandable. Too many eyes and ears."

He gives a chin lift. "These fuckers new?"

He nods. "Need the muscle. Apparently, there's a bounty on my head now that I'm in control."

Forger grunts. "I know the feelin'."

Why the fuck these two are such good buddies, I don't know. Or should I say *were*. We all know both would shoot the other without even blinking if it came down to it.

"The mafioso wants a sample of the coke," Forger goes on. "Thought it might be a good time to meet, get acquainted with the deadliest family in Houston, never know when you may need allies."

"Truest words ever spoken, also won't hurt for them to see how things are done around here."

Forger chuckles. "You know they used to run this town?"

"Right. But that was then, this is now. Shit's changed. They have no power here, not anymore."

Forger just stares back blankly then, abruptly, he stands. Jett, Priest, and I all reach for our guns at the same time, and Forger smirks, his men doing the same. My hands still beneath my cut, and Big Papa turns and laughs.

"Told you they were good."

Forger shakes his head. "Let's not get into a pissin' contest. We need to get out of here."

"You got any money on the fight?"

Motherfucker has everything rigged. Of course he does.

He grins. "Of course. You know the house always wins."

Twenty minutes later, we're inside a van, moving to an undisclosed location.

This feeling I get, it ain't good. The only thing that makes me realize that we're not in peril is the fact that Big Papa is needed and heavily guarded. It's our one saving grace.

Rock

All the while, I have an undetectable earpiece with Cash talking to me. They're following us. It almost feels too good to be true. Getting Forger away from the fight so we can kill him without the watchful eyes and ears all around us.

But nothing is ever that simple. Either Forger got way too cocky, or he's onto us.

If he is, then we're all ready, but then again, so is he. They all are.

His need for power and control has him dealing with all sides. This isn't going to end well. We already know that, but involving the Italians, it's not something that we bargained for. It's gonna make things harder. To kill Forger in front of them will pose a problem, but I tend to think that Cash must have another plan up his sleeve.

So the most likely scenario is that we wait for the meeting to be over, then follow Forger and kill him then. There is no way that he's getting away this time.

I feel the tension mounting, and I'm trying not to sweat. Nothing looks guiltier than a sudden rush of perspiration.

As we head down toward the docks, I can smell the sea.

Every now and again, Big Papa flicks his eyes over to us, and I have to ask myself whether he is truly on our side. The fact that I may never see my girl again tightens in my chest. *Could this really be it? I haven't even had a chance to get to know her yet. There are so many things that I want to know...*

I shake myself out of my reverie. No good can come from that. I'll see her again.

Even though I know that if something happens to me, I never told her what I really wanted to say. I didn't tell her, but she's the greatest thing that has happened to me in a very long time. That it's crazy, but I'm falling for her. She's all I think about when I wake up, all I dream about when we're apart. And I never took myself for a goddamn romantic, but here we are.

If I get out of this mess, I'm gonna show her exactly what I want. She'll never have to wonder about my feelings, or if she's important to me, because she'll know.

I don't know what love is. But I think it comes close to how I feel about Aspyn. Which again, is crazy, as I barely know anything about this chick, but I know how I feel. And I'm rarely ever wrong.

My brother was probably thinking the same thing about his ol' lady, Summer. But maybe she had a heads up about what was really going on tonight.

It's not like I can tell Aspyn all about club business when she's not my ol' lady. Not yet, anyway.

When we park, we climb out cautiously, and two black, unmarked cars are waiting.

Forger moves ahead with his men, and we tail behind. I take this as a good sign that we're not in the firing line.

Never turn your back, no matter what.

I learned that when I was on the streets all those years ago. Mistake number one.

Maybe Forger isn't exactly the genius we thought he was. And this might just be his undoing.

Of course, Jett and I did research on the Caruso family. It's not like there aren't pictures of them on the internet. The head of the family, Don Carlo and his underboss and brother Salerno, run the family business. Only Salerno is here, with another man who I don't recognize to his right.

They really want to do fuckin' business if they sent the underboss and his muscle.

All the while, the Irish are getting fucked over from all sides. If we ever get out of this, Cash will have some explaining to do.

"Salerno," Forger says. The men don't shake hands. In fact, armed men stand all around, looking as grim as you'd imagine any crime boss family security to look.

This isn't going as planned.

"Forger, I hear you've been a busy man."

Forger chuckles as we move closer. "That I have. Securing the underworld crime syndicate for your family's return."

What in the actual fuck?

Forger is insane.

If he's planning on sniffing out the Irish, then he doesn't care about backlash. The man must have a serious fuckin' death wish.

"This is my consigliere, Este." Salerno gestures to the man, but my eyes are locked on him.

There's something about him that's familiar. Vaguely.

Big Papa moves with Forger as I stick to him like glue until we're face to face with the other men. "These are my friends," Forger says. "Big Papa, who I'm sure you know all about."

Salerno looks up at me, and I freeze.

Why is this man so familiar? Who the fuck is he?

He glances away, lighting up a thin cigar… The scent wafts over and cloaks me in dread and bitterness. Memories…and an empty house. A mother who was constantly out of it.

Then it all clicks into place.

When I look at Jett, and he's gone rigid, his stance alarming as I see his hand on his belt, close to his hidden gun.

I glance back at Salerno.

His suit.

His gold medallion.

The ring on his pinkie finger.

No fucking way.

I swallow hard, the pain beginning in the back of my head as I will myself not to have a panic attack.

Jett's hands turn to fists as Salerno smiles at something his confidant says and I cringe.

It's him.

The man who…the man who haunts my dreams. The man who took everything from me and my brother. Who used our mother like a whore and beat her, then took her children in the vilest of ways.

I feel the bile rising in my throat. As if I could ever forget.

He's really here... After all these years, the bastard finally showed his face.

I never knew his name, but I'll never forget that smirk. The way he stinks like cigars and then when he finally speaks, his voice makes me want to vomit.

I feel Jett's eyes on me, and I nod once without looking at him.

The men begin looking at the product while Big Papa talks, all the while I'm sizing up the men around, trying to gauge how many there are and how we can kill this motherfucker without all dying tonight.

So many nights I've dreamed of ending his life, and what it would feel like to have his blood on my hands. To feel his heartbeat slowing as he took his last breath. To remind him of all he took while he died an insufferably slow and painful death.

Sometimes it's all that's kept me going. Even though I never had a clue how to find him or who he even was. And now he's here.

My throat feels like sandpaper. I'm trying to think before my brother reacts... Then again, he's probably thinking the same thing about me because I'm the wild card out of the two of us. Seeing him rigid like this, his eyes saying a thousand words, makes me want to put a bullet between this man's eyes and not even care about the consequences.

The worst part: I can't even tell Cash. I can hear him, and he can hear around us, but I can't risk getting caught talking, or else they'll know something's up. I don't wanna be the one to blow this, not with so much at stake.

Do we do it now? Or do we wait until Salerno is least suspecting. I don't want him to live another day. I don't want that. I want him to die tonight. There is no other way.

The main problem is that Big Papa talks a lot and Forger acts if they're best friends.

I can't believe the nerve of this man. It's like he revels in the idea of everybody at war.

He gets off on it.

He gets off on trying to kill his own kid.

I zone out for most of the conversation. I'm still trying to will myself not to go into panic mode. If I do, that could blow everything.

Of course, he wouldn't recognize us now. We're grown men.

Would he even remember?

Big Papa gives me a look, noticing a change in me, but the others are too engrossed in conversation.

Cash is in my ear.

"We're gonna move in. Whatever the fuck you do, don't get shot again."

I close my eyes briefly. Priest behind, my brother in front, as I touch Big Papa on the shoulder, my signal to the others.

"Ready," I mutter.

All of a sudden when Salerno begins to speak, bullets fly out of nowhere and everyone ducks as mayhem erupts.

I knock my brother sideways, just like I've done in the past, at the same time a bullet hits Forger between the eyes. I don't know if Tag or Harlem perfected their shot lately, but he's dead. Finally, one asshole is gone forever.

I'd take a bet that was Harlem. If not, he'll be pissed someone got to Forger first.

I fire, aiming at one of the guards shielding Salerno. Este ducks for cover like a goddamn pussy. The guard goes down, and I feel Jett behind me.

"You hit?"

"Nah, I'm good."

"Priest?"

"Copped a scratch, I'm good." He pushes to his feet as we

stay low. I see blood pooling through Priest's shirt at his shoulder.

"Fuckin' piece of shit," I growl. "Fuck, Jett."

"It's him, isn't it?" I hear the terror in his voice. "He's the guy…"

I feel someone pull back on my cut, and I glance around. Cash.

"Y'all hit?"

I shake my head. "Forger's dead."

"Yeah, I saw. About fuckin' time."

"Harlem got him?"

"Yep. Couldn't risk havin' him escape. He might never resurface again."

Cash fires as the Italians duck for cover. I have to say, for a big guy, Big Papa is certainly light on his feet and he's a good shot.

"*Cash*," I start as we keep low. "Salerno…the underboss, he's…he's the guy who…"

I can't even say the words.

"Wasn't plannin' on the underboss bein' here, or the Italians," Cash grumbles. "But it is what it is."

"No," I start again, unable to form words.

"Spit it out." Cash reloads his gun. "Gotta make sure every fucker here tonight is fuckin' gone."

"He…he's the one who molested us," I say as my eyes meet Cash's.

He frowns. "What?"

"You heard me."

"Salerno Caruso?"

I nod. I've no words.

"Are you…"

"I'm sure."

Cash's eyes darken. His entire demeanor changes. "He's a dead man."

I swallow hard, my head hasn't stopped spinning this whole time.

I can't fuckin' do this. I can't...

"You want him dead, or captured?" Priest cuts in.

I turn to Jett, and we both say, "Dead," at the same time.

Cash stands and, in a moment of absolute madness, he surges forward, shooting as he goes. Men are flying this way and that as I see Harlem, Tag, Bronco, Nevada, JJ, and Hawk coming up from the rear. If anyone escapes tonight and sees what we did, we're all dead.

I flag Cash, Jett, and Priest as Big Papa's men circle behind, some dead, some still standing. It's a mess.

Salerno makes it to the car, but two of his men covering his side go down.

Holy fuck.

Salerno turns, a gun in his hand as he points at Cash. Cash is faster, running toward him as he sprays the man with bullets. "Motherfucker!" he screams. Salerno's eyes go wide as he drops his gun, slumping back against the car door as we surround him.

"This is for my boys, Jett and Rock, you motherfuckin' piece of shit. You molested them when they were children, and now you're gonna meet the devil himself."

Recognition flashes through his eyes for a brief moment as his eyes shift.

"Don't fuckin' look at them!" Cash head butts him so fuckn' hard, I don't know how the man won't injure himself in the process. Salerno's head flies back but Cash is quicker. He holds the gun to his head and pulls the trigger. No hesitation.

I turn away, the sight too gruesome even for me.

We all stand there, bodies strewn around us, everywhere we look.

I stare at the man as Cash lets the corpse slide down the car.

"Big Papa?" Tag pulls him to his feet. "You good?"

He pats himself down, his face frantic. "Holy fuck."

"Yeah," Tag grumbles.

"We were meant to kill Forger, not Salerno Caruso," he says, rubbing his head.

His men are all dead.

I hope to God none of ours are.

Cash sees Priest bleeding. "Need to get outta here," he says. "Call Crystal, get Casey over pronto." Casey is Crystal's sister and an EMT. She helps the club in times of trouble.

"Fuck," I mutter, but Priest waves his hand.

"I'm gonna be okay," he says. "Just a graze."

"Whatever happens," Cash says, breaths heavy, "it's a drug deal gone wrong with Forger and Caruso."

Jett meets my eye, and he looks as pale as I feel. I grip his shoulder. "It's over now."

He nods. "Over."

"He can't hurt us." I grip my brother's neck and pull him to me. Our foreheads touch. "Nobody can."

"I know. It's just...*a lot,*" he whispers.

I let him go, ready to be gone before I throw up at this carnage.

"Go!" Cash orders. "Tag and Harlem will make sure nothin' is here that can tie us to this, but we need to get out of here."

I'm shaking. I take one long last look, and even though Priest is shot, he pulls me by my cut, Jett too, and we make our way to the van.

Tonight didn't go as planned.

We killed the mafia underboss. Carlo Caruso's brother.

But we were never here.

24

ASPYN

I'm exhausted after tonight, but so eager to get to Rock.

Tara, however, needs soothing.

"The thing I'm mad about most," she goes on when we're alone, "is the fact that you think you *love* this man." She snorts like I'm crazy.

I frown. "T, I can only tell you what I feel, and that's how I've always been…"

"And look where it got you." She shakes her head. "Hurt and humiliated."

"You just can't let it go, can you?" I fire back.

She looks affronted. "What do you mean?"

I don't want to hurt her, but she has to stop trying to control my life, just like my father. "I love you, T, but you have to let me make my own choices and, ultimately, my own mistakes. Not every guy I'm gonna meet is bad."

She looks enraged. I've never seen her like this. "Fine, make your own mistakes, just don't come crying to me when it all falls down, which it will, *again*."

I stand there, shocked at her cold words. "Why are you being like this? Especially after tonight. Beth has been arrested…" My father called me earlier, and I'm still trying to get my head around it.

Tara pushes her hair back behind her ears as she begins to fidget with her hands. "Why has Beth been arrested?"

I sigh. "The cops found stuff on her computer. Where some of the emails came from when that crazy person decided to threaten to kill me."

Her face softens slightly. "I'm glad she's been arrested. They need to lock her away permanently."

I shake my head. "I can't believe Beth would do something like this."

"Well, it's probably a good thing that she hasn't been able to message and email you. She may have lured you back and God knows what would've happened."

The news seems to have softened some of her icy demeanor. "I agree. Look, I don't want to fight, T, okay? Maybe I am confusing lust with love, I don't know, but after what I've been through, it feels good to feel good, you know? To be wanted and it isn't just about the sex."

"Just promise me that you'll take a step back, look at this objectively. Are you really going to come and live in *New Orleans?*" She accentuates the word like it's insanity. "He sure as hell isn't gonna move to LA."

"It's early days yet, nobody is moving anywhere," I say gently. "If you're saying this because you think I don't need you anymore, you're wrong. I will always need you. You're my best friend. We've been through so much together."

Tara nods. "I'm sorry that I said those things." All the anger has disappeared from her face. "I'm going to go home tomorrow so you can spend some time with Rock and work out what you want to do now that Beth is under arrest. Maybe if I'm out of the picture, then things may be clearer."

"You don't have to do that. Honestly, Rock will keep his distance while you're here."

She laughs without humor. "Like you said, you deserve a

chance at being happy. Will you just look at things from my perspective? That's all I ask."

"Of course I will."

She smiles. "Okay."

I lean in to give her a hug, feeling better about things. I know it's always hard for her to let go, but something has to give. I respect her opinion, and I understand her point of view that Rock is a biker and, from her standpoint, it looks like I don't know what the fuck I'm doing.

She thinks it's all based on lust, but she couldn't be further from the truth.

"I have an early cab."

"I wish you wouldn't leave."

We pull back, and she's back to her old self, thank God. "It's all gonna be okay. Beth isn't going to hurt you anymore. Things can go back to the way they were."

I try not to show my disappointment.

No.

Things are not going to go back to the way they were. I've changed.

Rather than start another argument, I nod and back off. "I need to go get some sleep."

"I'll see you early."

Closing her door, I breathe a sigh of relief. I pad down the hallway, scooping up Pirate as I kiss him on the head and lay him on the bed.

When I hear the shower water running, I don't even hesitate to strip down to nothing and join Rock. I need to be close to him.

He looks up when I enter. His eyes skate down my body as he takes me in.

He's washed all the blood off of him, his clothes in a pile on the floor.

I climb in, taking tentative steps as we watch one another.

"Rock?" I say. "Is everything okay?"

"How is Tara?"

I smile. "She's fine. She's going home tomorrow."

He doesn't say anything.

"She'll be leaving early. I'll see her out."

He nods. "I never wanted to come between you two."

"I know that. She knows it, too. She's just being overprotective."

A long silence hangs between us.

"Never wanted you to find out this way," he mutters with a shake of his head.

He turns his back on me and dips his head under the water, pushing the hair off his face before his gaze meets mine again.

As he pulls me to his body, I wrap my arms around his neck and reach up onto my tiptoes. "Find out what?"

He sighs. "If I tell you, you can't say shit to anyone. If you do, it'll be the end of us."

I shake my head. "I won't say a thing."

"It involves...killing people."

My eyes go wide. "Oh, Rock, what did you do?"

He shakes his head, pain laced in his words and in his eyes as he lets me go. "We got into a bad situation, and guns were used. You don't need to know who or where, just that it happened, and they were bad guys..."

"I'm just glad you're okay." If he had to do this, there's a reason.

"Remember when I said that I'm not a good guy, that there isn't anything redeemable in me?"

I nod. "Yes, and you're still wrong about that."

He stares at me, his beautiful eyes dark and dangerous as my breath hitches in my chest. "What if I said I enjoyed it?"

I swallow hard. "Enjoyed killing people?"

"Yes."

"I'd say that you'd have good reason to feel that way."

He laughs without humor. "You're too trusting, *Trouble*. It's one of the things I love about you the most."

My eyes go wide. "You really love me?"

"Yes. I love you. When I thought that I might never see you again tonight, it made me afraid. More afraid than I'd ever been because I never got to tell you."

My stomach swirls with butterflies as I step closer. "There is good in you. I believe it."

"Then you believe a lie."

"No."

He runs a hand through his hair and shakes his head. "Tonight...something happened we didn't expect. There was a man...he...wasn't a good guy."

"You knew him?"

Rock nods. "A long time ago. I'd buried the memory of him, and what he did to me and Jett..."

Oh, fuck.

"Rock?"

He looks off toward the door, his face so lost that I want to hold him in my arms and never let go.

"He molested us, that's all you need to know. It started when we were seven."

My breath hitches, but it sounds more like a gasp. "Oh my god, Rock."

His eyes don't meet mine. They look anywhere but. "Maybe that's why I'm depraved. Why I am the way I am and I enjoy hurting others, or maybe I'm just a sick fuck."

"No." I cup his face and make him look at me. "You're none of those things, Rock. You hurt bad people, not good or innocent people. You don't hurt kids. There's a big difference between you and a murderer."

"But I still did it. I was still there, with a gun in my hand. Even if I didn't deliver his final blow, I was part of it."

"Good. One less pedo on the streets has to be a good thing."

"He's not a man whose disappearance is gonna go unnoticed."

"What does Cash say?"

A slow smile spreads across his face. "No regrets."

I smile too. "Thank you for sharing that. I know I'm not supposed to know anything about 'club business,' but I'd never tell anyone, Rock. whatever you say to me, stays with me."

His eyes meet mine. "You'd make a good ol' lady."

My lips part. "What if I want that? To try."

His eyebrows knit together. "You'd move here?"

I nod. "I like it here. Living here with you… If you promise to take me out on a proper date to a restaurant that the club doesn't own."

He bends and kisses my lips. "I think I can do that."

I sober for a second. "I'm so sorry about what happened to you."

He strokes my hair. "Me and Jett didn't have a great upbringing. Our mom was a crack whore, as you already know, and she died young. After we got taken away, we were passed from pillar to post and never settled anywhere. None of our foster parents were good people. We were in and out of foster homes up until we ran away at fifteen. Livin' on the streets was better than puttin' up with what they were doin'."

"I'm sorry, Rock. People are so fucking shitty."

"Tell me about it."

"Did you ever speak to anyone about it?"

"Jett did counseling, but I didn't have the stomach for it. I self-medicated with drugs and alcohol for a long time. Soothing the pain, though that never lasted long. Trouble also seemed to find me—not that I was an angel, far from it. But we were innocent kids. Sometimes I wonder how different things could've been if we'd had a mother who cared about us instead of passin' us around to her boyfriends."

"Jesus. That's just so disgusting. I don't have any words

for how that must've been for you." I feel like such a sap for complaining about my poor little life, when in truth, I haven't had it that bad. Okay, my relationship with my dad is strained, but he loves me. He'd never hurt me or pass me around to his friends. God, the idea is sickening.

My beautiful Rock. I reach up to kiss him, needing to be closer. Needing to feel him skin to skin.

"I love you," I whisper. "I love you so damn much."

He presses his forehead to mine. "You barely know me."

"I know enough."

"I feel the same way. This isn't just sex, Aspyn. At first, I thought I was just infatuated with you, and I am, but it's so much more than that. I've never told a living soul what happened. I've never been this close to a woman, emotionally."

My heart soars hearing his words. I love that I do this to him. That we have this connection that nobody, especially Tara, can deny. She doesn't know him like I do. Our hearts and our souls have aligned, and that's how I know this is real.

"I love that I'm the first."

I look up and he grins. "I love how I'm the first at a few things, too."

I roll my lips, knowing what he's referring to.

"Is it okay to…" As I slip one hand down his torso, he groans.

"You never have to ask."

I stop, my hand resting on the hair at his navel. "But I don't want to mix these emotions and feelings we're having with sex. It isn't about that."

"I know. The sex just makes all of what I'm feeling all the more special."

I never want to mask sex as compensation. It's easy to fall into his bed but not really deal with the other issues going on. Sex can only last so long unless we communicate.

He tilts my chin up. "You know how I feel about you…"

"Do I?"

He kisses me again as my hand lowers to cup his heavy dick.

"Yes. You know I'd do anythin' for you. I'd protect you with my life. Not gonna say no to sex, babe, but it's you I want. I want to hear everythin' you've got to say. I want to be there when you wake up and be the last thing you see at night."

"It's you I want too, Rock. I want all of those things."

I run my other hand up his muscled torso, tracing the tattoos on his chest. He's completely covered, and I love every inch of him.

"I want to show you," I whisper. I drop down to my knees, and he groans when I fondle his balls, cupping him as I lick his tip with my tongue.

As I glance up, he's watching me with hooded eyes. The rumble in his chest seems to reverberate through his body as I take him farther into my mouth, squeezing his dick as I bob my head.

"Fuck," he mutters, bracing one hand against the wall. "Babe…"

I look up but continue sucking. His eyes are on fire as he stares at me ablaze. His body is so lean and taut, flexing as his other hand grips my hair. "I took you too hard at the club," he mutters. "I was rough with you."

I shake my head.

"I just… I just needed to be close to you. To feel your heart beating with mine…"

I suck harder, and he blanches, his breathing getting ragged. Then I'm being pulled up as he lifts me, yelping as he pushes me against the tile.

He reaches between us and slides his dick through my folds as I wrap my arms around his neck. His tongue is in my mouth before I can even get a word out. I'm so wet for him that he chuckles when he runs flat fingers through me and circles my clit.

"Need to make you come," he mutters, sliding his cock through me again. His length pushes against my clit as I groan wildly.

"I need it too," I gasp.

He keeps rubbing, and I close my eyes as the burn in my lower belly increases. When he dips his mouth to my nipple and sucks hard, I scream his name as I let go and my orgasm takes over me.

Grinning against my flesh, he lines up and pushes himself in. I groan at the intrusion, but I need him so much. As he lifts me, I wrap my arms around him, his pumps never pausing. Not furious, like back at the club, but at a steady pace that makes my heart race.

"Tell me you love me when you come," he whispers against my mouth. "I wanna hear it."

His mouth wanders to my neck, where he kisses me and teases me with his teeth. I cry out when he begins to thrust harder, and I know I'm not going to last.

"Rock!" I moan.

"Tell me, baby, tell me."

"Rock, I love you... Oh, oh, Rock..." He keeps banging me as I bounce up and down on his dick and I wonder how I ever enjoyed sex before I met him.

He cries out as he climaxes, grunting, "I love you, too, *Trouble*. Oh, fuck..."

Stilling, he continues to unleash streams of cum inside me as I gasp at the roar that leaves his chest.

As we slow, I'm panting hard. "Twice in one night?" I gasp.

He rubs his nose against mine. "Oh, babe. I'm just gettin' started."

Hearing a noise at the door, I sit up in bed. A shadow moves, but then I see Pirate as he launches himself up on the bed.

I rest back against the pillows, Rock spooning me from behind as I revel in his warmth.

We moved into another realm tonight.

When I think about him and Jett as frightened little children, I want to throw up. What they had to go through, no child should ever have to go through. A protective urge tightens my chest when I think about how scared they would have been. How violated, and their mom did nothing because she was too high to give a shit? I turn in his arms, moving to face him so I can watch him sleep.

He's so peaceful.

He doesn't have the mind of a killer, not a real one. Those men who were killed, I know they all deserved it. There isn't a mean bone in Rock's body. He'd never hurt anyone without good reason. So he can go to Hell when he tells me he's a bad person. I don't believe it.

I stroke his face. I love how he looks so content like this. All the strain and stress have left him as he lays on my pillows, his warm body pressed up against mine.

He made love to me when we got to bed. It was gentle and soft. Him on top of me, as I scratched the shit out of his back to speed up. But he didn't. He wanted to show me that he can be gentle, and I know that he can. That this is so much stronger than just physical.

But being in his arms is the safest place in the world. Maybe Tara is right, and we need this time for ourselves. I need to figure out exactly what I want, and if me and Rock can make a go of things. I'm not attached to my life in LA. I don't even have a life, and I can do my charity work here. I want to help Luna and Tag with Faux Paws and put my time to much better use. Maybe I'll even get a job. I could help Rock at his shop... I giggle at the idea. I wouldn't know where to start, but the possibilities are endless.

Rock

I know he said some bad things. That he *did* bad things, but it doesn't make me love him any less. In fact, him sticking up to the man who hurt him only makes me love him all the more.

I want to give it a shot.

For once in my life, I'm choosing what *I* want. Not what anyone else wants.

And it feels like such a blessing.

25

ROCK

I wake with a start, momentarily unsure of where I am.

Then I realize I'm in Aspyn's bed.

I feel across, but her side of the bed is cold.

Yawning, I roll the comforter off and go take a leak.

Just as I'm about to go looking for her, my phone rings.

"Rock?" I hear Linc through the phone.

He's a guy me and Jett often call for help when we need it. He's a great tracker and an even better hacker. I asked him to do some snooping, and I hope that he's ringing to tell me good news. Even though it looks and sounds like this Beth chick is guilty.

"Yeah, bud."

"Sorry it's early."

"All good, how's it goin'?"

"Listen. I got a friend in LA to check up with some of the people on the list you sent me."

If I thought I knew people in low places, I underestimated Linc.

"They arrested Beth Fields yesterday. She's Aspyn's agent. Looks like she's been the one sending those emails."

"She's not the one I'm concerned with," he says gravely.

"Sendin' a screenshot now. Had a guy follow her friend, Tara Conway. She got on a flight to New Orleans yesterday…"

"She's here," I sputter. "In our apartment. What happened?"

"Fuck, Rock. Get Aspyn the fuck away from her."

My heart begins to race, stomach sinking. "Why?" I'm already moving to pull my boxer briefs on as I run out into the apartment. It's silent. Empty. I check both bedrooms as Linc prattles on.

Then I pull my phone back when the text comes through, and I stop to look at the images.

"What the fuck is this?"

"A shrine to your girlfriend," he says. "I think Tara Conway is obsessed with Aspyn, and has been for a long time. This is her closet wall. She keeps it locked, though my guy didn't find it hard to break in."

There are pictures of Aspyn all over. Literally hundreds of pictures. Some of them just her, some of them together. Candid ones of her in the street, getting coffee by herself or driving. I stare at it in shock.

"Fuck, Linc, they're gone. I've got prospects downstairs."

"I'll pull up the footage from surveillance and call you back."

As soon as we hang up, I try Aspyn's phone. It goes straight to voice message. So I dial Pipes. He was downstairs last night, along with Rodeo. He doesn't pick up either.

I run back into the bedroom and dial Rodeo, and he picks up after two rings.

"Where are you?" I bark.

"Out front."

"Where is Aspyn?"

"She said goodbye to her friend and went back upstairs."

Relief floods me until I ask, "How long ago was that?"

"Uh, maybe, like, ten minutes ago."

My heart stutters. She isn't here. *Where the fuck is she?*

"Where the fuck is Pipes?"

I hear a strangled noise, and then it sounds like Rodeo drops the phone.

"Rodeo?" I bark. "What the fuck is goin' on?"

"Fuck. It's Pipes, he's...*unconscious.*"

My eyes go wide. "Is he breathin'?"

A few more moments pass as I tug my jeans on and then my boots.

"Yeah, he's groggy..."

"I'm comin' down."

I hang up and then dial my brother.

"What time do you call this?" he mutters.

"Aspyn's gone," I blurt out. "Tara's the stalker. She's obsessed with her. Linc sent some photos of her wall, and this chick is next level. Pipes was attacked..."

"I'm comin' over. I'll call the boys."

"No, the best thing you can do is help Linc. I'm gonna get in my truck with Rodeo and—"

"You saved my life again last night. If you think I'm lettin' you do this alone, you can think again."

"Fine. I'll pick you up. We'll be there in ten."

Panic ripples through me as I take off for the elevator.

It can't go fast enough as I pace inside, my hands in my hair, trying to wonder how I didn't see this coming. Tara fooled us all.

As I pace, I suddenly remember about GPS tracking. Fumbling with my phone, I hope to God she has her phone on her. Even if she has it turned off, location services should still work or give a general location, but that takes time...

When the elevator finally stops and the doors open, I see Rodeo pulling Pipe's limp body over to the truck.

"What the fuck?"

"Suspectin' chloroform," he says. "Someone must've jumped him when Aspyn was gettin' in the elevator."

"Where the fuck were you?" I bark.

Rock

"Out front. A car came and the friend got in."

I shake my head, unlocking my truck as we haul Pipes in the back. "If anyone harms a hair on her head, I'm gonna hold you personally responsible." I point at him.

He has the good sense to look sheepish as he climbs into the passenger seat.

"Tell me what you saw."

He explains the dark sedan pulled up, that he assumed it was an Uber, and Tara got in. Aspyn leaned in to give her friend one last hug and that was that. Then he went back out front to man the doors.

"Fuck!" I hiss, hitting the steering wheel as I fumble to start the damn thing, reversing like a bat out of hell.

My phone rings, and I answer on Bluetooth.

"Heard about Aspyn," Cash says, sounding very unhappy.

Great. Now I've let him down too. All of this took place under my fuckin' nose.

"I'm on it, Cash. Not gonna let that stupid fuckin' bitch do this."

"Woah, slow down. Jett told me somethin' about Tara?"

I relay what I know, then toss my phone to Rodeo. "Send the picture I just sent to Jett to Cash."

He takes my phone and does as I say.

"Fuck," Cash mutters.

"She's obsessed with her. Fuck knows what else she's had planned all this time. The fact that Tommy trusted her enough to send her here and she was right under our noses the whole time…" I say. "I have GPS tracker, but her phone's off. Even though it's takin' longer to track with cellular data, it's my only option until Linc gets back to me."

"We'll find her."

"I'm pickin' up Jett. Though I don't know where the fuck I'm headin'."

Linc's call pops up on the screen. "Gotta go, Linc's callin'."

"We'll meet you. Just let me know where you're headed when you can."

I hang up. "Linc?"

"Sendin' the surveillance," he says as I give Rodeo a chin lift. "Looks like she was dragged into the car and some asshole was drivin'."

"Fuck." I feel like I can't even breathe.

Rodeo holds up the screen as we see Pipes bein' grabbed from behind, a cloth placed over his mouth by the driver.

Holy fuckin' shit.

What the fuck do they plan on doing with Aspyn?

All of the worst-case scenarios fly through my mind as I try to get a grip on what the fuck I'm seeing.

I should've fuckin' known.

Here we were thinking that Tara was just a concerned friend, terrified of Aspyn being hurt again and she was the instigator all along. What for? Why the fuck would she do this?

"Got a partial plate," Linc says. "Runnin' a scan now. From what I can see, they turned north onto the highway from the turnpike. Don't got a bead on them yet, but workin' on it."

"Okay. Call me back when you have somethin'. Pickin' up my brother, trying to use triangulation of signals, but Jett is better at this shit than me."

"Let me know when you have somethin'. I'll keep lookin'."

I hang up, running a hand through my hair.

"I'm sorry, Rock," Rodeo begins.

I can't even deal with him right now.

"Just make sure Pipes keeps breathin'."

I know Pipes will be angry with himself. I just wish Aspyn had woken me to escort her downstairs. I know she didn't because it isn't like Tara and I were seeing eye to eye, but if I would've…we probably wouldn't be in this position now.

Rock

I need to think.

I get to Jett's in record time, and Rodeo moves into the back with Pipes, who's starting to wake up.

"The fuck happened?" Jett says, jumping in the front.

"Fuckin' Tara," I mutter. "Should've seen it comin'. She had it in for me the minute she laid eyes on me. She just wanted Aspyn for herself. There's an entire wall dedicated to my girl in her goddamn closet."

Jett doesn't comment about the "my girl" bit, which is probably for the best.

"We'll get her back," he assures me. "What did Linc say?"

"That they headed north, but without proper directions, we're flyin' around blind. Need you to work your magic on GPS trackin', but she has her phone turned off."

Rodeo chucks Jett my phone.

"This is fucked!" I hammer my palm against the wheel as Jett looks at me sideways.

"What the fuck are we gonna do if GPS won't work and Linc can't find the car..."

He places a hand on my shoulder. This is a lot after last night.

I texted Jett to make sure he was okay before I went to sleep. Yesterday was a lot.

"It's gonna be alright, just take a breath." He starts to press buttons on my phone, and I wonder why the fuck I didn't grab my goddamn laptop or some equipment.

He's trying to make me feel better, but right now I feel like shit.

I let this happen.

Aspyn was in my care, and now she's gone.

Her father doesn't even know.

This is so fucked.

"She's not gonna drive all the way back to LA," I say. "But they can't put an unconscious woman on a plane. She could be anywhere by now."

"Thinkin' Tara will be tryin' to lay low," Jett says. "She probably thinks she's gotten away with it, which could be to our advantage."

"Yeah, that's all well and dandy if we knew where she was."

He taps away on his phone as I keep driving, not knowing where the fuck I'm going.

"Jett," I mutter. "We gotta find her."

"I'm tryin', brother."

A few anxious minutes pass, and Jett says, "Need to get onto the North Causeway Boulevard."

"You got her?"

"Yeah, but who knows how delayed this is."

My heart rate spikes. At least it's something.

We're right on the north side, so I make the next turn and keep heading in the direction Jett calls out.

I swear to God, if she's hurt Aspyn, I'll fuckin' rip her vocal cords from her throat.

The wrath she'll suffer from me won't be anything that I'll regret. She'll be begging me to end her life.

"Looks as if they're headin' off to Causeway Road, leads to the river."

"What else is there?"

He clicks away. "Close to Jefferson Park. There's a marine repair place… Lots of open space."

He frowns, and I notice. "What?"

"Signal dropped out."

"Wait," Rodeo calls from the back as I make the turn onto Causeway Road, "Look! That's the car, I'm sure of it."

I turn and see a dark sedan turning toward the south ahead of us.

Adrenaline rushes through my veins as Jett answers Linc's call. "Think we've got them," Jett says through the speaker.

"South on Causeway?"

Rock

"Just lost GPS tracking, but the prospect saw the car. Followin' 'em now."

"Roger."

Jett dials Cash and gives him the details. The club's on their way.

"Gonna have to call it in," Cash says. "Can't be dealin' with any more murders after last night."

I shake my head. "Not possible."

"Listen to me, I'm not gonna see you in a concrete cell, Rock. We've worked too hard to get this far. She'll be goin' to jail for a very long time, plus, it'll give us favor with that goddamn asshole Callaghan. We throw him a bone, and he'll throw one our way."

Jett snorts. "You really believe that? The man is by the book."

"Unless it's self-defense, we need her alive."

I'm pissed. More than pissed. Cash can't ask that of me, and what about her accomplice? I don't mention that. The less Cash knows, the better.

"We also need Aspyn alive," I say, my agitation showing. "I'm not gonna say I'll hold back if she's hurt, Cash. You can't ask that."

"Sit tight." He hangs up.

Fuck him.

Fuck everyone.

I don't give a shit about my life. All I care about is her.

About my mystery girl and if I'm ever gonna see her again.

We temporarily lose the car, and I panic, only to see it again on the far south side.

"Losin' 'em," Rodeo says from the back.

"Goin' as fast as I can without killin' us," I mutter.

"Cash said we need *her* alive," Jett says as I glance at him. "So?"

"So? The motherfuckin' driver is fair game."

For the first time, I smile. "Now you're speakin' my type of language."

"Let's just be cool. Bullets can be traced," he reminds me. "Even self-defense is gonna require jail time. Just remember that. When we get Aspyn back, she's not gonna want to visit you in a prison cell. Can fuck him up without killin' him."

Even though I've not had a real conversation with my brother about her, it's clear he knows what's going on. You don't have to be Sherlock Holmes to see it if you look hard enough.

Ignoring Rodeo and Pipes, who's stirring and mumbling, I lower my voice. "Don't know what I'm capable of after last night. You processed it yet?"

He shakes his head. "Maybe I never will."

Touche.

I keep driving and relief floods me when we see the parked car. They're still ahead of us, though, and anything could've happened to my girl.

I don't like the fact they've driven to the edge of the Mississippi River.

A cold panic blankets me when I think about what could've happened in that car.

Aspyn never saw it coming.

Even though her friend had her own fair share of shortcomings, Aspyn was too nice to let her go. I wonder how long this obsessive behavior has been going on. Probably years, by the looks of things. Aspyn had told me they had an on again, off again friendship.

No wonder she hated me getting in the way. It all makes sense now.

We park, then hop out of the truck, leaving Pipes to sleep it off.

"Not splittin' up," Jett tells me.

"Hate it when they do that in the movies," Rodeo pipes up as we turn to shoot him a glare.

Rock

"Keep your eyes and ears open," I whisper-shout. With any luck, they didn't see us tail-gaiting, and I hope to hell that this is the car and we haven't just followed some tourist here to take some happy snaps.

We pull out our guns one after the other. Cash said not to shoot, but you can still fire and not kill someone. Not that he'd know that.

Images of Cash putting a bullet in Salerno's brain will haunt me for the rest of my time.

It sucks the asshole didn't have time to suffer, and by now I'm sure that the mafiosos are well aware of what's taken place, setting Forger and the Devils up to take the heat.

"Fuck," Jett whispers. "They're down by the scrub."

Along this part of the river, where the tourists don't go, it's a breeding ground for seedy shit.

Looks like Tara and her little friend know what they're doing, but what is their plan?

We follow down a small path, leading farther into the scrub. The wind picks up as Rodeo hangs behind.

When we spot them, Tara doesn't even try to hide. "I knew you'd come," she says. She almost sounds cheerful about it and not at all surprised.

"What the fuck are you doin'?" I call out, holding my gun pointed at her, even though her accomplice is pointing one at me. "Tara!"

Jett follows suit, aiming his gun. "Don't move, asshole."

"The way I see it is one of you dies," Tara says, eerily calm. She's holding a small gun, pointed toward Aspyn. "I wonder how one twin brother would do without the other. Aspyn told me how close you are."

Did I never notice how evil her tone is? How evil she is?

Aspyn is conscious but sprawled on the ground. Drugged, it seems. The thought of that makes me nauseous.

I crack my neck. I know that if I shot this bitch right now, there's no way I'd feel guilty about it. Even though I've never killed a woman before.

"Shut the fuck up," I tell her. "You can't get out of this. The cops are on their way. "You might even get a leaner sentence if you come quietly."

She snorts. "Do you know how long I've sat in the wings waiting for Aspyn to see what we have? Don't you get it, *Rock*? We're supposed to be together, but not in this life."

It's then I realize what she means.

As if reading my mind, she smiles. "So do it, Rock. Shoot me. Just know that Aspyn and I will be together, no matter what."

"Who's the bum?" Jett nods to the guy who looks piss weak by now. He may be large in stature, but he looks like a scared sheep.

She shrugs. "Some asshole I hired to take down one of your guys. You seriously need to invest in some better manpower. It was almost too easy."

"Fuck you."

She shoves Aspyn forward, pulling her to her knees, head bobbing.

"Don't tempt me, Rock. I don't miss. A nice tidy double murder suicide will clear all of this right up. Nobody has to take the fall." She actually smiles.

"Why are you doing this?" I manage.

Keep them talking... Rule number one of taking down your opponent. One thing people like Tara love to do is talk...

"I've tried so many times to convey to Aspyn that we're meant to be together. All through high school, I watched her fuck up. Nobody was ever worthy of her. I even made up a guy once on Facebook just to mess with her head, and it did. She fell for a dude that she'd never even met." She laughs. "When things fizzled out, she came running back to me. That's what she does, you see. I'm her fall guy. I'm reliable. And that whole disaster with Dylan? Oh my god. Aspyn never was very clued in on who was good and bad. You can blame her father for that one, for never letting her do anything. She just sees the good in everyone.'

"Another evil way to get into her head? I smirk. "Pretendin' to be someone else? I can see you're a really good friend. Just tell me this, what did she ever do to you?"

She smirks. "She never picked me, Rock. I'm sure you know what that's like. I bet you were a lot like me, a loser. An outcast. Somebody people just forgot about and bypassed like they're some kind of nuisance."

"I'm nothin' like you."

"You're right. You're not." She turns and shoots the schmuck in the chest as he falls and drops the gun he's holding, squirming around as blood fills his lungs. I wince at the sight.

She immediately points her gun back at Aspyn's head. "What a waste," she mutters.

I tighten my finger on the trigger, signaling to Jett not to shoot. It's what she wants. If we shoot her, the gun goes off and kills Aspyn. "You're fuckin' crazy, but I know you don't really want to hurt Aspyn."

Her eyes find mine again. "I bet you want to make me pay, don't you, Rock? And you're right, I don't want to hurt Aspyn, but she keeps hurting me. I've been here this whole time, and you just had to swoop in, just as I was getting through to her."

I laugh. "You're kiddin' yourself. Do you know how crazy she told me she thought you were?"

Her face falls. "What?"

"Especially when you showed up unannounced. She moved from LA to get away from you and your control." While that isn't exactly the truth, I want to make her mad so I get an opportunity to end this. "We joked about it often."

Her lips part, and her eyes narrow. "She'd never…"

I laugh again. "Seriously, you're one deluded chick. She

couldn't wait to get away from you. Maybe she told you it was her father's controlling ways, but that isn't the truth. It was you."

"You asshole!" She turns the gun on me, and I take my shot, hitting her in the shoulder as she releases a horrible scream and falls backward. Before she hits the ground, I'm rushing over to Aspyn at the same time Jett does. Aspyn falls sideways, and I just catch her before her head hits the ground.

Jett kicks the gun away from Tara as she howls in pain. We need her alive. Death is too good for her. She needs to suffer just like my girl has. She has to pay for her sins.

"I've got you," I whisper, holding Aspyn to my chest. "I'm here now. Nobody is ever gonna hurt you again."

EPILOGUE

Aspyn

I wake and immediately wince.

Pain shoots through me as I hear voices and a machine beeping.

Then I feel hands on me as I open my eyes.

"Rock?" I squeak.

"Babe." His voice is smooth and full of worry.

When my eyes eventually focus, I realize I'm sitting on a bed.

"Where am I?"

"The hospital."

"Oh, God. Tara…"

"It's okay, she's been arrested." He sits up, and I snake my arms around his waist. "Your father's on his way."

I start to cry. "She's the one behind all of this?"

He strokes my back. "Yes, I'm sorry to say she was. I had a guy break into her house…"

"You what?"

"Anyone close to you was bein' watched, thoroughly. We were just too late in realizing what she was up to."

"Why would she do this to me?"

He holds me as I try to find the words without breaking down. "To hurt you because she's obsessed with being with you. I figured the relationship had its challenges from what you told me, but I never suspected she was bat-shit crazy."

"What happened?"

He sighs. "You need to rest."

"No, Rock. You need to tell me, *please.*"

He relents. "She was going to kill you, so I'd kill her. Then you could be together."

My breath hitches in my chest. "She... Why?"

I know I'm repeating myself, but none of this adds up.

Tara and I have had our ups and downs in the past, but I never thought she was capable of this.

"To make sure she got to be the last. She was tired of living in the shadows and wanted to have a real relationship with you. She pretended to be some guy on Facebook to taunt you, never feeling bad about what she did. In fact, she found it amusing."

I screw my face up. "She did that? Oh my god..."

He kisses the top of my head. "I'm sorry, babe. She admitted it. You moving away didn't help. She couldn't cope without having you there. I guess when we got together and she didn't get her way, it was the final straw."

"How do you know..."

He pulls out his phone. "I never wanted you to see this, but once you do, you might understand the level of depravity she was sufferin'."

Sliding his thumb over his phone, he shows me a photo. It's a wall covered in pictures of me. The entire wall. She's even drawn pictures on my face and torn off the place where Dylan was on one of them.

"Oh God."

"I know. She's goin' to jail for a very long time."

"How did you find us?" I was out of it for most of the journey after Tara drugged me.

"It's a long story. Just know that I'm sorry. I should've known sooner…"

I cup his face, shaking my head. "You don't have to be sorry, Rock. None of this is your fault. I swear. I always knew Tara was controlling, but I thought it was coming from a place of concern and love, not…not *this.*" My nose wrinkles in disgust.

"I shot her," Rock says as I gasp.

"What?"

"I had to. She pointed the gun at me when I riled her, and I took my chance. I didn't want her to die because the real punishment is lettin' her suffer, just like you've done thinkin' she was your friend for such a long time when she was the enemy all along."

I curl closer into his side. "I want to go home."

He kisses the top of my head. "Where is home, Aspyn?"

"Wherever you are, Rock."

He pulls back to look down at me. "I love you."

My breathing hitches as I stare at him. "I love you, too."

"I'm so sorry you got hurt." I see the pain in his eyes, and it breaks my heart.

"I'm just sorry that it went on this long and she fooled us all."

"It's over now. It's finally over." I can't help but feel joyful, even though I should feel remorse and sorrow.

"You're gonna have some shitty days ahead," he tells me as he holds me tight. "Some questions we may not even be able to answer. Who knows why she did any of it. In her mind, she was protectin' you."

"She wanted to kill me!"

He soothes me as I cradle once more into his shoulder. "I know. Which is why I'm never lettin' you go ever again."

I take a deep breath. "I want to tell my dad about us."

Rock pulls back to look at me again. "You sure about that?"

I nod. "Yes. of course I'm sure. I wanted to make sure you loved me back. I mean, you're not just saying that because you almost died yesterday and I almost died today, right?"

He chuckles. "I think I loved you when I first rescued that suitcase from the conveyor belt. My heart skipped a beat when our eyes met."

I run my hand over his face, my fingers brushing his beard. Suddenly, I need all of him.

Pressing my lips against his, he cups my face with both hands.

"Aspyn, not here."

"Shhh! Near-death experience here, let me have this."

I love the feel of his lips on mine.

But before we can fully kiss, someone clears their throat.

Turning my head, I see my dad is standing in the doorway. I gasp and Rock squeezes my hand even tighter. He doesn't move off the bed and my dad eyes him warily.

"What the hell is going on?" he barks.

"Dad," I say as he rushes to me, side-eyeing Rock as he pulls me into his arms. "My princess, are you alright? Are you hurt? The doctor said you hit your head, that Tara drugged you?"

Cash walks in behind him, giving Rock a pointed look.

All the warnings he gave Rock and he didn't listen to any one of them.

I try not to laugh as Dad pulls back. This is no laughing matter.

"What's so funny?" He quirks a brow.

I shake my head. "Hysterical reaction. I'm fine. I had a mild concussion."

"Cash told me everything." He glances at Rock. "What he didn't tell me was about you. The man hired to guard my princess. Why are you holding my daughter's hand and sitting so close to her?"

Rock

"Dad," I start. "Something happened while I was down here."

"In a week?" He shakes his head. "Aspyn, that is utterly ridiculous. You don't even know this man."

"It's been more than a week," I start lamely, my head throbbing.

"I know that I'm in love with your daughter," Rock says. "I know I've never felt this way before, and we didn't mean for it to happen."

"You're the reason she was kidnapped!" he snaps.

"No!" I cry. "It wasn't Rock's fault. I slipped out of bed, and he was still sleeping…"

"Jesus Christ."

Oops, wrong thing to say.

"What I meant was, I was supposed to wake Rock up when Tara left, and I didn't. That's on me, not him."

"Please, Mr. Huntley. Don't be mad at her. I should've been there, and I wasn't. That's on me," Rock says.

I glance at him, confused.

My dad isn't having it. "This could've been a disaster, look at you! Bruised and battered." He turns to Cash, eyes narrowed. "I thought you said your men could be trusted!"

"They can," Cash replies, leaning against the door jam. "But it looks like the two of them found one another regardless."

"Your daughter is amazing," Rock says. "I never meant for this to happen, but it happened fast. Even if I wanted to stop it, I'm not sure I could."

"I don't have to sit here and listen to this!"

"Dad," I plead. "*Please!* For once in your life, listen! This is what I want. I want to get to know Rock. We've fallen fast, I admit that, but if you could just see how happy he makes me. How much I want this… You'd be happy for us."

Dad searches my eyes and sobers, pressing a kiss to my

forehead. "We'll talk about this later, when you're feeling better."

"I'm feeling better now, and I'm not changing my mind," I state firmly.

"What are you saying?"

I take a breath. "I'm staying in New Orleans, Dad."

He shakes his head, huffing out a breath. "Clearly, she has a concussion, she's not thinking straight."

"I *am* thinking straight!" I fire back. "For the first time in my life, I see things so much more clearly. I want to work some things out for myself. I'm a grown woman, Dad. I love you so much, but you have to let me live my life."

He doesn't say anything and stands to leave. "I need a moment."

Rock nods, and we watch as he leaves the room. I can tell he's angry and wants to knock Rock into next week, but he also doesn't want to upset me.

Cash moves closer. "What did I tell you?" he says, like Rock is a child. "But I should've known you'd put your hand in the goddamn cookie jar before long." There's amusement in his tone as I settle back into the pillows.

Rock shrugs. "Can't help how we feel," he says. Pure adrenaline, fueled by the rush of hearing him say that, runs through my veins. "I've got a long way to go in provin' it to her father, but we're not gonna be kept apart."

Cash regards him for a moment before his eyes move to me. "I'll let you get some rest."

Smiling softly, I nod. "Thank you, Cash."

As soon as the door closes, I turn to Rock. "That didn't go as planned."

He chuckles. "Yes, it did. Your dad was never gonna be okay with it. I just have to bide my time and prove to him that I'm worthy of you."

I bite my lip. "Do you mean that?"

"Of course I mean it. You're his daughter. I get he's not gonna be happy about it. You almost died!"

"Don't be angry with yourself," I say. "Please, Rock. I don't blame you. I should've seen the signs. Poor Beth…"

"Tara broke into Beth's office," he goes on. "Framed her for the whole thing. She wasn't smart enough to cover her tracks."

"Let me guess, security cameras?"

He smiles, kissing me chastely. "You got it."

"Take me home, Rock. I don't want to be here."

"The doc said a few hours, need to make sure you have nothin' more than a concussion. Then we'll go."

"Promise?"

He smiles, looking down at me with adoration. "Promise."

"I meant what I said to my dad. I want us to be together, to try, anyway."

"I want that too."

"Even if I'm a complete nightmare to live with?"

He smirks. "Long as one of us learns to cook and clean, then I think we're gonna be just fine."

I smile against his mouth. "That's not gonna be me, bozo."

He kisses me again. "Looks like we're gonna be orderin' take-out and hirin' a maid, then."

"Suits me."

Chuckling, he grins. "*You* suit me, and I'm gonna do everythin' I can to make you see how much you mean to me."

"I love you."

His eyes burn into mine, and I feel it in my very soul when he says, "Right back at ya, *Trouble*."

Rock

One month later

Priest winces at the bar as I slap him on the shoulder.

"You still sore?"

He rolls his eyes. "I've turned to the bottle, so that should answer your question."

Priest has been necking a little more whiskey these days. After being grazed by the bullet, he was lucky the damn thing didn't do more damage. Still, he's milking it for all it's worth.

I chuckle. "Don't tell me your still abstainin'?"

He takes another sip. "Sweet butts testin' a man's patience, that much I'll say."

I shake my head. "I don't know why you do it to yourself."

"That's because you have a beautiful woman in your bed every night. Trust me, if I had that, I'd be worshippin' her too. Until then…"

"So you're not abstainin' for good? Just until the right woman comes along?"

"Somethin' like that."

"You sure you didn't get hit in the head?"

"Nope. I remember havin' this conversation before I got shot."

"Least we can compare scars now," I say as he sighs.

"Mine's always gonna be bigger than yours, Rock," he says, patting me on the shoulder. "At least, that's what I've been told."

I grin as the clubhouse doors open and Manny, Luna, and Aspyn walk in.

Ever since that night when Tara was shot and arrested, things between us have been calm and almost blissful. We've been enjoying each other's company. Learning about one another. Talking.

So much about both our pasts has had me in a trigger hold and now all of that is gone. Having Salerno finally rid off the face of the earth has brought me a lot of peace and clarity.

Rock

I was holding on to so much resentment that I'd long since buried.

I'll never be able to thank Cash enough for doing what he did. For taking the lead, like a true father figure and protector.

"Hello, *Trouble*," I say when my girl slides onto my lap and reaches her arms around my neck.

"Hello, sexy."

Priest groans next to me. "You two need to go get a room."

"Nah, we've got my desk in the back," I say. "I'd recommend sanitizin' it if you plan on usin' it for work purposes."

He groans again. "Fuckin' coupla horny adolescents," he mutters under his breath.

Aspyn slaps me playfully on the arm as our lips meet. "Where have you been?" I ask.

She rubs her nose against mine. "As if you don't know."

I smile. She knows me too well.

"I don't need a tracker to know you're either at the coffee shop, the salon, or buyin' more blankets we don't need in Target."

She pouts. "But those blankets are for snuggle time."

"I think we need to go and snuggle right now," I coax, waggling my eyebrows.

"I think I just threw up a little," Priest complains.

I slap his back, not the side where he was hurt. "Don't worry about him, his dick hasn't been wet for a while. He's just bein' grumpy."

Aspyn looks over at him. "You've not, uh, indulged for over a month?"

I snort. "Longer than that."

"Shut up, asshole," Priest says, shoving me back.

He looks at Aspyn pointedly. "I'm choosin' to abstain for my mental health," he says. "It's not because I can't *get* any."

She rolls her lips. "I can see that."

I pinch her on the ass, and she yelps. My possessive side hasn't gotten any better with time.

"Chicks are trouble," I grumble, smiling when Aspyn pinches my ass this time.

"Hey!"

"What? Just sayin' it like it is."

That earns me another pinch.

"Makin' BLTs, who wants one?" Manny sings-songs as he pours himself a Diet Coke.

Luna screws up her nose. "Can you make anything other than BLTs and Gumbo?"

Manny gives her a look. "Makin' pumpkin pie this afternoon, but I don't suppose you'll be wanting any of that?"

They bicker all the way to the kitchen as I chuckle. "Better get you home, you must be tired after listenin' to those two."

"I am," she says, pouting.

Priest sighs again. "I know that's code for 'we're goin' to go fuck' so off you go. Scram."

Aspyn giggles as I move her off my lap and we head off.

"Have fun tuggin' your purple helmet, bud."

I don't even have to turn to see that he's flipping me the bird.

An hour later, I'm sinking my dick into Aspyn's tight, newly waxed pussy as she lies back on the couch and I hold her legs over my shoulders. I've taken it easy with her for a while because of her bruising. Aside from her concussion and being drugged, she also had bruising to her hip and shoulder where that asshole Tara hired dragged her in and out of the car.

He deserved a bullet just for that.

Tara is awaiting sentencing and has been flown back to LA until the trial.

For now, Aspyn can rest easy until she has to testify, something I know she isn't looking forward to. Getting her head around her friend's betrayal has been hard on her.

"Oh, Rock," she groans when I slide in and out, torturously slow. "So good."

I already got her off, and she did me, at the same time when we were sixty-nining on the couch. Fuck, that was hot. Tasting myself on her lips is something I know still shocks her as much as it excites her.

"Better than my tongue, babe?" I thrust a little harder.

"Oh!"

"Better than my fingers findin' that spot inside you that drives you wild?"

"Harder!"

I don't listen. I keep up my steady, slow but brutal rhythm. Knowing I'm driving her crazy makes me dick swell even more.

"You wax this pussy for me, *Trouble?*"

"Who else?" she cries.

I pinch her nipple in reprimand, and she gasps. Trouble is, she likes my punishment.

"Cheeky."

She runs her hands up my body and groans when she feels my muscles, gripping onto my shoulders. Thank God my girl is bendy. This angle is so damn deep.

"Should see how good you look like this," I moan when I dip my eyes to watch myself moving in and out of her.

I know I'm keeping her on the edge, but I can't help it. I love every single thing about her.

"I need you, Rock."

"Me?"

"Uh huh."

When I slam in, she yelps. "Or my cock?"

"You!" she pants.

"I don't know…"

I do it again, and she jolts as I enjoy watching her tits bounce.

"Could tie you up to my bed and never let you leave," I mutter.

Her eyes flutter open, and I see the flush in her cheeks. I never cease to not shock her.

"But you'd like that too much," I add.

She smiles. "So deep, Rock..."

I move in and out, increasing pace until she's grinding back against me. Her pretty blue eyes meet mine as I stare down at her. Enjoying every single clench of her gripping my cock.

"You love it, don't you, *Trouble?*"

"Yes," she gasps when I thrust harder. "I love you, Rock..."

I groan as I feel my balls tighten at her words. "Again."

"I love you, Rock, *oh!*"

I pound her until she screams my name and I spill inside her, telling her over and over how much I love her until I'm spent.

Letting her legs go, I collapse on top of her.

I don't know how long we lie there for, but when I feel a furry critter brushing up against my foot, I know it's time to move.

I pull out, enjoying watching myself spill out of her as I brush one hand over the cat before he runs away, and one hand over her thigh.

"Why do you love watching yourself leak out of me?" she asks, sitting up, watching what I'm doing.

I glance up. "It's hot, that's why."

She pulls me to her and kisses me until my cocks stirring again. This woman is insatiable.

"Uh huh."

I move so I'm flat against the couch and she's straddled over me.

"We're gonna need a new couch the amount of fucking we do on it," she mumbles against my mouth.

I smile against her lips. "So when you buy a new blanket, I know it's code for sex." I glance down at all the blankets along the couch, protecting it from my cum. Fuck knows we have done it a lot. On every surface of the house. Even out on the patio.

I never knew my girl was an exhibitionist, though the day she got off on my sled should've been a sure indication.

"I think my dad's coming into town this weekend."

I smile. "Good. Maybe this trip will be the one where he speaks to me."

Things have been slow going with Tommy, but I think in time we'll get there.

Having his daughter move down here permanently was hard on him, but he knows that Aspyn has wings and it's time for her to fly. I'm never gonna give him a reason to doubt me, or to make her cry.

I fell hard and fast, and I make no apologies for it.

Jett was right. When you know, you know.

"He'll love you soon, he just takes a while to get used to."

"As long as you love me, that's all I care about."

She tugs on my beard, and I growl in response, feeling the tug down in my balls. "I love you if you keep doing that thing you do."

"Hey, I thought you loved me for me," I chuckle.

"I do, but I also love that pretty mouth." She kisses me. "And these pretty eyes." She kisses those too. "And that big nose."

"Big?"

She squeals when I cup and squeeze her ass. Reaching between her legs, I spread our slickness all the way back to her ass. She knows what this means.

"Ooh," she coos. "Am I gonna be punished?"

"Nope. You're gonna be pleasured until you're forgettin' all about my big nose and focusin' on my big dick instead."

I take her mouth and groan when her hand slides down to my erect dick.

"Jesus, does this thing ever go down?" she laughs.

I shake my head. "Nope. Permanently up around you."

I stare at her in awe. She's mine. And I'm hers.

My heart constricts at the very feeling.

One I know I deserve and have been waiting for, for a very long time.

"How did I ever get so lucky?" she asks, her voice soft, eyes burning into mine.

With a grin, I pull her to me. "Took the words right out of my mouth."

ACKNOWLEDGMENTS

Thank you for reading Rock and Aspyn.

For everyone who took an ARC; I appreciate you giving me a chance if you're a new reader. And for those of you that have a previous MC ARC – I hope you enjoyed Rock!

Thank you to all my loyal readers that begged for Rock's book. I appreciate your support so much. NOLA Rebels is a spin-off from my best selling series Bracken Ridge Rebels MC set in Arizona. That series is complete with 12 books 😊

Thanks as always to D, my twin sister, for not only keeping me sane during the difficult time of writing and fitting everything in. Also you're a proofreading genius and thank you for Beta reading!

Thank you to my Alpha reader Michelle – The Outgoing Bookworm (follow her on IG) for all of your comments and suggestions

Thank you to my BETA Girlies (follow them on IG): Angelica – angelicareads92 Kylie – caffeinatedfitmama and Anshul – stories.buddy

To Alana my PA @thenovelassistant for all of your help and services in getting this one to the finish line, also for formatting beautifully as always!

Thanks again to Monique from MoSa Designs for Rocks cover, I love it and the hot pink

Thanks again to my editor, Kenzie from Nice Girl, Naughty Edits

Eric Battershell Photography for the model photo – he's perfect

To Josh Lamech (jay_lem89) for being not only handsome with the best smile in the business (I know Rock's cover he isn't smiling, but check his IG page!) I've wanted you on a cover for so long, and we got there. Truly you are perfect for my character, and I love that you have so many tat's that I didn't have to add any LOL x

Thank you to @theauthoragency for doing my PR and blog tour/Arc's again for all your amazingness.

To my amazing ARC & Street team for your continued support as always a pleasure to see how much you enjoy my books. Truly, I appreciate all your help.

If you can spare the time to leave a review on GR and/or Amazon and BookBub if you loved Rock or any of my books that would be greatly appreciated and helps me so much as an indie author. Links are on the following pages.

The next book in the series will be Priest and Bella. Release date is 16th June 2024.

I have been dyinggggg to writing Priest for so long and can't wait to get into his head LOL and Bella will be a new to the MC character, but interlaces in an unexpected way. She's very innocent in the ways of the world, but I can assure you that she won't be once Priest is done with her LOL Check out a sneak preview and pre-order link below.

Be sure to check out my private Facebook group (links below) as I update this page regularly before anything gets released on other social media channels.

Love from Australia, MF xx

ABOUT THE AUTHOR

Mackenzy Fox is an author of contemporary, enemies to lovers, motorcycle and dark themed romance novels. When she's not writing she loves vegan cooking, walking her beloved pooch's, reading books and is an expert on online shopping.

She's slightly obsessed with drinking tea, testing bubbly Moscato, watching home decorating shows and has a black belt in origami. She strives to live a quiet and introverted life in Western Australia's South-West with her hubby, twin sister and her dogs.

FIND ME HERE:

Tiktok: https://www.tiktok.com/@mackenzyfoxauthor

Tiktok backup account: https://www.tiktok.com/@mackenzyfoxbooks

Tiktok Fox sisters: https://www.tiktok.com/@thefoxsisterswrite

Face book: https://www.facebook.com/mackenzy.foxauthor.5

Instagram: https://www.instagram.com/mackenzyfoxbooks/

Goodreads: http://bit.ly/3ql07a7

Don't forget to join my and Dakotah's private Facebook Group: The Den – A Mackenzy & Dakotah Fox Readers Group here: https://bit.ly/3dgQfKk

Sign up for my newsletter:

https://landing.mailerlite.com/webforms/landing/g2l8y8

Find all my books, ARC sign ups, book links and giveaways here in one easy spot: https://linktr.ee/mackenzyfox

Checkout my website:

https://mackenzyfox.com

ALSO BY MACKENZY FOX

Bracken Ridge Rebels MC:

Steel

Gunner

Brock

Colt

Rubble

Bones

Axton

Nitro

Gears

Knox

Hutch

(Series complete)

A Bracken Ridge Christmas – extended epilogues

NOLA Rebels MC:

Cash

Jett

Hawk

Harlem

Tag

Bad Boys of New York:

Jaxon

Taboo Collection

Mr. Bentley

Mr Petrov

Mr Devereaux

ALSO BY MACKENZY FOX & DAKOTAH FOX

Medici Mafia Series:

Fortress of the King

Fortress of the Queen

Fortress of the Heart

Fortress of the Soul

Fortress of the Damned

Fortress of the Brave

Fortress of the Cursed

(Series complete)

Quick Burn Series:

Ruler Breaker Romance – Sports

Huxley

Nash

Wolf

Shepherd

Silver Pines Series:

Small Town Christmas Novels

Snowed In

Snowed Out

Snowed Under - coming December 2024

Standalone:

Broken Wings

Basset Brothers Bourbon - Stoney Creek Series:

Celeste and Callan - Prequel Novella

Grayson & Hartley

WANT MORE?

Priest

Tropes:
MC vs Mafia
He's the club's spiritual advisor
Identity deception
Homeless heroine
Age gap
Virgin FMC
Biker who vows celibacy in order to start over
He has a dark past
He teaches her

SNEAK PEEK - PRIEST

Excerpt (subject to change) before editing:

10 years ago
New Orleans Correctional Facility

I held my hands around the man's throat, and not for the first time I wondered about how it would feel to choke this piece of shit for real.

I may only be twenty-one years old, but the men here fear me. If not for my size alone, standing at six-foot-four inches, I'm also wide set and muscled with a mean streak some call vengeful. My mother once said I had the face of an angel, but the mind of a little devil. Then again, she didn't turn out to be much of a mother to begin with, so maybe she got it wrong. I can't deny I've used my looks to my advantage, but it isn't like the chicks I've been with don't know what we're there for.

Women seem to like me — or they did until I wound up in NOLA Correctional Facility on a bullshit charge. I swear the fuckers around here have it in for me, but that won't exactly help me now. Then again, beating my step-father, Eric, to a pulp was what got me locked up here in the first place. As it was ruled self defense — and I didn't manage to kill the fucker — I got a lesser sentence of six months with probation. Still. The Correctional Facility isn't Disneyland. You've still gotta watch your back. There are slimy fucks everywhere.

I'm known on the streets of New Orleans, and not for anything good.

The cops sprung me for selling drugs here and there, luckily I didn't have shit on me when I beat Eric, or I know I'd be suffering a worse fate than I am now. Still, two months into my sentence, and I've made allegiance and allies. That's how you win in prison. I didn't come here to be pushed around by other inmates, but survival is key.

Which is why I've lived in this low down place as long as I have. Make no mistake, correctional facilities are no walk in the park.

"You're doin' it wrong," Riot says from behind me. My cellmate, as well as resident yapper.

I turn around. "Fuck off."

"He's turnin' blue, better give him air unless you got a plan?"

Riot got his name for obvious reasons, but since he's part of the NOLA Rebels MC, he has a price on his back which is why a lot of the cell mates protect him. They want in at the club, and the MC holds a lot of weight around here. They accept ex-cons, but their prez, Cash, is notorious for being a hard ass. I guess he took my cell mate in, and Riot is a good guy when all's said and done. Riot man may be shorter than me, and far too cocky for his own good, but he can fight. The little shit is dirty though, like all street brawlers are. I'm glad I have him as my cellmate and not the motherfucker who just jumped me.

"I've got a plan." I punch my cell mate in the ribs and he gasps for air when I let him go. "The question is, do you, motherfucker?"

He gasps and sputters, trying to catch his breath.

Riot keeps guard while I fuck him up a little. "The fuck was he thinkin' jumpin' you here?"

"Judgin' by the state of him, he's cooked." Most of the inmates here are big-time drug addicts. Me? I don't touch the stuff, only to deal. "What I wanna know is who wants me deal, shit head."

I slap him around a little. "You think I'm some fish who hasn't been here before, asshole?"

In here, they call me Shadow; because I possess the ability to go reasonably unnoticed. Keeping to myself, silently observing the intricate dynamics. But now I'm thinking they should change it to Cobra. Because when I strike, I'm deadly.

He shakes his head.

"Who was it?" Of course, I know who it was; the same assholes who think they run this joint.

The Beast and his crew who think they run shit around here. Sure, he's thick as fuck, but I've watched his fighting skills, and he's just solid. He has no skill at all. In a fight, I know I could take him. But they fight dirty. Every last one of them.

"The beast?" I prompt.

He nods. I punch him again and again and again. It'll send a message, not before I handle the Beast myself. I knew I had it coming, but his time is gonna be up soon.

"You know they're gonna retaliate." Riot leans against the wall, unaffected by my actions. He's seen it all before.

"I don't give a fuck. They wanna come for me? Come for me. I have nothin' to live for anyway." That's mostly true. Staying alive just to drink and get pussy is getting pretty old.

Coming in here again has made me realize that.

Riot chuckles. "Whatever you say, bro."

I lean toward the asshole's ear. "Next time, that blade will be spurting your blood all over my feet while I mop it up with your lifeless corpse, understand?"

"Y– yes," he gasps. I shove him toward the bars and kick his ass to help him out.

"Fuck. I wouldn't mess with you," Riot chuckles after he's gone.

I glance at him. "Luckily I like you. Fuck knows why, you whine like a little bitch."

Riot is one of the good guys. Maybe when I get out, I might look at joining the MC.

He holds his hand up. "My mama always said if I can use humor to get out of any situation, I should do that, before resorting to violence."

"That's why you're known as Riot?" I shake my head, picking up the switchblade and placing it under my mattress. Of course, it can't stay there, but it'll do for now.

"Hey, not my fault I also inherited my father's temper."

I grunt and give him a chin lift. "We're gonna need it if we ever plan on walkin' out of here."

He taps his nose. "Leave it to me."

"I hate it when you say that."

He grins. "Say, Shadow, you ever met a holy man?"

I frown. "Nope, and I don't plan to."

"I really think you and Big Apple might hit it off." Big Apple is the spiritual counselor who assists inmates in finding God, as well as listening to their concerns and fears. He's respected in here, though. They leave him alone because he's an old man. Even the Beast and the other miscreants. I'd say Big Apple holds a lot of secrets, and to me, that means he's a liability.

I snort. "You think I can pray my way out of this hell?"

Riot shrugs. "Maybe. He doesn't just pray, though. He's taught me a lot; how to control my anger and seek guidance when I need it."

"Sounds like he's pussy whippin' you. What's next, do we all sit around chanting?" I don't need saving.

"Just sayin'. It's only a matter of time until you get jumped again."

"And how is Big Apple gonna help with that?" I turn to face him, annoyed.

"You have an advantage. You're known as the Shadow. When Fat Harry gets back to his cell, they're all gonna know you're a dark horse. They're gonna come for you, and you gotta know when to pick your battles. When to cause havoc and when to lie low."

I point in his face. "You think I haven't been doin' that? How do you think I got my nickname?"

He shakes his head. "That's not what I'm sayin'. Trust me, I didn't get my name by bein' the quiet one amongst these four walls. But I'm still here. Still breathin'. There's a lot of guys who just wanna do their time, but the systems is fucked and you know it." he says.

"What has any of that shit gotta do with me?"

He shrugs. "Big Apple will be gettin' out soon enough. He's gonna need a successor."

"I'm here for three more months, big shot. Then I'm gone."

"You really think you're gonna keep your nose clean in here and you'll be out in three months?" He holds in his laughter. Asshole.

"I don't think it, I *know* it."

"What about on the outside?"

"Speak English, brother."

"When you get out. You know you can prospect, but I know a way you could get in the NOLA Rebels and fast track all that bullshit."

This piques my interest. "So speak."

"Cash has been talkin' about lookin' for someone to guide the club, spiritually. He used to be one percent, you know what that is?" He gives me a chin lift and I nod. "Well, now he's legit.

The whole club is. But obviously some of us go off the rails and get mixed up in bad shit from time to time. Havin' someone in the club like Big Apple, who tends to the needs of the members has worked in lots of other clubs. A chaplain, or spiritual guide."

I laugh. "Chaplain? I prefer Priest. Believe or not, I grew up catholic, not that I practice any of that now. I don't even know what I believe anymore."

"Is that why you have that cross tattoo?"

I shoot him a look. "Let's not get into that, it'll make your eyes water, pretty boy."

He sighs. "Just think about it. Like I said, it's two years minimum as a prospect, and trust me when I say, you don't wanna be doin' that if you can help it."

I honestly don't know why he's telling me this. I guess he really does want me to join the MC, and what I've heard about being a prospect sounds like no picnic.

"If it'll keep you off my back and talkin' for five seconds, then I'll think about it."

He grins. "Good. I think you'd get along with the guys."

"Are they as yappy as you?"

"No, but free snatch, grub and all the beer you can drink gotta be worth it. And a roof over your head."

"Cash okay with ex-cons?" I already know the answer to that, but I wanna hear it from him.

"If he likes you, then yeah. I fucked up, but he knows I was in the wrong place at the wrong time. It's tight knit, you know that by reputation. Cash won't just let anyone in, but he trusts me."

"I'll take your word on it."

He pushes off the wall. "So, what are you gonna do with that blade?"

I face him and grin. "I'm gonna bury it in the Beast's neck. What do you think I'm gonna do with it?"

He doesn't flinch. Going up against the worst criminal in here is potential suicide, but right now, I've nothing to live for. I have no prospects at all, even if joining the MC has piqued my interest. "I wanna be there when he's on his knees pleadin'."

I rub my chin. "Maybe I should talk to Big Apple after all, I need to be able to know how to read someone their last rights."

He chuckles. "Penance, my friend? And you said you weren't catholic."

I reach for the blade, tucking it into my shoe. Who knows how soon I'm gonna need it.

"By the time I'm done with the Beast, or any other jailbird around here who wants to fuck with me, they'll all be on their knees praying for mercy." It won't be the first time I've killed a man. Not that I've ever been locked up for it. But trust me, the assholes deserved it. The more I think about it, I'm starting to like this idea more and more.

He whacks me on the back. "That's what I like to hear."

Club Chaplain? It has a ring to it.

I could do that. I could fast-track into the MC and get my life back on track. Or I could die here in prison.

The only question is, can I really hand myself over to the almighty? Faking it could come as naturally as breathing, but even I have my superstitions. I don't mess with holy shit.

I've always had a sixth sense, and it's eerily accurate. People have always confided in me, and I've no idea why. It's like I'm the flame to the moth and they just can't help themselves.

One thing I do know is that the Beast is going to die in this jail, and it'll be at my hands. I also know I'll get away with it, easily. The question of what to do with myself after that remains.

It could be a way out. The brotherhood I've always craved and wanted. To belong, to be needed; deep down that is my ultimate desire and is what's kept me alive this long.

I rub my chin once more. Maybe all of this hell on earth

I've been suffering was for a reason. Maybe this is my calling? And if I get free grub, snatch and a place to live, how bad could it be? I could even start to like it.

I smile. "Come to think of it, I'm sure I could be reformed for the right situation." I lean back on my bunk and my smile spreads into a grin. "I think finding the lord could be my meal ticket outta here."

He nods his head. "Best thing I've heard all day." He reaches out to clasp my hand. "I'll join the dots with Cash, you've just gotta do the leg work."

"Best go find a bible then, hadn't I?"

Grab it here for release on 16th June 2024: https://books2read.com/NOLAPriest

Made in United States
Orlando, FL
27 May 2025

61627289R00215